Praise for *The Wonder Garden*

"[Acampora] accomplishes great depth of characterization, in no small part because [she] doesn't shy from the unpalatable . . . There is a barbed honesty to the stories that brushes up against Acampora's lovely prose to interesting effect."

—*New York Times Book Review*

"[*The Wonder Garden*] is reminiscent of John Cheever in its anatomizing of suburban ennui and of Ann Beattie in its bemused dissection of a colorful cast of eccentrics. But Acampora's is entirely her own book . . . [her] ability to lay bare the heartaches of complex individuals within an utterly unique imaginative world is worthy of high praise."

—*Boston Globe*

"Acampora's stories show that an *Anna Karenina* principle still applies: All happy families are the same; the unhappy ones are miserable in their own special way. Or to boil it down to modern terms: mo' money, mo' problems . . . Add well-drawn characters, interesting plots, cultural zingers and dead-on critiques of consumerism and Acampora delivers a page-turner."

—*Dallas Morning News*

"A smashing debut, with range, subtlety and bite. Reading Acampora, we're in Cheever country, with hints of Flannery O'Connor."

—BBC.com

"Well-plotted, incisive and beautifully written fiction."

—Bookreporter.com

"Acampora's debut creates a portrait of a fictional upscale New York suburb, Old Cranbury, through a series of linked stories that are intelligent, unnerving, and very often strange . . . In each story, Acampora examines the tensions, longings, and mild lunacies underlying the 'beady-eyed mommy culture' and socio-political 'forgetfulness' marking Old Cranbury. At the same time, Acampora's picture of the town—rendered in crisp prose and drawing on extensive architectural detail—is as irresistible as it is disturbing." —*Publishers Weekly* (starred, boxed review)

"The stories in Acampora's first collection are so vivid, tightly plotted, and expertly woven that they make you look forward to reading more by this accomplished author."

—*Library Journal* (starred review)

"Spooky and fabulous . . . A cleareyed lens into the strange, human wants of upper-class suburbia."

—*Kirkus* (starred review)

"Acampora wields prose with the precision of a scalpel, insightfully dissecting people's desperate emotions and most cherished hopes . . . Acampora not only meticulously conveys the allure of an outwardly paradisiacal suburban community, with its perfectly restored Victorian homes and well-tended lawns; she also clearly captures the inner turmoil of its residents, honing in on their darkest impulses and beliefs. Some of the stories' starring characters make cameos in others, adding considerable complexity to the whole. Like Evan S. Connell in his iconic novels, *Mrs. Bridge* (1958) and *Mr. Bridge* (1969), Acampora brilliantly captures the heartaches and delusions of American suburbanites." —*Booklist* (starred review)

"A dark and brilliant collection of stories. Lauren Acampora is a terrific writer."

—Joseph O'Neill, author of *Netherland* and *The Dog*

"The world depicted in Lauren Acampora's stories seems reassuringly familiar, until it becomes unaccountably strange and unsettling. One moment we seem to be in Cheever's Westchester, the next we plunge through the looking glass into realms that may remind some readers of George Saunders or Robert Coover or the David Lynch of *Blue Velvet,* though, inevitably, all resemblances prove to be superficial. Acampora is an original and *The Wonder Garden* is an outstanding debut."

—Jay McInerney, author of *Bright Lights, Big City*

"*The Wonder Garden* is a beautiful book: witty, intelligent, deeply compassionate and gorgeously crafted. Lauren Acampora is uncannily skilled at chronicling the emotional lives of her characters with the same razor-sharp precision as she does the suburban landscape that surrounds them. I can't stop thinking about these stories." —Molly Antopol, author of *The UnAmericans*

"Like the famous opening scene in *Blue Velvet,* Lauren Acampora's *The Wonder Garden* pulls us under the surface of that most carefully tended American garden, the prosperous suburb, to lay bare its dark underbelly. *The Wonder Garden* is wondrous, and its stories are addictive. I dreaded coming to the end."

—Susan Choi, author of *My Education*

"Lauren Acampora's linked stories, about one Connecticut town, vividly explore dark interiors as well as polished facades. *The Wonder Garden* is an elegant construction and a chronicle of the surprising ways in which suburban lives intersect. Lauren Acampora is a writer of extraordinary dexterity."

—Elliott Holt, author of *You Are One of Them*

"I loved *The Wonder Garden*. Acampora's writing moves like a laser through her characters' souls, finding the deepest, darkest truths and delusions. Every story surprises. Every story is devastating. Like *Mad Men* set in the present day, but better."

—Heidi Pitlor, author of *The Daylight Marriage*

"Here in the suburb of Old Cranbury, where the lawns are carefully tended and life is coated with a veneer of normalcy, Lauren Acampora shines a bright light on the mysteries of human emotions. These perceptive, riveting stories give us the opportunity to explore the hidden tumult of a prosperous community and to discover its dramatic secrets."

—Joanna Scott, author of *De Potter's Grand Tour*

The Wonder Garden

The Wonder Garden

Lauren Acampora

Grove Press
New York

"Swarm" previously appeared in *The Missouri Review.*

Published simultaneously in Canada
Printed in the United States of America

ISBN 978-0-8021-2481-4
eISBN 978-0-8021-9129-8

Grove Press
an imprint of Grove Atlantic
154 West 14th Street
New York, NY 10011

Distributed by Publishers Group West

groveatlantic.com

16 17 18 19 10 9 8 7 6 5 4 3 2 1

In memory of my father

Contents

Ground Fault 1
The Wonder Garden 29
Afterglow 59
The Umbrella Bird 89
Swarm 111
Visa 135
The Virginals 163
Floortime 197
Sentry 223
Elevations 245
Aether 273
Moon Roof 309
Wampum 327

Ground Fault

John likes to arrive first. He enjoys standing quietly with a house before his clients arrive, and today, although he feels pinned beneath an invisible weight, he resolves to savor this solitary moment. It's one of those overhauled ranches so common to Old Cranbury these days, swollen and dressed to resemble a colonial. White, of course, with ornamental shutters and latches pretending to hold them open. A close echo of its renovated sisters on Whistle Hill Road, garnished with hostas and glitzed with azaleas. He has seen too many of these to count, but today he feels newly affronted.

He begins with the property. The front grade of this particular address slopes gently away from the structure, ideal from a topographical standpoint. There are no real trees to speak of, only snug rows of adolescent pines at either side of the property, screening the house from its neighbors in the most neighborly possible way.

He strides slowly up the front path in his work boots, noting the fine condition of the brick pavers, flush to the ground with just the slightest efflorescence. On the porch, he squats to finger a pile of fine orange frass. Carpenter ants—nothing unusual this time of year. He goes around the side of the property, surveys the TruWood siding, the tidy soffits and fascias. A quick survey of the back lawn gives the septic risers away: two low welts in the soil. The grass itself is the jolly green attainable only through obsessive fertilization and well-paid maintenance.

Foraging for the well head, John pauses for a moment and listens to the ambient sounds of yard work and birdcalls. From time to time he might experience a mystical flash on a job, a brief collapse of boundaries between himself and the house he is about to examine. He might divine a premonitory sketch of a structure, what its trouble spots might be—foundation, floor, or roof—like those men attuned to the silent thoughts of animals. John closes his eyes, stands upon the pampered grass, and waits. The sun touches the roots of his waning hairline and presses against his eyelids until he sees the red throb of his own blood vessels. No presentiment comes to him. Instead, he finds himself replaying last night, starting with the phone call from Diana. When he opens his eyes again, they catch sight of a neighbor watching from the far side of the privacy pines. The man is buffing a vintage MG and pauses to give a soldier's salute.

Of course, John Duffy's work is not remotely psychic. His skills have been carefully honed over two decades in the field, and he takes pride in their hard-won mastery. As a young man, he itched to be outdoors, driving a vehicle, autonomous. In a moment of bold lucidity, he'd quit his deadening job at a mortgage bank and enrolled in a home inspectors' certification course. After passing the exam, he apprenticed himself to a crabby old man for five years, paid his dues. Knowing that his employer would never retire, John did what every warm-blooded American has at one time or another dreamed of doing: he plucked the dangling fruit of self-employment, turned fantasy into fact. After that, no one could put John Duffy down or undermine him, no one could second-guess the calls he made on site visits or apologize to *his* clients for an alleged mistake in a report. He has no one to answer to but himself, his clients, and the all-inspecting eye of God.

As he turns back toward this particular front porch on Whistle Hill, a silver Audi pulls into the driveway, and a woman emerges from the passenger door. John sees a short triangular dress and uninterrupted legs, and even from this distance his blood responds. The woman glides up the path beside a man whose pale skin and squinted eyes suggest a good deal of time spent indoors. Her dress vibrates with a kind of 1960s optical illusion pattern, white with orange circles embedded within one another. His eyes are drawn into these mini-vortexes, and only after an overlong stare does he recognize that she is pregnant. The woman smiles.

"I hope you haven't been waiting long," she says.

"No, you're right on time." The husband's hand, when John shakes it, feels like chilled meat. Hers is narrow, paper-dry, the bones discernible beneath skin.

"First-time buyers?" John asks.

"Yes," answers the husband.

"We have a lot to learn about houses," the wife says. "I've been looking forward to this." Her voice hits John's ear like a tuning fork, a silver bell.

"Well, I hope to help educate you," says John.

Indeed, on his website John emphasizes that the mission of Argus Home Inspections, Inc., is not only to protect consumers from unwise investments but also to educate them about the properties they intend to purchase. The company is named for the all-seeing giant of Greek mythology. Its logo is elegant, designed by Diana's artist cousin—a spray of blue peacock feathers, each tipped with a human eye.

"What's that, I wonder." The wife points at a conical hive at the crease of the porch ceiling.

"Wasp's nest," John reports. "You can get it down with a broom but they'll keep coming back. Welcome to country life." He lifts his clipboard and pencils a desultory note about the hive. "You're from the city, aren't you?"

"Mmm," says the wife.

"Manhattan, yes," the husband adds.

John nods. These two will be easy, reasonable clients. Something about the husband's manner suggests a wish for swiftness. This is a formality for him, John suspects. The wife is easy in her own way: a wide-eyed beginner, trusting of John's expertise and secretly confident that the house they've chosen is faultless. She has the crescent-shaped eyes of an optimist. Sky blue in color, these are eyes accustomed to admiring and being admired, that dare anyone to make them unhappy. If it weren't for the tiny creases like gentle comb marks at their outer corners, John might mistake her for a very young woman.

As it happens, John does not really enjoy educating the consumer. He prefers inspections during which the client does *not* follow him like a lapdog, asking questions and taking notes. And he prefers most of all those clients who are too busy to even show up to an inspection, who take him at his word and are satisfied with a handwritten report. The truth is that John does his best work solo. Like a doctor making a diagnosis, he believes a good home inspector shines best when unmolested.

The three of them stand on the porch for a prolonged moment broken finally by the arrival of Lori Hatfield. Lori is John's favorite broker. No other broker consistently refers clients to him, and he might even go as far as to call her a friend. He supposes that he has, without really intending to, seen her through some bad times. They've gone out for a few drinks in days past and found themselves trading heartaches. There has been no romantic angle to this whatsoever; Lori is a mousy woman in her fifties with a string of dirty pearls forever at her neck. But they respect each other. John knows her to be one of the few right-minded brokers, a woman with an intrinsic inability to profit from a customer's ignorance. And Lori understands that John, too, is haunted by his own honesty. Other brokers hate him for the deals his inspections have ruined, but Lori knows that he is the consumer's best friend, a kind of superhero who saves buyers from their own mistakes.

Reputations, after all, are everything in this field, and John carefully guards his own. He serves as vice president of the local branch of the American Society of Home Inspectors, dutifully collecting news for the quarterly newsletter. His colleagues think well of him. They know he adheres like flypaper to the ASHI code of ethics: integrity, honesty, objectivity. And he, in turn, knows all the guys in the business. He knows who is too lazy or chicken to climb on a customer's roof; who overcharges for flashy computerized reports; who has been sued, lost his business, and been forced to change his name.

Lori slams the door of her Lexus and rushes up the front walk to her clients. "Sorry I'm late," she wheezes. "David, Madeleine, I see you've met John." She smiles toward him, her tired eyes smudged with liner. Dog hair is visible on her black pants and, from beneath a colorful neck scarf, the dingy pearls peek out. John pictures her applying makeup in the car with a shaky hand.

"He's one of the best," she says.

John does not know the asking price of this house, but he is certain it will be high enough to make Lori's year. He blinks and breaks her gaze. "Well, should we get going? I'll start with the roof."

He ambles to his GMC, hauls the articulated folding ladder from the back, and braces it against the front elevation of the house. His first step on the ladder is unsteady, and for a moment he feels fatigue overtake him, the undertow of his sleepless night. By the third and fourth steps he regains his composure and scales the rest of the ladder as effortlessly as a lemur. His footing established on the roof, he looks down to his audience and sees the tops of their heads, triangulated, as they chat among themselves. A gust of laughter reaches his ears. Not one of them looks up to where he balances on an eave. Quickly, he takes in the condition of the roof. Standard three-tab asphalt shingles, two layers, unremarkable.

"It's really one of the most desirable neighborhoods in town," Lori is saying as he returns to the ground. "I think you've made a great choice."

"Oh, good . . ." The wife trails off, her eyes turning toward the house next door. The neighbor is still there with his MG, wielding a shammy cloth.

John suspects these two young people to be the type who will hire landscapers to trim their bushes. They will hire handymen to clean their gutters, plumbers to tighten their pipes. He is well aware that he is among the few in this town who prefer to do things himself; who would rather drown than pay a professional; who insulates his own attic, extends his own drain pipes, replaces his own cracked shingles. Most others treat home ownership as an entitlement, trusting that their house will provide shelter from the elements without strenuous effort on their part. Few seem to respect the marvel of engineering and ingenuity that a house represents.

Only once has John overestimated his abilities. Without the help of an electrician, he'd attempted to replace several two-pronged outlets with three-pronged grounded outlets and had been flattened by a forceful shock. As he lay prone on the dining room floor, Diana had shrieked that he was foolish and egotistical, that he would never admit there were things he was not qualified to do.

Lori opens the lockbox. Inside, the house is bright and cold as an art museum. John does not usually notice a home's decor any more than a woman's nail polish, but today his senses are uncomfortably heightened, and as the party steps through the living room, he is sharply aware of its spare furnishings. There is a low-slung orange sofa fronted by a coffee table, a glossy black oval at knee-banging height. What person enjoys sitting on such a sofa? Where does a man put down a drink? The wife who lives here, he is sure, would scowl at a glass placed upon the table. She would be a woman who slides a coaster beneath her husband's tumbler and moves it away from the table's edge, as if he were a child. The kind of woman who picks lint from his shirt without asking, who brushes crumbs from his chin in public.

John's own home boasts original geometric linoleum from 1941, and its bathrooms are lined with veteran baby-blue tile. The furniture, however, is only eighteen years old, chosen by himself and his wife during a giddy shopping spree the day after closing. He remembers that day as one of the most joyful of their marriage. He and Diana had been buoyed by the same warm wave of exhilaration, tasted the same salt of home ownership. They'd spun through the furniture showroom, laying claim to a sectional sofa, a king-sized sleigh bed, a dining set for eight. Styles have changed since then, of course, but Diana has nimbly updated the existing pieces. The sectional has been disguised with slipcovers over the years, each retiring to the linen closet after its tour of duty. The huge oak bookshelf—forever displaying John's building code manuals and Diana's archive of *House Beautiful*—has been renewed with countless coats of color. The marriage may have slipped into obsolescence, but the house has always remained painstakingly fresh. For eighteen years John has been comfortable within its confines, surveying the world from its windows, watching the daffodils bloom in spring, rose of Sharon in summer, sunflowers in fall. At no juncture has he felt the desire to trade it for any of these nouveau colonials. He loves and respects the house and the ghosts it contains, of his own life and of those who came before. The previous owners had remained there well into their eighties, and John wholly expects to do the same, with or without Diana. He intends to keep the bones of the house strong and its organs clean for decades to come, even as the skeletons of newer houses rise and fall around it.

Most inspectors make a beeline for the basement mechanicals, then vet the rest of a structure. John knows that he is a bit of a renegade in that he prefers to reverse the order. In his opinion, kicking off with heavy-duty items like the service panel and furnace is a sure way to unsettle a buyer, and once the questions start coming, it can take hours to get to the first floor. He prefers to start with attics, sparse and innocuous, and work his way down so that, by the time they reach the water heater, his customers are limp and glazed over.

So he leads Lori and her buyers to the attic first. Inhaling deeply, he ventures out along the narrow beams. The wood beneath his feet feels solid and sure, and he marks this on his clipboard. He follows the beams as far as he can in each direction, feeling the slabs of the sloped ceiling with his hand. Dry and clean. The insulation is new, mirror-tight. He stands for another moment, listening. There have been times when he's detected the scratching of hidden animals in attics, even in daylight, so brash and accustomed to privacy they are. He holds still for a long quiet moment, breathing the fishy smell of fiberglass, before turning and stepping back.

"How does it look?" the wife asks.

"Good," John replies. "Solid."

He leads them back down the stairs, feeling a flick of pleasure in the sound of footsteps tapping obediently behind him. The second floor of the house is clearly an addition, fitted upon the old house like a plastic lid. It is a classic layout, devoid of interest: three bedrooms with a shared full bath and, at the east end of the floor, a vast master bedroom with triple exposure, skylight, walk-in closet, crown molding. The Tuscan-tiled master bath features a Jacuzzi, towel warmer, and half-moon window with a view of treetops.

There is no texture to any of these rooms, no place for defects to hide. John spends no more than a few minutes in each, checking the registers, feeling the frigid central air pushing through. He moves independently of the group now, hearing snippets of the wife's comments as the group serpentines slowly behind him.

"I love this little catwalk balcony," she says brightly. "And I love that the laundry room is upstairs."

Lori murmurs encouragingly. John is relieved to be alone as he tests the water pressure in the master bathroom sink. He flushes the toilet. He takes the bottle of fluorescent tracer dye from his fanny pack, measures and pours the liquid into the bowl, flushes again. He tests the showerhead, then moves to the Jacuzzi tub. It is degrading, he feels, for a serious home inspector to examine a Jacuzzi—to stoop to a brass faucet embellished like the knob of a palace entry and wait for the jets to gush. This is a gray area in ASHI's standards of practice, something he could justify omitting, but he senses that these buyers would not appreciate that. As he stands watching the tub fill, he allows himself to picture the wife introducing a toe to scalding water, then easing her leg in so that the skin turns a slow scarlet. Gingerly, she would lower her body into the water until only her head and neck cleared the surface. Then she would relax and survey the vista beyond the arched window, the trees and sky every inch her own.

The jets come on strong and sure. John drains the water, leaves the bathroom, and moves downstairs. In the kitchen, he turns on the tap and leaves it running for the septic dye test.

"Beautiful cabinets," Lori is saying. "You can tell they were just done."

The wife nods. "They're gorgeous. And I love the tiled backsplash, don't you, honey?"

The husband stands vacantly at the far side of the kitchen island, his hands deep in his pockets. He does not reply at once. His gaze is abstracted, perhaps focused on an evening in his future when he'll come home to this kitchen and greet his family. When John catches the man's eye, he thinks he sees a flicker of apprehension.

"They're very nice," the husband replies.

If all goes well with the inspection, this man will live here. This will be the landscape upon which fresh chapters of his life and marriage will play out, for better or worse. John doesn't purport to be a gauge of the intimate lives of others, but he imagines that this couple is vulnerable to the same blights as any. Perhaps this wife will become callous and antagonistic like Diana. Perhaps all women do, eventually. If John were a different sort of man, he might beckon the husband into a corner and caution him about wives turning against husbands without warning. He might alert him to the perverse importance of *talking*. He might tell him how he'd always believed he and Diana were viscerally linked, that she'd been as much a part of him as his lungs or liver, that their communication had approached telepathy. So then, how, in nineteen years of marriage, had he failed to notice what she one day referred to as a "brick wall" between them? All at once, it was too late for endearments; all the talking they'd ever done was meaningless, abruptly sealed away behind them.

John opens the cabinet doors beneath the kitchen sink. Bottles of cleaning fluid are organized around beautiful new PVC piping. There is still sawdust in the corners of the cabinetwork. He turns off the tap and circles the kitchen, opening and closing drawers. He checks the countertops, above and below, feeling the weight of Lori's eyes on him.

"Granite," John mumbles. "There's a small possibility of radon, in case you'd like to order a test."

When he looks up, he sees the wife leaning against the counter, her inflated middle tapering to the implausible pair of tanned legs.

"No, I think we'll pass," the husband says.

John clears his throat. "Otherwise everything looks clean."

"Oh, good." The woman smiles and, after a moment, asks, "So, how long have you been an inspector?"

John hesitates before answering. He is unable to tell from the tone of her voice whether she is asking out of polite curiosity or skepticism.

"About twenty years," he says. "Truth is, I know more about the houses in this town than anyone should be allowed to know."

"Oh, do you live here?" The surprise in the woman's voice is undisguised.

"Since before you were born, probably." At this, Lori shoots him a look.

The wife nods at John. There is something appraising in her face that makes him uneasy.

"I think you'll love it here," he goes on. "It's a great school system. I'm on the school board myself, making sure of it." He glances at her belly and attempts an avuncular grin. "Girl or boy, do you know?"

The woman's smile dims. "It's a surprise."

"I have a daughter." John hears his voice echo in the kitchen. "She's in the high school now."

The woman nods. She now strikes him as much older than before, too old to be having a baby.

"We have a terrific theater program," he continues aimlessly, "and the football team does very well."

Again, the dim smile.

"All I can say is, enjoy them when they're little. You'll see how fast it goes." As John speaks, he feels a thickening at his tonsils. Bethany's childhood has sluiced past like water.

The husband has come to his wife's side now. Neither of them responds to John's last comment, and he can't blame them. He always hates it himself, when others proffer such insulting banalities. Children grow up, everyone knows that. He feels humiliation brush his cheeks like sandpaper. The prickling migrates to his neck and chest, inflaming the skin beneath his shirt.

Husband and wife lean together against the granite countertop, unfazed by the radon progeny that may or may not be forming a particulate cloud around them. It is now clear to John that these are unapologetic members of the city rich, that breed of newcomers who've been slowly infiltrating the town, contracting showy new construction or transforming the abodes of the dead and elderly. John has watched modest, well-loved homes grow extra limbs overnight, become burdened with columns and porticos, moated with wrought-iron gates. He's seen bumper-stickered Volkswagens give way to army-sized SUVs. And in his rearview mirror, more and more often, he finds shadowed drivers behind gleaming windshields, clutching cell phones, tailgating.

"So, what's next?" the man asks. His arms are crossed over his chest, and the vulnerability in his eyes has vanished. This is a man in control of his life, proprietor of home and family, and John feels the cool, professional distance between them.

He leads them back through the icy living room and into a smaller room with a piano and built-in window seats. This room, some kind of parlor, is obviously another addition. It is crisp, with unclouded windowpanes that give an impartial view of the outdoors. The window seats are covered with blue velvet cushioning suitable for a royal family portrait. It is difficult to believe that the same wife responsible for the stiff orange sofa has chosen the upholstery here. Just as Diana loved to do, this other woman must have sat with fabric swatches and held them to the light. Whenever he came upon his wife in such a pose, he would be struck by the distant focus in her eyes, as if she were envisioning a life somewhere beyond the walls of the room, a life more captivating than her own, a life that he suspected did not include him.

It's impossible to think their bond had been so tenuous. After all these years, Diana's insistence that there was a fault line all along—that they communicated poorly, that he'd always been self-involved, unromantic—does not jibe. Her dissatisfaction had congealed too suddenly; her voice was too sharply contemptuous. Any man would be suspicious. And then, in January, the odd phone calls in the morning began, followed by lengthy, unfruitful trips to the mall. John had more than once thought of trailing her car, but resisted. What a pathetic thing it would be to usher his proud GMC behind her Impala. And worse than the ugly possibility of being detected, of course, was the calamity of being correct.

So he did nothing, and in March the paperwork appeared on his night table on the letterhead of their family attorney. Diana did not come home from work. Prowling the hallway in the night, stunned and sleepless, John found a strip of light beneath his daughter's door. Entering the room, he met Bethany's eyes where she lay propped in bed with a book. The look she gave him was flatly unsurprised and, he swore, held a glint of mockery.

John bends to check the electrical outlets beneath the velvet window seats: three-pronged and modern. As he stands, he sees the husband tentatively run a finger over the glossy fall board of the piano and catches the private smile his wife gives him.

"He used to play," she explains, then looks back to her husband. "We could get a piano and put it right here. We should do it."

"What a wonderful idea," Lori chimes.

John has no doubt they will do it. This wife will surely surprise her husband one Christmas morning with a grand piano wrapped in a bow. It's the sort of purchase people like these make without undue concern, rooted in the belief that everyone deserves the things that attract them.

John's house, too, holds a piano—an old upright from the elementary school, which Diana was savvy enough to procure when the district sprang for concert grands. It makes John crazy that the board squanders property taxes on such extravagances, but at least Bethany has had her own instrument to play at home. It is a blond wood Kimball with shallow graffiti inscribed on its lid, and Bethany had sat dutifully at its bench for a few months, picking out commercial jingles and television theme songs. Then she quit and turned to acting. It's normal, John supposes, for his daughter to aspire to stardom. It's normal for a girl her age to paint her eyelids with pink glitter and wear rhinestones on her jean pockets. And yet John notices that Bethany dresses differently from most girls in town. He isn't sure what is influencing her: music videos or supermarket magazines. Her friends seem coarse, with pitted faces like moonscapes and suggestive phrases across the rears of their shorts. Bethany herself is delicate-featured and thick-haired. When she leaves her hair long and simple, John thinks she is as lovely as any actress in a photograph.

Earlier that month, she played Holly Golightly in the school's unlikely musical production of *Breakfast at Tiffany's*. The director had caused a near scandal by casting Bethany—an eleventh grader—as the lead, but apparently no senior was able to carry the role. John came to the play alone and sat apart from Diana, the back of whose head he could see several rows ahead of him. He watched his daughter pretend to smoke from a cigarette holder onstage and give a real kiss to her costar. She made up for her middling singing voice in brass and volume, and her potholed melodies soared gloriously across the auditorium.

After the play, John rushed to arrive backstage before Diana. He stood at the periphery of a squealing huddle around Bethany, holding a bouquet of red roses and waiting his turn to commend her. She smiled politely as he gave her the flowers, as if indulging a misguided suitor. He found himself stumbling as he told his daughter how well she'd acted, how much like

Holly she'd been. He left her holding the bouquet tentatively, as if it were not hers, and when he turned back saw that she'd rested it on the floor beneath a school desk.

John tests the windows of the piano room, noting the fluid opening of the sashes. Lori stands in a shaft of sunlight, saying, "It's a lovely room, don't you think? So bright and pleasant."

It must be almost four o'clock, judging from the slant of light through the glass. A single home inspection always seems to occupy the whole afternoon, no matter how quickly he works. He thinks longingly of his couch at home—truly *his* couch now, no one else's—and its burgundy slipcover. He thinks of the Michelob bottles in the refrigerator. Closing the windows in the parlor one at a time, he seals out the warm breath of spring that has already begun to mix in the room. The dry chill of central air returns, and John's fatigue becomes an aching, shrunken feeling in his skull.

He exits the parlor at a clip, not waiting for his flock to keep pace, and heads for the basement steps. The air, as he descends, takes on a more humane humidity for which he is grateful. The basement is refreshingly raw, lined with ripped industrial floor covering and sided with cinder block. The only untouched, indigenous part of the house. A tower of softened cardboard boxes tilts in a corner along with a dusty bicycle and snowboard. Several cobwebbed windows are level with the ground, framing the undersides of azaleas. These, he is sure, are the original basement windows, thick and invincible. John tests one, finds it sealed shut.

He takes a breath and concentrates on the low humming sound at the far side of the basement. Here are the mechanicals, enclosed within plywood walls. This is his favorite part of an inspection. More than anything he enjoys scanning the maintenance history stickers on the sides of oil tanks and water heaters, the old names and dates scrawled in faded ink. John feels the old gallop in his pulse return as he slips behind the thin walls, out of the group's view.

The furnace is dormant for summer, a run-of-the-mill American Standard. There is some rust on the belly of the oil tank, like the barnacled hull of a ship. The maintenance dates go back fifteen years, but this tank is older than that. *It's a workhorse,* John thinks of telling the clients, but knows they won't appreciate the meaning of this. To him, looking at the tank is like looking at a stalwart old man, a veteran of important wars. These machines are the pumping heart of the house; everything else is frivolous and disposable in comparison. He hears snippets of discussion on the other side of the wall, Lori's voice, small and obsequious. "Definitely, definitely."

He recalls the evening he and Lori talked over drinks at Charley's. She'd confided in him some garden-variety disappointment with her husband, and he'd complained about some small failing or other of Diana's. They'd sat together amicably in the tavern's wooden booth, pints of amber ale between them, the tableau dimly lit by a wall sconce. There had been a warmth to their rapport, made possible by the relative mildness of their grievances, and when they parted, it had been with the lightness of friends returning to safe and familiar quarters.

After Diana's sudden departure, John hired his own lawyer out of the yellow pages. The lawyer assumed that John would request custody of Bethany, and he hadn't contradicted this. He knew he would have a case. Diana had abandoned them both without warning, without a hint to her whereabouts, leaving father and daughter as awkward housemates.

The strange thing was that Bethany hadn't complained. Day after day she came home from school as if nothing had changed. She sat across from John at the dinner table, Diana's empty seat at her side. As her eyes lowered to the microwaved lasagna on her plate, John felt certain that she knew where her mother was. They were in secret contact, he surmised, and Diana was bracing for battle. One night, when John could no longer stand watching his daughter's prim, calculated motions at the table, he cleared his throat and heard himself tell her that he did not intend to fight for custody. She was old enough to decide for herself, and that was what he expected.

Over the following weeks, he felt himself on trial. He made genuine overtures to his daughter—offered to take her shopping for summer clothes, to host an end-of-school party for her friends—but feared that these efforts seemed forced and transparent. He wanted to remind Bethany of the way she'd squealed in delight when he lifted her into the air as a child, but he sensed the powerlessness of nostalgia against the new barrier of womanhood she'd erected. This, he imagined, was the loss felt by every man who'd ever raised a daughter into adulthood, been through that tragedy. Bethany responded coolly to his efforts, and finally he let them drop.

The days seemed to accelerate then, jerking out of his grasp like a violently unspooling fishing line. And then, last night, he had the phone call from Diana. Abruptly, after weeks of silence, her voice. Bethany was going to pack some things, she said, and come stay with her.

"What do you mean, stay with you?" John asked, his voice tight. "Where are you?"

Diana sighed through the receiver. "What does it matter, really." Her tone was no longer resentful—just tired.

After dinner, Bethany came out of her room with an overstuffed duffel bag.

"That's a big bag" was what John had said. She smiled, a shadow of wistfulness at the corners of her lips, and tugged the bag behind her.

"Here, let me take that."

He carried his daughter's bag out of the house and onto the porch. Diana's Impala was waiting in the driveway, its headlights shining in their faces. Bethany hugged John guardedly, and he returned the hug in the same way, so that there was a gap of several inches between them. Then she went out to the car, her figure silhouetted. For a moment, after the passenger door slammed shut, the faces of mother and daughter were briefly illuminated by the interior ceiling light. Then the light faded, and the car backed out of the driveway into the dark.

It is this image that returns to John as he stands between oil tank and furnace. He can still see the faces aglow in the car, already like relics, unreachable.

Lori pokes her head into the mechanicals room. "You okay in here?"

John ignores her winking, confidential tone. "Fine," he grumbles.

As he emerges, he hears the wife saying, "I'm just surprised they left it this way." She gestures to the floor, frowning. "But we can rip this up and put down some good carpeting." She brushes a hand over a wall of aged corkboard, breaking off crumbs. "And this stuff has to go. We can put up new drywall and recessed lighting and make a really nice playroom."

John's jaw tightens, and he walks away from the voices. He comes to a halt by the electrical service panel and slowly unscrews its cover. It's a 200-amp panel with no fewer than five GFCI breakers. Overkill, maybe, but he feels a prick of envy. He is ashamed to never have invested in GFCIs for his own house, despite the cautionary tales. He remembers clearly the chapter on electrical safety from his certification course, what happens when a loose current finds a ground fault in an unsuspecting human body. It would have been so easy to install circuit interrupters himself when Diana was out of the house, and yet something had made him forget. It is inexcusable for a professional to expose himself and his family to such a simple and unnecessary danger. Their home, after all his vain attentions, is nothing but a coiled snake, charged and capricious. As he thinks of this, a knot tightens in his gut, and his hands tremble as he screws the cover back onto the panel.

He takes measured steps around the perimeter of the basement and pauses beside the corkboard, littered with staples and ripped paper corners. Upon closer examination, he finds traces of scribbled crayon—the outlines of horses, rabbits, trees—like cave paintings. And, faintly, a ladder of penciled parallel lines rises from the floor, labeled with initials and dates: *'62, '63, '64*. Looking at these hieroglyphics, John feels a squeeze in his chest, akin to the ache he'd once felt watching his daughter sleep in her crib.

He turns to Lori and the clients. The husband now stands with an arm around his wife's waist, a bright wristwatch flashing at her belly. John finds himself transfixed by its luster, by the hallucinogenic circles of the wife's dress, the miraculous swell beneath. They are the uncontested, oblivious owners of all of it. They lack even the awareness to doubt this.

"Are we all done?" the husband asks.

John coughs artificially. "Yup, that's about it." His own voice sounds muted to him, muffled by the basement walls.

"Everything looks all right?" the wife asks.

John meets her open, girlish gaze for a moment, the crystalline irises with nothing in them but confidence in the universe. He feels nearly dead in comparison, wearier by the moment, as if he were being depleted by her presence. It seems that there is a lack of air in this place, that the windows have been sealed shut for decades, since the long-ago children were last measured.

A slow moment elapses. In the space of this pause, John feels the breath of the past, the cumulative exhalations of the house and its lost inhabitants. They seem to gather in the basement's webbed corners, fuzzed with dust and dead skin. It strikes him that this is a last capsule of memory, that when it is swept and painted, the raw floor carpeted and windows unstuck, no trace of life will remain. The history of the house will persist only in the memories of its former residents, those far-flung stewards of dwindling, inexact images.

These meditations visit John as he stands, breathing stale air, and fuse into a beam of insight. The house, in that moment, speaks to him. Suddenly, he sees this basement as an invaluable artifact. Perhaps another set of purchasers will understand, and preserve it.

He inhales purposefully. His eyes turn away from the clients and fix upon a clouded window, its smear of dull sunlight.

"Well, not everything," he hears himself say. "You've got some pretty decrepit machinery here. The furnace is inefficient, water heater's on its last legs, and the oil tank's vintage Watergate."

Lori jerks around to look at him.

"And I don't feel good about the WDI situation."

"WDI?"

"Wood-destroying insects. Termites, carpenter ants. I can't get inside the walls to diagnose how much damage there might be, but I saw a few red flags. You can try preventative measures, of course, like a baiting system, but that'll be a few thousand bucks and it's basically a crapshoot. It might already be too late. The structure could already be compromised."

The husband's pale face flushes. "You didn't say anything about red flags."

John shrugs, drops his gaze to his clipboard. "I'm just mentioning it now as part of the wrap-up. There was wood dust on the porch. No visible mud tubes, but there are signs of chronic dampness near the foundation, under the azaleas. Very attractive for termites."

"And the machinery," the wife says calmly, "does it all have to be replaced?"

"Ma'am," John hears himself say, "it would be irresponsible of me to recommend anything else."

"Well, that's something we can bring to the bargaining table," Lori interjects. "You could ask for a credit to cover the costs."

"But what about the insects? That sounds like a deal breaker to me," the husband speaks in the deep voice of pragmatism.

"We don't know for sure if there's a problem," answers Lori, looking to John. Her head tilts slightly and her eyes blink rapidly.

"No, you're right. There's a possibility there's no damage." John pauses, swallows. "You could certainly take that chance."

The wife stands in place, her optimism still there like firelight, undimmed. John's eyes are repelled from her as from a blaze. "Another thing I remarked before you arrived, during my exterior inspection, is a questionable septic. You'll notice the grass in the back is bright green. That's the classic sign of an overworked field. It's hard to say how many years might be left, but you'd be wise to be careful with your water usage. Short showers, easy on the laundry, and so on."

The woman stands silent, clear-eyed, watching John. Then she turns an expressionless face toward her husband, a barely perceptible quiver at the lips.

"Here's your report summary," John murmurs, handing the clipboard to the husband. "Excuse the chicken scratch. The full, typed report should arrive in the mail within forty-eight hours."

Lori stands in place, smirking slightly, the creases beneath her eyes etched in a kind of shallow mirth. It's as if she is waiting for the joke to reveal itself, for John to break into a grin and rip the report in two.

Instead, the husband signs the paper, and John tears the top sheet across its perforated line, leaving the carbon copy beneath. He touches his ear involuntarily. His voice catches as he speaks, croaking.

"Nice to see you, Lori."

She opens her mouth, then lets it close again. She nods and crosses her arms over her chest, as if concealing an unbuttoned blouse. After he leaves, John imagines, she will use her most coaxing broker's tone to try to allay the damage. She will return her clients' attention to the granite countertops, Jacuzzi tub, piano room. There will be no one to stop her from trying. John turns and leaves them in the basement.

He drives silently home. As he moves through town, he is aware only of the blunt power of his truck gripping the road. He concentrates on this feeling, the simple momentum of driving, of making a dull push upon the world. On Mercy Avenue, the town's main concourse, he does not slow, as is his habit, to take proud note of the properties he's inspected. He lets the houses blur past.

John turns onto Iron Horse, beneath the mature oaks and maples that have shaded his walks with Bethany and Diana on so many summertime mornings. He presses the brake gently as the roof of his own house comes into view, its chimney like a snorkel. Drawing closer, he views it the way another inspector might. The house is a plain brown box, on its fifth year of paint. It rests at the base of an incline that turns icy in winter and channels storm water in spring. The basement is prone to flooding. This is an error of siting, impossible to solve.

The growl of John's truck dies as he cuts the ignition. He steps along the front walk, over the same seven cracks in the flagstone that grow wider each year. The boxwood still needs pruning. The porch steps list, and the railing bobs under his hand. His work boots are heavy and slow, but they bring him to the door before he is ready. He pauses there for a long moment, his key in the knob, suspended between the sidelights' dark margins.

The Wonder Garden

JFK is disgraceful. The arrivals hall is dirty, sickly lit, clogged with sour-mouthed taxi drivers. What a shameful first face for the country to offer its rosy visitors and inspirited immigrants, Rosalie thinks, this unpainted face of neglectful contempt. *You're on your own* is what it seems to say. She holds up a sign with the girl's name on it and attempts a smile sunny enough to obliterate the gloom.

She and her family have been standing for nearly an hour behind a metal barrier, like cattle, waiting for the passengers of Etihad Flight 101 to come through baggage claim. Finally, a river of new arrivals comes into view: tight-lipped, dark-skinned people hunched jealously over mounded baggage carts. A woman with an airline badge stops in front of them, a scrawny girl at her side. During the handoff, Rosalie maintains her smile, but is unnerved by how strongly the girl resembles a mongoose, with round black eyes and a pointed chin. Her hair is severely parted down the center, and a tight ponytail exposes elfin ears. She is dressed in a blue T-shirt and lightweight olive pants, not the elaborate native costume Rosalie had expected.

Hannah vibrates with excitement like a dog who would bound upon the girl, licking. There is no doubt for her that this will be a great new friend, plain and malleable.

"Hi!" she cries. "Welcome to America!"

Rosalie extends a hand and squeezes the girl's damp, wormlike fingers. In contrast to this diminutive person, her own children are giants. Their faces are assertively sculpted, with patrician brows and jawbones. It's striking, seeing these young people together, how God is capable of carving such variety from the same stone. As Rosalie studies the girl's face, she decides there is a slanted kind of prettiness there—something that flickers in and out, dodging and diving.

In the short-term parking lot, Rosalie gestures to the titanic Grand Caravan, gleaming silver. "Here it is," she says. The girl's pointed face shows no change. For a moment, Rosalie sinks with the suspicion that this was all a mistake, that they have gotten a dud, that the next several months will be suffocating. But, no. It is her job to make it work. She is a mother, first and foremost, and this stranger will soon be like her own child. She takes a quick gauge of the girl's height and weight: borderline. To be safe, she gestures her into the middle booster seat. The girl fidgets but does not resist as Rosalie buckles her in.

On the Hutchinson River Parkway, Rosalie keeps to the center lane, tolerating the maniacs weaving around her. These initial surroundings are disappointing, the cramped multifamily dwellings along the exit lane, the frightful megaliths of Co-op City.

"Don't look!" Hannah says jubilantly to the girl. "This isn't where we live. I'll tell you when to look."

"How was the flight?" Rosalie attempts in her best motherly tone.

The girl's voice barely rises above the sound of the car engine, soft and musical. "It was okay, thank you."

"You must be tired."

"Yes."

The Grand Caravan finally merges onto an emptier highway, wide and clean, edged with lush leafwork, and Rosalie feels a familiar sense of relief, of spatial freedom. As they pull off the exit and drive through the center of Old Cranbury, she prickles with a feeling of pride for this place, its preserved character, the quality of its people.

"That's the hardware store," Hannah says, "and the handbag store, and the health food store, and there's where we get our hair cut."

Rosalie glimpses the girl's profile as she looks out the window, brightened by the lucid and fair New England sun. She has cleared her own calendar these first few weeks. She'll write her "In the Spectators' Stand" column at night, after the children are asleep. She will devote her daylight hours to acclimating the student to her family and its roster of enriching activities.

"This is it," Hannah announces as they pull into the driveway. Rosalie tries to see her home through the girl's eyes and imagines it looks like paradise. There is a barn-style garage door, borders of neat Belgium block, stone pillars flanking the driveway. The flower boxes are full. She has added these careful details to the property over the years without ever altering the original structure. She is proud not to have wasted money on expansion, even as her family has burgeoned. The boys occupy two bedrooms, and she has transformed an attic storage space into a funky, garret-like room for the girls.

This is the room that Nayana will share. Rosalie has purchased a roll-out trundle for her, along with cheerful bedding, careful to avoid television characters she might not recognize. At home in Bangladesh, according to the exchange agency, the girl sleeps in a single room with her entire family. Rosalie has a picture in her mind of this room, of disheveled blankets, stained mattresses on the floor. The mother probably sweeps with a straw broom, ushers the dirt right out the door. Is there electricity? This point has been omitted by the agency. Rosalie has warned her children that this might be the student's first experience with it.

At dinner, the family eats quietly, a kind of humming suspense in the air. Rosalie is pleased that the kids have remembered her guidelines, to not ask too many questions and to speak more softly than usual. Nayana's family is probably not as rambunctious as the Warrens. There are cultural differences that need to be respected. Rosalie sorts through a muddle of feelings as she watches Nayana pick at her macaroni and cheese: pity for the girl, mixed with pride in herself for having invited her here, and a surging affection for her own children, sitting respectfully with their forks and knives, each of them excellent in his or her own way.

The girl is obviously exhausted. She lays her fork down as if its weight is too much for her and looks up to Rosalie in supplication.

"Why don't you go ahead and get ready for bed, Nayana. I'll show you where everything is."

Rosalie leads her down the hall, past the framed array of black-and-white photographs, a gallery of family joy. As they walk, Rosalie is almost ashamed of her tremendous fortune, and feels a shiver of gratitude for who she is, for what she has been given.

In the girls' bedroom, Nayana opens her suitcase, revealing a compact mound of clothing, and pulls out a pilled pajama set the color of mud. Rosalie waits outside the bathroom as she brushes her teeth, or completes whatever cleansing rituals she has learned at home. Before the rest of the family has finished eating, she is under her generic pink blanket, asleep.

In bed, Michael remarks, "She's quiet."

Rosalie stiffens. "Well, that's to be expected."

"I know. I was just making an observation."

She lets a beat pass. "It's going to be a great experience for the kids."

"I'm sure it will be. You always do wonderful things for them."

There is, Rosalie thinks, a sardonic inflection in his voice, passing beneath the words like a water moccasin. What is wrong with doing wonderful things for her children? This is an argument not worth having before bed. She has every confidence that, by inviting this girl into their home, they will all learn about the world. They have not traveled since Ethan was a baby, when they'd visited Mexico and Rosalie had gotten sick from the water. Now that they are a family of seven, now that Michael's work has intensified and airfares have risen, now that places like Mexico have dropped into the quicksand of crime, it makes more sense to stay home and bring the world to them.

The agency had allowed her to choose the nationality of her student. To Rosalie's dismay, many of the available students seemed to be from Middle Eastern and North African countries. Muslim. Rosalie had to admit she felt unprepared for that. She was more open-minded than most, but as a Christian and peace-loving American, she had mixed feelings about certain tenets of the Islamic faith. Not to mention that she was uncertain as to how her own community, having lost so many husbands and fathers in the terror attacks, would react to such a youth in its midst. And what would such a youth have in common with the Warrens? Wouldn't she feel uncomfortable, out of place, in her burka, or face veil, or whatever covering she was required to wear? Rosalie had to be honest with herself: it would make *her* uncomfortable to share space with a veiled child. She was afraid she might slip and say something that might offend the girl, defame her culture. It was one thing to host a foreign student, another to incite a political skirmish.

So she'd chosen a girl from a Hindu region of Bangladesh. A little less obvious than India, a little more exotic. She taught her children to find the country on the map. They took out books from the library to learn about the customs and habits, dress and language. Rosalie emphasized that this was a thoroughly poor country, devoid of glittery urban pockets and mirrored skyscrapers. There was no question that they would be hosting an underprivileged child, introducing her to the dizzying freedoms and opportunities of American life. She pointed out that only a minority of Bangladeshi children have a chance to learn English in addition to their native language—the implication being that her own children, in their fortunate circumstances, should be grateful for their grade-level Spanish. Together, they learned about the Hindu religion, the meaning of the gods. Her children were entertained by the idea of so many deities for so many oddball things.

It's a thrill to bring Nayana on Sunday to outdoor church services at St. John's Chapel in the woods. The possibility flits through Rosalie's mind that mere exposure to such a parish, so humbly and effortlessly in harmony with Nature, will be enough to snap the girl out of her yoke of archaic, superstitious beliefs. At the end of a wooded path, the congregation is seated upon log benches facing the young pastor beneath his rustic trellis. The Warrens usher Nayana onto the wood-chip path in her white cotton dress like a shy debutante.

The pastor begins the service by announcing the presence of a special guest from afar, whom he is confident everyone will treat as an honorary member of the congregation. Faces turn and smile at the Warrens, and Rosalie feels lifted by the collective tide of goodwill. It is so strong, she thinks, that Nayana must feel it, too, the pure force of decency in these people around her. The pastor then leads the group in song, and Rosalie lifts her voice to meet the others, twisting and braiding in the air. Rosalie glances at Nayana and wonders what revelations might be occurring inside her brain at this moment.

Back in the car, Rachel asks, "Nayana, what is your church like at home?"

"They don't have church," Noah calls from the far backseat.

"He's right," Jonah says from the middle backseat. "Don't you remember? They have temples and icons. They paste silver foil on rocks and paint them orange."

Rosalie intervenes. "Why don't we ask Nayana what she thought of the service?"

There is a pause, then the girl's voice lilts, "I thought it was very nice."

Noah grunts. "She *has* to say that."

Rosalie glances in the rearview mirror to where her youngest son sits behind his brothers. He alone among her children remains pale after three months of summer vacation, three months of dazzling afternoons spent in his room, sorting minerals and dead insects.

"Put your seat belt on, Noah," she tells him, and watches him yank the strap from its sheath. It kills her that the belt hits him just at the neck, denting the skin, but she fights the urge to adjust it. He could technically still be in a booster—he has yet to surpass the weight requirements—but she would not point this out. Any scrap of dignity, she knows, is crucial to a boy this age. Even his face reflects the torture of pubescence. The eyebrows are too low, left behind by the reckless rise of his forehead, and there is a permanent look of scorn in his eyes, set temporarily too close together. Rosalie has faith that his features will soon adopt more regular proportions, as his older brothers' have, but knows better than to assure him of this.

Rosalie meets Nayana's eyes in the rearview mirror and smiles. She is not a true "exchange" student, in that no child from Old

Cranbury will be spending equal time in Bangladesh. Instead, one of Noah's eighth-grade classmates will stay with a family in Australia for the semester. Noah had wanted to do this, but Rosalie had told him no. She can't fathom one of her children being absent for so long, coming home taller and heavier, full of meals she hasn't prepared.

There is no higher directive than motherhood, she believes, no better purpose than shepherding new life through the world. She is continually transfixed by her own offspring, these five miraculous iterations of her own genes. What a pity, those women who choose not to have children, who deny the clamoring souls inside them. She disapproves, too, of those women who have children casually, who treat them as accessories, or worse, burdens—those women who continue to chase power careers, who hire live-in nannies who keep the television on all day, as she has witnessed through the window of Suzanne Crawford's home. It's no wonder her little boy still hasn't spoken a word.

The sad fact is that Rosalie is nearing fifty. She might have tried for another child, but her husband had been firmly opposed, and now the stockades of menopause are undeniable. Still, she takes comfort in the fact that there is no family in town larger than her own. Because of this, she enjoys a kind of celebrity. She is always the class parent in one grade or another at any given time. She knows every teacher and parent in the elementary, middle, and high schools. It is difficult to complete any grocery trip for all the chatting she is obliged to do. It was inevitable, of course, that she'd eventually run for school board and be elected. She understands what children need. She'd begun her first term this summer, an intrepid foot soldier in the battle of the budget. The numbers are daunting to her, the spreadsheets with rows of digits like crawling ants, but she knows better than to worry over them. What matters are the values those digits represent: each a history teacher, a soccer field, a new set of school bus tires. The decisions are, after all, basic. The board doesn't need another mumbling accountant. It needs Rosalie Warren, clearheaded and largehearted, mother of all.

As the late August sun dries the leaves, Rosalie feels the first stirrings of autumn. This is her favorite time of year, these last breaths of summer, the store-fresh smell of new denim. She drives the children to the mall and sets them loose in a pack, keeping Nayana to herself. The girl touches the clothing in Aéropostale as if it were powdered with gold dust. Rosalie takes the liberty of choosing things for her, hanging them in a dressing room, and shutting her inside. After several moments of silence, the door opens, and the girl stands dangle-limbed in a bumpy knit sweater dress, a crooked smile at her lips.

"Oh, don't you look fabulous!" Rosalie croons.

"Everything is so *short*," the girl says thinly.

"That's okay." Rosalie nods. "It shows off your long legs."

The girl flushes and retreats into the dressing room so that only her bony ankles are visible. Rosalie buys her the dress, along with a jean skirt, colored tights, and a pair of faddish ankle boots. She barely has time to review her own children's selections as they pile into the Grand Caravan like a winning team.

At their annual barbecue, Rosalie directs guests to the cholar dal platter that Nayana has helped prepare. As the guests make astonished noises with their mouths full, Rosalie puts a hand on Nayana's shoulder and tells the anecdote from the mall.

"Everything is so *short!*" she repeats.

John Duffy approaches Rosalie with a strained smile. His cheerful summer attire is like a costume on him, she thinks. The pink polo shirt and shorts are unable to disguise his cold-weather disposition, best suited to Carhartts and work boots. He is a home inspector—the most stringent in the business, he claims—and insufferable in his arrogance. The constant reminders that he is an entrepreneur, a self-made man, reek of a sense of inferiority and resentment. It is too late to get away. Rosalie gives him her best summertime smile, praying he knows better than to talk board business now. The other guests pull away, and even Nayana takes the opportunity to escape.

John launches right into it. "The cuts aren't even close to adequate." He thrusts his hands into his shorts pockets. "You have to admit that the high school was a mistake."

"Do you really think so?"

"Come on, Rosalie." He laughs drily. "It's bigger than some college campuses. Who are we trying to impress? With the economy the way it is? Come on. Would you have green-lighted it if you'd been on the board then?"

A chill shoots through Rosalie's veins, as if John has insulted one of her children. The new high school is like a Renaissance cathedral compared to the former cinder block cloister with its dank cells. The children of Old Cranbury deserve their new building. They deserve light and space and air. They deserve the new indoor stadium, the undented gym lockers, the Olympic-sized pool.

Rosalie shows her teeth in a smile. "I think I would have, yes."

"Well, we'll have to pay for it now," he snorts. "We'll have to cut electives, like it or not. Music, art, languages. And even, God forbid, sports."

"No." Rosalie shakes her head calmly. This speech, she suspects, is one that she will have to repeat all year. "We'll only need to cut some administrative and janitorial positions. And the busing will have to be doubled up. We'll just have to tighten our belts a little bit, John, until we get back on our feet. Every school district is going through this right now."

As she is cleaning up after the party, putting potato salad into Tupperware and throwing out broken tortilla chips, Rosalie feels unaccountably drained. She is not a person who naps, but she feels that if she were to lie down now, she would stay down for hours. The way to fight this drag, she knows, is to keep moving. She moves on to the buffet table and is rewarded with the gratifying vision of the empty cholar dal platter.

Early on the first morning of school, Rosalie prepares six lunches. She prints the name of each of her children on a brown paper bag and feels the usual sense of dislocation at seeing the names written out. The children will carry these names into the world, beyond the scope of her sight. There is a rush to the breakfast table, the plumage of self-selected fashions. Nayana sits quietly in her lilac tights and denim skirt, the battered satchel at her side full of crisp school supplies. At Rosalie's request, she will share a homeroom with Noah, who has promised to escort her to all her classes.

After they are gone, the house falls into bittersweet silence. Rosalie does not pause, but packs the breakfast bowls into the dishwasher and sits back down at the table with a notebook to plan the family commemoration event for September 11. Each year—each additional year of mourning for innocent lives lost, of troops crushed overseas—this project holds more meaning for her. It has never seemed adequate to observe a moment of silence at 8:46 A.M., to privately replay the barbarity of that day. This energy should be directed outward, she believes, funneled into a constructive project. This year, she decides, the focus of the event will be assembling care packages for the troops. The fighting is necessary, she believes, and ultimately for a righteous purpose, the most Christian purpose of all: peace on earth. Rosalie is embarrassed by Americans who remain willfully ignorant of the sacrifices their soldiers make every day to defend them and to bring stability to others. No one ties a yellow ribbon around a tree anymore, but Rosalie still does this every September and leaves it up until someone or something pulls it down.

She purchases thick wool socks for the soldiers, bottles of sunscreen, Sudoku puzzles, powdered Gatorade, boxes of Nilla Wafers. Her children float in and out of the dining room, where she has set up the boxes, helping to pack them in shifts. Only Nayana stays all day, sitting beside Rosalie. As they fill the boxes with foam peanuts, Rosalie allows herself to ask cautious questions about the girl's family.

"What does your father do for a living?"

"He was a construction worker," the girl answers simply. "But he died in the floods."

Rosalie is silent, arranging pink peanuts around a stack of socks. Her face heats. It is inexcusable, she thinks, that the exchange agency failed to include this information.

"How terrible," she says gently. "It must be very difficult not to have your father."

The girl nods. There are two older sisters, she says, who help their mother and who looked after Nayana when she was younger. Her sisters and mother worked in a rice mill, but lost their jobs when the mill went automatic. Now they are in the city, where Nayana goes to a special girls' school. Her family refuses to let her work. She is better than the boys in math and science, and they hope someday she will go to the polytechnic college and become an engineer, that she will move to America and bring them with her. This fulfillment of stereotype is exciting to Rosalie. The student will be, as she had hoped, an example of diligence and ambition to her own girls.

"That's exactly what America is for," she tells Nayana firmly. "There's no reason you shouldn't achieve your dreams here. You should start looking at colleges. I'll help you with your applications when the time comes, and serve as a reference or sponsor, or whatever you need."

Rosalie feels a swelling of thanks to God for choosing her as His servant for this task. Its significance is more than she can comfortably process, and she is humbled by it. She thinks with a knot in her throat of that mother, on the other side of the world—of the incredible flash of fortune that has sent her daughter to the United States. What a tangled gratitude that woman must feel. How awful to not be able to provide opportunities for her own children, to be forever occupied with the basics, with paying for sustenance, keeping the house from falling apart. Rosalie knows that she is among a lucky percentage of the world's women whose husbands go to work and return.

Of course, there are drawbacks. Michael stays late at the hospital and is rarely home for dinner. You would think he was a martyr, the way he talks about sacrificing for the family. Obviously, she'd known life with a brain surgeon would be like this. She'd managed her expectations from the start, filled her days with activity. She is not the type of woman who depends on her husband for constant companionship and emotional fulfillment. The ideal wife of a professional is able to provide much of this for herself, and does not begrudge her husband the scraps of personal space he needs, the odd hour or two he takes in his workshop: a detached tool shed outfitted with hammers and wood, out of which no construction ever emerges.

Autumn progresses. Hannah is abandoned by her best friend; Rachel can't shake off a clinger. Ethan falls on the field with another ACL tear, benched for the season. Rosalie scraps her varsity football column and rewrites it on sports injuries, the need to guard our children's long-term health while promoting victory on the field. Noah and Nayana quietly ride bicycles around the neighborhood and collect bugs. It gladdens Rosalie to see that he has taken her under his wing. She is touchingly young, much less sophisticated than the girls in town. One evening, Rosalie notices that the door to the den is closed, but she cannot imagine her son being interested in a girl like this. Rosalie knocks and opens the door to find them sitting primly together, watching *Nova*.

For Halloween, Rosalie solicits Nayana's help in creating the family costume. She has thought that, this year, they might all go as Bollywood stars. Nayana seems glad to accompany her to the fabric store, where they select jewel-toned silks and gold trim. After Nayana has finished her homework and the other children are visiting friends, they sew glittering saris and head scarves for the girls, tunics and turbans for Michael and the boys.

On Halloween, Rosalie reserves a table for eight at Gulliver's. The other patrons look up from their meals as the Warrens enter like a dinner-theater performance troupe. Rosalie and Nayana giggle together, and Rosalie feels hot, as if in a spotlight. The boys position themselves at the table so that they face the football game on the television screens above the bar.

"Fifteen dollars for a burger?" Michael grumbles.

"Oh, we only go out a few times a year," Rosalie says.

By the time the drinks and the plate of onion blossoms come, they have forgotten their costumes. Rebecca Lamb and her family stop by the table, her boys dressed halfheartedly as astronauts.

"You guys look amazing," she exclaims, "even better than last year. What were you, crayons?"

The burgers come, and Nayana's bland-looking penne primavera. The girl is especially talkative tonight, perhaps more at ease in East Asian garb. Hannah sits transfixed as she animatedly describes an amusement park near her home.

"It's called Wonder Garden, and it has water rides and a very big pool, and a motorcycle show called *Danger Game*." Nayana giggles. "I and my sisters want to go very much. But my mother does not like for us to talk about it. It is too much money, she says, and not necessary."

"We'll pay for it!" Jonah shouts. "We can pay for your whole family to go!"

"Oh." Nayana's smile fades. "No, no."

"Well," Rosalie says gently, "we can talk about that later."

As she eats, Rosalie becomes aware of a woman with a sullen little girl at a nearby table. The woman keeps looking at them, and in particular at Michael. Rosalie wipes her chin with her napkin. Michael, she notices, is chewing with a strange twist on his lips. He laughs loudly at something Jonah has said. Rosalie glances at the woman again—an attractive blonde in a cowl-neck sweater—and catches her eye. There is something in the woman's gaze, something flinty and unpleasant, that makes Rosalie look away.

Out of her costume, later, she is caught for a moment by her own image in the bathroom mirror. At a glance, she sees that the black eyeliner has miraculously succeeded in conjuring its illusion. It makes Rosalie look like a different woman, younger and more dangerous. This kind of thing rarely matters to Rosalie. She is not like other women whose appearances are paramount to their sense of worth. To her, the face she has at forty-eight is not so much aged as broken in. It is stretched and wrinkled in the right places, like a pair of soft jeans, a reflection of her character. Still, she is reluctant to wash her face tonight. She gazes for a prolonged moment at this new permutation of herself, lifting her chin to different angles, until the tiny fissures in the drying makeup begin to predominate and the effect shifts from sex appeal to mild derangement.

Michael is already in his pajamas when she comes out of the bathroom. She stands for a moment, watching him get into bed. He does not look at her in the bathroom doorway.

"Who was that woman in the restaurant?" she asks, careful to keep her voice light, curious.

"What woman?" Michael says, too quickly.

"The one who was looking at you."

"Who's that? I didn't notice anyone looking at me." He now looks toward Rosalie, in her pale blue nightgown with satin smocking. "Do you mean the waitress?"

There is something scripted in his delivery. Rosalie has never heard him speak in quite this way.

"There was a woman," she says more plainly, "looking at you like she knew you. Who was that?"

Rosalie's heart beats quickly, uncertainly, unsure of how to pilot such an exchange, of which there is no precedent in their twenty-two years of marriage.

"I'm sorry, honey," Michael continues in his theatric tone. "I really don't know who you mean. Maybe she was looking at our costumes."

Rosalie does not speak. She stands in front of her jewelry box and, with a snag of regret, takes the gold hoops out of her earlobes. Delicately, she places them in their blue velveteen slots and, as she executes this motion, seems to tap into a deep, primal stream that delivers the truth to all women. She holds on to the edge of the dresser for a moment and closes her eyes. Then she turns around and smiles flatly at her husband.

"You're probably right," she says.

When she wakes in the morning, Halloween has rotted away. There is a string of bright, hard days ahead of her leading up to the school board meeting. While the kids are out, she burrows into the budget numbers, taps them into her calculator. Michael returns home after dark each night and seems to avoid looking directly at her. Perhaps this is not strange, she thinks. Perhaps he never did.

For the board meeting, Rosalie chooses a charcoal pantsuit. She puts on a string of pearls and paints her nails with opaline polish. The message, she hopes, is elegant austerity. She is the newest member and the only woman on the board. Her fellow members are businessmen, financiers, lawyers, and accountants, or think they are. They wear the set jowls of stoic beleaguerment. They are accustomed to daily, unsentimental spinning of numbers and whiteboard presentations. John Duffy is in his habitual undertaker's suit. As the attendees convene in the high school library, Rosalie sits calmly behind her microphone, sipping at her water cup. All at once, she feels that she understands the plight of the politician, burdened with the expectations of an untutored public.

A group of adorable first graders, up past their bedtimes, leads the group in the Pledge of Allegiance. Their parents snap pictures, then usher the children home, vacating the front rows of seats. No one moves up to fill these, so that there is a yawning gap between the board and the seated public. All at once, Rosalie feels a sharp longing for her own children.

Gary Tighe leans toward his microphone and launches into the preliminary budget discussion. When he mentions the projected rise in expenses, there is audible rumbling. Rosalie makes eye contact with a fleshy, slit-mouthed woman she doesn't know, most likely a woman with no children of her own in the schools. The woman's hair is gray and frizzed, and she wears glasses that are too small for her face. This is exactly the type of person who comes religiously to board meetings. Rosalie can already predict her grievances: Property taxes are already too high—who can afford living here anymore?

When Gary finishes, he glances at Rosalie. She feels her shoulders contract into an involuntary shrug as she breathes into her microphone.

"I'm proud of the budget that we've been putting together," she says in a squeaking falsetto. "Given the restrictions we're facing, that every district is facing, I think we've done a fantastic job of putting our students first."

She grasps a sheet of paper and waves it in panicked illustration.

"I'm especially proud of the cost cutting we're going to do through retirement buyouts. It's a great way to infuse the district with fresh blood, and the only way to avoid losing extracurriculars."

John Duffy clears his throat. "If I may respectfully interject," he says in a voice like a sludge-filled river. "It's just not enough, Rosalie."

There is a whisper of fabric in the audience, as people shift in their seats.

"We can't expect the community to accept another tax hike. The high school was irresponsible, and it's time to pay the piper."

Gary Tighe begins to mutter something in defense, but John continues. His eyes are trained only on Rosalie.

"The taxpayers have sacrificed enough. Now it's time for our students to sacrifice. They've been coddled, they've never been told *no.* It won't kill them to go a few years without new sports uniforms, without another school psychologist."

"John," Rosalie begins, fighting to keep her voice level, "our job as adults is to make sure our students don't *have* to sacrifice." As she speaks, she thinks of him on her lawn in his pink polo shirt, eating from a paper plate, and hates herself for having fed him.

"Rosalie, that's just not realistic. I know you're new to the board, but you're not *that* young."

There is a rumble of laughter from the public.

"It's not just about sports games and bake sales," John continues. "Really, sometimes I think this board needs to be clearer about its expectations for candidacy. If you don't understand business, you can't understand budgets, and you're not qualified for a seat. It's a disservice to our students and to our community."

"Okay," Gary interjects. "Thank you, John. I think that's enough. Why don't we go ahead and open the public forum."

Rosalie's mouth is dry. She lifts her water cup and maintains a wry smile directed at the far wall of the library. She stares at the display of periodicals, crammed with arguments and opinion, words printed in aggressive black text, the voices of everyone but herself.

As expected, the gray-haired woman is the first at the podium. Her words are more spat than spoken, like gun spray. Rosalie leans back into her seat and tries to relax her shoulders. No one is going to make her speak anymore. The other board members respond to the woman's speech with their masculine drones, extinguishing it. She listens, then, to the mothers who rise, one by one, and put their fears into the microphone, their voices transformed into overamplified bird chirps. She sits back and becomes like a coral reef, allowing the voices to mingle and wave over her. After the public has risen to go, after the A/V staff has dismantled the overhead projector, she rises and smooths down the creases in her charcoal pants. The wry smile has hardened on her face. She nods at her colleagues, collects her notebook, and drives home.

At dinner the next night, Rosalie detects tension at the table. Noah does not look up from his plate, and there is a slight distortion on Nayana's face. Rosalie has the sudden suspicion that the children know about the board meeting, that they've heard about it at school. She wonders whether the other parents might have criticized her by name. She does not taste her dinner.

Afterward, while Noah is helping in the kitchen, she asks lightly, "Is everything okay, honey?"

"Of course," he says, wiping the counter. "Why wouldn't it be?"

These words are spoken frankly, with no note of sarcasm or accusation. Rosalie turns to look at her son, but he does not meet her eye, and his face reveals nothing.

That night, Rosalie adds another blanket to the bed. It is, incredibly, already November. Like every year, the autumn has swept past too quickly and been stripped bare. These unadorned days will soon be gone, too, cloaked by the holidays. Then the year will end and Nayana will fly away.

It would be right, Rosalie thinks, to secure some time alone with the girl while she can. She schedules a Saturday appointment at a salon. They can get manicures and have their hair done, and perhaps Nayana can have her eyebrows and facial hair waxed before Thanksgiving. It must be hard for her, Rosalie thinks, living with dark tufts over her lip and at the sides of her face. She wonders if there are opportunities for basic grooming in Bangladesh, of if girls just have to make the best of their lots.

At the salon, they sit together, their fingertips dipped in cuticle-softening solution.

"Are you close with your mother, at home?" Rosalie ventures.

"Yes, of course," Nayana says in her forever lilting voice. "She has no one except me and my sisters."

It is very difficult, Nayana explains, to be a widow in her country. There is virtually no chance of her mother finding another man to marry. Rosalie is impressed by the girl's unsentimental understanding of this, her poise in speaking about it. "That's very sad," she comments.

"It's different here," Nayana says, glancing at Rosalie. "People can find another chance. Women can marry again. Orphaned children can go to new families."

Rosalie nods, enjoying the cool sensation of the solution at her knuckles. She lifts her fingertips from the bowl and admires the softened, pinkened skin. When she looks at Nayana, the girl's face is somber.

"Noah told me about his father," she says. "I am very sorry."

Rosalie holds her fingertips aloft, glistening.

"What about his father?"

The girl stares with her overlarge mongoose eyes. She speaks again in a softened voice. "That he was a victim of the terrible day, in the offices of the World Trade Center."

Rosalie brings her hands into her lap and wipes the fingertips on her jeans. She feels the usual knife stab at the sound of the words *World Trade Center*, but it takes a long moment for her to parse the rest of the girl's sentence. She turns it over in her mind, but it still makes no sense. Michael, thank God, had been nowhere near the towers that day. This is something she has reflected upon innumerable times, and for which she has offered prayers of thanksgiving along with those of healing for the less fortunate.

"He showed me the name, the . . . plaque in the park," Nayana continues. "He showed me his birth father's name."

Rosalie stares at Nayana. "His birth father? What are you talking about?"

Nayana looks back in terror. "He told me how his birth mother died when he was a baby, and how, after 9/11, he was an orphan. You and Dr. Warren were very kind to take him in. Especially with so many children already."

Rosalie feels the blood hammer in her eardrums. She forces a plastic smile.

"I see. You say that he showed you a name on a plaque? What was the name?"

"Thomas Callahan," the girl whispers.

The blood has entered Rosalie's face now and fills the vessels behind her eyeballs. She nods and blinks slowly, spinning for a moment the way she had that cyclonic morning, grasping for new bearings. She remembers the name Thomas Callahan. He'd been a trader at Cantor Fitzgerald, she believes, one of the five local men incinerated that day. She knows the plaque, of course, though she hasn't looked at it for a long time. It's become part of the scenery, embedded in the boxwood shrubs, as invisible as the flagpole beside it. With the passing years, the names in the granite have lost their raw wrongness and assumed a permanent, fated quality.

Rosalie and Nayana are quiet while the manicurist girls dab their fingers dry and paint their nails with cool brushstrokes. As they are rising to leave, Rosalie looks at Nayana and sees that the girl has been transformed. Her eyebrows are thin and arched. Cleared of its brush, her face is arrestingly intelligent. A new pair of earrings catches the light at either side of her head, and there is an iridescent blue sheen to her hair, inimitable by any Caucasian. Her body is lithe and graceful as she stands and puts her purse over her shoulder.

"Thank you," she says to Rosalie with a slight bow of the head.

Noah does not look up when his mother enters the room. He is seated on the braided rug in his underwear, examining some jarred specimen. There is a greasy cowlick at his hairline, exposing a set of blackheads. His mouth twitches as he peers into the jar.

"Noah, can I ask you a question? Nayana told me something strange today."

"She's lying," Noah says simply, after Rosalie has finished.

"Why would she lie?"

"How should I know? I don't know what makes her do things." His eyes rise but stop short of his mother's face, somewhere near the clavicle. "I don't even know why she's here, to be honest."

Rosalie blinks. "I thought you liked having her here."

Noah scoffs quietly, in a way that makes her think of his father, then lowers his eyes again. "All I mean is that it's not like it's *helping* her, living here."

Rosalie feels the floor spin beneath her feet. She has a momentary flash of the school board meeting, feels that whirlpool wanting to tug her under. She lifts her chin, breathes in.

"Why did you lie?" she asks firmly.

"I told you, she's making it up. Why would you believe her and not me?"

Rosalie does not answer. All at once, she wishes that Nayana had never come. She wishes she had never volunteered her home to any stranger.

"What difference does it make, anyway?" Noah says. "It might as well be true."

"What might as well be true?"

"You know, about my *birth father*." Noah's voice lowers, trembles. "He's never here anyway. It might as well have been him."

"Pardon me?"

Noah is silent, holding the jar to his eye.

"What did you say?"

Noah shrugs, and his mouth squeezes to the size of a button.

Rosalie stands dumbly in the doorway for another second, a wax mold of a mother. Then, as if enough applied heat has melted her joints, she moves swiftly. In one fluent gesture, she takes the jar from her son's hand and catapults it to the wall. She is surprised by the momentum. The thick glass cracks cleanly on impact and shatters upon the hardwood floor, radiating shards onto the rug where Noah sits. His hand is still aloft, cupping air, and he raises his eyes to his mother in pale alarm.

The floor whirls as she turns and goes back through the door, closes it behind her and makes the latch snap shut.

When Michael comes home from the hospital, Rosalie sits mutely beside him as he watches the news. He leans back into the couch cushions and assumes a pose of relaxation, of a neurosurgeon having met the demands of his day. She will never know what his eyes witness within hospital walls, what scans of clotted lobes they examine, what eddies of blighted tissue. She does not presume to fathom any of it, has learned not to ask. Tonight, he has disrobed to a black T-shirt. Sitting beside him, the spinning feeling, which had subsided during dinner, returns. There is something disruptive about his presence, as if he were a dark magnet with alternating charges, first attracting, then repelling.

Michael turns his head and looks at her. She wants to speak, to force the moment into normalcy, but her larynx is constricted. She should, she knows, tell him about their son's transgression, but there is something in the way he looks at her, something blunt in his eyes that muffles her. She scrambles to rationalize this. There are, of course, many things that she does not talk with Michael about, things too complicated to discuss in the short time they have together, things not worth unloading, not worth confusing or burdening him with. All she wants to do now is stand up. She just wants to stand from the couch and go somewhere else, into some other room. But she is strangely unable to move.

Sinking into the cushion, captive, she thinks of Thomas Callahan. She hadn't known him when he was alive, but had seen his photograph and obituary in the newspaper. A kind, competent face. A father of three: a boy and two girls. His face comes to her now, in the colors of life, and she pictures him here on the cushion beside her, an unborn moment. She thinks of the phone call he might have made from his desk in the last clear seconds before the world caved. For a moment she wishes she'd been the one he'd called, the wife who'd heard his warm breath in the mouthpiece. She feels the collapse as if it were happening inside her. She feels a plunging grief for his children. A plunging grief for Noah.

The television news purrs on, and she remains in place beside her husband, pinned in his shadow. The collapse is still happening, always happening. She feels herself shrinking, becoming infinitesimal, a cone of dust. The children are in bed in their rooms, their little hive cells, asleep or awake. Rosalie sits far apart from everything, disintegrating.

She opens her eyes and looks at the television, a car commercial. An American couple achieves the top of a mountain, commanding a vista. She breathes in and breathes out. It is all right to retreat. She will pull back, she will redraw her boundaries. She will find her balance. When she emerges again, she will be refreshed, reenergized. She will be the best Rosalie she can be. The best and only.

Afterglow

HAROLD'S WIFE is up on a stepladder, doing something to the drapes. A pattern of leaves and vines, framing a point-blank view of the sound.

"How strange," she says, "I'm having such a sense of déjà vu right now."

"To do with the drapes?"

"Yes, to do with the drapes. And also you saying that. And this right now, too . . ." She turns from her perch on the stepladder and looks with wide eyes at Harold. "Now it's gone. But it felt so real, like I knew what was going to happen next."

Harold nods.

"It's been happening a lot lately." Carol steps down from the ladder, turning her head from side to side. "And you know what I keep thinking of? You know what keeps popping into my head? That time when we were in Spain, when we had our first paella together, at that restaurant with the flamenco dancer. Remember? The very dark restaurant that felt like a cave. All the candlelight. The flamenco dancer had a yellow dress, and you were wearing a red shirt."

"Seville."

"Right, Seville. It's funny. I don't have many vivid memories from that long ago, but that one just popped back. It feels like it happened yesterday."

"It's a nice memory"—Harold's stomach clenches—"I wish I could remember it."

"It keeps coming back now." His wife shakes her head again, as if shaking the memory away.

Thinking of Spain, Harold can resurrect only one moment: sitting on a hill in La Mancha, looking over the arid landscape. There had been a bare tinge of evening's approach, a retreating glow on the scrublands, an advancing mineral tint. They'd looked out at the distant town of Cuenca, its ancient stone houses jutting over a cliff, and he'd absorbed that picture into his brain, imprinted it there. He had deliberately frozen that moment when he turned to the woman at his side, soon to be his wife, and told her that he was happy.

Now Carol disappears into another room of the house. The tap of her clogs on hardwood floor punctuates the quiet. His brain continues to hold aloft the image of the Spanish vista. Then it quavers in his mind's eye and goes dim.

From outside comes the bleat of a bird. An ugly tune. His wife's clomping, too, has become irritating. Harold goes into his office, closes the door, and turns on his jungle sounds—a gift from one or another of his children. He sits on the easy chair and lets the jungle wash over him. With the shades drawn, the bright Sunday afternoon progresses unseen. The weekends are beginning to make him feel old. He is aware of vague aches in his body. His jog was hard this morning, and his cholesterol count is a problem, a maddening genetic hand-me-down. There are cocky young bastards in his office with designs on his leadership. Fifty-nine, he reminds them, is the prime of a man's life.

But one day, he knows, the board will elect to force him out. They'll retire him, impose a blank second act for his life. At that juncture, perhaps, he might like to enroll in medical school. People begin new careers all the time. His business experience would be helpful, he thinks, in making difficult judgments, dealing with difficult patients.

He sits at the computer and looks again at the admissions page for Harvard Medical School. They require a college transcript, test scores, letters of recommendation, an essay. He chuckles at the thought of the essay, his explanation of this sudden shift in his life, a man who could buy the whole medical school if he wanted.

He thinks about that. He thinks about buying a medical school, enrolling himself in it, paying the doctors to teach him.

The sound of raindrops and monkey calls deepens his reverie. Curiosity, he read somewhere, is part of the recipe for happiness. Perhaps following its pull is the only way to upend the mind's more tedious, workaday functions. Perhaps happiness is nothing more than that—the cessation of logistics, a broad clearing of the decks.

He feels that his own potential for curiosity is still there, but atrophying more each year. Math and science had come so easily to him when he was younger. He'd always assumed that his life would follow that path—a brightly studded path of organs and numbers and knives. Instead, he found economics. It's true that his inquisitiveness has served him well in his chosen field. He's absorbed the tenets of finance, learned to handle the instruments of business the way a surgeon handles his scalpels, with a sure grip and steady purpose. He's made leveraged buyouts, one by one, with clinical precision, taking his targets by surprise. In the best cases, it feels like hunting. Stalking a company, studying its inner workings down to the behavior of individual executives. He predicts the moment of weakness, then waits for it, sometimes for years. It is obsessive, he knows, but he always takes his quarry. It has kept him limber for decades.

Ultimately, he has no regrets about the direction his life has taken. He is a businessman who enjoys reading science magazines in the evening. His is a comfortable living, with three substantial cars, a number of well-tended acres on the water.

On vacation in Kauai, the Christensens buy coconut halves from the barefoot men on the beach, and the almost-grown daughters learn to make leis. Near the end of the trip, Harold's wife lies flat on a towel under the sun.

"I'm thinking about Spain again."

"Again? The paella?"

"It's so strange, it's like I can taste it again. It actually feels like I'm eating paella right now."

Hearing this, Harold feels his body tense. The lulling seaside heat turns hostile.

"Maybe it's the sun," he says. "You should go under the umbrella."

"Hmm," she says, her eyes closed. Then her eyes open and she sits up on the towel. She stares intently at the ocean, as if seeing something approach, some strange ship. Harold follows her gaze, but finds nothing but water and empty horizon. He looks back at Carol, whose right arm lifts and stretches in front of her. Harold can see the beginning of sunburn on the skin.

"Honey, are you all right? What are you doing?"

She doesn't answer, but continues to stare straight ahead, her arm stretched. Her lips move soundlessly.

"I think you should go under the umbrella."

Her arm stretch lasts another moment, and then another. She appears to be reaching for something. Then her arm slackens and relaxes at her side. She lies back down on the towel.

"What just happened?" Harold asks her.

"I don't know." Carol says. "What happened?"

"Honey, come under the umbrella. The sun is doing something to you."

That evening, her arm stretches out during dinner. She topples a water glass, and her fork falls from her hand.

The Hawaiian hospital admits her overnight. Their test results are inconclusive. The doctors recommend she follow up at home. The Christensens are lucky to live in a place with some of the best neurological facilities in the country.

Harold's family spends a tame New Year's Eve at the hotel bar. Carol maintains her muted good spirits, sipping sparkling cider. Their daughters are determinedly upbeat, and no one mentions the episode.

* * *

The day of their return, Harold makes a few strategic phone calls and secures an appointment with the best doctor in the field. According to his chief operating officer, who's survived an aneurysm, there is no one but Michael Warren, head of neurosurgery at St. Joseph's.

Harold takes the afternoon off work to accompany his wife to the hospital. Dr. Warren is young, at least a decade younger than Harold, with a full head of dark wavy hair. They sit in his office, a cold shell of a room with few embellishments, and Harold describes the nature of Carol's episodes.

Dr. Warren listens closely. When Harold finishes, the doctor says, "I should tell you that I'm not usually involved in diagnosis."

"Usually," Harold repeats.

Dr. Warren looks silently at Harold for a moment. He has quick, intelligent eyes.

"How long have you been practicing?" Harold asks.

The doctor blinks, sits back in his chair. "Well, I finished medical school twenty-one years ago."

"Oh, I'm not questioning your credentials. Just curious. I wanted to be a doctor myself when I was a kid."

"A doctor is always practicing. That's a bad joke in the medical field." The doctor sits forward again, begins to stand.

"This seems like a very good hospital," Harold says, standing first. His shoulders square instinctively and he feels the clean, masculine lines of his suit. "I shouldn't speak so soon, I mean not until my wife has been diagnosed." He tilts his head toward Carol, who is gathering herself up from her chair. "But this seems like the kind of institution that might be worthy of financial support."

"Well." The doctor pauses, smiles. "There's always room for improvement—and for fighting malpractice lawsuits."

There. They have an understanding.

Harold chuckles. "And there's always room for grants for talented doctors, I bet."

Dr. Warren sends Carol for an MRI the same day. Harold watches her frame disappear into the space-age tunnel, then asks the radiology technician for permission to come inside the booth where they study the scan of her brain. The technician hesitates, but looks steadily at Harold, a gray-haired man in a gray pin-striped suit, and cautiously assents.

"Just don't touch anything," he says.

The technician sits at what appears to be a desktop computer. Harold hovers at his side, watching the monitor. All at once, the brain shape appears, ruffled and white, like a cauliflower cut in half. Harold stares. His breath catches, and he has the irrational desire to touch the screen.

The radiology technician speaks into a headset. "You'll hear some banging sounds. They'll just last a few seconds."

"Who are you talking to?" Harold whispers.

The technician glances coldly at him. "Your wife. There's a speaker in the machine, so she can hear my voice. It's comforting for patients to know that what's happening in there is normal." He looks back at the machine. "Now you'll hear a buzzing noise and some high-pitched beeping. It will last about a minute. Just close your eyes and try to relax."

"What's happening now?"

The technician presses a button and writes something down. The image on the screen flips to a side view, showing the profile of Carol's face, the bone of her nose. "We're checking for abnormalities in the hippocampus."

Harold stares at the brain. Viewed from the side, there is a breathtaking architecture of curved vaults and aqueducts, and a purposeful canal leading to the rest of the body. It seems far too complex a thing to be inside Carol. Harold feels an itch at the top inner part of his right thigh, near his groin. He resists the urge to scratch it, and considers the elaborate circuitry that makes him aware of the itch and that keeps his hand in place despite the overwhelming desire to move it. He wonders what that particular neural scenario would look like on the brain screen. Perhaps the arising itch might appear as a spontaneous bright dot in one of the brain lobes. Which lobe, he cannot hope to know. It would be improper to ask now, of course, and distract the technician from the medical attention he is supposed to be giving his wife.

Several moments of silence pass. Harold takes his eyes from the screen and looks through the lab window to the colossal machine that contains Carol. He can see the hem of her hospital gown, the soles of her socks, her bare legs tan from Hawaii. The top part of her body is hidden. She looks like a magician's assistant about to be cut in half. What is she thinking in there? Is she thinking about drapes? Death? Handbags? She looks lonely in the tube. The brain on the screen looks lonely, too. It feels like a strange sort of perfidy, to examine her mind in this way, to ogle it with these other men. The most surprising part of it, so far, is that her brain is exactly the shape he expected. It is the shape of all brains in the world.

"What are you looking for, exactly?" Harold asks.

"Any lesions or abnormalities in the brain's anatomy," the technician mutters, "that might help us determine the cause of your wife's seizures."

"Any indication yet?"

"You'll have to discuss the results with the doctor."

Harold looks back through the glass and sees Carol's foot jiggle. What if she has an itch inside the tube? How terrible, he thinks, not to be able to scratch it.

Harold watches the technician's face in profile, lit up by the glow of the screen. The face contains godly knowledge. What, on the other hand, does Harold know? Cash-flow projections? Imaginary galaxies of real use to no one. He feels the same hunger that he felt as a boy, a driving need to know, to be taught.

"Now twenty seconds of clicking," the technician says.

Harold thinks he can hear the clicking sounds himself. Like the sound of a fork tapping a glass bowl around his head.

Carol emerges, whole, from the MRI tube. She emerges fully clothed from the hospital, and Harold escorts her back to the car. She is a civilian again, with makeup and high-heeled shoes. The only difference is the slightly shaken look on her face, the lips flexed in a strained half-smile.

"The doctor said we'll hear in a few days. I'm sure everything's fine," says Harold.

"Yes, I know. I'm just glad it's over."

The MRI was nothing, thinks Harold. If there is bad news, she might have to undergo brain surgery. No one has told him this, but he's sure it is true. Bad news always means surgery.

"It didn't hurt, did it?"

"Not at all, but the noises were unpleasant."

Harold tries not to grin.

"You mean the bangs and taps and whirs?"

"Yes, how did you know?"

"I talked to the doctor about it. I wanted to know what you were experiencing."

"That was sweet of you, honey. But really, it wasn't that bad. I'm just glad to be out of that tube."

"It looked claustrophobic."

"It was! I had a terrible itch on my nose and there was nothing I could do!"

"I can imagine, sweetheart. It sounds terrible." But not as terrible as brain surgery, he thinks.

They are relieved when the doctor reports that Carol's brain has no anatomical malformation they can find. The seizure could have been an anomaly, possibly even an allergic reaction to something. That sounds likely, the family agrees. They'd been in Hawaii, after all, eating unusual foods and breathing unusual air.

Back home, Harold watches his wife flip through fabric swatches. She's returned to her work, reupholstering everything in the house. A diamond twinkles from the lobe of her ear, that weird, primitive organ. Harold thinks of what brain surgery might entail, whether a piece of skull would need to be removed like a door, whether the brain matter itself could stand to be touched by an instrument, or if it is done in some other way—maybe with lasers.

He spends an hour after dinner thumbing through *Scientific American*. As he sits, he tries to discern the workings of his own brain. The transmitters, he imagines, fire more slowly while he listens to the calming jungle tones, and faster when he looks at the magazine. His brain feels powerfully charged, marvelously elastic. He imagines how it might look on an MRI screen, color-coded.

But this is nothing, this armchair science. There are men who spend their whole lives studying the human brain. Others study outer space. How about that? There are men who do nothing but study the human brain—or the universe—each day, who are excited by pictures that are meaningless to the rest of the world. Harold feels a gnawing envy. The magazine pictures of the brain and of the cosmos are beautiful and not dissimilar—abstract smudges of color against the same fluid black background. Brains and galaxies, these places where everyone lives, where everyone floats in an enormous black egg. Every surgeon and astrophysicist and Wall Street banker alive.

His own house, deep within the egg, features leafy drapes, decorative wreaths, patterns around the rims of dishes, everything made to chase fear away.

Several weeks later, Carol has another episode. It happens while she is out walking on Pelican Point's narrow finger of land, past its string of hermetic mansions. It is a stroke of luck that the driver of a passing car happens to find her on the side of the road, jolting in a patch of pachysandra.

Dr. Warren prescribes medication for her seizures—for her *epilepsy*—and Harold's family gets used to the word. Over the following year the seizures seem to come at random intervals, often preceded by a vivid memory or sensory experience.

Harold leaves *Scientific American* behind. He buys neuroscience books and learns all he can about the brain's structure and functions. He is beginning to see the connection, now, between the recurring paella taste and the rigid grasping motions that follow. And now he knows that the brain has no sensory nerves of its own. It is, in fact, dead to the touch.

The more he learns about the brain's curled geography, its mystifying functions, the more he needs to know. He wants to see the organ up close. He even considers buying a brain in a jar—an authentic cross section for sale on the Internet—but knows his wife would not be happy about it. In any case, a preserved specimen is no substitute for the real, living thing.

There are so many questions. Harold tells himself that it is his responsibility to answer them, to gain uncommon insight into the nature of his wife's trouble. But, he knows, this is not just about Carol. The truth is that he wants total access, total knowledge. So when Dr. Warren orders a PET-CT scan, Harold requests the doctor's presence. They stand together in the technician's booth. Harold watches his wife slide into the scanner's mouth and waits for her brain to appear. It swims onto the screen, this time in vibrant colors like a flamboyant fish, and the doctor's face glows aquamarine.

The technician picks up his headset.

Harold coughs. "Dr. Warren, before we start, may I speak to you privately?"

The technician puts the headset down, as if offended, and the doctor looks at Harold. They step into the corner of the room, and Harold whispers, "May I ask you an unusual question?" He straightens his posture, tries to picture an admiring board of directors sitting before him. "Would it be possible for a patient to touch his own brain?" He is dismayed to feel his face heat.

The doctor levels a blank gaze, then smiles slightly.

"Perhaps, yes. I mean, it's hypothetically possible. There could be local anesthesia on the skull area and nowhere else. In fact, it's sometimes preferable that a patient remains conscious during an open-brain test. So, yes, it's technically feasible that a patient could touch the surface of his own brain."

Harold nods. "I'm sure it would be a very strange feeling."

The doctor pauses. "Yes, I'm sure," he says, stepping back toward the monitors.

Harold is quiet, focusing on a yellow cloud in the back of Carol's brain. The occipital lobe, he knows.

It isn't difficult to convince Dr. Warren to speak to him privately. All men are vain, in one way or another, Harold knows, and this request would appeal directly to his ego and professional sense of duty.

"I've been thinking of making a donation toward your work," Harold says. "A substantial one."

"That's terrific news." The doctor smiles genuinely as the men walk together down the hall.

"Yes, well, it hasn't happened yet," says Harold as they enter the doctor's office. He sits down without being asked. "The thing is, I think of philanthropy as an investment. And, as a businessman, I like to know what, exactly, I'm investing in."

"Understandable," the doctor replies after a moment's hesitation, taking the seat behind the desk. "I'd be happy to put you in touch with our development office."

"No." Harold leans forward. "You see, I'm particularly interested in neurosurgery, as you might gather. I'd like to learn more of the specifics about what *you* do here, what sort of advances make your own work stand out."

"I see."

"I don't want some dry, deadly report. I don't want to read a bunch of medical lingo." Harold looks the doctor in the eye. "I want you to give me the real juice, man-to-man."

Dr. Warren shifts back in his chair. "I'd be happy to help you however I can," he says tentatively.

"Well then, let's schedule a time to talk."

"Schedule a time? Oh. Well, I'm afraid that won't be easy. I'm usually booked solid."

Harold stands. "Let me know when you have time to spare. I'll buy you a drink and pick your brain, so to speak. Maybe give you a few tips of my own, if you like. Business insight." Harold taps his forehead with a forefinger.

The doctor tilts his head and smiles up at Harold, looking for that moment like a teenager in a beam of praise.

* * *

The doctor chooses the bar, a generic Irish pub that Harold has never noticed, just off the main street near the hospital. There are television sets showing the same frantic basketball game. In the dim light, the doctor's features are softer, more human. He is a handsome man with a pair of strong eyebrows and a turned-up curl at one corner of the lips, as if he is harboring illicit thoughts.

The first half hour is useless, a banter of commonplaces. Like a bad date. But Harold is patient. It is impolite to rush things.

Finally, after his second Scotch, they get into it. "What was your first surgery like?" Harold asks, and the next hour swarms with tales of the doctor's first year in the operating room, its triumphs and missteps and ultimate mysteries. So many mysteries remain, the doctor says, shaking his head.

"That's it," says Harold quietly. "That's exactly what this is about."

They meet again two weeks later, at the same bar. The doctor's love of his work is evident, as is his satisfaction in being so queried. Harold reciprocates with his own insights, where appropriate, into the market, amused by the doctor's intent stare. It is a beautiful joining of minds, Harold thinks, a fruit-bearing tree.

They meet every other week for the rest of that year. Finally, on a bitter December evening, Harold tells Dr. Warren that he is ready to make his donation.

* * *

Two hundred grand is more than reasonable for the fulfillment of his purpose. The doctor's only condition is that the payment be in cash. Harold nods in understanding, fired by such backroom collusion.

Harold is exhilarated with himself, with this, his greatest investment of all. After just three whiskeys, the doctor has agreed to grant him access to the operating room, where he will be able to observe a neurosurgical procedure.

The next several days are limned with anticipation. Christmas passes in a blur. Harold feels a physical rush each time he thinks of his secret, each time he considers the prospect of encountering a stranger's brain—another person's memories and experiences contained in one unit, exposed.

Harold returns to the hospital on the agreed-upon day in January, without Carol. Like a boy, he nearly jogs from the car to the front entrance, past the stocky hospital shrubs, through the enchanted automatic doors. He nods to the nurses and winks at the pretty ones. They walk obliviously past him in their tropical uniforms, South Pacific blue. He, in his gray suit, is invisible. Visitors have disturbingly free rein here. It is almost insolent, this lack of concern on the part of the staff, who are all but chained to their little clipboards. Harold takes the wrong route to the neurosurgery wing, but finally finds the way to Dr. Warren's door. He knocks. He imagines that when he emerges from this office in just a few minutes, he'll be wearing the tropical uniform, too.

Dr. Warren takes him in and closes the door. Harold still thinks the doctor, his friend, seems suspiciously young with his wavy Roman hair and unlined brow. He motions briefly to the visitor's chair.

"I'm sorry to tell you this, but I won't be able to help you today." The doctor speaks strongly, not meeting Harold's eye, as if afraid of faltering. "I just can't be held responsible for a breach of security."

Harold sits quietly as the doctor goes on. A sudden flashback to his Hippocratic oath, perhaps. Or, simply, sobriety. The money is attractive, the doctor admits, but he can't hazard going to jail.

"Dr. Warren, we had an agreement."

"I'm sorry, Harold, but I've thought about it, and it's just too risky."

"But it wouldn't be you at fault, it would be me," Harold reminds him.

The doctor smiles sadly. "I'm the one who'd be fired."

"But our story is solid."

The surgeon shakes his head. Harold increases his offer. Dr. Warren flinches, but still refuses.

By the spring, Carol still hasn't responded to medications. Further tests continue to show what appears to be a normal organ.

Harold is now sixty years old. Not truly old, but well past the block of time known as "youth" in the life span of a human being. There is no longer any way he can pinpoint what each year has meant to him specifically. There have been too many of them, one leaking into the other.

He sits on the wing chair, near the picture window. His wife sits on the couch nearby, on the phone with another wife. Harold listens to her as she listens to her friend's voice on the receiver, nodding and responding in the tuneful, sympathetic monosyllables unique to women on telephones. The women are starting to succumb to illnesses, to accidents, a creeping string of minor disorders that will ultimately take them under. There is a look on his wife's face lately, as if she knows something that he is failing to grasp. A searching, disbelieving look. Her eyes, like her hair, have begun to show sage flecks of silver, and her face is more angular. She will never be one of those women who spreads out in her own flesh. She is already contracting, minimizing, as if making herself more efficient for the next, most difficult stretch ahead.

They've had a good life. Compatible from the start, a smooth coast. Like a pair of cross-country skis, Harold imagines, never straying far from each other's sight, but keeping separate enough, with plenty of room to maneuver and come together again. It had never occurred to him that her course might veer, that he would ever find her out of reach.

At their next appointment, Dr. Warren finds a tumor in her brain. Harold and his wife sit together as he shows them the results of the MRI with a double dose of contrast. Looking back on the prior imaging now, he explains, the tumor was just barely visible.

"So you missed it the first time," Harold says.

"Sometimes that happens," Dr. Warren clips. "Only in retrospect do we see the clues. It would have been impossible to identify the abnormality without this additional test."

"A year later."

The doctor does not respond or meet Harold's eyes.

"Well, we've found it now," Harold says calmly.

The doctor's shoulders hunch slightly as he speaks. The tumor is not necessarily bad news, he explains. It has clear borders and is most likely benign, but is not far from the hippocampus, which explains her strange memory relapses. The condition causes abnormal electrical bursts in the temporal lobe, the seat of sensory organization. This can create unpleasant sensations, like the perception of invisible presences. Some people with the condition become delusional, believing themselves to have contact with supernatural entities. Moses was likely a sufferer of temporal lobe epilepsy, as was Joan of Arc.

Carol flashes Harold a look of terror.

"Well, it will be all right, now. Won't it?" Harold asks.

"Surgery would be the best option," Dr. Warren says gently. "The success rate is remarkably high."

Carol's face turns pale and pinched, as if she would sink into her turtleneck sweater. They drive home in silence.

When Harold approaches Dr. Warren with his new idea, the surgeon responds with a blunt mix of disbelief and admiration. They sit together at O'Reilly's, at their usual table. Their meetings have become a favorite ritual of Harold's, and he suspects they are a highlight for the doctor, too. He has continued to meet Harold after their failed scheme, as if nothing untoward has happened. Now, the doctor shakes his head.

"I thought brain surgeons were known for being mavericks," Harold says.

It's true. He's heard that they are addicted to adrenaline: juggling patients' lives in their hands, screwing nurses in the locker room. Of course there must be quiet, steady neurosurgeons, too—men like himself, with stable marriages and rain forest sound tracks at home. Even after their hours of conversation, he still isn't entirely sure which type of surgeon Dr. Warren is.

"Who's going to complain about it?" Harold presses. "I'm the only one who would complain. I'm the only one who would sue."

Harold actually flashes a thick roll of hundred-dollar bills for effect. The surgeon looks gravely at it.

"And I'm the one who *won't* sue over a certain botched diagnosis."

Dr. Warren is silent. Harold tucks the cash away in his jacket pocket and pats the bulge that it makes.

The girls come home, and the night before the operation, the Christensens gather for dinner at a high-end Spanish restaurant. This is Carol's idea. She's been wanting to try the place for years, she says, but no occasion has ever seemed special enough. It's as if she expects this dinner to be her last. She orders paella and a pitcher of sangria for the table, but there is a weight in her eyes, as if she can't bear to look at her family. Even the girls are subdued as they take turns filling their glasses.

"Listen, kids. Carol," Harold speaks with conviction. "I'm just as nervous about this as you are. But you have to look at the facts here. Modern science is more precise than you realize. Operations like this happen hundreds of times a day, all over the world."

His daughters nod and force smiles. Carol looks down at her plate.

"It's more dangerous to cross a busy street than to have surgery nowadays. And these surgeons are experts, remember. They wouldn't operate if they weren't very, very confident of their success. Their own careers are on the line, after all. Think of all the lawsuits. They wouldn't do it unless they were sure."

The more Harold speaks, the more certain he feels about the truth of these words. He looks at his younger daughter, only nineteen. She is on her second glass of sangria, but nobody stops her. Tonight is beyond such trivialities as underage drinking. Harold watches her chew a wine-soaked orange rind and feels a rising apprehension. She is too young to be motherless.

Later that night, as he watches his wife cleanse her face with a tissue and cream, the apprehension returns. He feels it as a push inside his chest. His wife drops a used tissue into the trash, draws a new one out of its box, and pats her face in the mirror. For a moment, he questions his plan.

As Carol lies in bed beside him in her yellow nightgown, Harold tries to sort the problem out logically. He is not a man accustomed to second-guessing himself. He lies still and tries to shepherd his thoughts into a rational row. They will all make perfect sense together, he is sure, even if they are disjointed and unruly now.

He remembers dissecting a cow's heart in school. He feels keenly again the thrill of encountering on the outside those secrets that belonged on the inside. He hadn't been brought up with religion, but he felt he was touching a machine manufactured by God. He stood at the front of the class and explained what he knew about ventricles and valves and the unknown motor that made the pump run. A girl wrinkled her face as he put a finger in the aortic artery. Harold squeezed the heart. He stood holding the heart, memorizing the cool smooth feel of it, until the teacher asked him to give it back and sit down.

His wife rustles in the bed. She wants to talk, he can tell.

"What is it, honey?"

Carol is quiet for a moment.

"I'm afraid," she says softly into Harold's arm.

"Oh, you know there's nothing to be afraid of, sweetheart. It's a safe operation."

"It's brain surgery. What if I die, or end up brain damaged?"

"Yes, it's brain surgery. But they do it all the time. You won't die, and you won't be brain damaged, I promise. You'll be much better when it's over."

"I think I'd rather have the fits."

Carol's face is still pressed against his arm. He looks down at the top of her head, the waves of meandering hair that he's looked down upon for years. Just a single prod to the correct fold of her motor cortex, he knows, could cause her knee to bend or fingers to curl. The thought brings a sense of almost excruciating intimacy.

"Trust me, honey. You'll be fine."

She whimpers slightly and pushes her face harder against him. He wraps her in his arms and squeezes. He will never know anyone so fully, that much is certain. He keeps her tightly in his arms until her breathing slows and she sleeps. He relaxes his hold then and takes a long look at her, the slackened mouth and crinkled eyelids. He lies beside her, feeling his worries wash out in a pool of tenderness.

He can still feel the dinner stir in his stomach, the rice and wine and spices breaking down to a pool of sharp juice. The echo of garlic rises into his mouth as he silently belches. It is the taste of Spain, of their courtship in its early days. All at once he remembers Seville, remembers the restaurant, the dancer. Carol had cried that night, he remembers. She had sat at the table with trembling lips. It was a white frilled top that she wore, that she'd bought at an outdoor market that day. He remembers how it had made her look like a young girl, like a peasant's daughter. The trip had been perfect until then. Carol's face had colored in the sun despite her straw hats. Her skin had been smooth and youthful, and she'd been eager to disrobe in the hotel, with the shades drawn or apart. She had been his then, unquestioningly, and exalted to be far from home.

Why he'd chosen that moment, he'll never know. He understands now that every man keeps a detail or two in a neutral place inside his own brain, and the wise ones never enter that particular cabinet. To speak at that moment must have been a decision brought on by a young man's misguided idea of honor, or an obscure brand of perversity.

"Her name was Jacqueline," he said.

Carol did not respond. There was a happy buzz in the restaurant, the whirl of the dancer, the aching, adamant guitars propelling everything forward.

The rest of the evening unraveled. He told her the details—she questioning and he answering calmly. He apologized with what was, he thought, inviolable sincerity. The tears came, predictably, and spoiled her face. They finished their meal, or left it, and concluded the rest of the trip in a kind of muffled, vacuumed atmosphere, as if a giant bowl in the sky had descended upon them. In the days after the trip, he wanted to take the words back. He lay beside her in bed and stroked her hair. It had been nothing, he told her, which was true; it had been only a kink in his sanity. They would go back to being the same. She nodded and smiled blandly and said she believed him.

Before leaving for the hospital, Carol puts on makeup. Harold waits, feeling a slight burn of impatience as she spreads foundation over her face, brushes her cheeks with powder, and applies bronze eye shadow. The color she dabs onto her lips is a shade of red more suited to a Hollywood premiere than the operating table. She even puts hot rollers in her hair, the way she used to do when they were first married.

Harold goes out to the living room to wait on an upholstered chair. When Carol emerges from the bedroom, she looks younger, almost pretty. She smiles shyly, and he notices that she is wearing the necklace he gave her for their twentieth wedding anniversary, diamonds in the shape of a heart.

"I don't think they'll let you wear that, honey," Harold says, coming close. "They'll probably take it from you."

"Well, it's not going to get in the way of my brain, is it?"

"No, but I'm sure it's hospital policy. You don't usually see patients wearing diamonds with their hospital gowns, do you?"

She is silent, but keeps the necklace on. She is still wearing it when he hugs her in the hospital corridor and they lead her away to the neurosurgery wing.

Harold feels a twinge as he watches her go. It is natural to be worried, he reasons, and ultimately maybe a positive thing. The concern on his face might help him blend in with the other husbands in the waiting room. He imagines that he looks generic, forgettable enough. Just another gray-haired gentleman.

He sits patiently for several long minutes before Dr. Warren appears and signals to him from the corridor. With a friendly nod to his neighbors, he rises and follows.

He doesn't know how the doctor has managed to circumvent security protocol, but with a swipe of an identification card, they are in the surgical suite. Dr. Warren leads him through the fastidious stages of "scrubbing in," and Harold is frustrated by the exaggerated and time-consuming insistence on sterility. At the scrub sink, Dr. Warren uses his elbows to pump the soap. They are to spend no fewer than ten minutes, each, washing. Harold watches the clock above the sink and feels like a schoolboy again, his eyes fixed on a motionless minute hand. When they are finished, the doctor uses his elbow to turn off the tap. In the sterile prep room, he prepares the surgical gown and mask for Harold and directs him in putting them on. Donning surgical gloves requires a further set of calisthenics. Harold must not touch any unsterile object—even his own face—the doctor warns him, or he will have to rescrub, regown, reglove.

Harold realizes too late that he will not be able to consult the decidedly unsterile piece of paper he's brought with him—a map of the brain's specialized areas: vision, memory, emotion, motion. He isn't entirely sure exactly where Carol's tumor is located. It had been hard to tell from the MRI scan.

Dr. Warren and Harold enter the operating room together. The rest of the surgery team is already there, waiting. The doctor introduces Harold as Dr. Kaminski, a visiting neurosurgeon from Poland, here to observe the procedure. His English, Dr. Warren explains to the team, is extremely limited.

Harold concentrates on keeping his face muscles loose, relaxed. Skeptical eyes gaze back at him.

"Poland?" a nurse asks.

There is a faint murmur amid the surgery staff.

"All right, everyone, let's go," Dr. Warren interjects, moving toward the operating table. Harold follows.

All at once, he sees what must be his wife's body in the room, hidden beneath a blue canopy like a pup tent. It reminds Harold of war, of the makeshift shelters used by medics in battle zones, or what he's seen of them in movies.

The doctor motions to Harold, who joins the others at the tent. He is aware of an ambient sound of machines. A nurse operates a console like something from a recording studio. A monitor graphs an undulating line: his wife's heartbeat. Across the tent, a row of nurses stand, their faces uniformly serious.

Harold focuses on one nurse whose brow comprises thin utilitarian lines above searing blue eyes. When she suddenly raises those eyes to his, he winks reflexively, then feels a buzz of shame.

He cannot see any part of his wife's body. Still, it feels dangerously devious to be here, so close beside her. His instinct tells him to hide. But Harold reminds himself that she is anesthetized. Entirely unaware of his presence.

Dr. Warren moves a sheet to one side, and Harold finds himself staring down all at once at a small patch of bare brain. He looks away involuntarily. What have they done with the piece of missing skull? Is the hair still stuck to it? There are so many questions, but he can't keep them together. His heart quickens. Looking up, he takes stock of the surgery room and feels disoriented, as if awaking in an airplane thirty thousand feet above land.

Harold looks back down. He concentrates on maintaining an air of calm, confident superiority; an air he's mastered over the years. Nonetheless, he feels increasingly conscious of eyes upon him. He stares at the brain. The window itself is disappointingly tiny, revealing just a glimpse of a pale reflective substance. Over this surface runs a faint, spidery red road map. Blood vessels, Harold assumes. Exposed within its drab skull, the brain strikes him as a delicate animal whose stone shelter has been removed. A snail in an overturned shell. It is amazing to think that every human thought and action arises from this weird matter. There is something divine about the sight of it, and Harold thinks he can detect a hush beneath the low bustle in the operating room, as if in religious observance.

He stares for another moment. Then, all at once, his hand reaches toward the brain. His rubber glove is thin as a condom and, like a condom, he would prefer not to wear it. But when his little finger makes contact, the texture of the brain is gloriously discernible. Wet and gelatinous, like custard. It feels marvelously supple—not the dense muscle he'd imagined. He is unsure of what this particular lobe represents, with what expertise he is meddling, but he pushes the thought away and tries to memorize the moment. This is the highlight of a lifetime, he knows, something he'll never experience again.

He removes his finger as quickly as he'd positioned it, before Dr. Warren can take it away. The surgeon stares, stupefied. Harold nods authoritatively and stands back, letting the team close in, shielding the view of his wife.

The whole episode cannot have taken more than two seconds. There is still a thrill in Harold's hand, spiking his blood. He stands back from the table, feeling a sweet numbness in his own brain. The operating room is eerily quiet, with only the sounds of shifting fabric and the occasional clink of metal. Harold is not sure how long to linger. It is somewhat comforting to be in the room; it takes away the fear of an emergency happening out of his sight. But finally Dr. Warren catches Harold's eye and nods curtly toward the door.

Harold returns to the waiting room, feeling conspicuous, oversized. Most of his neighbors are still there, largely unchanged. One man now holds his head in his hands, perhaps coping with bad news, or taking a nap. A mother and daughter play cards together cheerfully, as if this were their living room.

The receptionist sits at her desk quietly, with hair like coral, pasted in solid swirls against her head. No one approaches her to ask after anyone. It isn't like the movies. There is no urgency here, no tears.

Harold takes a seat among the others, clutching his secret. As he sits, a wheelchair passes through the room slowly, bearing a very elderly man with thin, bare legs and feet in beige ped socks. An IV drip rolls along with him, and a glum nurse. The man gazes straight ahead, as if looking upon an enthralling, faraway place. It comes to Harold in a sudden dart that he will be like that someday. Carol will push him in a wheelchair just like that. *Maybe,* he thinks. If he is lucky, she'll still be there to push him.

The nurse wheels the old man out of sight, her wide rump emphatically not belonging to Carol. Harold feels a horrible, baffling loss as he watches the man disappear.

Later, a nurse comes out to the waiting room and calls for him. He rises expectantly, and the nurse approaches and hands him Carol's necklace. For a moment he feels certain, deep in his bones, that his wife is dead. He teeters on the lip of that canyon, feeling its cold wind rise up to his face. But then the nurse grins and tells him that Carol is ready to see him.

The recovery room is small with wood paneling, like a sauna. Carol sits up in a cot, looking small in her yellow nightgown. Her legs are bare up to the knees. Harold pulls up a chair and gives her a loving smile. There is a white bandage, cartoonlike, around her head. Nothing can improve on the old-fashioned bandage, he supposes, wrapped around heads for millennia.

"How do you feel?" he asks.

"Weak, but all right. A little woozy."

Her face is blurred, like a child waking from a long sleep. Her eyes focus slowly on him, and she smiles back at him—that same impish smile that had stolen his balance twenty-five years ago. At this moment, he wants desperately to tell her about the incredible thing that has happened, the secret inside him that threatens to pop. He is suddenly hit by the full truth of it: the strange new closeness that they share, profound and singular. Even unspoken, he imagines she might already be able to sense it. It is a miracle, an uncanny dream. It is as deep as anything else in their lives.

"I brought your necklace," Harold says gently, and Carol's eyes travel down to the gleam in his hand. They register the necklace. In her brain, she still stores a picture of it. She remembers Harold, too, amazingly; the shapes that make up the face of her husband.

"Thank you," she says quietly.

Harold stands. He comes close, brings the chain around her neck to the front, and fastens the clasp.

The Umbrella Bird

It had been a touch of incredible fortune to find David one spring night at a dive on Houston Street. He'd been attending a coworker's farewell gathering, an anomalous outing for him. He was short-haired and clean against the peeling paint and graffiti. That he'd been there that night nursing a Stella Artois, and had needed the restroom at the same time as she, had upended statistical logic. He was taller than everyone, and thinner, as if streamlined for air travel. Not conventionally handsome, but with a narrow, austere face. His green irises seemed lit, like dappled leaves on a forest floor. When he looked at Madeleine, she was briefly paralyzed, a field mouse in a clearing. He bought her a vodka tonic and left a three-dollar tip for the bartender. As he handed the glass to her, turning the tiny straw in her direction, she'd felt the dizzy euphoria of a traveler who has turned onto the right road, the easy expansion of lungs as the horizon opens before her.

He was an account supervisor at a big advertising firm in midtown, he explained breezily, coordinating campaigns for sneakers and tortilla chips. But later, over a series of ardent dinner dates, she learned that he'd grown up in the country—on a farm, no less—and had never felt truly at peace in an apartment building. Lately he felt that he was being gradually drawn back to Nature, and now that he'd found her, he suggested with elaborate, soft-forested eyes, perhaps his quest was complete. Within six months, they were married and looking at real estate listings.

The house has been sweepingly renovated, the front door framed by columns and topped by a counterfeit balcony. It's what the real estate agent had termed a *center-hall colonial,* with the kind of timeless architecture and rigorous symmetry designed to leverage a calming effect on its inhabitants. Paired with precise, harmonious details, she implied, a house like this had the power to transform its owners' experience of the world, to render any obstacle—any boiler failure or termite siege—surmountable.

Nearly all their money has gone to the down payment, and with the little that remains, Madeleine is scrambling to furnish. With a Sharpie, she circles furniture in soft-lit catalogs: a sectional sofa, a leather armchair, a mirrored console table. Deliverymen put them in place. Still, the rooms echo.

Alone, she wanders the house on the balls of her feet. It is preternaturally quiet, the walls themselves thick with insulation, sealing out the buzz of the world. A sliding glass door displays a wide lawn tumbling to a thumb-smudge of trees. She has reached it at last: this asylum, this glorious valve. Madeleine had first glimpsed this kind of life as a girl, visiting a friend who'd moved to a verdant nook of New Jersey. Entering that house had been like entering a palace: the soaring entrance hall, floors that didn't sag toward the middle, bay windows looking onto wanton grass and trees, the great yawn of sky. There, she'd learned to ride a bicycle. Pedaling back and forth on that wide blacktop driveway, she'd felt the first ecstasy of flight.

She has never lived anywhere but in a gerbil cage. She has never had money. Her father was a bag-eyed jazz musician—dead in middle age—her mother a schoolteacher who supported them all. Madeleine had diligently sidestepped adulthood in her parents' lopsided brownstone on Charles Street, among the aging socialists and drag queens. Before meeting David, she had acquired the habits of every cynical city girl: shutting down dirty bars, flattering scrawny musicians, waking Sundays on ripped Naugahyde couches.

Tonight, he is out in the woods, building a tree house for their daughter who is due in a month. Although she will not use it for years, he has thrown himself into the project as if on a deadline. Each evening, when he comes home from work, he puts on old jeans, disappears into the garage, and cuts lumber with a power saw. Madeleine has agreed not to visit the tree house until it is finished. She watches David carry wooden planks over the grass to the woods, the late-summer sun casting his long shadow before him. His hands have become splintered and raw, his forearms welted from the ash tree he has selected.

This is his nature, she knows, this kind of focused work ethic. He lugs home stacks of library books about tree house architecture. At night, he comes into the house with the look of an outdoorsman, in soiled plaid shirts and patch-kneed jeans. Perhaps he has reverted to a forgotten self, his childhood on the farm, when he'd spent whole days in the woods hunting for turtle shells, mouse skulls, snake skins. He works on the tree house later and later each night, until he is coming indoors well after dark. Madeleine does not want to complain. She wants him to feel free in his life with her. For years he has lived as an independent man—but now, with parenthood advancing upon him, perhaps he feels invisible ropes tightening. She wants to show that she understands. He can build a tree house if he wants to.

Alone, she watches the evening news, its galloping sound track bridging one bleak segment to the next. Beyond the glass door, she sees David cross slowly over the grass, his figure becoming part of the deepening evening. At last, his silhouette melts into the dark line of trees. The glass door frames a phantasmagoric reflection of the room's interior, of Madeleine's own bulging form. The news anchor begins a dirge about home foreclosures. There is talk of a stimulus package. People will be given old-fashioned things to do with their hands. Madeleine herself is fabulously idle, having finally quit her series of temp jobs. This had been David's idea. He'd encouraged her to enjoy her pregnancy, to not feel ashamed for staying home with their child if that was what she wanted to do.

She is not accustomed to so much aloneness. Nothing in her old life had ever approached this depth of quiet, this vacuum of night. She imagines animals in the woods surrounding the house, emerging when the sun sets to carry on their dark pursuits. She does not like to think of David out there, but restrains herself from going to retrieve him, from begging him to come inside and sit with her. She does not want to be that kind of woman.

At last, after she has gone to bed, she hears the sliding door. Moments later, he is with her beneath the blanket, whispering apologies. There is a chill in his touch, a suggestion of autumn. He slides up against her spine and a coil loosens inside her. What extraordinary luck, after all: this beautiful place, this wonderful man. At last, a real house with a mailbox and garden hose. A desirable suburb in a sterling school district, not too far from the city. A kind, intelligent husband with a lucrative career and domestic leanings. The child inside her settles itself, and she falls into dreamless sleep.

Over the summer weeks that follow, David returns from work earlier in the afternoon. "Light day," he tells her, and disappears into the garage. He rushes into the trees with his planks. He comes in only to eat whatever dinner she has made, then goes back out until dark. One night, he does not come in for dinner at all, and Madeleine finds herself crying over turkey tetrazzini. Finally, she puts the food away and climbs into bed in her clothes. After midnight, she hears the sliding glass door. "I'm so sorry," he tells her in bed. "Sometimes I just lose track of time out there." Madeleine turns over, too spent to protest, and allows him to put an arm around her. "I know you're tired of this, but I'm almost done building, I promise. I can't wait to show it to you."

She has been sleeping badly, staring through the skylight in the bedroom ceiling, convinced she can see the stars move. David has become progressively more restless at night, twitching his legs like a cricket, muttering garbled syllables. She listens closely, but is unable to decipher any meaning. Tonight, his vague murmurs become louder, insistent. He repeats a strange phrase that sounds like "Up a cat I kill." His face tightens and he jerks upright, eyes open. A cold current passes through Madeleine's veins, and she turns on the bedside lamp. David stares at her for a moment without recognition. She rubs his arm tentatively.

"It's okay, honey. You were just dreaming."

He gazes for another blank moment, until something in his eyes folds inward and he softens into himself again. He shakes his head. "I'm sorry."

She keeps rubbing his arm. "What were you dreaming about?"

He is quiet for a moment. "The same dream I've been having all week. I'm in the tree house and a strange bird lands on a branch and talks to me."

"It talks to you? What does it say?"

"Nothing, really. Nonsense."

"You've been having the same dream every night?"

"More or less."

"Anxiety, I guess," Madeleine says.

"Probably."

She turns the light off, and David is silent for the rest of the night. But she stays awake, watching the vibrations of stars through the skylight until they vanish into dawn. It is impractical to have a skylight in the bedroom, of course. Uncovered like this, it allows the morning light into the room—but Madeleine has not yet found an elegant shade for it.

When the alarm rings, David unfolds himself from bed and lurches into the bathroom, pale and dazed as if hungover. Still, he emerges showered and shaven, and in a white button-down shirt and pressed chinos he is an advertising executive again. He kisses Madeleine and goes out to catch the 7:09 to the city.

That afternoon, Madeleine shops for baby clothes and returns to find David lying on the couch with an arm over his face. She feels a primal rush of alarm, as if she has walked in on an intruder. She rests the shopping bag on the mirrored console table.

"What's wrong?"

"Terrible headache," he says drily. "It's been happening a lot lately, but today I just couldn't get through it."

Madeleine sits on the edge of a cushion, puts a hand to his forehead.

"You never said anything about headaches. Why didn't you say something?"

"It was just a headache before. Now it's worse."

"You're warm. Did you take something?"

He blinks at her. "Of course. Nothing helps. It's like an ache in my whole body. Even my scalp hurts."

"You need to see a doctor."

He closes his eyes again. "We don't have a doctor here."

"We'll find one."

"Just let me rest right now."

She kisses his forehead and retreats. While she is upstairs arranging the baby clothes in dresser drawers, she hears the sound of the sliding glass door. Outside the nursery window, she sees David go over the grass toward the woods.

* * *

"I can't help myself," he says, when he comes to bed after midnight again. "It's like the woods are calling me. The only time I feel all right is when I'm up in that ash tree. At work, I can't sit near the computer. There's no air in the building."

"Honey, what's going on? You never had this problem before," Madeleine says.

He looks at her for a long moment, then asks quietly, "Do you remember the bird in my dreams?"

She nods.

"My mother used to talk about things like that. Dream visitors. I remember she used to have recurring dreams of a mountain lion. It was her guardian animal, she said. She used to ask me if I ever had animal friends in my dreams. I told her I didn't know what she was talking about." David smiles weakly. "I used to think she was crazy, or pretending to be eccentric. Once, she made a big papier-mâché sculpture in the yard, a big yellow mountain lion. It was supposed to be a totem to her animal."

Madeleine does not respond. The sky is clouded tonight, and there is no moon through the skylight, no stars. David's face is just a shifting patchwork of shadows.

"Anyway, I've been thinking about that," David continues. "I took some books out from the library, just for the heck of it. New Age stuff, about animal dreams and their meanings. There's a lot out there."

"I'm sure," Madeleine says.

He props himself up on an elbow.

"Can I read you something?"

He turns on the bedside lamp, and Madeleine squeezes her eyes shut. She hears him slide out of bed. When he returns, he is holding a book with a cover illustration of a neon figure shooting laser beams from its fingers and toes. "This one has a whole section about physical symptoms like the ones I've been having." David glances at her with flashing eyes. "Listen to this."

> An individual may be chosen by the spirits to act as a go-between, a kind of messenger between worlds, entrusted with the role of community healer. The chosen individual may be awakened to his calling in a number of ways. He may hear voices or encounter animal spirits in his dreams. He may undergo a profound trial in Nature, characterized by physical symptoms such as headaches, general numbness, and tingling in the scalp. Often, the chosen individual is initially fearful or confused by these signals from the spirit world. He may feel cursed, angry, and resistant to adopting such responsibility. But the alternative is typically worse; rejecting the spirits' calling may put him at risk of severe depression, even suicide.

Madeleine listens quietly, unable to absorb the words. They arch over her head, as if she is standing behind a waterfall. As she watches David's face, his latticed irises, a memory comes to her of their first date, when they'd walked downtown along the Hudson. When they'd reached Trinity Church, he had led her through the gate to its weathered graveyard, and they'd wandered among the mildewed headstones. She remembers the way he'd run his hand over the grave markers. As a boy, he told her, he'd spent hours in the old cemetery near his house. He'd made grave rubbings, memorized names, birth dates, death dates. He'd devised detailed life stories for those people: the wives who'd died in childbirth, the grieving husbands who remarried only to be left again. At the time, this had not struck her as peculiar, but as exquisitely sensitive, the mark of a man with untold depths.

He begins to skip shaving in the morning and wears the same pants three days in a row. He leaves the house so late on some mornings that Madeleine knows he will miss his train. There is nothing she can do, she tells herself, except trust. He has come this far in his life without her. He is more of an adult than anyone else she knows. Men, of course, go through transitions and investigations like anyone else. This is normal, healthy. No one is—or should be—completely stagnant and predictable, year after year. This will prove a brief episode, she assures herself. At worst, a midlife crisis.

She goes about her own concerns: choosing paint for the nursery, a runner for the upstairs hall. She prepares a macaroni-and-cheese casserole for her first book club meeting. The invitation had come from a neighbor named Rosalie Warren, who'd swooped in the wake of their moving van with a tray of lemon bars. Her army of children is impossible to ignore, patrolling Whistle Hill Road on bikes and scooters, peering into the windows of parked cars.

Madeleine pulls on a white eyelet maternity dress and carries the casserole the half mile to Rosalie's house. Arms aching, she shuffles up to the brick facade with an oval window like a third eye above the door. Flowering shrubs flank the walkway, and on the front step a shoe brush grows from a stone hedgehog's back. Feeling watched, she rubs the soles of her sandals over it.

Inside, women mingle in shades of melon and chartreuse. The furniture is permanent-looking: a vast coffee table of distressed wood, armchairs of cream-colored linen. Madeleine's tub of macaroni sits on the buffet like a fat girl among asparagus wraps. The women gather on tufted dining chairs and discuss the book selection, *In the Path of Poseidon,* a memoir of a man who sailed around the world with his family. They dive right in. The author was reckless, they agree, to endanger his wife and children in this way. *They could have been killed.*

Madeleine listens, nodding when appropriate. She thinks of David, surely home already, huddled in the woods. A flare of something like dread goes through her body. She is uncomfortable in her chair, unable to cross her legs, forced to squeeze them together. She curses herself for wearing such a short dress. The women volley their opinions around her. Within half an hour, the conversation has devolved into a lament about the economy, worry that husbands will be laid off, that home renovations will have to wait. The book is not mentioned again.

After the meeting, Madeleine walks home. Some of the women drive past, their headlights illuminating the macaroni tub in her arms, still nearly full. Her next-door neighbor Suzanne—whom she has just met—rolls slowly alongside in a Range Rover like an abductor, but Madeleine politely tells her she prefers to walk. It is good to do this, she thinks, to breathe the night air, absorb her new habitat. As Suzanne's engine dies out, the only sound remaining is that of her own sandal steps. The darkening sky is the color of the open sea, bare and boatless. All around, windows smolder with lamplight. The seafaring author is indoors somewhere with his family now, sheltered in some American home, perhaps looking out a window at this same nautical sky, pining for the sway and jostle of water beneath him.

She finds David on the couch, barefoot, eating ice cream. He smiles as she comes in the door, as if he has been waiting for her.

"It's the end of an era," he says, holding up his bowl. "I'm done with work."

Madeleine puts the casserole on the console table. "What do you mean?"

David sucks on his spoon. "I mean I'm not going back."

She steps into the living room. "You didn't quit."

"No, not exactly." He crosses his legs, exposing overgrown toenails, curled and yellow as claws. "They asked me to leave."

"You were fired?"

"I would have left anyway."

Madeleine feels an immediate numbness in her face, as if the blood is blockaded in her veins. She drops onto the large leather easy chair, newly purchased for a thousand dollars.

"I can't use the computer anymore," David says simply. "The sound is awful, and it gives off a toxic emanation. I know I've been sensitive lately, but I can't even sit at my desk when it's on."

Madeleine stares at him, at the ice cream bowl in his hand, the simian feet. "David, this was never a problem before."

He shrugs.

Madeleine leans forward, grips the arms of the chair. Controlling her breath, she says, "What are you telling me? You're telling me they fired you."

David looks away, giving her his profile. He seems to be playing some memory in his mind. There is an unnerving little smile on his lips. A long moment extends, a bloated silence, and Madeleine realizes she has been holding her breath. She lets out a slow wheeze.

"How are we going to pay the mortgage?" she says softly.

"I have a plan." He glances at her with a weird light in his eyes. "You have to trust me."

In the pause that follows, Madeleine remembers her first visit to his childhood home in Pennsylvania, with wind chimes on the porch and laundry in the front yard. Inside, David's gray-braided parents sat at a big wooden table, churning apple butter. Incense burned on the counter beside a statuette of Krishna. In his oxford shirt and loafers, David appeared as foreign to this environment as his parents were native. How strange, she'd thought, that something so strong and unbendable had been forged by this queer fire.

"Trust me," David repeats.

Madeleine studies his face. He appears to be the same man. A man who has never given her a reason not to trust him. She had so easily, eagerly, fallen into the habit of trust. In their wedding vows, when they had promised to help each other achieve their dreams, to stand beside each other through any difficulty, it had seemed that the words were skewed to her benefit. It had never occurred to her, really, that she would be called upon.

"I think I can find a way to harness this," David says.

"Harness what?" Madeleine asks. "I don't understand."

"I'm thinking I can learn traditional healing techniques and open an independent practice."

Madeleine stares. "You've been in advertising for fifteen years."

"It's a career change, yes. People change careers all the time."

"But the timing, David. We're about to have a baby."

He smiles. "Babies are born all over the world, to all kinds of people."

"What does that mean?"

David is quiet. After a moment, he says, "What if I wanted to go to law school? Would you support that?"

There is a touch of impatience in his voice that Madeleine has never heard before. She sits for another moment, then rises to her feet, steadying herself on the back of the chair.

"Listen," she says. "You can keep talking, but I'm going to go make dinner."

He follows her into the kitchen. "I know you're upset."

She pours rice into a measuring cup without measuring it and fills a pot with water. She seizes a blind assortment of vegetables from the refrigerator and begins chopping. He stands beside her. "Listen to me. I think the bird is a messenger inviting me to change course. I'm luckier than some people, who never receive a tangible sign. They just feel sick and never know why."

Madeleine gazes at the cutting board, where she has created a heap of cubed carrot, potato, cucumber. She slides the vegetables into a pot and her eyes alight on the backsplash behind the stove, a grid of glossy bloodred tiles. This is one of the details she'd loved about the house, but which now strikes her as superfluous.

David puts a hand on her arm. "I believe I've received a gift, Madeleine. I believe I've been selected for something very strange and wonderful."

She turns to him and sees the fevered eyes of a teenager who has just discovered beat poetry. Her own face heats. She should have known that this was inside him all along, like a time bomb. This is what he came from, what he is made of. His corporate adventure—his visit to the culture of work, of responsibility—was just that, an adventure. A rebellion against his upbringing, short-lived. What she is witnessing now, she suddenly understands, is a return to his roots, his true character. The truth detonates before her.

And is it surprising that she would align herself with someone like this, after all? People are drawn to those like themselves. On a deep level, they recognize themselves in others, so that every couple is, at the core, properly matched. Like his corporate charade, her own transformation into suburban housewife has been a hoax. She is an imposter in this place, in this house. She stands at the kitchen sink, before the wide window that is still missing treatments, and feels that the whole town can see in.

"I think a healing practice would fill a real need," David is saying. "People are looking for release from the ills of modern culture. So many of us are disconnected from Nature, from our spiritual selves, and it's making us sick. It's endemic to the whole country, don't you think? It's something I've always suspected in some low-grade way, but kept pushing aside. Don't you feel like that, deep down? Don't you just rationalize it away?"

Madeleine takes the pot from the burner and slops the vegetables onto a platter.

"Maybe they'll take you back," she says.

David stares. "Haven't you been listening? I don't want to go back."

Madeleine brings the platter down on the counter. "I can't believe I'm hearing this. We just bought this house, David. We're having a baby."

As she speaks, her body sways as if upon a boat. Another memory returns from her visit to David's childhood home, one curious moment. Washing her hands in the rustic powder room, Madeleine had looked out the window to see David in the yard, standing beside a pole birdfeeder, its clear plastic silo filled with seed. As he stood, tall and still, Madeleine watched a sparrow circle the feeder and alight. Then a crow. As she stood at the powder room window, the feeder had swelled with birds.

David spends his first day of unemployment thumbing library books on the couch. Madeleine slips out of the air-conditioned house and into a kiln. She lumbers down Whistle Hill Road, past flat-faced houses blinking back the noonday sun, past the little pond furred with algae. She keeps a small, purposeful smile on her face, but is unable to rid herself of the sense that she is being watched, as if her husband's aberration is visible upon her like a jumpsuit. There are men in the periphery of her vision, trimming bushes, washing cars. There are the low growls of lawnmowers and chain saws. David hasn't mowed their lawn in over a month.

That night, David stays in the woods, in the ripped blue sleeping bag of his boyhood. Madeleine lies alone in bed with a hand on the globe of her belly, deciphering the changes in its temper. There is a sense of agitation, of looming implosion. There is a swoon of adrenaline as her abdomen stiffens, becomes hard as a watermelon. She gasps and fixes her eyes on the skylight, a black velvet kerchief crusted with stars.

The adrenaline waves proliferate, building on themselves, in the pattern of the panic attacks she'd had as a younger woman. She has learned to breathe through these, to carve a space for herself, as she would do when negotiating a crowd in Midtown.

At last, when the breathing becomes impossible, she crawls from bed and goes outside with a flashlight. She edges over the dark carpet of grass, stopping to clutch herself. In the woods, she follows a narrow path, twigs snapping, and sweeps her flashlight over the barbed branches. At last she illuminates a crude box suspended in a forked tree trunk. She calls to David.

They name the baby Annabel. The first weeks are suspended out of time, a dream of sleeping and nursing. David is mercifully silent on the topic of his spiritual vocation. It isn't until Annabel is two months old that he comes to Madeleine with a library book, an almanac of South American fauna. Without speaking, he opens the book to a full-page photograph of an ebony bird poised upon a branch, a crest like a standing wave upon its head. Its eye is small and hard, a jet bead ringed with white, and there is a long protuberance like an empty black kneesock beneath its beak. The bird gives an impression of cool majesty, of indifference to human quandary.

"It's an Amazonian umbrella bird," David whispers after a moment. "All I know is that it has a loud call, but is rarely seen. It lives its whole life in the rain forest canopy in Brazil and Peru. The male courts the female by stretching out his wattle, but then the female builds the nest and raises the chicks alone."

"Leave it to Nature," Madeleine says.

"I'd love to see it in person one day."

He spends the rest of the week designing a logo—a black silhouette of a crested bird in flight—for an ad that will run in the local newspaper and the kinds of free magazines provided at spas and yoga studios. By the end of the month, he has his first appointment.

When the client arrives at the house, Madeleine hides in the bedroom with the baby. She watches from the upstairs window as a young man approaches the door, a silver bull ring glinting at his nose. The Warren children are probably running indoors right now, she imagines, calling to their mother. Perhaps Rosalie, at this moment, is dialing for a patrol car.

For the hour that David spends in the tree house with the stranger, Madeleine sits nursing Annabel, examining the same few pages of a novel. When the men finally come back through the house, they are laughing. She remains upstairs until David knocks.

"It went amazingly well," he announces. "Rufus was perfect to work with, so cooperative. He's trying to overcome a drug addiction." He holds up a bouquet of twenty-dollar bills. "Not bad for an hour."

Madeleine closes her book and funnels her whole heart into a smile.

More clients come in the next few months, smiling bashfully at Madeleine and Annabel as they pass through the house to the backyard. They go over the grass and into the woods: large women in caftans, thin girls in yoga pants, ponytailed men. At first there are two or three a week. Then one a day. By the winter, David is juggling several appointments on each square of the kitchen calendar.

"Where do they come from?" Madeleine asks.

"All over. My client this morning came down from Hartford."

"How do they know about you?"

"There's a very tight community. Word spreads fast."

Today he is wearing something new: a leather cord necklace with a small pouch attached.

"It's a medicine bundle," he says, following her gaze. "It's where I keep tokens that bring me closer to my spirit animal."

Madeleine asks what kind of animal this might be.

"I'm not supposed to tell you, but I bet you can guess." From a pocket, he removes a second leather pouch and shows it to her. "A bundle for the baby."

Madeleine gazes at the pouch. It is made of soft leather that begs to be touched. She reaches for it, takes it from David's hand. The leather is puckered neatly at the top, and there is a clink of hidden objects within. An amulet.

"I'd like to journey on her behalf," David says. "And meet with her animal. Would you help me?"

"Journey where?"

"To the Lower World," he answers matter-of-factly.

Madeleine is quiet. Her husband is in front of her, behind the rough reddish growth of beard, speaking of spirit worlds. She looks at the leather pouch again. She looks at the baby in her arms, built from nothing.

That night, she sits on the nursery floor with a drum in her lap. On the baby's changing table is a plastic bag labeled *Spirit Warrior Music & Instruments.*

"It's not perfect, but it's something to practice on for now. Eventually I'll make my own drum out of maple and rawhide."

David stretches out on the sand-colored carpet. Annabel lies on her back in the bassinet, cycling her legs. The winter sun has gone down, and the room is quiet and dark. The windows make a grid of indigo sky. It is not difficult to imagine that the three of them are alone in the universe.

"The drumbeat is a bridge to the World Tree," David tells her from the floor, "giving me access to the branches that lead to the Upper World, or to the roots that tunnel to the Lower World."

"Is that in one of your books?"

"More than one." David closes his eyes. "Check your watch before you start drumming. Just start out with a nice, slow beat.

When you've been going for about ten minutes, go ahead and change to a callback rhythm. Something faster, like a gallop."

"To call you back?"

"I'll hopefully be down pretty deep, but I'll perceive the change in the drum's tempo and know it's time to return."

Madeleine tests the drum. The hard surface is made of a polished synthetic that stings her palms. The sound it makes is flat and unsubtle, like something heavy dropping to the floor again and again. The effect is the opposite of soothing.

"There, keep it going like that."

Madeleine's legs are already starting to cramp in their pretzeled arrangement. Although there is no direct sight line from neighboring houses, she wishes with a sudden fervor that she had closed the curtains. She wishes that she had not agreed to do this, that she could switch bodies with any of her neighbors. She thinks of Suzanne Crawford in the irreproachable house next door and desperately wants to be doing whatever she is doing—sipping Pinot Grigio at a kitchen island, loading the dishwasher, paying bills.

The drumbeat is tediously slow, the plodding of an old draft horse. Within a few moments Madeleine's hands have begun to fall mechanically, driven by their own momentum, and the strident thumps have dulled into sameness. David appears to go to sleep. She continues to hit the drum, resigned, a trudging giant in the nursery.

Watching, she notices gradual changes in David's face. His eyeballs flicker under the lids like goldfish in a bag. His mouth moves slightly, as if he is speaking to an unseen companion. The baby's legs finally stop cycling. Squares of blue light fall upon the carpet, and the room is suffused with something sublime and church-like. Madeleine closes her eyes. She pictures David's tree house, dimly, in the branches of the ash. She entertains the idea of embracing the trunk of the tree and being pulled downward into the ground. Is this how it goes? As she drums, she extends the script, sinking down through the earth, following the tree roots through the soil, to—what?—a sloping underground tunnel. Here, her imagination stalls. What should lie at the bottom? A dark pool of water, or a grassy clearing, or a cave of molten rock. She settles on the pool of water, hovers above it, conjures murky creatures beneath the surface.

When she opens her eyes again, Annabel appears to be asleep. It has easily been ten minutes since she began drumming. At last, her hands pause, then drum again faster. As she does this, she imagines David racing up through a tunnel as through a mine shaft. She looks for evidence of this effort in his face, but it remains placid, as serene as the face of their sleeping daughter. She beats the drum and closes her eyes. She is in a coal car barreling underground, dimly aware of the turns and dips ahead. There may be water, there may be rock. It is not for her to know the way.

Swarm

The new house is a horror. Martin and his wife remark on it each time they turn onto Minuteman Road and are struck by the bald ostentation. The house, constructed in just three months, appears to have been modeled after a Palladian villa. It is fronted by a columned entry with a pediment like a dunce cap, and its symmetrical wings are shot through with fussy, arched windows. Although the structure is set back from the road, the owners have perversely removed the trees at the property's front edge and installed a squat stone wall flecked with mica. They don't believe themselves to be prone to prejudgment, but Martin and Philomena are people of modest leanings and allow themselves the small, wicked gratification of condemning the owners' taste.

So Martin detects a tone of abashment in his wife's voice when, over dinner, she tells him she has met their new neighbors.

"The wife's name is Coraline," she says between bites. "I was driving past and she was out by the mailbox, so I stopped to say hello. Anyway"—Philomena sighs—"she seemed very nice. Maybe in her midfifties."

"Fifties?"

"They just moved up from the city. Their kids are already grown."

"You mean it's just the two of them?" Martin says. "In that palazzo?"

"Yes, I guess so." Philomena sighs again. "Anyway, I invited them over for Saturday. It seemed the hospitable thing to do."

"I wish you would've asked me first."

"Why? What would you have said? No?"

Martin looks down to the burnt orange weave of the chair upholstery, then back up to his wife. She is in her usual spot, across from him at the table, her plump form silhouetted by the window behind her, glazed with late-afternoon sun. Her hair shines white gold.

Martin has seen forty years of skies pass by that window. The interior of the dining room is still lined with wood paneling, as it was the day they moved in. Like a ski lodge. He has stared at the same wooden slabs for forty years, too, his eye settling on their natural flaws, the dark knots in the grain like stationary whirlpools. Forty winters in this room, with chili and cocoa. The zero sound of snow. The shifting, lenticular sky.

In the summer, Philomena's garden opens like a garden in a children's book. Her climbing-rose trellis blooms, and the diagonal rows of marigold. The little pond in the woods comes alive with turtles and frogs. And over those forty years, property values have blossomed, too. Their four-bedroom colonial with green shutters and charmingly darkened shingles is now worth at least a million dollars. Nearly a full acre on a desirable street between train line and school. If this is possible—if it is possible that a boy who sucked licorice on the sidewalks of Flatbush could be a millionaire now, inflation notwithstanding—then the world is a spooky and fabulous place indeed.

Martin hated their house at first. It took him too far from the city and the cramped studio on Fourteenth Street he'd come to romanticize. He enjoyed watching the restless parade of crooks, bums, and nuns beneath his window. He enjoyed putting a canvas against a wall and making brash marks that clanged like music. But this house has endeared itself to him over the years. The rooms have absorbed something of him, and he of them. And he knows that it was a fortunate confluence of timing and geography that softly deposited him upon a tenure track at the neighboring state university, just a twenty-minute drive from Minuteman Road.

They'd grown fairly close with some of the neighbors, a handful of couples with children the same age as theirs, with whom they took turns hosting dinners. Martin always had the feeling that these gatherings were building toward some ultimate consummation of friendship that hovered just one or two dinners away. The Loomises were the first to sell. They traded their lovely, weatherworn home on the sound for a Spanish-tiled monster in Jupiter. The Petries were next, once their children were safely launched onto Wall Street. For them it was Sanibel Island. Then the Henrys and the Callahans. They all fell, as if to gravity, to that southerly force so much like the grip of death. They all bequeathed their houses to sweet, anxious families like mirror images of their younger selves.

Philomena broached Florida just once, and just once Martin said *never.*

After dinner, he helps his wife with the dishes, then retires to the studio. In one corner, a sawhorse sits idle. In another, a tower of brittle sketchbooks leans into the wall. The easel wears a thin pelt of dust. Martin settles into the worn easy chair and opens an issue of *Time* magazine. A fly orbits his head, alights on his ear, clings. There is the brief, eerie feeling of miniature appendages taking purchase on flesh before his hand rises reflexively. The fly finds a perch on the edge of the gummed-up turpentine jar, and Martin sinks deeper into his chair. He skims the pages of *Time* and naps, as has become his evening ritual.

The Gregorys come on Saturday. Coraline is a doll, he has to admit, with a fit body beneath her cable-knit sweater and pedal pushers. He shakes her hand firmly—he is still a robust man and wants to demonstrate this—and returns her smile with a handsome set of teeth, still his own. The husband, too, Martin finds likable. Bill Gregory wears a pair of wide-wale corduroys with a brass-buttoned blazer. His collar parts, revealing the pink flesh of a happy businessman. It seems impossible that these are the philistines behind the nouveau concoction on the corner.

They exchange pleasantries and take seats around the wooden coffee table that still bears the scars of children's homework. Philomena serves tall glasses of Campari and soda with lemon crescents. Coraline and Bill share the old brown couch, and their hosts flank them in armchairs.

Bill leans forward toward Martin. "So, Philomena tells us you're an artist."

"Oh." Martin glances at his wife. "Well, yes."

"What kind of work do you do?" Coraline asks.

Martin looks again toward Philomena, who returns his glance with an encouraging smile.

"Well, I've always been a painter, primarily," he begins, "but really I've dipped into everything."

"The Carnegie Museum owns one of his paintings." Philomena swirls her glass. "So does the Menil Collection in Texas."

"Really?" Coraline puts down her Campari. "I wonder if we may have seen your work."

"Oh, probably not. It hasn't been on view in a while," says Martin, sipping his drink too quickly, the herbal syrup delightfully bitter.

"Do you work here at home?" asks Bill.

Martin nods.

"Could we"—Bill looks at Philomena—"come visit the studio sometime, maybe have a tour?"

Martin clings to his drink and considers for a moment its wedge of lemon, curled at the rim like a banana slug. He puts the glass down and stands.

"Well, why not. Let's go do it now."

For a moment he stands alone, fearing that he has misread the moment. This is the time for dinner, of course, not a studio visit. But the Gregorys stand, and then his wife. He leads them through the breezeway to the studio, which was once the garage.

He begins with the vertical painting rack. One by one he slides the dusty old abstracts into the light and perches them on the easel. The Gregorys make complimentary noises. Then he moves to the later, experimental sculptures, arachnid shapes. There are many more of these to show, their production having aligned with the art world's lamentable shift toward performance and politics. He'd been offered only two solo shows between 1970 and 1985. After that, his gallery had relegated him to summer group exhibitions, then ceased to invite him at all. He tries not to mind this. He has no reason to complain, having earned a comfortable living from teaching, having raised two children to adulthood, having stayed happily married. He has retained his health well into retirement, and although he's never warmed to golfing, he has found ways to stay occupied. It makes no sense to generate more art at this point. It would only take up space.

"Martin, this is phenomenal work," Bill says gravely.

"We're art collectors, you know," Coraline adds. "So this is very exciting for us."

"What are you working on now, if I may ask?" Bill's eyes scan the room.

"Well, to be honest, I've been resting on my laurels." Martin chuckles. "Just a few drawings here and there." He pauses. "I've always wanted to try something large-scale, actually, but it's a question of space. And funding."

Bill and Coraline are quiet. Philomena stares.

"Let me ask you something," says Bill, turning to face Martin, his hands thrust into corduroy pockets. "If you had a commission, let's say, and could do any project you wanted right now, what would you do?"

There is a long pause. In a dresser drawer upstairs, beneath his underpants, Martin keeps the carefully drawn plans from his youth. The papers are yellowed and the pencil lines faded, but the finished image remains bright in his mind. When he proposed the idea to his dealer years ago, he'd received a look of amused incredulity—an unfair response, given the blatant hoaxes other artists were permitted. It was true that the idea might have seemed a departure, but to Martin it was an extension of his vision, its shadow side. He rarely thinks of the project anymore, but every so often it appears to him in a dream, magically realized, and he feels an exhilaration so complete it brings tears to his eyes.

He stands for another moment, looking at Bill and Coraline Gregory. Then he goes out the studio door and hurries upstairs to his underwear drawer.

The Gregorys return the next week to formally commission the work. After their visit, Philomena is strangely quiet. In front of the bathroom mirror, she puts her toothbrush down and finally speaks. "Are you crazy? Do you understand how big their house is?"

Yes, Martin says, he is aware of the size. It's perfect. Monumental. He'd seen the excitement in Bill Gregory's eyes when he unfolded the first drawing. Yes, Martin had explained, those *were* insects, each individually sculpted and affixed to the exterior of a house. Spiders, moths, beetles, grasshoppers. The house in the picture was a generic 1950s ranch, nearly obscured by a mass of clinging bodies, an enchanting tangle of wings, legs, and antennae.

"You'd need millions of them to cover it," Philomena says. "Who's going to model each one?"

Martin brushes his teeth calmly.

"And the Gregorys are lunatics, too. Who do they think they are? The de' Medicis?"

"What's wrong with that?"

Philomena looks at him in the mirror. They lock eyes for a moment, and her face softens. "I just don't want to see you disappointed."

"That won't happen."

"I hope you're right."

"They're serious about this. You heard what they said. They'll cover the cost of materials and pay me the rest when it's finished." Martin smiles at himself. "This could be really big. Hell, it can't be anything *but* big."

"I'm just saying you should measure the house first. You're not twenty-five anymore. You've never even done an outdoor project before."

Martin seizes his wife's soft body. He kisses her forehead and bends her backward, hearing the faint click of her bones. "You worry too much," he says.

Bill Gregory gives him a copy of the blueprints, but Martin barely looks at them. He understands that the house is large; he doesn't need to know the exact square footage. First he will need a stockpile of closed-cell foam, dense enough to carve and score.

At the lumber yard, he puts in an order for a hundred sheets of pink insulation board. From the hardware store, he buys spools of black electrical wire and tubes of foam adhesive. The owner calls a supplier in California for a roll of fine-gauge stainless mesh. Lastly, he buys paint. Gallons of all-weather coating in a spectrum of colors. He already has a stack of nature books, including a five-pound insect encyclopedia with color illustrations of specimens cataloged by continent.

After the insulation sheets arrive and the men deposit them in the backyard, Martin sits at the kitchen table with a glass of lemonade. Outside, a mountain of pink foam waits beyond the marigolds, topped with cinder block weights. He feels giddy, feverish to begin.

"I hope you're not planning on leaving that there," says Philomena, coming through the kitchen in gardening gloves. "It'll kill the grass."

"Don't worry, they won't be there for long."

On Friday, Martin begins to make the first bug. He goes outdoors, saws a chunk from a sheet of foam, and clamps it into the vise on his workbench. With a coping saw, he shapes the piece, then refines it with an X-Acto knife and sandpaper. He carves textured ribbing along the thorax and abdomen. After lunch, he cuts wing shapes from the stainless mesh and carefully glues wire to their undersides, creating the illusion of veins. Finally, he pierces the thorax with six thick wires: three sets of legs. When Philomena calls him for dinner, he has not yet begun painting.

He finishes the first insect at ten o'clock that night. There were a few setbacks after dinner—a lost leg, a vein peeled away from its wing—but nothing Martin hasn't been able to rectify with invisible glue. Finally, he sets about painting the iridescent dragonfly body. Although he is yawning by the time he finishes, adrenaline courses through his bloodstream. He fairly jogs up the stairs holding the piece and carries it to Philomena in bed.

"What do you think?" he pants, holding the insect in front of her. "It's a blue darner, *Aeschna cyanea*."

She looks up from her book. "It's wonderful."

"That's all?"

"It's lovely. But at this rate, it's going to take you ten years to finish."

Martin is silent, holding the dragonfly. "It'll go faster once I get in the swing of things."

Philomena smiles and goes back to her book.

"Or if I had an assistant." Martin puts a hand to his wife's shoulder.

"You can put an ad in the paper," she says without looking up.

By Tuesday, Martin has completed two dragonflies, two spiders, and one perfect ladybug. On Wednesday, Philomena agrees to help glue the wings to a gypsy moth, and by the weekend she is sitting with him through whole days, helping to carve new creatures from scratch. The production doubles, then triples—as Martin predicted it would—as they become more adept. Together, they fall into a kind of shared trance, bending wires and sculpting foam as the summer progresses and weeds crawl up the sides of the pink pyramid behind the house.

Slowly, they produce each species in the book. Despite her bad back and creeping arthritis, Philomena works unflagging hours, fashioning the spiky hairs on fly legs, painting the chartreuse wings of a luna moth. She works with a beatific look on her face, like a woman deep in her knitting. By September, they have made a hundred insects. Martin is reluctant to store them in boxes, where they might be damaged. Instead, they rest upon every available surface, until they crowd the studio and overflow into the breezeway. *Swarm,* Martin decides, will be the title of the piece.

When the Gregorys invite them for dinner, Martin and Philomena walk down Minuteman Road to the glittering stone wall. On foot, the house is more imposing than ever—six thousand square feet at least. Martin says nothing as his wife glances at him and presses the musical doorbell.

Bill leads the tour of the interior, pausing to highlight the artwork. The paintings tend to be oversized, lacking in nuance. The artists' names are unfamiliar. Several gallery pedestals surround the dinner table, supporting bronze blobs. Martin sits quietly beneath the vaulted ceiling as the others converse and a chef serves steak tartare.

Martin chooses not to return the dinner invitation, despite Philomena's protests. It is unwise to give his patrons a preview of the piece before it's complete, he argues, and it will be too much trouble to stow it away.

By November, a phalanx of insects occupies the kitchen. The first snow comes and lays a clean blanket upon the hill of insulation boards. Alone in the house, Martin and Philomena slide into the timeless ski-lodge feeling. With the exception of supermarket cashiers and hardware store clerks, they speak only to each other. It has been a long time since they were together like this—really together—doing something. Something about their shared concentration on the same objective spurs easy conversation. They talk about people they've known, relive their children's blunders, make each other laugh.

From time to time, there are phone calls, the ring resounding like a siren through the house, rattling Martin out of his chair. Philomena speaks to their daughter, Melinda, divorced in San Francisco, and their son, Claude, living in Nashville with their two granddaughters.

"Will we come down there for Christmas? He wants to know."

Martin does not respond. He has resorted to fingernail scissors for fashioning the knobs of a millipede's body, and his fingers are blistered from it.

"Martin, I just spoke to you."

"I heard you, love. I just don't know the answer yet."

"The answer to whether you'll fly to see your son and grandchildren for Christmas?"

"That's right. I don't know the answer. I don't think they'll be too happy with my bug-making at the dinner table." He chuckles. "I might get foam dust in the turkey."

"What's so funny? Do you think you're funny?"

"Come on, Phil, I'm only joking. I wouldn't really bring my bugs to Nashville." He pauses, breathes in. "But I don't think I should go. I've got too much work to do."

His wife stares at him, her eyes stygian. He looks back at his millipede.

"You can go if you want, of course," he adds. "I wouldn't want to stop you from going."

"Well, you don't have to worry about that," she says, and heaves herself up from the couch.

After that, Martin works alone. He becomes bogged down with a monarch butterfly whose colors are coming out muddy. It is important, he knows, to create a few really vibrant pieces. Among the monochromes of the insect world, there is always an occasional peacock—a spirit-lifting splash of color. He repaints the butterfly's wings, then puts them aside to dry before setting to the delicate task of adding the black veins and spots. As he holds the fine-tipped brush, Martin's fingers tremble. He commands them to steady, but they shake until he is forced to put the brush down.

After breakfast each morning, he goes into the studio and sits alone. All around him, arthropods stare with vacant eyes. Their bodies appear flimsy and childish to him now, the work of a deluded fool. To begin work on a new creature would be to waste another scrap of his life. Whether he'd be better off wasting the same time in Nashville, cramped in his son's frilly guest room, he doesn't know. He picks up *Time* magazine and stares at the cover: a soldier poised on a hill in Afghanistan. The world is a mess. Here is a young man, younger than Claude, forsaken upon a barren land in the sights of hidden riflescopes. Martin, with his ladybugs, might be on another planet.

When Philomena startles him awake, he sees that the sun has gone down. He comes groggily to the dinner table and looks at his wife. Perhaps she sees the entreaty in his look, because the next day she comes wordlessly to the studio and helps him again.

They do not go to Nashville. Martin hasn't needed to argue the issue. He heard Philomena on the phone one evening. *You know your father,* she was saying quietly. *That's true, but still, it means a lot to him.* And finally, wearily, *Next year, I promise. But you'll still come up for Easter, I hope?*

They decorate the tree to the songs of Bing Crosby, as is their tradition. Philomena, in an act of clemency that warms Martin's heart, eschews the usual angel and ties his monarch butterfly to the top.

The day before Christmas, the Gregorys surprise them at the front door with a ginger cake.

"Will you come in for tea? A cocktail?" Philomena asks, while Martin scrambles to hide insects in the broom closet.

"No, no, we're on our way to the city," Bill says. "We just wanted to spread some cheer." He shades his eyes and peers into the house. "The project going well?"

Yes, of course, Martin assures him. He'll be done by New Year's. Philomena glances at him.

"Wonderful," Bill booms. "Well, don't be strangers," he calls as they go back out into the snow and climb into their carriage, a Mercedes SUV.

By the time they finish the last insect, in April, the house is overrun. Together, Martin and Philomena joyfully hack the last lonely pink slab apart where it lies. A flattened yellow patch of grass remains while the rest turns green and Philomena's marigolds sprout their first leaves.

Martin goes on foot down Minuteman Road to report the good news. Although he's been forced to avoid the Gregorys all winter, his embarrassment evaporates as he inhales the spring air. He feels almost young as he trots up their driveway and rings the musical doorbell. And yet he finds himself out of breath when Coraline answers. He gasps, "It's finished."

She wears a look of concern. "What's finished?"

He laughs, bending to catch his breath. "The project is ready to go. When can we start installation?"

"Come in," she says, smiling, and calls for her husband.

They are set to begin work the week before Easter. The timing is bad, Martin admits. He wants to see the kids as much as his wife does, but the project can't be delayed any longer. He doesn't want to lose credibility. To his surprise, Philomena smiles. She calmly goes to the phone, asks Claude and Melinda if they can postpone their visits until summer. It will be better this way, Martin assures her after she hangs up the receiver. When the project is finished, they'll have time to relax together, to grill outside and go to the beach as a family.

"It's all right," she tells him, putting a hand to his shoulder. "We're almost there."

She is, at that moment, the woman he unveiled at the altar forty years ago, the flash of her jet eyes like a stomp to the chest.

Together, they pack insects into cardboard boxes and load the car. The Gregorys have considerately vacated their home for a fortnight, allowing the artist to work undisturbed. The house is already decked in scaffolding. Anyone passing would assume that the new neighbors are simply adding some finishing touches, a few last details to bring the preposterous house completely over the top. Martin smiles to himself. No one would guess the nature of those details. No one would imagine, in a thousand years, the kind of creative risk the Gregorys are about to embrace—the rare kind of people they really are.

It makes sense to start at the front, where the impact will be instantly felt, and so they will be sure not to run out of bugs for the facade. Martin gingerly climbs the scaffolding to the top plank of plywood. The platform feels solid enough, but when he glances at Philomena on the ground, he feels the beginnings of vertigo and clutches a pole.

"Why don't I stay up here, honey, and you can bring the insects up to me a few at a time," he calls, keeping his gaze firmly on the bricks of the house. "Just whatever you can handle at once."

Several moments later, he hears the heavy creaking of the scaffolding ladder, and then his wife's hand is there, offering a tarantula. He laughs. "Good place to start."

Philomena continues up and down the ladder each day of the week, and Martin uses industrial epoxy to affix the insects to the house at the painstaking rate she brings them up. It's a lot of climbing, he knows, but she does not complain. On Good Friday, she wheezes up the ladder, smiles at Martin, then dips into her bucket and presents a swallowtail. It is a splendid specimen, zigzagged with yellow. He finds a spot for it next to a welter of houseflies, where it will glow brilliantly. Philomena balances patiently at the top rung, gripping the plywood plank with one hand and using the other to unload another insect. Martin reaches down for a praying mantis at the moment her grip relaxes. He watches as her fingers release the plank slowly, gracefully, without understanding the meaning of it. Then there is a judder of scaffolding poles as her body crumples and drops to the ground.

Martin feels suspended high above the earth for an instant, saying, "Phil?," even as he moves to scramble down the ladder. The ground is soft, still muddy from spring rain. Philomena lies on her back. Her face is pale, and she looks at him in a kind of bemused surprise. He begins to feel for her pulse, but considers the passing moments, and instead runs down Minuteman Road to their home telephone.

When the ambulance comes, he rides in the back and watches the medical men. Their huddle obscures his wife from view. He feels absent from the vehicle, as if he is still on the scaffolding platform, holding the praying mantis. He continues to feel absent at the hospital as the doctor lays a hand on his shoulder. *Sudden coronary arrest.* A main artery jammed with plaque, narrowed over the years. Martin walks away from the hospital, through the parking lot and driveway, to the edge of the street. Then he turns and looks at the building that holds his wife, built of plain white cement blocks. It looks back at him, brutally mute.

The kids stay with him after the services. Claude and his wife settle into the guest room, and their two girls use the trundle bed in Claude's old bedroom. Melinda chooses to sleep on the old brown couch. She dusts the house and vacuums, sucking up bits of foam that have found their way into the braid of the rugs. She cooks vegetarian dinners in the wok she gave them one Christmas, which they'd never used. Martin walks from room to room and sits in every chair. He cannot find a comfortable spot. Every place has Philomena in it.

The Gregorys leave a condolence card in the mailbox. Martin is glad they didn't knock. He remains in pajamas, unshowered. He sleeps long, dreamless nights and takes ugly afternoon naps. He speaks only when necessary. The grandkids grow tired of playing board games and begin to whine softly, but are chastised by their parents. One morning, Martin walks through the house—past Melinda brewing coffee in the kitchen, Claude and the girls playing outside the window—and goes into the studio. There is still a square of insulation board remaining. With the blind motions of habit, he takes a serrated knife and carves the tapered abdomen of a wasp.

An unknown period of time passes before his daughter appears in the doorway.

"What are you doing, Dad?"

"Just keeping my hands busy."

He knows how he must look, the few tufts of dirty white hair fanning out from his head, his pajama top buttoned haphazardly.

"Would you like to help?" he asks.

"What do you mean? Help with what?" Melinda stands stolidly in a clean black sweater and jeans. There is a tone in her voice that Martin doesn't like.

"What do you think? With the project," he answers, keeping his eyes on the bug.

There is a long pause, and then Melinda speaks with open rancor. "You have to be kidding me. You're still doing this? Don't you understand that Mom is gone?" She takes a breath. "She died, Dad. Doing your stupid project."

Martin does not speak. Melinda turns and leaves the doorway. He takes an X-Acto knife and begins scoring the foam.

They are quiet at the dinner table. Melinda forks the salad into bowls with obvious anger, and Claude will not look at his father. At the end of the meal, Martin pushes his chair out from the table and says, "I know what you're all thinking. That I'm a selfish bastard for trying to finish this damn project." His voice quavers, and he glances at the grandchildren whose eyes stare back roundly. "But I have a commission, and I'm expected to deliver it. I am a professional."

He takes his empty plate to the kitchen and rinses it, then strides into the studio. A terrible draining sensation takes hold of his stomach as he stands in the room, surrounded by insects. Slowly, he fills a cardboard box with painted bodies.

The following day, he drives a loaded car to the Gregorys' house. The draining sensation in his gut has been replaced by something heavy and solid like an iron brick. He drives up to the scene of his wife's collapse and feels a dull distance, as if he were viewing it through a periscope. He sees, through the periscope's tunnel, that the scaffolding has been removed. A small group of insects clings to the upper corner of the house's face like a mole.

Martin goes to the door, clothed in his denim work shirt, and shakes Bill Gregory's hand. He accepts repeat condolences, and then asks when he might resume work.

The Gregorys cautiously express their appreciation that he intends to finish. They consult briefly, out of earshot. Finally they agree to let the project recommence, with the condition that they hire a crew to install the rest of the piece. Martin, of course, will serve as artistic supervisor.

It feels good to get out of the house. Martin's family has made no move to decamp, nor have they sought rapprochement. The accusation in the air is oppressive. He goes out into a fine spring day and walks along the side of the road to the site. The iron brick remains lodged in his gut, and the periscope vision persists. Far away, he hears a sound that he identifies as the trill of birds. The scaffolding is in the process of being replaced by men who do not appear to be artist assistants but construction workers.

The Gregorys give Martin a pair of binoculars, with which he can survey the work from a director's chair on the ground, and for several weeks he enjoys shouting out the names of the insects to the men. Despite their casual manner, the men are prodigious and accurate workers, and Martin watches as, day by day, the house grows a beard of exoskeletons and wings.

At last, Martin's family takes their leave. He observes their preparations through the periscope and feels little emotion as they load Claude's car with luggage and some of Philomena's things. He knows that he should be affected. He should plead with them to stay, ask for more time to grieve, more consolation. Or perhaps he should ask to accompany them, sell the house and live the rest of his days warm and watched over in Nashville. Instead, he bends down to let his granddaughters hug him and waves from the front door as the car reverses out of the driveway.

The men affix the final insect on the last day of May. When they take the tarps and scaffolding down and pack up their equipment, the house looks dazzling in the noon sun. Martin backs away, all the way to the road. Not a glimpse of the original brick is visible. The entire facade is completely shrouded in dark, voluptuous texture. Here and there, dashes of color—fuchsia butterfly, lime-green caterpillar—pop like jewels. It is exactly, incredibly, the way Martin imagined it. The manifestation of the house from his dreams, the improbable pinnacle of his career. As he stands at the end of the driveway, he sobs like a child.

The Gregorys come out to join him. Bill pats him on the back and Coraline holds his hand kindly. They are very pleased with how it has turned out, Bill says. It is a masterpiece, unlike anything they've ever encountered.

Martin is unable to speak for a moment. "I just wish Phil were here to see it," he says.

Within days, the first phone calls come in. The Gregorys field these with aplomb, listening to the neighbors' grievances and politely asserting their own rights as Old Cranbury property owners. They've been preparing for this kind of reaction, they tell Martin. They know that not everyone shares their avant-garde tastes. With a little time, they predict, the calls will taper off. People will grow accustomed to the sight, perhaps begin to appreciate its aesthetic value. Eventually, *Swarm* might even become a beloved town landmark.

But, over the summer months, the calls overflow to the town hall. The house is a travesty, disgusting to look at. It is bringing property values down. One passerby telephones in a panic, thinking the creatures are real. The house was already bad enough, some snap, but this is a middle finger to the rest of the town. There need to be regulations to suppress people like the Gregorys who believe the world is theirs to deface.

Finally, in November, Martin reads in the *Old Cranbury Gazette* about the lawsuit against his patrons. The art installation is incorrigibly offensive to the residents of the town. A black-and-white photograph of the house accompanies the front-page article. Martin sees his own name captioned beneath the image, and his breath catches for a moment. In the fuzzy photograph, of substandard resolution, the piece does look horrific, like the scene of a crime.

All publicity is good publicity, he reminds himself. Lying alone in bed, habitually on the right-hand side, he allows his mind to drift through the possibilities. The art media will surely catch wind of the controversy, and there might be a write-up in one of the monthly publications. The longer the Gregorys resist, the better for his own career. Perhaps other suburban iconoclasts will contact him about commissions. He feels a sweet shudder at the thought, despite the heavy awareness of the empty space at his left.

Later that week, Bill Gregory comes to the door. He shakes Martin's hand firmly, gives a brief, beleaguered smile, and announces that they are going to take the piece down. The battle is grueling already, and it has only begun. The situation is emotionally depleting for his wife, in particular, who has not taken well to being the town pariah.

They will cover the cost of de-installation, Bill says as he rises from the couch. And Martin, of course, will keep his commission payment. As Bill speaks, Martin sits quietly and watches his neighbor's gesturing hands, the gold wedding band making designs in the air. He watches the knob in Bill's throat move up and down the pink column of his neck. When Bill shakes his hand, Martin receives the grip impassively. As Bill leaves, the storm door lets in a crisp breeze before closing with a flatulent sigh.

The next week, a truck comes to Martin's house. A man rings his doorbell and asks where they can put the crates. There is no room in the studio—the garage—he tells them. He signs a paper and closes the door. He watches through the window as the men unload wooden crates onto the driveway. Then the truck pulls away.

Martin steps outside, and the autumn sun hits him flat in the face. He walks, partly blinded, toward the maze of crates on the pavement, each sealed tight. Fingering the perimeter of one lid, he feels the divots where each screw is firmly countersunk. There are at least twenty screws in this one lid. He sits down on the box. The sunlight crowns his head, indiscriminately loving. The fiery trees flap their excitable hands.

He thinks of the little pond behind the house, icy in winter, covered with algae in summer. He remembers chasing frogs with the kids, capturing dragonflies. Just now, the water would be clean and cold beneath a scrim of vibrant leaves. He entertains a vision: a pond bejeweled by insects. Floating grasshoppers and bees, the water shuddering alive. The foam would keep them afloat, and he would go in after them, sink down among them. He would drop through them with his iron weight, completing the piece and bestowing its meaning.

Martin sits for another moment, then uses both hands to push himself up. He leans down to the crate he'd been sitting on and tries to lift it, but the strain on his back is too much and he lets it drop back to the ground. Straightening, he surveys the jumble of boxes—too many to count, identical, equally impossible. He squints into the sun. A car approaches, loud and filled with children. A boy sees him with his boxes and waves. He waves back instinctively. The car rumbles out of earshot, and the small sounds of birds return.

Visa

They meet in the parking lot. She supposes that this is one of the more dampening aspects of suburban dating, this kind of public, day-lit rendezvous. They shake hands on the strip mall sidewalk like business associates. He is tall—taller than she remembers—with a pronounced jaw that hinges on the brink of ugliness. For a moment, she is thrown. In the blush-toned glow of O'Reilly's Pub, postmidnight, his profile had reminded her of a Roman statue. It is possible that she had even said this. Now, studying the flat-sloped nose and deep, suggestive cleft at the top lip, she understands that this is the kind of face that defies easy categorization. The kind of face that does not reveal itself at once, but alters with the faintest breeze of feeling.

In the Japanese restaurant they are enveloped by cool, regulated air, the sounds of synthesizers and burbling water. As they settle at their table, Camille watches his hands. Smooth and slender with neat oval-shaped nails, the type of quasi-feminine, erotic hands she notices on men from time to time. She meets his eyes—granite gray, dominating—and her initial distaste is interrupted by a slight shudder. All at once, the patchwork of his face seems to harmonize and become familiar, inevitable.

"So," he begins, without prelude. "How old is your daughter?"

Camille smiles sourly. It is unfair to start this way. "She's three."

He nods. This is the moment when another woman might take the bait and lightly ask if he'd like to have children of his own someday. Perhaps he is already testing her. She drops her eyes to the menu, allows the moment to extend uncomfortably.

"You don't look like a mother." He is not smiling, but staring with a directness that creates an animal confusion in her, a concurrent swelling and shrinking.

They eat their sushi rolls carefully, with strict restraint. She has heard it said that surgeons are wild. As he looks at her over the bamboo bento trays, she feels a pull from these darkening eyes that seem to tunnel away light.

He's never been married, he confirms in a neutral voice that reveals neither regret nor pride. A surgeon's life doesn't leave much time for meeting women, he says, especially in a place like this.

She pictures his condominium, a spare shelter like her own with few furnishings. He must make money, she thinks, and have nothing to spend it on. She can tell from his clothing, a pale gray dress shirt with mother-of-pearl buttons, that he has a foundation for elegance.

"You must feel isolated," Camille suggests.

"Sometimes," he says.

Camille wants to reach across the table and squeeze his hand, tell him that she knows. Things are impossible here. Since Nick left, she's been locked in a prison of women. Her days are nearly bereft of the male sex. She rarely sees Mark and Harris anymore and, anyway, they don't count. From time to time a rogue father will join the crowd of mothers for preschool pickup. When this happens, she finds herself standing differently, out of habit, generating the old energy regardless of what the poor man looks like, however paunchy or beaten down. And he looks at her. They always do. She supposes that she receives some trifling pleasure from this, some pellet of reward, like a pigeon that pecks a lever for birdseed. But afterward, the satisfaction fizzles and she's left with a vacant feeling, as if she's shoplifted something too easily.

They finish a bottle of sake together. He asks questions and listens intently, gravely, as if the answers were credo. She hardly notices her noodle dish vanish and be replaced by pistachio ice cream, which vanishes in turn.

"I've always dreamed of living in Paris." Camille allows herself to shift into a kittenish purr, leaning closer. "I was there once, during college. I thought someday I'd find an apartment with big windows and a fluffy white bed."

"Mmm." He smiles.

She laughs a tinkling arpeggio. But it is the truth. She has always romanticized living abroad—Paris, Barcelona, Rome—imagined herself living alone, the way a man might live. It is a quaint, clichéd nineteenth-century idea of liberation, perhaps, but the impulse to roam is native in her, and its continued denial a source of panic.

Of course, living alone is impossible now with Avis. So Camille has revised her vision of Paris to include a partner. The fluffy bed, she reasons, would be even better with a man in it. Now it's only a matter of finding him, whose passion is equal to hers. Sadly, it's nearly impossible to imagine such a man in a town like this, for whom the hills beyond the supermarket beckon with urgent promise. Nick, she has to admit, had been like that. He'd had that hunger in him. That much they had shared.

She does not mention Paris again, but it floats in the air between them like a specter. And the brief kiss they share in the parking lot, amid the doltish Volvos and Volkswagens, is like a pact, the first upward tug of a kite.

At home, the babysitter already has her coat on. Camille can hear Avis still awake in her room, singing to herself.

"I was supposed to be home by ten," the girl grumbles.

"Can your mom pick you up?"

"I told her you were driving me home."

On the road, Avis sits in her car seat in her pajamas and screams for a cookie. The cookies are in her other purse, Camille patiently explains, but her daughter does not relent. Already, within moments, she feels herself deflating.

"I wonder what your *father's* doing right now," she calls back, unconcerned about the preteen slumped in the passenger seat, listening. Let her hear it, let her be warned. Camille laughs bitterly. "Definitely not this, that's for sure."

Avis shrieks, and Camille rolls down the rear window to give her daughter a blast of cold air. Nick is fifty miles to the south, elevated in his pseudo loft on Spring Street, living some approximation of a 1980s fantasy with his black-haired, thin-lipped dominatrix. This is how Camille pictures the woman, anyway, the older coworker whose name, *Victoria,* she'd found infesting his call history. The fact that this Victoria is allegedly pregnant, thanks to some medical miracle, does not change the picture.

On the way back from the babysitter's house, Avis falls asleep in her seat, and Camille carries her to bed. Asleep, she is a dreamy thing. Her eyelashes form a golden mesh, and her face is innocent, forgetful of the dramas and torments of the day. Camille puts her face close, inhales the sweet breath. These little moments are hers alone now. Let Nick try to find them with his new child.

The next morning, the sake has receded like the tide and left her brain dry and seaweed strewn. She goes out in big sunglasses, a shearling coat, and boots over jeans. The sun throbs in the sky as she leads Avis to the entrance of Bright Beginnings. The two self-appointed "class mothers" are there, flanking the door, smiling with their horse teeth. One of them thrusts a flyer at her.

"Hope you'll contribute!"

Her hand trembles as she takes the sheet. A bake sale. *All families are invited to contribute a healthful, nut-free treat. Gluten-free and vegan especially encouraged!* She would like to throw the flyer into the recycling bin. In these first few weeks, she has received flyers discouraging plastic utensils at school, prohibiting tree nuts in the building, requesting awareness of branded clothing in the classroom.

"Twinkies okay?" Camille smiles broadly at the mothers, despite the pain of it, and herds her daughter through the door. Avis's hair is still matted from sleep, gathered in two stubby pigtails like horns on top of her head. Still, she is the prettiest girl in the classroom. The other children are cropped and bobbed, uniformed in drab organic clothing. Avis regards them coolly through glass-blue eyes, her father's best feature. She is long lashed and bubblegum pink in her ruffled skirt and sequined Mary Janes.

It delights Camille to dress her daughter this way, in the frothiest clothing she can find, if only to scandalize the other mothers. You would think the Disney princesses were succubi by the way these women talk. *I just don't understand why so many parents buy into the marketing,* they say. *They're basically grooming their girls to become appearance-obsessed little consumers.* These are the kind of primitive feminists, she is certain, who began referring to themselves as "women" at age eighteen, who sat with straight faces through college demonstrations of dental dams. She has no use for women like these, who would keep musty, second-wave feminism on life support. The rest of the world has moved on. It has thanked the poor, neutered mothers and grandmothers for the dreary work they did, and put on stilettos again with free-ranging pride.

So when Camille comes across such women standing together, their faces grave as crusaders, she finds herself pausing, despite herself, pretending to look for something in her bag. Always, she tells herself to back away, but feels her face heat. It is a public service to shut them down.

Excuse me, she'll say. *But I can't help overhearing, and I have to ask, do you really have a problem with little girls playing dress-up?*

The mothers will glare in their oatmeal bouclé-knit sweaters. After a moment, the most emboldened, ugliest mother will collect herself and reply, *We don't mean that they shouldn't play dress-up. We just think it's important to put some thought into what we offer our daughters. You know, rather than just accepting whatever's marketed to them?*

Mmm, right. The personal is political. Camille nods. *But you know this stuff is marketed to little girls for a reason. Because they* love *it.*

She knows they talk about her. That's what happens to independent-minded people in this place, to anyone who isn't brainwashed by beady-eyed mommy culture. They resent her, she knows, for preserving her pre-parent self, for dressing like a woman, for not surrendering to the dowdy, practical fashions that make the rest of them look like they've always just come from the gym, or bed.

Her only female friend in town is Madeleine Gaines, who'd risen from the city like a benevolent spirit. Her husband had been a colleague of Nick's at Clarkson-Ross, and they had all gotten together once for tapas in Union Square. When Camille first saw Madeleine in town, shuffling through the grocery aisles in a fabulous retro block-print maternity dress, she called and jogged up to her in a rush of bonhomie. She'd invited her over that very afternoon, and their roles were set from there: Camille was the outrageous, demonstrative one; Madeleine the good listener.

Perhaps she calls too often. Madeleine would be too polite to ever say so. But, today, she doesn't care; she's just happy to have a confidante she can tell about her date. Her old city friends would be too loyal, or hostile, to Nick's memory—like Mark and Harris, whose shared distaste for her ex still unaccountably rankles her. It is liberating to detach from them all, to begin a fresh history here.

They sit on beanbags in Camille's bedroom, like college roommates, sipping Cape Codders from margarita glasses.

"Where does he work?" Madeleine asks.

"Some hospital around here, I guess. I didn't ask."

"What kind of surgery does he do?"

Camille looks curiously at her friend. This is the difference between them, she decides. This anchor of practicality—or its sweet absence.

"What the hell should I care?" Camille smiles and takes a drink. Madeleine lifts her eyebrows and smiles in return, then tucks her feet under herself like a cat. She had removed her shoes at the door, although Camille had asked her not to. This is one of the small changes she's noticed in Madeleine lately. Concern about floors. Clothing that has shifted away from bright, geometric prints to dull plaids and country colors. Today she is wearing, of all things, a quilted vest.

"I think you should consider joining the book group," Madeleine says, swirling her glass. "At least come with me to a meeting and see what it's like. Really, it's just an excuse to get together with other women."

Camille stares. Madeleine, she knows, can do better than that. Last year, she and her husband had gone to South America and brought the baby. It was part of some spiritual quest of

David's, something that Madeleine does not like to discuss, but that thrills Camille. She knows that, since moving to the suburbs, David has undergone a drastic and mysterious change—abandoning convention rather than embracing it. According to Nick, he stopped attending client meetings at work and refused to use the computer. After his dismissal, he started hosting "clients" at home. This all makes Camille like Madeleine even more. To be married to a man like that, she must be a dissident, too. Camille praises herself for having unearthed a kindred spirit, for allying herself with the town's only other fearless woman.

"Mmm." Camille grins, holding her stare. "You know what I miss? The Cooler. Passerby. Do you remember those?"

"Of course," Madeleine says, her face neither brightened nor clouded by memory.

"I wonder if we might have seen each other out somewhere. Oh, and remember Lit Lounge on Second Avenue? I think it's still there."

She keeps a lock on Madeleine's eyes, seeking a hint of understanding. What she really wants to know is whether she still feels the burn. Does she, too, listen to music from her youth while driving and detect a carnal urge inside the traffic, catch the glances of strangers through car windows? It is an accepted truth, of course, that the reckless impulses of that music are dead now. There is nothing useful to be done with them. Still, the old rhythm catches in her, and she feels like a club princess trapped in a Toyota. In this state, she becomes aware of the hidden, parallel world beneath the mundane. Just beneath the surface of every defunct moment—waiting at a stoplight, finding a spot in the supermarket parking lot—lurks another moment, sexual, adulterous, waiting to be chosen. It shimmers faintly, a phosphorescent arc of lighter fluid ready to catch fire, detectable only to those attuned to it. She parks the car and watches the men and women going in and out through the automatic doors. Which of them are alight, secretly smoldering?

Madeleine waves her hand dismissively. She reaches into her tote bag and retrieves a copy of the book that her group will be discussing. Camille looks at the cover, a tablescape with dropped flower petals. Some bleak, bestselling woman's memoir. She can think of no book she'd less like to read. Without checking the jacket flap, she is certain that the book has been marketed as "empowering," that it is tailored to a nation of dispirited women looking for someone to pity, some way to cheer themselves.

"It's a good way of meeting people around here. Really, it's an excuse to get together," Madeleine repeats.

Camille softens her eyes and smiles. What she wants to say is that she has no need to meet people. She only needs one friend, and Madeleine is it.

"I appreciate the offer, I really do. I guess I'm just not in the mood for reading right now."

Later that night, Camille allows herself to type the doctor's name into the computer. As she'd suspected, the name is so commonplace that nothing useful surfaces. She checks the rosters of local hospitals, hoping for a photograph of him, but there is no matching name, no matching picture.

"Oh, they never update their websites," he says about the hospitals later. They are tucked at a corner table in a Spanish restaurant in the woods. "I'm at St. Joseph's." The way he says this is so offhand, so uninterested, that whatever seed of doubt Camille might have had is hurriedly interred.

His condominium complex has just been fumigated for termites, he tells her, so they go to her house instead. They wait in the driveway until the babysitter comes out to the car. The girl stares, and Camille widens her eyes in imitation.

"Yep, home early." She fights back tentacles of embarrassment while rummaging for cash in her purse. "Get in, let's go."

The babysitter sits in the back of the car, behind Camille and the doctor. It's only a five-minute drive to her house—easily walkable, but nobody lets their kids live anymore—and Avis is safely asleep in her bed. Camille has no patience for the kinds of people who consider it criminal to leave a sleeping child alone for ten minutes. Those are the kinds of people whose lives are governed by fear, or at least fear of vilification by their peers. The kinds of people who, with all the late-night news they watch, remain ignorant of the practices of the real world outside their bubbles: the contortions and improvisations of those without resources, the risible logistics of single parenthood.

Still, the awkwardness inside the car is painful. Camille feels a slight irritation with the doctor for forcing her into this situation. She would rather screw in a fumigation tent for twenty minutes than go through this whole production. After dropping off the babysitter, they drive back to the house in silence, toward a flat moon netted behind tree branches. Camille watches her feet pass over the concrete walkway and, inhaling the sharp night air, is stunned for a moment by her own autonomy, the giddy sweep of her jurisdiction, so completely and finally adult. She can choose whatever she wants. And she chooses this. There is a feeling like expanding helium in her as she thinks of it, filling her head and groin.

A draft comes through the bedroom window, itself marked with dried edges of paint and the residue of old decals. Usually, while dressing and undressing, she prefers to leave the window shade open, just for kicks, but tonight she pulls it down. Her bed is a futon on the floor, the same she's had since graduating from college, the same she and Nick shared for ten years. Beside it rests a stereo and vintage turntable, and above hangs a battered poster for Le Chat Noir, its slanted yellow eyes like a call to a more instinctual, hedonistic time. This futon and poster have been pillars of Camille's environment for decades. She hasn't bought a new item of furniture or decor in years—just entering a Bed Bath & Beyond gives her an anxiety attack—but that's all right. It's better to keep her bedroom minimalistic, unobtrusive, deferential to the sovereignty of its inhabitant.

Tonight, she goes through her box of vinyl and settles on Nina Simone. The doctor smiles in comprehension, and they fold together onto the futon. Camille is grateful not to be one of those women for whom beds are ruined by past partners. For her, history is continually erased so that each man is the first. There is no trace of Nick on this mattress. The doctor puts his hands in her hair and presses his fingertips into her scalp.

Only once does she think of Avis, asleep in her bed, but this comes to her from afar. There is nothing to keep her from falling, spiraling back to the raw sensations of her younger days. Each touch of this man is a discovery, and she nearly cries with gratitude for this renewal, this unexpected springtime.

He does not spend the night. This is an important trait, Camille recognizes, this unspoken consideration of her circumstances.

They spend an evening in the city. Camille drops Avis off with the housekeeper at Nick's apartment, wishing that her date were beside her instead of waiting downstairs in his double-parked BMW. She wants the housekeeper to see him, so that she might describe him to Nick. Looking over the woman's shoulder, she glowers at the loft's furnishings, the antiseptic white and chrome, backlit by a wall of blinding windows. She nearly throws Avis's toy bag inside, and presses a baggie of cookies into the housekeeper's hand.

Within an hour, she is on a hotel bed with the doctor, talking about Paris. He's been there several times, it turns out, and speaks workable French. There may be opportunities for him abroad. Camille expresses disbelief that he'd be so easy to sway, so amenable to adventure.

He kisses her. "If not now, when?" As simple as that.

When the night is fully dark, they wander down White Street to a new restaurant with black leather banquettes and brushed nickel sconces. She appreciates the gesture, but her head is already in Paris. The preening patrons of this restaurant—of

Manhattan, of America—strike her as uptight and vainglorious. Even the food is pert and prude. She longs for the bloody steaks and stained-wood bistros of the Left Bank. She longs for the rancid smell of the Métro. She grips his hand under the table, and he gives her the thundercloud look.

"Let's do it," he says. "Let's go for a week or two, just look around, see what the properties are like."

Camille lances an endive and brings it to her mouth. It is inexpressibly tender. The space it leaves on her plate is like an opening to the future, a smooth white channel. She chews slowly. This is a moment to capture. The doctor is in front of her, staring in his turbid way, his protean face taking on new and amazing arrangements. His lips lift in a sly smile meant only for her, those devastating, cloven lips.

"We could look at Montmartre," he says with a convincing French inflection. "Or the Marais. It's very hip right now."

Camille sips her Grenache. This bottle—his choice—is like none she's ever tasted, with a palate of blackberry, chocolate, and things that couldn't possibly be there, like roses and pine needles. She waits until the last of the taste has dwindled in her mouth before speaking.

"You should get to know Avis," she says quietly.

The doctor takes a drink of water, nods.

"Maybe we could spend a Saturday together," Camille ventures.

"That's a fine idea," he says.

When he drops them at the house late that night, he pets Avis on the head tentatively, and Camille thinks she sees something recoil in his eyes, as if he's received an electric shock from her hair. This is to be expected, of course, from a man without children.

Avis pulls back and clings to her mother's leg.

"It's all right," Camille says with a little laugh. "She'll get used to you."

The fact that he's here is what matters. He does not need to be a father. Camille will make certain that Avis does not require more than he can comfortably give. She will make certain that this remains a pleasurable endeavor for him, all the way through.

It's already October, but she puts on a Betsey Johnson ikat dress over leggings. Little girls are right, she thinks, to wear their Easter best to school. Why not be beautiful every day? Today, it pleases her to watch the other mothers' eyes slide to her cleavage and vault back as if scalded. She feels sorry for them, without any hope of such regeneration in their lives. There is nothing newly available to these women, sunk as they are in the sludge of marriage and family, that could match this kind of elevation. Who can blame them for packing together like nervous ewes?

She has begun arriving a few minutes late for pickup to avoid the bleating flock. The school has yet to levy the ten-dollar penalty they are forever threatening. But today, the teacher meets her at the classroom door with a portentous smile. Camille prepares an excuse: broken traffic light, clogged parking lot.

"Mrs. Donovan," the teacher says in her nursery school falsetto, "do you have a few moments to talk?"

Ten dollars, Camille decides, is a fair price to pay for the benefit she receives. She smiles deferentially and enters the classroom. Avis is involved with a dollhouse, a pathetic thing built of unvarnished wood. The teacher gestures to a squat little table, and Camille lowers onto a tiny chair, her knees jutting up. Everything in the room is custom-built for children, so that she feels like Alice in a dream.

The teacher is younger than Camille, dressed in head-to-toe L.L.Bean. "We don't want you to be alarmed," she begins, "but we've noticed that Avis seems to be having some trouble expressing herself verbally. Of course, our children are all at different stages of development, but at this age, we encourage them to make their needs known with words rather than screeching or pushing. But this can be difficult when there are underlying problems." The teacher maintains sympathetic, professional eye contact as she speaks in her girlish voice. "We think it might be a good idea for you to bring her in for an evaluation."

Camille nods. She should have known this might happen. Every child seems to be diagnosed with something these days. The classroom is crowded with physical therapists, occupational therapists, speech therapists. There are new disorders now: attention deficit disorder, sensory processing disorder, oppositional defiant disorder. She supposes there's money in it somewhere. It must behoove someone to capitalize on the micromanaging compulsions and amorphous fears of all these hysterical mothers.

"Professional guidance can make a meaningful difference," the teacher continues.

"Thank you for the suggestion," Camille says, rising from the midget chair. There are plenty of things she could say, plenty of ways she could poke holes in this girl's authoritative facade, but it isn't worth it. Soon they will be a thousand miles over the ocean.

She researches visa requirements and buys a French language book. If they end up staying in Paris, she'll look for a waitressing job. Even better, the doctor will find a position in a hospital and she won't have to work at all. They'll hire a French nanny for Avis.

"When are you planning to do this?" Madeleine asks.

"Soon. November or December, maybe."

Madeleine nods. She glances at the floor, then back up. "How well do you know this person?"

Camille looks at her friend, the pleasingly regular features, smooth skin, thick auburn hair. There is nothing shadowed in her face, no canyon or concavity that speaks of pain or regret.

"How well do any of us know anyone?"

Madeleine is quiet. She smiles in a sad way, as if thinking of something private. She almost never talks about her own husband. When Camille brings him up, asks for details about his eccentric behavior, Madeleine changes the subject.

"What about Avis's school?" Madeleine asks. "Aren't you going to let her finish the year?"

Camille laughs. "It's nursery school. And she'll learn more from a nanny in Paris than she will here, don't you think? She'll become bilingual. Not to mention there's a healthier balance in Europe, for mothers. Women don't have to apologize for having lives, you know? They aren't expected to spend every minute of the day in the playground. Kids play with kids, like they're supposed to, and adults play with adults. That's the way it used to be here, too, until the mommy police came into power."

"Huh," says Madeleine. "Well, I've never been to France."

Camille sits straight up in her beanbag. "You should come! Well, not right away, of course. But after we get settled, if we decide to stay, you and David should come visit. We could show you around, and then who knows? Maybe you'll want to stay, too. We can be our own little expatriate community."

Madeleine smiles wistfully. "If we hadn't just bought the house, maybe I'd consider it."

"Oh, I could totally see you in Paris." Camille nods. "You'd fit right in. You'd flourish."

Again, a class mother stands sentinel at the preschool entrance, holding a clipboard with papers, an alert, searching smile on her face. Camille puts on a rushed, apologetic look and manages to duck past with Avis. But on her way back out of the building, the woman ambushes her.

"Please, would you sign? Here's a flyer."

> As many of you are aware, many citizens of Old Cranbury are unhappy with the nature of the "art installation" that is currently being displayed on the property of our neighbors on Minuteman Road. Please sign this petition if you would like to see this inconsiderate eyesore removed and the property values of our town restored. Thank you!!!

Camille reads the flyer again, unable to decipher its meaning. She looks at the woman. "What art installation?"

"Oh, I'm sure you've seen it. That big new house on the corner of Minuteman and Edgeware, all covered with rubber? Do you know what that *is*? It's thousands of foam insects. I'm sure you've seen it. It looks like the Swamp Thing."

"That's what this petition is about?"

"You bet. Here's a pen."

Camille studies the woman. She is petite and redheaded, with a bob cut and gray raincoat, like a little Joan of Arc. Her pretty, pointed chin is infuriating.

"I can't believe you people are serious."

The woman tilts her head and smiles, as if Camille has said something sweet. "Well, obviously when this kind of thing happens, it's very bad for property values. Not to mention that it's against town zoning. There's a standard of appropriateness that homeowners have to abide by, otherwise people could construct gas stations on their properties, or raise pigs in the front yard."

"God forbid," Camille says, rounding her eyes. She can only imagine what the neighbors must say about her own, unmolested property. They would probably bring her to court, if they could, for the bald patches in her grass.

It occurs to her that she is in a unique position, with one foot already out of this place. Before she leaves, perhaps it is her duty to provoke a little self-reflection. She meets the woman's sparkling gaze and smiles. Then, with one motion, she reaches out and plucks the papers from her hand. They make a rude, guttural sound as she rips them in half.

She takes the long way home and drives past the art installation. The impression is, in fact, disconcerting. The house is gigantic, encrusted with a dark carapace, as if diseased. Her first reaction is, strangely, of shame for the house, as if it were the victim of some practical joke. Then, as she looks, it occurs to her that the artwork is a perfect metaphor for this whole place: a grand structure overrun by controlling, suffocating little bugs. She laughs to herself in the car. Perhaps the artist feels the same way she does. Perhaps this is his—or her?—portrait of the town. She honks the horn a few times in solidarity, and waves as she pulls away.

Entering her own home, she is met with a peculiar, constricted feeling. It is as if she has grown larger, or the rooms have shrunk. This house, like the preschool classroom, seems to have been built for children. Setting her purse down in its usual spot on the kitchen counter, a simple motion laden with habit, she feels a sudden urgency. It has become impossible, she understands, to remain here any longer.

Before she can change her mind, she calls the doctor on his cell phone.

"Hi," she begins breathlessly. "I want to know, have you been thinking about Paris as much as I have?"

"Camille," he answers, "hello."

"I just wanted to say that I'm ready to go when you are." She takes a breath, feels a weird dizziness. "Let's do it. Let's buy the tickets."

There is an empty pause on the phone, as if the doctor is distracted. After a long moment, his voice comes back clear as the sky. "You're right," he says, "we should buy them. I'll do it. I'll do it as soon as I have a better sense of my schedule coming up."

Camille does not respond. It is as if she has been pushed gently into a seat like a little girl. She feels a slug of embarrassment. It had been childish of her to think he would drop everything, leave his patients on the operating table, and board an airplane.

"So," he says in a different, quieter voice, "would you like to get together tonight?"

At once, her disappointment is flushed away by gratitude. She remembers how fortunate she is to have found this person. Among a colony of creeping carpet beetles, here is a creature with true wingspan, capable of traversing oceans at will.

Still, she does not want to be in the house, does not want to look at the dried paint on the window glass, the old nail holes in the wall that Nick never bothered to patch. With her two hours of freedom, she goes shopping. She bypasses the overpriced boutiques in town and enters the consignment shop. Without looking at the price tags, she holds Paris in mind. In the dressing room, she tries on a low-backed silver dress with a matte sheen. It is too fine for any occasion here, but something she might wear on a weeknight in Paris. This, she realizes, is what attracts her to the European way of life, this offhand glamour in the quotidian: flowers on the breakfast table, aged cheese for lunch.

She turns away from the mirror and views herself over her shoulder. Looking at her own face, she sees an echo of the doctor there. How has she never noticed the resemblance in their features? Now that she has caught it, it is unmistakable. She has heard it said that people tend to be attracted to those they resemble, whose looks are familiar in some way. This is why so many couples look like they could be siblings. It is, apparently, a vanity shared by all.

She buys the dress.

"Good choice," the saleswoman says at the register. "A designer for the label lives here in town, you know."

"I didn't look at the label," Camille snips.

To her relief, the petition woman is gone when she returns to school. Avis's teacher meets her eyes in a meaningful way, as if they share a lovers' secret. Camille takes her daughter's hand and leaves the building. For the rest of the day, she finds herself thinking about having a child with the doctor. She does not particularly want another child, of course, but finds that it is impossible not to consider it, not to imagine what might arise from such magnetic coupledom. How strikingly gray-eyed their offspring would be. It is a universal impulse, perhaps, to follow this preordained script—Nature's way of ensuring that humanity continues to invent ever-refined hybrids, lifting the species to new pinnacles.

Later that night on the futon, she lies with her head on the doctor's chest. Staring at the ceiling, she feels the assertion of his heartbeat, a hidden fist clenching and unclenching beneath her skull. Scanning the ceiling's blank expanse, her eyes catch on a cobweb in the corner of the room, too high to bother sweeping. This is not a man who would notice such things, she thinks gratefully, although perhaps Madeleine has.

Without bidding, her friend's warning returns and resonates in her mind. There is no need to know everything about this man, of course. She knows all that matters. Still, she finds herself humoring the question, following its direction lazily.

"So, tell me what you were like when you were a kid," she asks him.

"I don't know," he replies, with an undertone of something like distaste. "Like this, I guess, but smaller."

"I can't picture you as a boy," Camille says, shifting her body to look at him. It's true, she thinks, as she examines his face. The nose and jaw seem hardened from a permanent mold, as if he had been conceived a full-grown man.

For Halloween, Avis dresses as Sleeping Beauty. The costume is stiff from its packaging, with its crinoline petticoat and rough glittered designs, and she fusses with the white collar that projects from her shoulders. Camille has lost the battle over shoes and allows her to wear the transparent plastic mules that have come with the dress.

"You can wear them if you want, honey, but they won't be comfortable for trick-or-treating," Camille reminds her.

"Yes, they will," Avis says, clicking over the bare floor. She turns and looks at Camille, her hair limp over her shoulders, un-princess-like. The teacher reported that she pushed another little girl this morning, just for sitting too close. The reproach in the teacher's eyes, as she said this, had heated Camille's blood.

"You dress up, too, Mommy."

"No, no," Camille says with forced sweetness, "I want to make sure *you* get all the candy."

"*Please* dress up!"

She is already exhausted. Being alone with her daughter has been draining lately, and it is only out of obligation that she has agreed to circle the neighborhood tonight at a toddler's pace. This is one of the times when being a mother feels like a form of slavery, this constant servitude to a tyrant's whims. Nothing can come fast enough for her daughter, nothing is enough.

"How about we watch a movie together before we go?" Camille offers. "What would you like to see?"

Avis chooses a DVD about Sleeping Beauty, or Beauty and the Beast, or whatever Beauty, and sinks to the rug as if tranquilized. On the screen, a golden-haired girl sits down at a spinning wheel and emits a perfect drop of ruby blood. Strangely, watching the horror dawn on the animated girl's face, Camille feels a sting of sympathy. It was just a simple, wrong motion that cannot be reversed. Before the creature understands the consequences, claws of sleep pull her under.

How smoothly Nick had slipped out of the yoke. Now, she supposes, he'll trap this new woman into it, who has no idea how thoroughly a strong woman can be bent and broken. Or maybe she does know. Maybe she has already made arrangements for exhaustive child care. Maybe Victoria is smarter than Camille will ever be.

"Are we going to the parade now?" Avis asks when the movie ends.

Camille looks at her daughter. She has forgotten the town parade. The tantrum comes immediately, subdued by an impulsive offer to have dinner at Gulliver's.

At the restaurant, Camille allows Avis to order whatever she wants. This, of course, is French fries and ice cream. Camille splurges on a fifteen-dollar grilled chicken salad for herself, in hopes of losing five pounds before Paris. The restaurant is full and loud. It was good, she tells herself, to take Avis out. It is something they should do more often. Perhaps Camille has failed her daughter in not orchestrating more contact with the world, not arranging the usual playdates or swim classes or story hours. She watches Avis across the table, bobbing for ice cubes in her water glass, and concedes that it would be nice for her to have some little friends of her own, little princes and princesses to accompany trick-or-treating. But not now. It makes more sense to start over in France. She hasn't told Avis about the plan, but perhaps she will tonight. This might be just the time for it.

As they are waiting for their food, a large family comes into the restaurant, all costumed in some kind of Arabic dress. Camille smiles wryly. This kind of team costume is perfect, so typical, just the kind of thing that people here think is cute. The mother of the clan—Jesus, how many kids are there, six?—wears a look of proud satisfaction, her eyes scanning the dining room as she steers her herd to their table. This is probably a major outing for her, a highlight of her year. Halloween, Camille thinks, is such an American holiday, so thoroughly geared to a country of frustrated adults desperate to play dress-up.

Her gaze travels over this family and freezes. What she is seeing does not register at first. Her eyes are telling her that her doctor is there, sitting down with this family, wearing some sort of tunic. Her breath stops. It is not unusual, she reminds herself, in times of infatuation, to see a man's face in all faces. She looks away, and then back. It is him, she is certain. But why is he with these people? Why is he dressed this way? He does not see her as the family settles around a table, and he takes a seat between two adolescent boys.

She does not notice her own food arrive. When she glances back at her daughter, who is methodically dipping French fries into apple juice, it is like viewing her through a glass wall. Her eyes return helplessly to the doctor and remain there, watching his movements. Finally, he looks up and sees her. There is a hollow instant before the glimmer of recognition, but that is all. There is no surprise on his face. Instead, his exquisite mouth forms a sly smile, as if they are sharing a joke. She goes cold.

His eyes slide away, and he laughs at something one of the boys is saying. Camille's ears fill with loud static, so that she can no longer hear the noise of the restaurant. The mother of the family glances toward her and gazes blankly for a moment. She is tragic in her sequined sari and painted eye makeup, her face round and overfed like a pink, all-American sow.

Camille forces herself to remain at the table until Avis has finished her ice cream. She leaves her own salad untouched, with its tight cranberries, baby oranges, and frilly wreath of greens, like a careful little Eden.

The static remains in her ears through the drive home and crackles as she climbs the chipped concrete steps of her house. Avis vanishes inside. Camille follows, closes the door, and sits. There on the battle-torn sofa that has served her through two decades, she sits very still and tries to unpuzzle the riddle.

"To what end?" is the phrase that comes to her. *To what end?* She is not upset, she tells herself, not really. Just mystified. The picture of Paris—the bed and windows, the little gilt breakfast tray with bread and cheese and honey, the silver dress—glides smoothly away. She looks down at her legs on the couch. She is still here, as she was before. She is still safe, intact, shod in calfskin Steve Madden boots. *To what end?*

She finds a rumpled blanket at the end of the couch and pulls it over herself. The chill she'd felt in the restaurant is still with her. Even now, in her own house, she feels exposed, unsheltered, as if the walls were translucent and she were on display like a lab rat.

Avis comes running out of her bedroom and rushes to the front door holding a pumpkin pail. Her little pink gown is blotched with ketchup, and her hair has already snagged in her tiara. She clutches the doorknob with such naked hope that Camille feels a roll of nausea. The idea of taking her daughter outside, of holding her hand along the night-shaded, sinister streets of this town, of any town, is too much. It would be better for both of them to stay inside, it seems, to find a spot in the center of the house, far from the windows, and huddle together for a little while.

"Are you sure you want to go back out?" Camille asks lightly. "Maybe we could have some candy here and watch TV instead."

"Mommy!" Avis shrieks.

"Come on, let's cuddle up on the couch together."

Her daughter's dress puddles as she collapses to the floor.

"All right, all right," Camille says, "let's go."

She wears a scarf and hat, although the night is not cold enough to steam her breath. The house next door is darkened. The couple who lives there is older, she believes, probably pretending not to be home. Camille is envious tonight of their immunity. She and Avis keep walking through the unlit span to the next house. There are far-off sounds of children's voices, beams of flashlights sweeping through the trees. Camille walks quickly, battling an icy dread. She nearly jogs from house to house, trailing her child princess behind. It is rude, she knows, how curtly she responds to the fawning of the neighbors who answer their doors. She just wants this night to be over, this night of all nights, this never-ending night. Her heart keeps a crazed beat. When she wakes in the morning, she tells herself, the sky will be white, scraped clean. It will be the first day of November. The winter will loom close.

As they walk, Avis helps herself to candy from her pail, and by the time they return home, her face is bloodied with chocolate. She stands patiently as Camille unfastens the costume and lets the pink cloud deflate at her feet. Her little girl's body is thin and swaybacked, painfully fragile. Camille draws a wet washcloth over the smeared face and puts her to bed. Avis lies with wide-open eyes as Camille pulls the covers to her chin and kisses her good night, then shuts off the porch light and drops the deadbolt on the door.

The Virginals

There are no boxwood wreaths on the Ezekiel Slater house, no pine garlands around the batten heart pine door. There is no amber candlelight behind the twelve-by-twelve, divided-light windows.

"They're not living there," Cheryl Foster tells her husband. "They're not even trying to pretend."

Everyone decorates for Christmas on Cannonfield Road. As early as the second week of November, dark workmen appear on ladders, affixing red ribbons to window sashes, installing real pineapples and holly berries into triangular cornices. Cheryl and Roger decorate, too, with the most understated of candle glow, if only to avoid derision. What they'd prefer to do is hang a banner informing the neighbors that all their ornamentations are historically incorrect. The original owners of these homes were strict Puritans, forbidden to acknowledge the popish holiday. The colonists, in their plain way, would have worked through Christmas as through any day of the year, not a pineapple in sight.

It would be a stretch of incredible naïveté, of course, to think that the new owners of the Slater house are adhering to historical authenticity. It's true that she knows nothing of these newcomers other than that they are young, childless, and in possession of a preposterous Aston Martin that appears in the driveway from time to time like a mute foreigner. Its owners have shown themselves in full form only once. Cheryl and Roger had watched from the kitchen window one summer morning as the young couple slowly circled the august white saltbox across the street, freshly theirs, with the assessment of predator birds. Finally they disappeared inside, and as evening fell, Cheryl and Roger had seen a cool unfamiliar light appear in the window of the second-floor bedroom. Harriet's bedroom. Harriet's window: one of the beautiful, spit-perfect windows that Lars had installed with his own hands when he and Harriet were newlyweds. Those windows, like all things with flawless beginnings, had slackened with age and begun to gap over the years. There were drafts, Cheryl knew, that kept Harriet beneath a stack of quilts on winter nights.

They haven't seen a light in that bedroom since. There has been no moving van, no contractor's truck, no roofing ladder, no silver car.

"It's the Spaulding house all over again," Cheryl says to Roger. "I was afraid this might happen."

She still has nightmares about the Spaulding house, the wrecking ball slamming into its cedar shingles again and again, the front elevation crumpling inward as from a punch in the gut. Just like that, in one spinning flash of stupidity, two hundred years of history obliterated.

"I'm going to say something," Cheryl states, "at the next meeting."

Roger nods. Now that winter has descended, he has brought his file and spokeshave into the kitchen and works continuously at shaping spindles. His decision to specialize in the art of steam bending has paid off splendidly. There may be more multitalented carpenters around, but now that the legendary Thomas Whitman has hung up his adz, there exists no better maker of eighteenth-century Windsor chairs on the planet. The jump in demand after the Colonial Faire suggests that Roger has been crowned the living history community's chair-maker of choice. And once these people have chosen, they are loyal for the duration.

Roger shakes his head. "It's a bloody shame, it is."

It irks Cheryl when he slips like this, tainting the colonial manner of speaking with cockney syntax. She presses her lips together. At least he is trying. At home, she grooms her own speech but does not force it. Even with years of practice, she is drained by the effort of sustaining proper diction for any length of time, and reserves her *thees* and *thous* for sanctioned gatherings.

"You know Harriet would be turning in her grave," she tells Roger. "And Lars, too. And Ezekiel Slater, for that matter, and Jeremiah and all the grandchildren. You can be sure that Benjamin and Comfort would have done something. It's the duty of friends, then as now."

Roger does not reply at once, but holds a spindle aloft and examines it. Watching him, Cheryl feels a crawling vexation. He has slipped so comfortably into success. He has absorbed the admiration so easily, as if it were long due. He has cut his billable hours at work without a jag of self-doubt. His transformation from lawyer to chair-maker has been as fluid as tadpole to toad.

Her own enterprise is a slower slog. She has to remind herself that only the most refined slice of the community will ever appreciate her work. Most are content to settle for buttons made of horn, pewter, or even tin. Among those who understand the superiority of thread, there are even fewer who recognize the beauty and accuracy of the death's-head tradition. In her workshop at the faire, she'd been visited by a small handful of exultant admirers in flawless midcentury dress and had sold three sets of astral-style buttons. She has to remind herself that it is her own choice to reject dressmaking, that wide and easy highway—and in no way is it Roger's fault.

"You're a good friend," he tells her at last, fitting the spindle into a chair seat.

Cheryl feels a sudden threat of tears. Harriet is there, all at once, in her vegetable garden, dwarfed by sunflowers and tomato plants, bending with a watering can of dented metal. To Cheryl's surprise, this old woman had twined her way into her heart. She had risen above the general populace of scuttling, self-involved citizens and demonstrated what a full human being should be. Faithful and industrious, there could be no better heir to Reverend Slater's homestead, no better steward of the virtues of loyalty, sacrifice, and humility.

This image of Harriet in her garden is what Cheryl holds in her mind, three weeks later, as she sits at the massive oak table with her fellow commission members.

"Before we begin our scheduled agenda," she says, making eye contact with each of them in turn, "I'd like to bring an urgent matter to your attention."

The other commission members are sloppily dressed, in today's way, and slump in their chairs. No particular light of attention springs to their eyes. Cheryl, however, has honed the forgotten art of rhetoric. She has learned to use her voice like an instrument, strong and clear. She likes to think that her immersion into the past has opened her to the voices of the ancestors, given her the ability to channel them for present-day purposes. There is no denying that exceptional fervor comes through her voice, like a clarion call, as she eloquently skewers applications for certificates of appropriateness. The renovation plans that homeowners submit would be laughable were they not so sickening, tantamount to decimating original structures and hiding vulgar McMansions behind their facades. The homeowners—usually young, urbane couples—stare at her as she lambasts their building plans. When the commission votes with her, the husbands protest like teenagers given a bad grade. The women clutch their designer purses with intertwined initials and push back their ironed hair. Sometimes they cry. They should have stayed in the city where they belong, Cheryl thinks, in their elevator buildings with awnings and entrance rugs and sycophantic doormen.

"As you may be aware," she begins, "the Ezekiel Slater house at 430 Cannonfield Road, built in 1740 by the Reverend Ezekiel Slater, has recently passed into new ownership. As a neighbor of close proximity to the Slater homestead, it has come to my attention that the new proprietors have been absent from the premises for months. As a confidante of the former owner, Mrs. Harriet Hertz, I am privy to the fact that the house has long been in need of substantial repair. Mrs. Hertz, having become infirm and impecunious in her final years, was unable to finance said repairs, but took solace in the certainty that they would be conscientiously performed after her passing by the purchasers of the home."

Cheryl pauses, glances at the faces around the table. Victor Conetta gazes up at her with the eyes of an elderly beagle.

"However"—she pauses as she imagines an ancestral orator would—"as further weeks pass without bodily sign of the purchasers, it has become apparent to me that the acquisition of this venerable home was in fact made with an eye to circumventing the regulations of this commission through gradual and insidious demolition by neglect."

She lets these final, horrible words settle upon the table. A long moment passes.

"It is imperative that the commission take immediate action. We delay at our peril. The fate of one of this region's most historic structures is at stake."

A chair creaks, and Edward Drayton clears his throat.

"Pardon me, Cheryl, but is there visible *evidence* of neglect?" he asks in his slow, weary voice, gesturing as if his hands were underwater. "Are there broken windows, missing shingles, water stains on the roof?"

Cheryl straightens her posture and meets his gaze. "No, of course not. Not as yet, anyway."

Drayton turns his palms to the ceiling. "Without visible *evidence,* we can't accuse the owners of wrongdoing." He smiles, as if speaking to a child. "You know that."

"I am giving the commission concrete information about the interior condition of a significant structure located within this town's defined historic district. Are you saying that we passively watch the house deteriorate until the owners waltz in with a demolition application?"

"If the house is truly in bad shape, we'll see it on the outside eventually. Then we can contact the owners and *discuss* it."

Cheryl sniffs. "Like we did with the Spaulding house? You may notice there is no more Spaulding house."

"Again, Cheryl, I must remind you that it's not within our jurisdiction to intervene into the upkeep of privately owned properties without cause, even within the historic district. Unless there is unmistakable *evidence* of neglect." Drayton joins his hands and fingers together like the laces of a woman's stays. "Thank you, regardless, for bringing this to the commission's attention. We'll keep an eye on it. Now, let's move on to the written agenda."

Cheryl breathes in and holds the air for a moment, feeling the boning of the hidden jumps beneath her own clothing. Most women save their stays for formal events, but Cheryl has found that wearing at least an informal pair of jumps on a daily basis has improved her posture and general outlook. She has grown to dislike how she feels without them.

After the meeting, she sits for a while before bed with her thread and button forms. She replays the commission meeting in her mind until the repetitive focus of her work calms her. Threading buttons never fails to renew her sense of simple purpose. Upstairs, in her chemise and cap, she tells Roger about the outcome of her appeal at the meeting.

He leans against the headboard. "Well then, like Drayton said, it falls to us to keep an eye on it."

Extinguishing the lantern, they draw the bed hangings around them. There is satisfaction in lying upon the four-post bedstead built by Roger, warming themselves with the coverlet embroidered by Cheryl, swaddling themselves in white linen sheets. Inside this soft fort, they can feel themselves recede from the arrhythmic thrum of the world outside, join the steady pulse of the past.

Winter is Cheryl's favorite season in the Cook house: the short, stark days and early nights beside the hearth. In the pink-and-blue twilight, when Roger is finishing his work in the barn, she sits at her virginals near the window and fills the house with its silvery music. These are her most treasured moments, when she draws closest to the spirits of the house and the heavens. As she plays, she sometimes senses a presence beside her on the bench, feels the breath of Comfort on her neck.

The instrument is an exquisite reproduction, with an inset keyboard true to seventeenth-century Flemish construction, the lid's interior hand-painted with a pastoral scene. She knows it's a stretch to think an instrument like this would have existed in Hiram Cook's house. There may have been spinets in some households, but few true, vintage virginals. Still, she likes to imagine that as well-heeled leaders of the community the Cooks might have been an exception, might have indulged themselves in this one small way.

The virginals was a gift from Roger upon their fifth anniversary of purchasing the Cook house, of truly beginning their lives here. Before that, they'd rented a ranch house in a neighborhood of matching houses. They had chosen Old Cranbury carefully. The schools were outstanding and crime nonexistent. But more crucially, they'd been drawn to the historic pedigree of the place. There would naturally be remnants of Puritan conservatism and modesty here. The people would show a corresponding moral fiber.

It did not take long to recognize their mistake. Their ranch-house neighbors did not acknowledge their arrival. The constant sound of weed whackers and lawn mowers disrupted their weekends. Barbecues, to which they were not invited, were visible on the back decks of adjacent homes. The children wore disposable clothing and used trashy language. If this was true here, then perhaps there was no untainted place left in the country.

But the history was everywhere. Together, Cheryl and Roger would drive in religious silence up and down Cannonfield Road, that alley of splendor, a mile-long corridor of heart-stopping antiques, untouched by the larger plague of neocolonials with fanlights and dormers. These houses were the uncontested patriarchs of the town, their faces proud and plain against the old wagon road, their date plaques like medals of honor. They researched the founders of the town, the original families, paged through archived letters and early land deeds at the library. During that first year, throughout the course of Cheryl's first pregnancy, their love affair with the town's brave settlers was ignited. It became evident that they had been summoned here, that they must act as torchbearers, defenders of the original residents and their ideals. In that first year, they had been delivered from the sidelines of town to the core, transformed from aliens to denizens.

When the Cook homestead had surfaced on the market, they were the first to arrive at the open house. They were instantly disappointed. The kitchen was painted a ghastly white that sheathed the ceiling beams like mold. There was a stainless steel refrigerator and marble countertops. They had considered letting the house go, in favor of something less corrupted, but now Cheryl appreciates their luck. Having been inside nearly every home on this stretch, she has seen the hidden grotesqueries, the interiors revamped without compunction. Relative to those, the Cook house is pristine. The original post and timber framing is intact, the catslide roof is solid. The exposed oak beams are as strong as ribs along the ceiling of the first floor, and the central chimney and hearth—spine and heart of the house—exude the smell of ancient smoke.

It hasn't been difficult to undo the past sins of previous owners. They've replaced areas of strip flooring with wide chestnut boards—each scrupulously pillowed, sanded, and planed to match the originals. The front door, incongruously Victorian with inset stained glass, has been swapped with a plank of reclaimed barnwood, unpainted and unsheltered. It gladdens Cheryl to know that whoever visits this house on a rainy day will get wet waiting to be let in, just as they would have in 1740. They have kept electricity and plumbing, but done away with the microwave oven and sprinkler system. They have removed recessed lighting in favor of sconces and lamps. Lastly, they've pulled off the shutters and blasted away the exterior paint, a silly periwinkle, and returned the house to its native state: the uniform, heat-saving brown alluded to in Hiram Cook's probate papers.

The Cook house has been re-crowned the king of Cannonfield Road. People stop their cars to take pictures in front of the Grand Union flag on the door. Magazine journalists visit. Cheryl and Roger pose for interior shots, dressed in period attire. Among those who enter the house and listen to them speak, there is a sense of awe, even bewilderment.

All this has been lost on the children, of course. Comfort Cook delivered seven babies in this house, she would remind her own pair of offspring in answer to complaints about cramped bedrooms. In lieu of frivolities like a finished basement, closets, a swimming pool, they should feel fortunate for the opportunity to grow up in the manner of their forebears, the chance to absorb history with every breath, to build their bones with it.

"Only three of those babies survived to adulthood," the children would reply.

Cheryl and Roger's compatriots had warned that this would happen. It had been easy when the children were young, when there was an element of play in dressing in period clothing, in using a loom or a lathe. But at the exact age of thirteen, just as the other parents predicted, each of their children had undergone a hideous transformation, questioning the efficiency of hearth cooking, demanding cheaply made store clothing, refusing to participate in tavern nights and encampments. This was a universal phase, the others assured them, every child's way of orienting himself to the whirl of modern life, of observing and assessing it, and then, with any luck—and assuming his education has been sound—choosing to reject it. Cheryl and Roger were not to worry; their children would come back to them.

And today they are coming back—flying home from their respective California colleges for four weeks of winter vacation. Before driving to the airport, Cheryl finishes sewing bobbin lace trim to the neckline of a linen chemise for Rebekah. For Amos, she's found a reproduction pocket watch: a nickel-plated beauty with beetle and poker hands and the old-style Roman numeral "IIII" on the face. These are things her children would never dream of buying for themselves. She knows they might prefer digital gadgets, video games, but as the years pass, she's found it increasingly difficult to purchase such ephemeral objects. She is more hopelessly drawn to the qualities of handmade things. There is something almost sentient about natural material: a warm consciousness in wood, a primal heat in forged iron.

She waits in the arrivals terminal, trussed in an anonymous black parka, her heart beating in her gullet as if awaiting a lover. She detests the airport. The overhead lights blare like interrogation lamps, designed to expose every ugliness, to illuminate with dumb democracy things not meant to be highlighted. Here is the same humming tension she feels in every modern public institution: supermarkets, chain pharmacies, post offices. Entering these places has become progressively disheartening, coloring her perceptions for the rest of the day. She finds herself juggling contempt and pity for the fretful people she sees around her, assiduously avoiding one another's eyes. Even when she frames them as tragic orphans disconnected from structural meaning, it is difficult not to place blame. Within the course of just a generation or two, the inviolable structures of religion, community, honest labor—the bedrock of this country—have been disposed of like used coffee cups, replaced by the dual Styrofoam obelisks of economy and convenience.

These ruminations fly away like dust the instant she catches sight of her children. Her lurching heart pauses and her mind goes blank as she meets their eyes and sees a sparkle of gladness there, undermining the slow indifference of their gaits, their hooded sweatshirts with dangling strings.

In the car, Cheryl cannot stop talking. Without pause, she finds herself itemizing the menu for Christmas dinner. It isn't remotely authentic to prepare a holiday feast, of course, but the children expect it, and she harbors a private enjoyment in making it. She imagines what Comfort might have cooked for her own children—the three who remained, whom she must have loved with violent passion.

The meal begins with an appetizer of Indian pudding, then roast turkey with onion, stewed pumpkin, and skillet cranberries. Cheryl and Roger alone have dressed for the occasion, Cheryl in her red satin Brunswick gown, and Roger in waistcoat and cravat. Rebekah wears another floppy sweatshirt, her hair cropped at the ears in blunt waves. Amos hunches in a tight black T-shirt, dark bangs fringing his eyes. He resembles a sprite of the woods more than a man, but Cheryl knows better than to comment.

Instead, she talks. She tells them about the Slater house, rolls out a diatribe against the commission.

"But how do you know for sure, Mom?" Rebekah asks. "Don't you think you're being a little paranoid? You haven't even met the new neighbors."

"I know enough about the kind of people they are," Cheryl answers. "And I know exactly how the house was marketed. The listing was shameless. *Gorgeous two-acre property with house.* It actually said that. *With house.* I truly doubt these people bought the Ezekiel Slater house for its historical importance. I know the type. They don't want small, they don't want charm." Cheryl hears the venom rising in her voice. "They want open floor plans, kitchen islands, Viking ranges. They want two-car garages and gunite swimming pools in the backyard."

Rebekah is silent. Amos pokes the turkey bones on his plate. After a moment, Roger lifts his flagon of ale.

"How are your classes going, Rebekah?"

Their daughter, eased by the release of tension, speaks at length, telling more than she normally might.

"I've decided to major in history," she announces, and Cheryl feels her head lift like a balloon. "With a focus on colonial Africa."

"Colonial Africa?" Cheryl echoes. "What about American history?"

"There's a requirement for that, of course." Rebekah grins.

"A requirement."

"And I'll be taking French, too, so I can read primary source documents. And I might audit a course in Afrikaans, if they offer it next year."

The word *Afrikaans* hovers in the air for a long moment.

"Well, that does sound interesting," Cheryl makes herself say. "I have to admit, though, I'm surprised they offer classes on the subject. Not to offend, but the African nations don't seem to have done much with their independence. Not compared to the United States. It seems to me that a *real* revolutionary success story is right here in front of us."

Rebekah stares. "I can't believe you just said that, Mom. That's cultural hegemony, pure and simple. Not to mention racist."

"Cultural hegemony?" Cheryl blinks her eyes and lays her silverware gently on her plate. "Whatever does that mean?"

Roger sets his flagon down. "Cheryl."

"I'm only asking. I've never heard of this term, this *cultural hegemony*."

"What it means," Rebekah says, "is that your definition of success doesn't apply to the whole world."

"Oh." Cheryl nods. "I didn't realize that."

"Coming back here, it just reminds me how insidious nationalism always is. This place especially, with its fetishization of history and patriotism, is unbelievable. So much pride, but in what? This great country was founded on *murder*. Do you know how many Native Americans were massacred in the colonies?"

"Well, aren't you a fount of knowledge."

"Why don't we talk about something else," Roger says.

"Wouldn't that be convenient," Rebekah mutters, but does not continue.

Cheryl rises from her chair and collects the dinner dishes. She carries them into the kitchen, her shoes marking a slow, hollow beat on the floorboards. Alone in the buttery, she breathes in and feels the pressure of the stays at her ribs. Comfort Cook, she is certain, would never have suffered such insult. No child of her day would have dreamed of challenging her elders in this way. Comfort may have faced terrible trials, but this aspect of Cheryl's work is undeniably harder. She imagines Comfort watching her, sympathizing. Strengthened by her commiseration, she retrieves the Marlborough pie for dessert.

When she returns to the table, Roger is straining to listen to Amos talk about core requirements.

"Econ," Amos mumbles, " . . . political science."

Cheryl suspects that her son has been spending most of this first semester with the crew of waifs he met during orientation. His roommate answers the phone every time she calls and tells her that Amos is in band practice. It seems that her son's obsession with music has only intensified, that his attachment to his keyboard—what he calls a "keytar"—has become surgical. She remembers how, as a boy, he would sit and plink away at her virginals. Part of the credit for his interest in music belongs to her, for better or worse. Now, sitting hunched in his father's handmade Windsor chair, he seems to be in physical pain just to be in the house.

During dessert, she asks about his band and he brightens as he tells about their performances on campus and off. Seniors are hiring them for parties, paying real money.

"Maybe you can minor in music?" Cheryl suggests.

Amos grimaces.

"Well, anyway, you know that you're always welcome to practice on the virginals while you're home."

His grimace tightens. Cheryl rises from her chair again, brings the dessert dishes to the buttery. When she returns to the table, Roger is visibly ruffled.

"I know you think we're too young," their son is saying, "but this is the peak age. By the time we graduate, we'll be older than half the guys out there."

"The answer is no," Roger says. "Education is a privilege and may not be thrown away so cavalierly. Our forefathers didn't lose their lives for your freedom so that you could trample all over it."

"What's this?" Cheryl asks.

"Wait a minute," Amos says, his voice rising in pitch. "If they fought so hard for my freedom, then shouldn't I be able to use that freedom to do what I want? Isn't that the whole point?"

"No." Roger pushes back his chair and stands. At his full height, in his ivory linen waistcoat, he is a commanding figure. His features—the high forehead, narrow nose, hooded eyes—are not unlike those of Hiram Cook himself, who gazes out from the portrait on the dining room wall. In the adjacent portrait, Comfort smiles gently, her open face framed by a ruffled cap. What would the Cooks think of this family? Cheryl puts this question to herself at least once a day. What would they think of this town, what's become of this country? They would appreciate her struggles, she knows. They would applaud what she and Roger are trying to do. Every day of her life, with every action and decision she makes, she endeavors to make Hiram and Comfort proud.

That night, the children lie quiet in their bedroom, in the same folding beds they slept in as toddlers. As they'd grown, she and Roger found themselves debating ever more torturous decisions, brokering compromises they'd sworn they'd never make, bending the rules to accommodate the culture's gluttonous demands. The children joined sports intramurals, attended gatherings at the mall. Cheryl and Roger insisted on certain activities over others: the debate team over the audiovisual club, for instance, in the hope they might absorb something of the classical art of rhetoric. Still, the children went to unruly pool parties and came home with favor bags full of plastic junk. Cheryl found herself capitulating to Chinese-made toys so her children wouldn't feel alienated. It hurt her to purchase Rebekah's first Barbie and Amos's first Game Boy.

Despite all their efforts, Rebekah had rebelled like any other teenager, dressing in showgirl ensembles, blasting music through her earphones, dating disgusting boys. It seemed an attack on Cheryl, the way she paraded them into the house as if to defile it. The culmination was an older boy—a stunted man, really—with the face of a vagrant, punctuated by an asinine earring between his nostrils. The boy was visibly on edge, a fact that Cheryl first attributed to drug use. She was surprised when, after peering into the stone hearth, he looked at her and asked point-blank, "Are there spirits here?"

"Y-yes," she stuttered, "I do believe there are."

Rebekah had kept seeing him through that summer, but did not bring him through the door again.

Lying in bed, Cheryl listens to the sounds of the house. There is an admonishing echo of history, of company, in each ghostly creak of the floorboards, each groan of the rafters. Scurrying in the walls, a mouse family keeps warm, as mice families have done in these walls for two centuries. Outside the bedroom window dwells the pale silhouette of the Slater house, grievously empty.

In the morning—Christmas morning—the sun is bright and cleansing. They exchange gifts. From Roger, Cheryl receives sheet music: "The Holly and the Ivy" and "My Days Have Been So Wondrous Free." She sits at the keyboard and attempts to sing while sight-reading, but stumbles over the words and bursts out laughing. Roger and the children laugh with her, and the hearth fire glows warm in the kitchen.

Roger hollers over the zinc flask Cheryl presents to him and proceeds to fill it with rum. Amos hands a sloppily wrapped bundle to each of his parents, containing baseball hats and sweatshirts printed with the name of his college. From Rebekah, they receive a basket of flavored coffee and a book entitled *An Alternative History of the United States.*

"It's really eye-opening," Rebekah says. "It's history as experienced from the perspective of the disenfranchised. Slaves, Native Americans, Mexicans." She looks at her mother with the mischievous glint of a child throwing oatmeal on the floor.

"I look forward to reading it," Cheryl responds equably.

The children open their gifts. Rebekah smiles at the chemise.

"It's not exactly sexy," she says, "but it does look comfortable."

Amos stares at the pocket watch in his palm for a long moment with undisguised admiration.

"It's battery operated so you don't have to remember to wind it all the time," Roger pipes in. "Other than that, it's the same kind of watch the soldiers carried in the war."

As Amos turns the watch over and runs a finger over the smooth casing, Cheryl feels a tug of sadness for him. Any true curiosity he may harbor will stand no chance against the brute crush of today's culture, the pressure to plasticize, to comply. He would have made a handsome soldier, tall and straight in his tricorn hat, rifle strapped slantwise, the image of all that was new and good in this land.

Her son slides the watch into his jeans pocket and says, "Thanks."

Later, Cheryl sits at the virginals and gets the new music right. She sings:

My days have been so wondrous free,
the little birds that fly
with careless ease from tree to tree,
were but as blest as I.

The harmonizing chords reverberate in the walls and ceiling beams. Cheryl closes her eyes. It is a love song to the house, to the people in it—then and now—and to everything that has been lost to make this moment real. How can we deign to know the pride of mothers whose sons' lives were welded into the iron scaffold of liberty? How can we approach the glory of those who did the great work, the first work, that enabled the people of this nation to fly like little birds?

As she plays, she feels the strong presence of the Cook family in the room. She sends a silent prayer of thanks for the beauty of this day, this Christmastide—for the fortune of living in this house, in this way.

Amos and Rebekah are all but ghosts over the next two weeks. They haunt the kitchen for food, argue over the use of Roger's car, then spirit away again. Cheryl sits with her buttons at the window, glancing periodically at the Slater house as at the face of a friend. In her mind, she converses with Edward Drayton, argues for swift intervention, hears his dull, bullfrog response. "How do you know they're not home?" he croaks. "Have you even knocked on the door?"

She finishes threading a set of buttons, then puts on her cloak, awaits a break in traffic and goes across the street. She stands, as she imagines Comfort Cook once stood at the home of her friend Abigail Slater, and knocks. After she has waited ten full beats, she walks around to the back of the house, to the battered remains of Harriet's garden.

When Lars died, a new desperation had come into Harriet's hugs and shoulder touches. She and Harriet had begun to see each other every day. Harriet taught her to stitch by hand, weaning her from the machine. Sewing had once been an act of patriotic rebellion, Harriet told her, during the years that colonists shunned British imports, when the boldest women gathered in public with needles and thread and stitched clothing for their families.

"You look beautiful," Harriet had told Cheryl when she stopped by in her first hand-sewn bedgown.

As Cheryl went deeper into the past, she brought back gifts for her friend, taught her to make candles, churn butter. She showed Harriet how to bake bread in the beehive oven of her hearth. Comfort and Abigail, she liked to think, might have baked together like this.

Now, Cheryl looks at the rear of Harriet's house. The panes are still there, the wavy vintage glass that Lars had located somewhere upstate. Cheryl peers into a window, but the reflection is too strong in the winter light, and she can't see anything in the dark kitchen.

It's easier to let Christmas slide, knowing that a real holiday is on the horizon. The Second Regiment Light Dragoons hosts its annual Twelveth Night celebration at a tavern in Sheffield the second week of January. This is an occasion the colonists would have acknowledged; this is the night they would have costumed themselves and danced and flirted. So Cheryl lays out her blue brocade Jesuit gown and silver-embroidered stomacher. Roger presses his best white shirt with pleated ruffles and his burgundy frock coat with matching silk death's heads. Cheryl pins and re-pins the stomacher to her corset. Roger slides his new flask into a trouser pocket.

The forecast is for snow. This, at least, is what Rebekah tells her parents, waving a glowing device.

"There's a severe weather warning," she says. "Heavy snow all night, accumulations up to twelve inches."

"It's winter in New England." Roger grins.

"Seriously, I don't think we should go," Rebekah says. "The roads will get worse while we're out."

"That's why we have four-wheel drive, isn't it?" Cheryl says. *Remember the colonists,* she wants to add. *They would have had to ride horses.*

They discuss it no further. Cheryl and Roger are united in the opinion that today's world is governed by fear, that full-grown adults have become paralyzed by a terror of Nature, that capable citizens have allowed themselves to become infantilized by alarmist authorities. They will be warm in their woolen stockings and outerwear. The kids zip parkas over their sweatshirts. Cheryl wishes that Rebekah might have at least put on a skirt or brushed her hair. Young people had once met matrimonial prospects at dances like this one. Why couldn't the same happen for her daughter? Would it be so unlikely that Rebekah might meet someone suitable tonight, one of the sons of the regiment commander?

The drive is an hour on back roads. When they arrive at the tavern—a pub with neon beer signs in the window—the snow is drifting down beautifully, patterning Roger's great coat with fleeting constellations. Inside, they are heartened to see that everyone has come. Cheryl shrugs off her cloak, does a twirl to show off her skirts. "Huzzah!" call the men, flush-faced and rowdy. She loves these people. What outstanding luck to have found this community, like a portal through time. When they are all together, there is a thrilling sense of covert celebration, something of a speakeasy in the way they drink and dance out of the view of the others, the "regulars," those who would judge and mock. Here, they are the real winners. They are the ones with ardent friendships, in the oldest sense. They are the ones guided by true principle.

Some are operating in first-person mode, the men speaking with loud round vowels, colonial gusto. Roger takes a tankard of porter. Cheryl accepts a mug of cider. The children recede to a corner table and drink soda.

When the contra dancing begins, Cheryl tries to pull Rebekah onto the floor to introduce her to a boy named Caleb, someone's visiting nephew, skinny but elegant in a pair of striped silk breeches. Rebekah shrinks away when her mother tries to grasp her hand. Finally, perhaps in sympathy for poor Caleb, Rebekah rises to her feet. The beginning of their dance is halting, embarrassing, but then it seems to return to Rebekah, the memory of dancing this way as a girl. Her face loses its wrenched smirk and relaxes into the anticipatory gaze of a woman. Her movements, even in sweatshirt and jeans, are graceful and fluid, and by the end of the dance, she is smiling. Caleb delivers a deep bow.

"Did he ask for your phone number?" Cheryl asks in the car.

"No. Well, yes," Rebekah murmurs from the backseat.

"Well then," Cheryl says.

"It doesn't mean anything."

"How do you know?"

Roger drives the Jeep slowly over the unplowed road. The snowflakes streak through the night, large and wet, splattering against the windshield. On the country road between towns, they notice that the houses are dark.

"Power's out," Roger says plainly.

No one speaks again for the rest of the ride. The Jeep grinds through the snow, the windshield wipers creating a blurred porthole. There are no other cars on the road. It is, indeed, like passing through an eighteenth-century night.

At last they are on Cannonfield Road, steering its familiar bends. When they reach the Slater house, Roger touches the brake.

"Do you think their water's turned off?" he asks.

"I don't know," Cheryl says. "I suppose it's none of our business." As she says this, a thought shoots through her, sly and precise, like a silver fish beneath a frozen lake.

Roger looks at her, then drives on.

As the rest of the family prepares for bed, Cheryl sits at the virginals for a few moments. She plays the first bars of "Greensleeves" quietly, intentionally. She plays the notes as a kind of invocation, tuning her ear to the spiritual guidance of the Cook family. She repeats the phrases, closes her eyes, and after a moment feels her spine straighten and her lungs expand, as if Comfort has joined her. Her hands stop playing and rest on the keys. She breathes deeply, gathering her courage like a minuteman before battle.

In the small hours of the night, she wakes her husband. She has been unable to sleep, she tells him, for fear that the water pipes will burst in the Slater house. She still has the key that Harriet gave her, she whispers. It's unlikely that they've changed the locks.

Without pause or complaint, he draws back the bed hangings. How she loves this man. Together, they walk downstairs in their stocking feet, avoiding the worst-creaking floorboards. There is a sense of completeness in the house tonight—their children asleep, the family sheltered together, safe from the snow. These nights, she understands, will become ever fewer with the years.

They slip outside in their boots and go silently through the snow. The road has not been plowed, and there is a hallowed quality in it. There is no sound other than the rasping of the trees, a cracking branch, the soft drop of snow.

They cross the road and walk along the edge of the woods where their footprints will be obscured. They go over the lumpy span behind the house, Harriet's dead garden, and let themselves in through the back door. Stepping over the threshold, Cheryl holds her breath in anticipation of what she might find, what disorder or disfigurement.

Inside, they are able to see dimly by the incandescence of the snow. The house is dusty, but otherwise unchanged. Cheryl tamps down the stubborn sensation that Harriet is present nearby, that she is about to emerge from the bathroom. The chunky pine butcher block, constructed by Lars, remains in the kitchen like an orphaned child. There are few indications of foreign influence—some unfamiliar pots and pans, hardcover books, months-old magazines. In the dining room, a Windsor chair dwells in the corner like a silent friend, built and bestowed by Roger himself.

Roger goes directly to the basement door, but Cheryl steps onto the stairs and turns to him.

"While we're here . . ."

He joins her, and together they ascend. The second floor is sliced low by the slanted ceiling. Harriet's horseshoe still hangs over the bedroom door, its lintel so low that Roger has to duck his head. Upon entering the room, Cheryl is enveloped by the musty kerosene smell that delivers her instantly back to Harriet's side, toward the end, reading to her from historical romance novels. The old lover's knot quilt is still on the bed. Cheryl is unsure how to feel about the new owners using it.

She goes to the window and peers through the grid of glass. There is her own home across the street, nestled and safe in the snow. Safe. She lays her hands on the window's lower muntin and, bending her knees, heaves it open. A cold gust enters the room, and a few snowflakes drift in.

"What are you doing?" Roger asks.

Cheryl steps to the next window, yanks it open wide.

She turns to her husband, raises her eyebrows. "Don't you know?"

"Cheryl," he begins, but does not continue. He follows her into the adjacent bedchamber and watches her open the windows there.

She leans out under one of the sashes, reaching her arm around, and calls, "Where's the downspout?"

"Cheryl, no."

She draws herself back in and faces her husband squarely. "It has to happen," she says. "There has to be exterior proof."

"But this isn't proof, this is sabotage."

"What's the alternative? Wait until the house decays from the inside? That's what they're hoping. There won't be any proof until it's too late. Just like the Spaulding house. There was nothing to see on the outside until the walls started to rot."

Roger doesn't answer. Cheryl thrusts her head and torso back through the window.

"I found it," she gasps, extending her arm to its limit. "Come here."

He goes out of the room. A moment later, he returns with a fireplace poker in hand. He moves Cheryl aside and leans out the window, straining. He grunts, and Cheryl flinches at the sound of metal popping loose. He pulls back into the room with a strange look on his face. She peers out the window, sees the drainpipe dangling like a broken limb, knocking against the siding. A wave of nausea comes through her, as if she has dismembered someone dear to her. She retreats into the bedroom and sits on Harriet's quilt. Through the nausea, she sends a message of apology to the house. Her intentions are noble. Only noble.

"Do you hear that?" Roger asks. There is a thumping sound coming from above, the step of heavy boots. "It's in the attic. Maybe animals."

Cheryl is frozen in place. Reverend Slater was a pious man, but not known as a kind one. He was notorious for his anger, for the violent outbursts that kept his family docile and his community subservient.

"Come," says Roger, infused with some strange new energy. "Who knows what we'll find. Maybe it will help our case."

He goes out of the bedroom with the poker. Cheryl senses a new, unpleasant charge in the air that prickles against her skin, compelling her to flee. Instead, she scurries after Roger like a nervous hunting dog. As they climb the narrow staircase to the attic, she sees a flickering form pass against the wall beside her, inches from her face. The shape, flat and phosphorescent, sweeps upward as Roger reaches the top of the stairs.

No sound comes from Cheryl's throat as he steps along a ceiling joist and raises the poker to the ceiling. Her scream emerges just as the rafters buckle. In the suspended moment before the crash, it seems as if someone has pulled a string, dropping the beams at a neat, choreographed diagonal. The next moment, Roger is sprawled upon the floorboards, pinned at the leg.

Dead. Martyred. Cheryl stands paralyzed on the stairs, awed by the swiftness of judgment.

Her husband lifts a hand. "Go," he chokes. "What are you doing?"

As she rushes down through the house, electrified air spangles the back of her neck. Outside, her cloak blows open and she stumbles through the snow in her chemise. The shimmering shape appears again beside her, skimming close upon the snow, licking at her heels, tripping her. She scrambles over Cannonfield Road and falls through the door of her own house. The power is still out, the telephone dead. Upstairs, her children grumble awake.

Amos, thank heaven, is able to find a signal on his cell phone, and within moments an ambulance and fire engine arrive at the Slater house with spinning lights. A brigade of brawny, yellow-suited men storms the attic and lifts the mighty beam from Roger's leg. For the moment, no one asks who he is, why he is here.

Cheryl lets Rebekah drive the Jeep to the hospital. Amos sits in the passenger seat, Cheryl in the back.

"We were just turning off the water," she mumbles in a flat voice, although no one has asked. "We just went in to make sure it was turned off. We were just turning off the water."

They are fortunate, the doctors say, that Roger escaped with just a broken tibia. They will need to introduce a metal rod to align the bone, and he may walk with a permanent limp. His chair-making, at least, will not be affected.

"You look like a wounded soldier," Cheryl tells him, patting his cast.

The questions come now, in an avalanche. A police detective questions them at the hospital. Cheryl answers, holds fast to her story. They were turning off the water. A neighborly favor. They did not forcibly enter, but came in with a key. They were doing what they hoped their own neighbors might do, had they been away from their home in a storm. They had gone to the attic to investigate animal sounds.

And the drainpipe? The windows?

"Strange, yes. We thought so, too."

* * *

A blue tarp appears on the roof of the Slater house like a draped flag. Cheryl feels a nervous thrill each time it catches her eye through the window. It is an emblem of her victory—its healing presence the result of her actions alone. The house will be saved now, it is certain. Regardless of the cost, she has won. The Aston Martin pulls into the driveway one morning while she is at her button work. Her hands pause in midair as she watches from across the street, waiting for the car doors to open. She notices that she is holding her breath. After several moments, the car slides back out of the driveway and creeps away down Cannonfield Road.

The following week, the commission holds a special meeting with the homeowners about repairing the Slater house under its guidelines. Cheryl sits quietly at the table and lets Edward Drayton preside. The owners are what she'd pictured—the woman lithe and manicured, the husband skittish in modern glasses. They sit, as so many others have sat, on the flimsy folding chairs facing the oak table.

Cheryl is aware of the uneasy glances of the other commission members. The serenity she feels is that of a warrior who has completed her work, laid down her bayonet. Barbara Underhill and Gordon Cassava, Richard Darch and Lori Hatfield will never hear the shrill call of liberty the way she has, will never swim the current of history.

The homeowners have chosen not to press charges. They could easily have sued, Roger reminds her, for trespassing and vandalism. They could have fingerprinted the window sashes and drainpipe if they wanted. Perhaps deep down, Cheryl thinks, they know better than to do so. Perhaps they hear the boot-drop of Ezekiel in their dreams.

Edward Drayton announces that the commission's structural engineer has been contacted and will begin consultations without delay.

"An appropriate plan for restoration will be determined," he drones, "with an architect approved by the commission. All critical structural problems will be addressed in addition to repairing the roof, including repointing the foundation and replacing aged timber sill plates. The full cost, naturally, will be borne by the property owners, to bring the house in line with the standards of the commission. With our guidance, the Ezekiel Slater house will be returned to its former grandeur."

Cheryl is grateful that her children are home for one more night, that she can declare this final triumph in person. They sit at the table, their faces in candlelight, as she repeats Edward Drayton's words. Cheryl wants to capture this moment, their features gilded in this way, their eyes mirroring twin flames. She would like to visit this image in her mind for years to come, on those winter nights when her children are far away, doing things she will never know with people she has never met. She finishes speaking and smiles in anticipation. Her children do not reply at once. After a moment, Amos mutters, "Congratulations," to a focal point near Cheryl's ear, then excuses himself and goes upstairs. Rebekah blinks her eyes, smiles in her supercilious new way, and returns to her plate of leftover bread pudding.

The next morning, Cheryl and Roger drive them to the airport. They embrace at the security gate. Both parents resist the itch to remind and advise, to command their son to complete the semester, to tell their daughter to skip Afrikaans. Instead, they let their children pull out of their arms and join the security line. They watch them remove their shoes and put their backpacks on the conveyor belt. They see Amos place his pocket watch into a plastic bucket and send it through the X-ray machine. They watch their children pass through the metal detector's trellis and, on the other side, give a brief wave and disappear around a corner. They will sit together for the six-hour flight, then part ways in San Francisco, one aimed south, the other east. By the time the sun sets in New England, they will be speeding over freeways their parents have never driven, along the lurid blue coastline at the edge of America. They will charge through dark belts of sequoias, close and brooding, toward the brightening valleys and swells of the Santa Cruz Mountains, the Sierra Nevada.

Cheryl and Roger drive home in silence. There will be plenty to do these next few months. The springtime circuit is on the horizon: Fort Frederick in April, Ticonderoga in June. There will be another tavern dance, and several Ordinary Evenings with games and ale. Cheryl will have twilights at her virginals. And, of course, there are buttons to be sewn. As many as she can manage.

Floortime

Suzanne is supposed to be playing with Elliot. He sits on the rug with a stacking toy, donut-shaped rings on a rod. When finished, the tower should represent the colors of the rainbow in sequence, but Suzanne is happy if he can just fit a ring on the pole. When he fails, when a ring tumbles to the floor, she can't resist the urge to pick it up and slide it on for him. She is not supposed to do this, she knows. It is important to observe and encourage without assisting. It is important to make frequent eye contact, to use an upbeat and affectionate tone of voice. If he will not look at her when she speaks, she is supposed to tilt his chin with her fingers, to insist that their eyes meet. She has never actually done this.

It is Saturday, the first true spring day. Carlota is off, and Brian is on the boat. She had not dissuaded him from going, had not played the guilt card. There is no need for both of them to stay home today. If she is bad at playing with their son, Brian is worse.

Elliot drops a red ring, and it rolls under the coffee table. Suzanne lets it go, places a larger yellow ring into his blunt little hands. She looks at the time: only 11:45. Her watch strikes her at this moment as ludicrously fine—an anniversary gift marking five years of marriage—the Ebel she'd been hinting for, with a gray satin dial ringed with diamonds. It is expertly engineered, exquisitely beautiful, splintering the overhead lights into a thousand blazing fragments.

It has been three weeks since Elliot's diagnosis. For months, Suzanne had been lying at pediatrician appointments. When the doctor had asked about Elliot's physical and verbal development, she forced a smile and said that, yes, he was running and jumping; yes, he had at least ten words. The truth was that she had never heard him speak. He had never muttered "Mama" or "Dada." He was just a late bloomer, she'd assumed. He was an introverted, thoughtful child with quiet considerations of his own. It was true that she rarely spent time with other children Elliot's age, and had little basis for comparison. Only once had she observed him alongside a boy of the same size, at a restaurant. That child had pointed at Suzanne's hoop earrings and said a word that sounded like "bubble." Suzanne had smiled in surprise and studied the boy's face for a discreet moment—his eyes blue and keen, blinking with attention—before looking to his mother, a woman younger than herself and not remarkable in any way, and asking, "Did you hear that?"

"Oh, I know," the woman had said, laughing and chewing. "He loves jewelry."

Suzanne had looked back at the boy, who was now spooning clam chowder into his mouth. Slumped in the highchair beside her, Elliot gravely and repeatedly raked a fork over a paper napkin.

After that, Suzanne avoided taking her son into public. Brian hadn't yet been awakened to Elliot's differences, and she did not bring them to his attention. Then, at Elliot's eighteen-month checkup, she couldn't make him sit up. He screamed when the nurse put him on the baby scale and arched his back like a swordfish. When the doctor came in, Elliot was squirming belly-down on the examining table, kicking his legs. Suzanne smiled and shrugged. She had dressed for the appointment in a tweed pencil skirt and black turtleneck, as if to convince the doctor of her competence.

The doctor had kept Elliot for longer than expected. Her usual reassuring manner was gone, replaced by a disconcerting professional gravity. She gave Suzanne the name of a specialist and urged her to schedule an evaluation quickly. Later, she and Brian watched helplessly as the specialist sat across from their son, spoke his name, waited for eye contact. He rolled a ball to see if Elliot would reciprocate. He showed Elliot a book with a picture of a monkey, then put the book on his own head. Throughout all this, Elliot stared into the middle distance, unsmiling, periodically slapping the table in front of him.

Early intervention was important, the specialist said. They should find a support group. They should investigate which therapies their insurance might cover: home-based speech therapy, occupational therapy, physical therapy. He recommended that they visit treatment centers in person, to determine which approach might be best for Elliot. And the most important intervention would have to come from the family itself. He smiled when he said this, rubbing his glasses. It would be optimal, of course, if one parent were able to stay home with the boy, to engage with him each day in a rigorous and focused manner.

Now, Suzanne's laptop computer rests on the kitchen table in the periphery of her vision, sleek and white, its little light pulsing with intelligence. She is conscious of its pull through every moment she spends on the floor, but girds herself against it. Finally, when Elliot wrangles the last ring onto his tower, she applauds, then rewards herself by getting up to check her e-mail. There is nothing of interest in her inbox, but she lingers anyway, browsing *Vogue*.

Elliot has abandoned the stacking toy and is now on his feet, turning circles on the carpet. Suzanne watches passively for a few moments, until he topples sideways onto the couch. The specialist has explained that such behavior is often caused by too little sensory input. Her fault, this time, for having left him alone. She goes to him, takes him gently by the shoulders, and pulls him into a bear hug, as instructed. After a moment of steady pressure, she feels his body relax. The next activity should be something physical, she knows, so she goes to retrieve the balance board. Her watch glitters. Noon. Brian won't be home until at least four. She is jealous of his being outdoors. The world shimmers with life, but she cannot muster the energy to shepherd Elliot into the yard.

Once he has begun on the balance board, Suzanne steps away again. She goes to the kitchen and pours a glass of lemonade, adding the ice afterward to avoid the clatter of the cubes, too harsh for Elliot's ears. Last, she adds a finger of chilled vodka from the freezer.

Outside the living room window, through the border of young pines, Suzanne sees a man cross the adjacent yard and disappear into the woods. Their next-door neighbor. She has often seen him skulking outside like this, even on the few weekdays she's been at home. It appears that he does not have a job.

She met his wife, Madeleine, after they first moved in. A pretty, bewildered pregnant woman. A few months later, pink balloons had appeared on the neighboring mailbox, and Suzanne had brought over a key lime pie. The husband had answered the door. He was tall and lean and not handsome, but his eyes were brazenly green and unapologetic, almost rude.

Suzanne had shaped her face into a neighborly smile. "Suzanne Crawford from next door."

There had been a smell of something earthy, spicy, inside the house. Incense? Marijuana? She'd glimpsed Madeleine in the background, holding a bundle close to her body, perhaps breast-feeding. The husband apologized that his wife wasn't able to come to the door. His voice was soft and resonant, in contrast to the impolite stare.

She felt herself redden, handed him the pie. "Well, I don't want to disturb her. Just a little something from us to you."

Walking home, she realized she'd neglected to ask the baby's name.

Since they moved in, the neighbors' front yard has become increasingly shaggy, the weeds in the grass growing hardy enough to flower, autumn leaves left to mulch beneath snowfall. Such neglect stands out in a neighborhood like this, and Suzanne chafes whenever she looks at the property. She has fleetingly considered leaving an anonymous note. Perhaps these are the distracted, dreamy kind of people who simply don't know, don't see; who just need a gentle nudge. It's true that she has sensed something different about Madeleine, something faltering and apologetic. There is something almost cowering about her, like a pursued animal.

Really, Suzanne would have preferred living somewhere with fewer neighbors, larger properties, more privacy. When she and Brian had first discussed moving to the country, she'd envisioned horse pastures, old farmhouses with original beams and barns. But the cost of rural living—the elegant kind—had proven higher than they'd guessed. For the price of their Chelsea apartment, they could afford only a midsized four-bedroom on a half acre. This did not seem to bother Brian, who was happy just to be near the water. Without asking, he'd taken a chunk of their remaining savings and bought the boat.

After Elliot's birth, Suzanne had not experienced the hormonal lift of new motherhood. Instead, she'd been pummeled by fatigue, bedeviled by a nagging melancholy. Brian had insisted that they hire help and had found Carlota himself. He'd encouraged Suzanne to use her maternity leave to get outside, meet the neighbors, find a network of like-minded women. *Join a book group,* he'd said. She'd resisted this idea—she was never much of a reader and feared sounding stupid in front of others—but had, finally, found a group and joined it. To her relief, the same few women dominated the discussions. Most of the women were fashionable in a subdued suburban way, with just a handful of unkempt, over-smiling types. Her husband had been right; it felt good to see these people in the supermarket, to greet them by name. There was a sense of potential, at least, for dinner parties and deepening friendship. A more cautious and formulaic sort of friendship, perhaps, but a version of friendship still. The seed of all this, of course, lay in their children who would attend the same schools, bring their mothers together through teachers and sports teams.

But now she doesn't know. Will Elliot attend a different kind of school? Perhaps the conversations she will have for the rest of her life will be unpleasant, taut with the discomfort and pity of others. Perhaps they will not be things to enjoy, but to be gotten through.

The night of Elliot's diagnosis, she and Brian had lain in bed in their separate whirlpools of thought, without speaking. What, Suzanne wondered privately, had gone wrong in this genetic experiment so clearly weighted toward success? She and Brian were both healthy, strong-boned, intelligent. Which of them had contributed the guilty gene? Which, hiding the dormant flaw of some great-grandparent, had dropped their end of the bargain? She had, after all, been careful in choosing her mate. She and Brian had met respectably, through a college friend. They had gone on proper dates, asked the right questions, discovered parallel values and preferences, complementary personality traits. They'd posed for a wedding announcement in the *Times,* their faces properly aligned.

She had never really felt the maternal craving that other women claimed to feel, but she knew her time was limited. If they didn't have a baby soon, they might end up a childless couple—that curiosity—to whom others give questioning, pitying looks. Is it possible, she wonders now, that she'd failed to transfer some vital maternal message to her son in utero? Is the fact that he does not meet her eyes, does not return her smile, evidence of some basic failure on her part? Babies sense truths about their parents, she believes. Her son has floated in her waters, absorbed them, known their makeup. There can be no greater, more frightening intimacy.

And she is horrified by the disappointment she sometimes feels, alternating with a helpless, almost violent love for her boy. *So what if he isn't normal?* she admonishes herself. Had she borne a child only to watch him succeed at the endeavors she values? Would she only prize a child who was like other people's children?

Elliot's features are delicate, symmetrical. The bridge of his nose is broad and thoughtful-seeming, but his hair is bran-colored and feral. Even when she manages to wrestle a comb through, it splits back into scrappy chunks. Her son pats his head compulsively while eating, so that his hair collects the juices of ham and salami and, by the end of the day, smells like a trash can. She is sorry to leave him each morning—she feels a cavity open in her chest as she kisses his indifferent head and closes the door—but once she is moving, once the terror of the train's velocity, the panic of physical distance, has diminished, her disorientation recedes and is replaced by a kind of light and floating relief. She closes her eyes. She goes to work.

* * *

This month's book selection is about an Ethiopian orphan adopted by Iowans. Suzanne has gotten through only twenty pages of it, but dresses in anticipation of the evening's meeting, to be hosted by Madeleine Gaines next door. She chooses a fawn-colored sheath with red slingback sandals. No accessories: just a stroke of ruby lipstick and an elastic for her hair. She girds herself for what she might encounter next door, what clutter or unseemliness—and is surprised to enter a house that is clean, sparsely furnished, nondescript. There is a mirrored console table in the entrance hall, imitation art deco. No one greets her at the door. Mingling voices lead her to the sunken living room, where women huddle near a card table with glasses of sangria. Madeleine herself shuttles to and from the kitchen, bringing out appetizer forks and little stacks of paper napkins.

Suzanne greets the other women and surveys the hors d'oeuvre table. Limp prosciutto rolls, pucks of bruschetta, stuffed mushrooms still on the baking sheet. As Suzanne pours herself sangria, a clump of messy fruit splashes into her glass. Sangria is a nice idea, but will never be as elegant as clean white wine.

"You know, I have to say, I feel bad for the children," April Carlson remarks, when they are all sitting. "I know they're lucky to escape Africa, I know things would have been worse for them there, but I can't help thinking how hard it must be to look so different from their adoptive families."

April is fresh and blond, in clam diggers and espadrilles, though it is barely Memorial Day. It is clear, just from hearing her glass-chime voice, that she has no real worries to speak of. But it is impossible to be sure. All these women guard the details of their lives. Like surfacing whales, they arch their smooth rounds only briefly into view. The great bulks remain underwater. Once a month, they appear, breathe one another in, then dive again. There are alcoholic husbands, certainly. There are prescription drugs, cosmetic surgeries, eating disorders. There must be shames in this room dark or darker than Suzanne's own.

The women nod at April's comment, some tightening their mouths as if in contemplation. Leanne Vogel tells of a friend with an adopted Chinese daughter, the quizzical looks they receive from supermarket cashiers. There is a general murmur. Swiftly, the discussion shifts to same-sex parenting, then to gay marriage, then to tax evasion.

When the conversation begins to splinter, the women rise and chatter, moving sinuously through the room in groups of two and three. Suzanne approaches Madeleine, who is standing with two other women. It is not difficult to insert herself here, and when she does, the other women shrink away. Alone with Madeleine, she begins with questions about the baby: *How has she been sleeping? Are you still nursing?* She adopts a tone of sisterly experience, but the truth is that the early days of Elliot's infancy feel as distant to her as something she has dreamed. Madeleine responds in a choppy fashion, nervously alert, running her fingers through her hair as if dislodging loose strands.

Suzanne lingers with Madeleine. Before she can weigh the wisdom of it, she hears herself asking, "What does your husband do?"

Madeleine smiles strangely and glances to the side. "Well, he just changed careers, actually. He worked in advertising for years, but now he's started a business of his own."

"Oh? What sort of business?"

She pauses. "A kind of holistic healing business, I guess you could say. Traditional medicine." Madeleine flushes. "It's something new for him."

Suzanne feels herself staring. "Eastern medicine, like acupuncture?"

"Not exactly." Madeleine trails off. "It's hard to explain." Her eyes dart to the side. "Excuse me," she mumbles, "I have to say good-bye to someone."

Suzanne is left standing alone, glass of clotted sangria in hand. The women are dispersing, the room is quieting. She waits, dumbly, for Madeleine to return. Through the side window, she can see a segment of her own house showing pale between the pines.

The process is a long and slow one, the specialist reminds them. Therapies that work for some children do nothing for others. There are no shortcuts, only trial and error, love and patience. Suzanne takes a day off work to bring Elliot to a treatment center an hour's drive away. There, she chats with a few of the other mothers—they are all mothers—who share a saintly aura. It seems to Suzanne that they have moved through the stages of denial and sorrow into a ferocious embrace of their children's conditions. They use foreign terminology—*stimming, perseveration*—that bespeaks years of reading, research, preoccupation.

She thinks she detects a condescending sympathy in their eyes when they listen to her speak about Elliot, when she tells them she is optimistic about his recovery. They smile kindly, creases of valiant exhaustion in their faces. Their hair is cropped or pulled back, and their clothing is utilitarian: cargo shorts and rubberized sport sandals. None of these women, she comes to understand, works outside the home. They do not have to announce this fact; it is evident by their casual camaraderie, their practiced stances and ritualized movements, that they come here every day. When she mentions having taken a personal day from work, they give her that same frustrating, patient smile. The work they do with their children—the grinding hours of floortime, of tantrum taming, of endless mopping and toileting—is bigger than any office job, the smile seems to say.

The next day, Suzanne returns to work, and Carlota brings Elliot to the center. At night, Brian is quiet in bed. It is as if Suzanne can read his mind, but she waits for him to speak, makes him work at shaping his words and finding a careful way of delivering them. He asks whether she would consider leaving her job, working with Elliot herself. When she does not respond, he gathers himself, as if to continue the discussion on a greater scale. *No.* She stops him. She does not want to hear about life's unpredictability, the necessity to reassess, reprioritize, to choose what must be sacrificed and what preserved. *No,* she tells him. *Not now.*

It is maddening that the question will never be whether he should leave his job. His salary is double hers, and without it they couldn't keep the house. But still: work, for him, is just work. It isn't oxygen. It took years to realize that she was unusual, that for most people work is a discrete and ill-fitting role, incompatible with their true pleasures and purposes. Few are fortunate to have been born, as she was, to a clear-cut ambition. As a girl, she'd brought a notebook and flashlight under the covers at night and drew women in dresses. By the time she reached high school, she'd completed a dozen such notebooks and developed what she thought was a recognizable style. Now, at thirty-five, she is a design director at a major fashion house, just one notch beneath the name on the label.

She never stops designing. On the train, she sketches. When her eyes close, patterns erupt before her. Her current obsession is chinoiserie. She is not alone in this, she knows, and fears that the classic motifs—birds on flowering vines, sleepy pagodas—won't be fresh much longer. Still, she is pushing it as a unifying theme for the spring line. The novelty will come from the colors and details she proposes: silken dresses in cream and ivory, printed with shades of citron, magenta, turquoise. Romantic pieces slashed by exposed zippers. And suede footwear in risky pastels and unwise whites, sexy in their vulnerability. Here is a woman above such concerns as mud and scuffing. Buff-colored boots, brushed to rabbit softness. Suzanne feels a sensuous rush through her body as she draws a figure in these boots, the neck customarily long, with short marks for the mouth and nose: disdainful, defiant.

The fall line, now in stores, is dark and billowy, unstructured. She has grown to hate it with the acid repulsion reserved for things most recently loved. She can't get away from it fast enough, can't draw pale, slim things quickly enough to obscure the fall collection from her mind, the wide navy capes and black duster coats, the models like dour crows.

Coming home from work, she pours a glass of Syrah and helps Carlota with dinner. Elliot sits in front of the television, his hair greased with its daily buildup. Suzanne asks about their visit to the center, and Carlota itemizes Elliot's activities: squeezing a ball, looking at pictures of faces, toeing a painted line.

"What did the therapists say? Did they mention how soon we might see progress?" Suzanne takes a breath and revises the question for Carlota. "Did the teachers say when he'll get better?"

Carlota shrugs, makes a sour face. "I don't know. The teachers, they don't really talk to me."

Suzanne is silent. Of course Carlota is the only nanny there. "It's okay," she says, and looks at the back of Elliot's head.

It's a lot to ask of both of them, this daily trek to the center. If Elliot doesn't begin to show improvement in a few weeks, she decides, she will tell Carlota to stop taking him. In the meantime, there are other options. She has trawled Internet forums devoted to every treatment imaginable. There is play therapy, music therapy, massage therapy. There are vitamin supplements and elimination diets and antifungal treatments. There is a detoxification procedure to remove metals from the system. There is acupuncture.

They begin with elimination diets. Suzanne instructs Carlota to remove all sugars from Elliot's food for two weeks. This proves more difficult than expected—nearly every food label lists some form of sugar: evaporated cane juice, high fructose corn syrup—so that for two weeks Elliot eats nothing but lentils and cooked vegetables. Next, they take away food dyes, then gluten. There is, Suzanne thinks, a brief spell during the gluten-free period when Elliot seems more attentive. His eyes meet hers briefly when she soaps him in the tub, and for a breathless moment she believes she can read a message there: that he is on his way to her. But this happens only once.

Suzanne takes another vacation day and brings him to an acupuncturist. A foolish idea, she realizes, when she sees the long needles. He will shriek; she will cry. She pays for the annulled appointment and takes Elliot home.

There is still chelation therapy. For this, a willing doctor inserts a formula designed to bind with metal in the bloodstream and flush out any mercury left by vaccines. Suzanne has never been one of the hysterics who demonize immunizations—but who knows? Some mothers insist their children have been cured by chelation. Others warn that it's quackery. Doctors have been sued. A little boy has died.

Suzanne lies awake while Brian sleeps untroubled beside her. No light comes through the window blinds of their bedroom; there are no streetlamps or passing headlights. The darkness of night here is complete. The city had offered unlikely comfort in its sheer, crazy numbers. Here, Suzanne feels stripped of such layered company. She finds the neighboring houses at their respectful distances to be curiously confining. Those houses are darkened now, dense with their respective sleepers and insomniacs, humming with individual dreams.

The pink balloons on the mailbox next door had eventually shrunk to limp mitts, drooping against the post, until someone finally removed them. Suzanne remembers the way the husband had looked at her. It hadn't been flirtatious, but clinical, diagnostic. *Holistic healing,* his wife had said. Perhaps he'd been appraising her as a potential client. Perhaps he is one of those men who believe every woman is sick at the core, corroded by toxic memories, in need of a deep-tissue massage or scalding with hot rocks.

She shaps a vague resolution as she drifts off to sleep, and a few days later goes to the phone like a somnambulist. Madeleine answers, her voice heartier than Suzanne remembers.

"Madeleine, it's Suzanne Crawford from next door." She pauses. "It's been a while. Just checking in to say hello."

There is a moment of silence in which Suzanne fears that Madeleine has forgotten her, followed by a rambling of thanks, apology, grateful effusiveness. Suzanne listens. Then a breath, a pause.

"Oh," Suzanne says breezily, "I think I remember you mentioning that your husband has a healing practice of some sort? Do you think you could tell me a little more about that?"

She puts a hand to the kitchen wall as she says this and focuses on a glass-paneled cabinet, rows of glass tumblers inside, layers of transparency. There is no reply on the other end of the line.

"Hello?"

Madeleine's voice returns. "Let me put David on the phone."

Suzanne briefly considers hanging up, pretending the connection has been cut. She grips the receiver to her ear as the husband's voice comes on, dark and mellifluous, a radio voice.

They make an appointment for Saturday, when Brian will be on the boat. Suzanne will not mention it to him. The chance is too great that he will interpret it as evidence of her desperation, her rejection of responsibility. Any defense she might make would only cement her guilt.

On Saturday, Suzanne chooses an easy chambray shirtdress and ballerina flats, just a touch of nude lip gloss. She gives Elliot a bath, hastily shampooing his hair before he thinks of screaming, and dresses him in short overalls. He is reasonably compliant this morning, for which she is grateful.

Madeleine answers the door in a flowered peasant blouse, holding a solid and very pink baby. She looks fresh, unruffled, and young—utterly unlike how Suzanne recalls her own first months of motherhood. Suzanne gives her widest, most sincere smile as she compliments her neighbor. When Madeleine steps to the side, Suzanne sees David in the living room. For a long moment, no one speaks, and she feels immediately sorry for coming.

"Would you like something to drink?" Madeleine finally asks. "Iced tea, coffee, water?"

"Some iced tea would be nice." Suzanne smiles, still holding Elliot in the entrance hall. She does not want to put him down near the mirrored table.

"Have a seat," David instructs her. "Make yourself comfortable."

With as much dignity as she can, Suzanne strides into the living room and smooths her skirt before sitting on the couch. Elliot reaches beneath her dress collar, as is his habit, and digs his fingernails into her shoulder, but she refrains from pulling his hand away. She does not want to start a conflict so soon.

Madeleine brings the iced tea and takes a seat at the other end of the couch. David stands facing them like a workshop leader, in jeans and a thin brown T-shirt. Some kind of leather pouch hangs around his neck, bound with string.

"What I'm going to do is a modified version of an ancient custom," he begins without prelude. "As Madeleine might have mentioned, I've recently been blessed with the ability to enter altered states of consciousness that allow me to access and diagnose hidden illnesses and blockages in people."

Elliot is now clawing forcefully at Suzanne's shoulder. She concentrates on keeping her face relaxed, her expression neutral. She hears what David is saying, but is unable to make meaning of the words. She gives an interested smile and nods for him to continue.

"What I'd like to do is spend a little time with Elliot and see if I can confront whatever it is that's obstructing his development. It's not uncommon for a young child to have problems on a spiritual level stemming from some early trauma, like a difficult birth. But most medical doctors don't consider this."

Suzanne's shoulder flinches involuntarily, and Elliot digs deeper. She registers the words *difficult birth*. It had, in fact, been difficult.

"The whole session shouldn't take more than an hour or so," David says, turning away. He goes out of the room and returns with a rough wooden tray holding a collection of objects: a long striped feather, a group of round stones, a small animal skull. The tray is a peculiar prop in this anodyne beige room with its microfiber sofa and leather armchair, its shag rug the color of milky tea.

David lifts the coffee table up from this rug and moves it to a corner of the room. He puts a match to a bundle of weeds in a little clay pot, and after a moment the fragrance reaches Suzanne. He dims the lights, then squats in front of the couch and asks if Elliot would like to lie on the floor.

To Suzanne's surprise, Elliot disengages his grip and allows himself to be placed on the rug. He does not lie down, but sits with his legs forked in front of him. Madeleine positions her own daughter into a saucer-shaped jumper seat. From a closet she retrieves a drum, moldy looking and embellished with bells and tassels. She lowers herself to the floor, legs crossed Indian-style, and nestles the drum in the crook of her knees. The herb bundle smokes, producing its exotic perfume. Suzanne looks instinctively to the window. The blinds are tightly closed.

David begins to walk a slow circle around Elliot, humming a meandering tune. After a number of circles, he lowers himself to the floor and stretches out beside the boy, while Madeleine begins to pat the drum. Elliot ignores both of them, picking at tufts of yarn on the rug.

Suzanne sits with her legs tight together, wishing herself out of the room. It is unpleasant to watch adults behave in this way. She does not like to see a grown man on the floor; she does not like to see a woman with a dirty drum. Madeleine increases her volume and tempo so that the drumbeats grow loud and insistent. At this, the baby girl stops bouncing. Her little face reddens and her mouth gapes silently for a moment. When the cries come, Madeleine looks up and falters in her drumming.

The baby's father, flat on the floor, appears unaware of the disturbance. He is absent from the room, the movement of his eyeballs perceptible beneath his closed lids. Suzanne hesitates, then goes to the bouncer and picks up the baby. She gazes into the fat, wet-lashed face, so different from Elliot's, and blinks her eyes playfully. To her amazement, the baby shows her nubby teeth in pleasure. For the rest of the ritual, she holds the little girl on her lap, breathing her smell of orange and vanilla.

The performance continues monotonously, tirelessly. Elliot has now slumped sideways onto the floor, his fingers meshed into the rug's fibers. David makes quick shapes with his mouth, as if speaking to an invisible entity. He snarls and clutches his hands into fists. Madeleine's tempo slows to a heartbeat, then quickens again. Finally, David's legs jerk and his eyes spring open. He stares blankly at the ceiling for a moment, then gives his wife a nod, releasing her from drum duty. Suzanne returns the baby to her, feeling a bittersweet tug as the girl's body is taken away, vibrating with health and potential.

David crawls to Elliot and leans over his prone form. He places his cupped hands to the back of the boy's head and blows a long breath into them. Elliot stirs and David carefully rolls him face upward, then blows the same way into his chest. Watching this, Suzanne realizes that she is holding her breath. Something is happening, she sees. Something is passing between them. Whether it is healing or not, she doesn't know, but there is a thickening in the air that seems to her full of her son, and for a moment she is certain that he has been tapped in some way, freed.

Finally David passes the feather over Elliot's body, and with a touch at the forehead, the boy awakens. David resumes his tuneless hum and walks a final circle around the child.

"I think that will help," David says, and puts a hand to Elliot's head. "It makes sense that he's been having trouble. He's battling powerful forces. But I located his guardian animal, and it's a good one. He's been fighting without any help up to this point, but now he'll have some backup."

Suzanne nods mutely.

"I think you'll start noticing some changes," David says, and lowers himself into the easy chair. He closes his eyes. There is a sense of dislocation that Suzanne imagines they all feel, as the reverberations of the drum linger in the air.

"Well, I'm so glad you could come," Madeleine says, walking Suzanne toward the door, as if she had stopped in for coffee.

In the entrance hall, Suzanne turns to her. "Does David . . ." she whispers. "How much does he . . . or should I expect an invoice?"

"No, no"—Madeleine shakes her head—"of course not."

"Well then. Thank you."

She carries Elliot home. The day is blinding, and she feels the disorientation of emerging from a matinee. Her son's body drapes against her shoulder. The weight of his arms around her neck is achingly pleasant, the closest she will get to a hug. They go slowly up their neighbors' driveway, over drifts of fallen catkins and past the overgrown yard, the wild violets humming with life. They step briefly along the hot-baked road, then turn into their own driveway, laid with cobblestone pavers. The driveway appears to Suzanne, in her mild delirium, as a throat connected to the house, swallowing her down.

The next morning, while Brian is on the computer, Suzanne brings Elliot out to the backyard. She spreads a blanket at the far edge of the lawn, out of view of the neighbors, and reads a picture book to him. As usual, he ignores her, fixated on combing his fingers through the freshly mown grass, frilled with clippings. She tries to put a melody in her voice as she reads, but keeps reverting to the same mechanical chant. She holds up the pictures, pointlessly, for Elliot to see. Finally, she stops reading. The silence is a balm, and she lies down in the sun, watching strings of red baubles float behind her lids.

After several drifting moments, she is surprised by a pressure on her chest. She opens her eyes to see Elliot resting there. He raises his head and looks at her. He smiles. It takes a beat to process this. She lifts herself on an elbow and looks deeply at him. They stare at each other for a long moment, and Suzanne feels as if her son is finally, lavishly pouring himself into her. She smiles back, and Elliot actually laughs. She laughs in return. She wants to gather him up in her arms, to tackle him with astonished joy. She wants to run through the clump of pine trees and bang on the window of the house next door, shouting. Instead, she keeps still, and for a few airborne moments, her son lolls on the blanket with her, and seems to know her. Tentatively, she puts a hand into Elliot's hair. Closing her eyes, she lobs up something like a prayer to the summer sky.

It's true, Brian agrees. He does seem better. They spend the day as a family, outdoors. They take a walk around the neighborhood with Elliot, docile in a stroller. Suzanne returns the waves of drivers in slow-moving cars. The houses they pass are faced with thin stone and brick, self-consciously substantial and too close to the road, but ultimately benign, even kindly. Elliot appears to notice them, too, for the first time.

Suzanne returns to work with fresh energy. *Notice,* she tells Carlota, as she steps out the door, *if he seems any different to you.* When she returns home that evening, she finds Carlota asleep on the couch. The television is on, and Elliot is seated on the floor in front of it, transfixed by the screen. Suzanne walks into his sight line and stops. He looks at her without recognition, his eyes dull.

Carlota stirs, shakes herself awake, apologizes. She comes to gather Elliot for bed.

"It's all right," Suzanne tells her. "I'll do it tonight."

Carlota studies Suzanne for a moment, as if searching for reprobation in her employer's face.

"Really, it's okay," Suzanne assures her. She sends her up to her room, which they have allowed her to decorate however she likes, with whatever religious icons and candles.

Suzanne is actually looking forward to putting her son to bed tonight. There is a new understanding between them now, she imagines—the bond of travelers who have been through a taxing journey together—and she is eager to explore its boundaries and variegations.

She turns the television off. As its strident chatter ceases and the screen dies to black, Elliot's fists clench and his body turns rigid. A low moan of protest emerges from his throat. It is the sound of a pained animal, a pup deserted in the woods. Suzanne squats down in front of her child and attempts eye contact. For a suspended instant, she is certain that he will return her gaze the way he had on the grass yesterday, that he will bestow that seal of recognition, of rightness. And she is confused when his eyes and mouth squeeze to slits, when his face seizes into a mask of outrage. And then, all at once, he is upon her.

The pain is a surprise. His teeth penetrate the linen of her trouser leg at the back of her calf. She yelps and stands, tries to yank away, but the clamp of his jaw is as strong as a dog's. The instinct to reach down and wrench him off, to hurl him away, is almost overwhelming, but with all her will she resists doing this. She stands in place as the boy bites with growing ferocity, deep into her flesh. She stands with her own teeth clenched and feels the force of it.

The pain burns through her like an electrical bolt. It keeps burning even after her son has released her leg and rolled onto the floor, sobbing. It keeps burning after she has picked him up, thrashing, and carried him upstairs, and after she has lowered him screaming into his crib, still in his clothing and wet diaper. It burns when she is lying in bed alone, and later when Brian lies down beside her and when he puts a lazy hand on her breast. It burns as she turns away toward the wall. It is there, sharp and searing, as she stares at the bedroom wallpaper, the delicate black-on-white toile she'd chosen for its delicacy, its smiling maidens with their lambs, shaded by trees in leaf.

Sentry

The little girl is trampling the flowers. For the past half hour, Helen has watched her move closer to the property line, then finally duck beneath the split-rail fence and edge into the garden. The peonies have only just sprung five days ago, have only just lifted their faces to the world, and Helen has felt the same quickening she does every May, the same pride of a new mother.

She sits with her tea, which she drinks from a fine, hand-painted cup passed down from her great-grandmother in Bremen. She sees no reason to store such treasures away, to use cheaper objects for everyday life. Her ethic is to live among beauty.

The girl next door is a garish bird, clumsy among the garden's tender shoots. She wears a blaring pink shirt and glittered sneakers. There had been another girl with her earlier—an underage babysitter, it seemed—who is now absent. Helen clinks the teacup onto its saucer and rises from her chair.

Outside, she walks with a measured step around the side of the house. As she approaches the garden, the girl freezes in place with the round eyes of a hatchling. Helen walks slowly closer, puts a kindly smile on her face. She peers over the fence to the scrubby yard next door. There is no one there that she can see, no one monitoring the situation.

"Where is your mother?" she enunciates carefully.

The girl shakes her head.

"Do you have a babysitter?"

The girl just looks at her. The pink T-shirt is pocked with faux jewels that spell the word DIVA. A cheap barrette hangs from her hair.

"Is anyone here with you?"

The girl continues to stare. It occurs to Helen that there might be something wrong with her.

"Come," Helen says. She takes the little girl's hand, plump and sticky. They walk up Helen's own driveway and down the one beside it.

The house next door is yellow, as it has always been, although the new occupants have removed the shutters for some reason, denuding it. The former owners had moved into the neighborhood the same year as Helen. One of the daughters had been in school with Rufus and went on to become a successful prosecutor. The parents were themselves professors, always somewhat disheveled, driving a wood-paneled station wagon and letting the house slide into neglect. After the children were gone, they retired to Maine of all places, and Helen had been heartened to see a young family replace them. They would renovate, she was certain, and bring the property up to neighborhood standards. She'd walked over with a batch of peppernuts and introduced herself. The young woman who answered had seemed harried, almost rude. The husband had not even come to the door. Peering inside, Helen had been discouraged to see the front hall still littered with moving boxes, a baby crawling on the dirty floor.

Now, the husband appears to be gone. His diminutive black sports car, with two white stripes like a skunk, no longer pulls out of the driveway in the morning. Helen no longer sees him on warm evenings, drinking beer on the back deck. She sees only the mother, in tight jeans and fur-collared jackets, her blond mane tousled, rushing her daughter to and from a white Toyota. At night, she lounges in her lighted window like an Amsterdam whore. On some days, babysitters make an appearance, girls no older than twelve. On other days, the little girl roams the property alone, wearing shorts in the unmowed grass, her bare legs exposed to deer ticks. Playthings are left out in all weather, gathering puddles in their plastic gullies.

As Helen mounts the neighbor's porch steps with the girl, she puts a hand to the original wrought-iron railing, its curves shamed by a rash of rust. There is a piece of paper stuck to the door.

My mom told me I have to go home. Sorry. Avis is playing outside. —Olivia

Helen whistles softly through her teeth. No ring sounds when she presses the grimy doorbell button, and after a moment she opens the screen door and knocks with her knuckles. When there is no answer, she tries the door handle, finds it unlocked. The hall, now divested of boxes, is stark and uncarpeted, toys scattered across the floor like land mines. There are patched places on the wall where pictures should hang. She calls out uselessly.

Back outside, she pulls the note off the door, puts it in her pocket, and takes the girl around the house's exterior, as if the babysitter might be hiding in a bush. The heels of her brown leather pumps sink into the moist grass, and she pauses to roll the cuffs of her slacks. The girl follows at a distance as Helen goes past the birdbath with its slimy basin of stagnant water, past the blue plastic toddler slide, faded by the sun.

"I'm hungry," Helen hears a small voice announce behind her.

She turns and looks at the girl. She is not a bad-looking child: blue-eyed and honey-haired, but with chubby limbs like bratwurst links.

"Well." Helen bends slightly at the knees, to approach the girl's level. "Why don't you come to my house and have a little snack while we wait for your mommy to come home?"

Helen instructs the girl to remove her muddy sneakers at the front door. After a moment's pause, she leans down to help with the shoelaces, ineffectual with her own long fingernails, and is suddenly revisited by the impatience of motherhood.

Inside, they sit quietly at the table where Helen has left her cup of tea. The girl gingerly eats slices of green apple, looking out the window at her own deserted house. Perhaps this is a good but unlucky child, at the mercy of lazy upbringing. Helen's husband dislikes her tendency to point out every set of incompetent guardians they encounter in public. It is none of her business how people raise their children, he tells her. But it matters, she answers. It matters more than she can explain.

"So, your name is Avis?" Helen asks.

The girl nods.

Helen smiles, cocks her head. "What an interesting name."

It is possible—though unlikely—that the girl's parents have named her for the Latin *avis,* or *bird.* If so, the name would be almost elegant. *Rara avis.* It seems to her that the inspiration here, more probably, was the car rental company.

After the apple, Helen brings the girl to the room where she works on her dollhouses. Avis is silent for a moment, then says, "Can I play with them?"

"These are not for playing," Helen answers. "I make these houses by myself. I make the furniture, too, and the little people."

The girl stares at the collection in front of her, and for the first time Helen sees it the way a child might. There are seven dollhouses in this room, painted shades of ice cream—pale pink, mint green, yellow—and frilled with sugar gables. A paradise.

Helen smiles. "Would you like to help me paint?"

The girl nods her head savagely.

It is easier than Helen might have thought. The girl is careful with the paintbrush, dipping it timidly into a jar of ochre. Helen has given her a simple chair to paint, a throwaway piece, one of several. She herself works on a canopy bed, gluing the blankets and floral-cased pillows into place. They sit in silence together, and it strikes Helen that perhaps it is just as simple as this. Children are, after all, wonderfully malleable at this age. All the girl needs is a model. Already, she is absorbing something of Helen, learning the virtues of quietude, focus, discipline. This, Helen muses, is how she might have spent time with a daughter, if she'd had one. Instead, in some perverse joke, she'd been given a son. If she were thoroughly religious, she might have viewed this as a test from God, customized to engage her individual shortcomings.

After half an hour or so, the girl begins to squirm, and Helen sees that she has turned the paintbrush on herself, making hatch marks along her lower arm.

Helen stands, removes the brush from the girl's hand. "Let's go and see if your mother is home yet."

There is still no car in the driveway, but they go next door anyway. Helen knocks, receives no answer. She and Avis stand on that concrete porch, looking at their own shadows on the door. Things like this happen, Helen knows. This is a country in which mothers sometimes don't come home. Often they are innocuous episodes—a stalled car, a delayed appointment—but equally often they are something worse. Helen begins to imagine the scenarios. A traffic accident, the Toyota overturned at the side of a highway. Or, more terrible, the Toyota driving onward—heading west, or south—with a tankful of fuel.

They return to Helen's house, remove their shoes again, come back inside. Gene and his crew are repairing a collapsed roof on Cannonfield Road today, and he will not be home until dinner.

"Are you tired?" Helen asks the girl.

She nods.

"Come upstairs, and we'll give you a nice bed."

Rufus's room has been transformed into a respectable place for guests. The moment he moved out, Helen had peeled off the dreadful posters with their macabre images and inscrutable words: *Ministry, Tool, Bauhaus.* She scrubbed the room clean, took up the crusted carpet, the blotched bedspread. The new rug is plush white, the walls a buttercup yellow. A vestige of masculinity has been retained in the nautical duvet and navy drapes. On the bookshelf, Helen has arranged framed photographs of Rufus as a little boy. His first-grade photo, with his missing front tooth and shirt collar turned up. A snapshot from a farm trip, with an ice cream cone, shaggy bangs shading one eye.

There are fewer photographs of him as an adolescent, but Helen remembers vividly the pebbled forehead, the dyed black hair incongruously long on top and shaved beneath. She remembers the rotation of concert T-shirts emblazoned with profanities and revolting images. Nude women with their hair on fire.

Her son is now twenty-seven. It has been six years since he dropped out of college and moved into an apartment in the town to the south with chain-smoking roommates. Since then he has been fleetingly employed and released by concerns such as Gold Soundz Records, the Coffee Bean, and the Donut Hole. There has been at least one flunked drug test, a vague cross-country road trip, stretches of unexplained absence. From what Helen can glean, he is now working as a counter boy at the Sweet Spot, wearing a hairnet over his ponytail.

Helen helps Avis out of the grimy DIVA shirt and gives her Rufus's old Block Island T-shirt, which comes down to her knees. She closes the drapes against the afternoon sun. The girl clambers into bed, nestles beneath the covers.

While Avis naps, Helen returns to her post at the kitchen table: her teacup, her window view of the flower garden and the house next door. What was previously a leisurely occupation now feels like a vigil. Still, Helen is caught off guard when the white Toyota turns into the neighbor's driveway, and the girl's mother—in a gauzy white top like a bandage—gets out and goes into the house. Helen sits unmoving, holding the handle of her cup for the few moments before the woman comes bursting back outside. The sound of the screen door banging shut makes Helen jump. She grips the handle of her teacup as she watches the woman walk across the grass, disappear around the far side of the house, and reappear in the driveway. Helen holds her teacup as the woman makes another circuit, calling her daughter's name. Helen sits quietly, as if watching a film reel, and does not move from her chair, does not go to wake the girl. The woman has begun to run in erratic patterns over the grass. Helen watches her bend to look under a rhododendron and beneath the plastic slide. There is a new tremor in her calls, discernible even through the window glass. Helen listens. No sound comes from Rufus's bedroom upstairs. She stands and goes to the stove, puts the teakettle on.

Later, Avis wakes, drowsy and rose-cheeked, and asks for her mother. Helen nearly replies that her mother is home now, that their little visit together is over, but the words do not come. Instead, she hears herself say soothingly, "Your mother called.

She said she'll be home soon, and that you should stay with me a little while longer."

Helen leads Avis to the master bedroom, where she closes the curtains and puts on the television. The girl sits on the bed in the draping Block Island shirt, a thumb in her mouth.

Helen searches the channels for a suitable program. She skips over the animated shows with their exaggerated colors and frenetic blinking. Whatever has become of the educational shows of Rufus's youth, she doesn't know. Everything seems frivolous now, designed to stimulate quickly and cheaply, to dazzle the eye and ear. Helen finally stops at a nature show about meerkats, a wholesome, slow-moving program that she herself finds tremendously calming. She appreciates the earnest faces of the animals, their clean, careful manner, the hushed, expert voice of the female narrator. Avis seems similarly transfixed, watching a mother meerkat shoo a snake out of the family den. A wordless emotion rises in Helen's heart. While the pack forages for food, one animal takes sentry duty, standing erect on its hind legs, exposing itself for the good of the group. Gene does not understand her fondness for this show. He accuses her of forcing human values onto nut-brained rodents. Perhaps this is true. But, she thinks, it is hard to ignore the light in their liquid eyes that suggests something more, an inner province of emotion. It seems to her that they really do mourn their young, that a mother really does wither when a predator enters the burrow in her absence.

Of course, Helen is unable to watch without thinking of Rufus. When he visits, when Helen can persuade him to drive the twenty minutes home, he greets her with the old teenage grimace. He rails against the changes in town, the renovated homes, the refurbished street signs, the expensive new high school building. The town was always bad, he grumbles, but has only grown worse. Everything has been scoured and polished to a cold, slick finish. The few warm shadows that used to exist, the only furrows where authenticity could hope to take refuge—the weedy alcove behind the high school science wing, the concrete-benched town plaza—sacred places to smoke and skateboard—have been expunged. Helen rankles at the moral superiority in his voice. She feels compelled to defend the town, insist that it is a good place to raise children. He does not respond to this, but looks away from her, a cloudy film over his eyes.

At such moments she is overtaken by a nebulous sense of regret. She is revisited primarily, curiously, by contrition for having discouraged his interest years ago in the professor-neighbors' daughter. At the time, Helen had considered the girl unfeminine and coarse-featured, of mediocre breeding. Now, she would be delighted, overjoyed—she would give almost anything—to see him with a woman like that.

She and Avis watch television on the bed until the sun goes down. At the start of a show about whales, Avis begins to wiggle and whine. Helen realizes she has eaten nothing more than an apple since noon.

"Would you like to help me cook dinner? What should we make?" Helen asks, hearing the nervous edge in her voice. She hasn't thought this far, hasn't considered dinner. She hasn't considered Gene's return from work.

Hastily, she helps Avis change back into her own clothing. Downstairs, they look in the kitchen cupboard together. Avis selects an ancient box of wagon wheel pasta, and Helen finds ingredients for brown gravy. She allows herself a glance at the house next door, sees the windows lit yellow. There is a falling feeling inside her, a kind of accelerating confusion, that she attributes to hunger.

When Gene comes in the door, Helen flashes a smile. She stirs the gravy with one hand, gesturing with the other to the girl standing stone-faced beside her.

"This is Avis from next door," she says brightly. "Her mother asked us to watch her tonight. Just a little favor."

Gene pauses in midstep, hugging a paper grocery bag. "What next door?"

"That house." Helen gestures briskly to the side. "We're making pasta for dinner. Right, honey?"

Avis stares dolefully at Gene, who comes in and puts the grocery bag into the refrigerator, minus one bottle. He loosens the cap with a claw-shaped toggle and takes a drink.

"What's this now? We're babysitting?"

"Just for tonight." Helen looks at Avis. "We've been having a lot of fun, right?"

Gene grumbles and retreats to the den. A moment later, Helen hears the sound of the television, rough male voices and gunshots.

When Helen turns around again, she sees that Avis has climbed onto a chair and is looking out the window toward her house. Helen comes up beside her, for a moment expecting to see police cars next door, and reaches to unhook the curtains.

"Come, honey, let's make the gravy together."

"Where's my mommy?"

Helen puts a hand to Avis's shoulder, feels the warmth of skin beneath the shirt. The girl flinches, pulls away.

"She'll be back tomorrow. She told me that you should stay here, just for tonight." Helen breathes in. "Don't worry, I'm going to take care of you."

Helen feels a tingle of pride as she says this, as if she has won some private contest. She thinks of the woman next door, hurriedly dialing the telephone right now, or perhaps sitting quietly by herself. Is there any chance that she is reviewing the course of her actions, narrowing them down, pinpointing the careless decisions that have led here? Most likely not, Helen concludes. She feels that she understands women like this. Avis's mother will not pause to examine her own role, but hasten to place blame. She will call the mother of the babysitter, Olivia, who'd left her daughter alone. She will blame that girl, that mother. Still, Helen feels a twist of pity. It is a harsh lesson for any parent, no matter how deserving.

When the gravy is done, the pasta cooked, Helen shows Avis where to place the cloth napkins on the table, where to put the forks and water glasses. This may be, as far as Helen knows, her first encounter with a fully set table, a family dinner. She calls Gene, who slouches out of the den and opens a new bottle. There is no booster seat in the house, so Avis sits sunken on a full-sized chair. Gene, at the head of the table, shifts uncomfortably. They eat quietly for a few minutes, the table trembling from some repetitive movement of Avis's. As Helen watches the girl spear her wagon wheels, one by one, she sways with the sudden premonition of a knock at the door. For a moment she waits—breathing deeply, composing herself—but the knock does not come.

It is good, Helen reminds herself, for the girl to be here, in a house like this. Her home is an extension of her own self as she would present it to the world. The structure, once a single-story ranch, the stylistic peer of its 1950s neighbors, is now indistinguishable from the newly built houses on teardown lots. She has added a second story, adorned it with arched-eyebrow gables. She has overlaid the concrete porch with bluestone, rebuilt the steps with ashlar risers. And, in keeping with the prevailing aesthetic, she has added craftsman-style columns and a vaulted beadboard ceiling.

Unlike Rufus, she has welcomed the changes around her. She appreciates the care that the town's meticulous new families have exhibited in their renovations and landscaping, bespeaking a larger set of kindred values. Rather than threatened, Helen feels comforted by this influx of discriminating young people, flush with money and beauty, who have chosen to live here. The appreciation is mutual, she imagines. As a longtime resident, she deserves part of the credit for making Old Cranbury so attractive to newcomers, a place with a well-rooted citizenry, upholders of community standards.

The interior of her home is equally reflective of her taste and character, and potentially instructive to a child. The living room is formal in the old style, with a Persian rug, Louis XVI settee, damask curtains edged with tassels. A large, gilt-lined table displays her most prized dollhouse, a three-story Victorian. A satinwood display cabinet showcases her family heirlooms—porcelain bells, plates, beer steins—emblazoned with the coat of arms of the Free Hanseatic City of Bremen. These are objects with roots in proven, time-tested culture. We are the stewards of our culture, Helen believes, responsible for shepherding it safely into the future. Helen feels pity for children of parents with no understanding of this, who dispose of the past like so much used toilet tissue.

Her own son has disparaged her concern for appearances. As she notes of so many American youths, he has learned to prize individual freedom above all else, even at the expense of civilized manners and common decency. It is, at the core, a sad misunderstanding. He has never been able to hear her, or has willfully blocked her out, when she tries to explain that her attention to dress, to housekeeping, to the front shrubs and flower boxes, is not about impressing others. There is no such servility in it. On the contrary, it is a matter of self-regard, a concerted lifting of the individual in example to the many. This is the way the world works, she has tried to tell him, the way it has always worked since the beginning. Those who miss this truth, or ignore it, will lose—and always have.

She looks at Avis in her gravy-dripped shirt, poking at a wagon wheel with her finger. The exertions of the day descend upon Helen all at once, make her posture begin to hunch. Still, she forces herself to make conversation with Gene, to ask about Cannonfield Road, pretend to listen. When there is a pause, she smiles at Avis and says, "And what did *we* do today?"

The girl looks down at her plate.

"Did we paint together? Did you help me paint furniture for the dollhouse?"

There is a quiver at the sides of the girl's lips, but she does not answer. Helen rises to clear the table. She goes into the kitchen with the stack of dishes and runs the water over them.

"Helen," Gene calls.

She comes back in and sees that Avis is crying, her face crumpled pink.

Gene stays in the den as Helen helps Avis wash her face and brush her teeth. Through the floor, she hears the jangling sound track of another 1970s vigilante film. She puts Avis back in the Block Island T-shirt and sits with her in Rufus's room. There are no longer any children's books in the house, so she retells the events of their day together. The girl looks at her without expression, then her face crumples again. The alarming pink color returns, the tears mingling with mucous and dripping into her mouth. Helen sits and waits, watching the contortions of the little girl's face until she finally expends herself. Within moments, she has dropped to the pillow, asleep.

Helen, too, feels ready to collapse. As she is pulling on her nightgown, Gene creaks up the stairs and puts his head into the bedroom.

"You didn't tell me she was *sleeping* here."

"It's just for one night."

"Who are these people again? I've never heard you mention them."

"The next-door neighbors. The mother couldn't find a babysitter." This is true in a way, Helen thinks.

"Well, you didn't ask me."

"Don't worry, you don't have to do anything. Just watch your *Death Wish*." She turns away.

Helen wakes early. She lies quietly, feeling an unidentified spark, and after a few moments remembers Avis. Slipping out of bed and into the hallway, she turns the knob of Rufus's bedroom. The girl's head is still there, resting on the pillow. From this distance, the unfamiliar mass of hair looks to Helen like the fur of a small animal. She closes the door and retreats, lets the girl sleep.

She dresses in front of the full-length mirror. She pins her hair in an artful fashion, arranging a swag to cover the thinning place at the hairline. In a buttoned blouse and bias-cut skirt, she believes herself to look younger and more feminine than other women her age, those who wear robes and slippers in the house and sometimes in public. Even if she doesn't step outdoors all day, even if it's only to please herself when she passes a mirror in her own home, it is always worth the effort to look nice.

Today, before bringing her home, Helen might like to take Avis shopping, buy her some pretty clothes. She pictures a scallop-collared shirt with pearly buttons, a skirt with pleats.

They will have to go quickly, before Gene awakes, before the lights come on in the house next door. If the clothing stores are not yet open for business, perhaps they will go for breakfast somewhere.

Helen rouses the girl, who whines and shrinks away. It takes a few struggling minutes to pull her into a sitting position and to squeeze her into her clothing. This is followed by a tumultuous visit to the bathroom, a discovery of wet underwear. This is all right, Helen thinks. They can buy new panties, too.

Downstairs, Helen helps Avis with her shoes, looping the laces in careful bows. Lastly, she tries to do something about the knotty hair—but when Helen applies her boar bristle hairbrush, the girl screeches and pulls away. Like a kitten, she bounds into the living room and climbs onto the settee, her shoe soles digging into the upholstery. Helen feels her blood ripple. So, here it is at last, true evidence of the girl's upbringing. She takes a breath. This is an important moment. It is crucial to control her response, to deliver her message correctly and firmly.

"Take your shoes off the sofa, please," she commands.

Avis looks at her, thumb in mouth, and Helen detects a dark glimmer in her stare. It strikes her as the practiced gaze of the chronically guilty, which the girl's mother has allowed her to master. Helen lowers her voice, steadies its tremor.

"I said take your shoes off the sofa, please. Now."

Avis scrambles off the settee altogether and begins a directionless sprint, crying, "No! I wan' my mommy!" Her sneakers slap through the hallway into the kitchen.

This is all theatrics, Helen understands. She knows the girl to be four years old, at least, and four-year-olds speak more fluently than this. She is positive that Rufus had composed complex sentences at this age.

Helen has just cornered the girl in the kitchen when the phone rings, and cannot risk going to answer it. She hears the vibrations of her husband's voice through the ceiling, then the drum of his footsteps on the stairs.

When he comes into the kitchen, Helen looks sternly at Avis. "Please say 'good morning' to Mr. Tanner," she commands.

Avis does not reply, but retreats farther into the corner, flanked by the trash can. Helen looks at her husband, the rigid mouth and scored forehead, and understands that something has happened.

"Rufus is in the hospital," Gene says. "They're saying he lost consciousness at a party. I don't know. Maybe it was drugs." Gene stands in the kitchen with his arms at his sides. "They said he's awake now. Being monitored."

"What?"

Gene turns from her, his hands shaking as he fumbles in the drawer for the car keys.

"Goddamn it," he mumbles.

Helen stands in the kitchen in her buttoned blouse and skirt, watching her husband's movements.

"Get your coat," he tells her.

It is May, of course, and getting a coat makes no sense. Helen does not move.

"What are you doing?" he asks.

"Nothing," she answers.

Her voice is faint, as if coming from a faraway place. She feels strangely weightless, plucked out of time. She struggles to picture her son in a hospital room. With a poor understanding of drugs, of what they might do to a person, all she can imagine is jaundiced skin, chapped lips. She has a vision of the room itself, the speckled gray visitor's chairs, the glowing green numbers of a heart rate monitor. In her mind, her son lies in a narrow bed, strapped to an IV. He looks at her accusingly through sunken eyes. The eyes of an intruder. She does not, she realizes, want to see any of this.

She continues to stand in place, blocking the little girl in the corner. The thing that Gene has presented her with is too large, like a wall of water rushing toward her. She must be absolved, for the moment, of any responsibility but survival.

When Gene asks, "Are you coming or not?" she shakes her head. No words come.

After he leaves, Helen lowers herself to the chair by the kitchen window. Avis has forgotten her game now, vacated the corner. Helen can only hope that she is still somewhere in the house. She draws back the window curtain, returns it to its hook. The white Toyota is no longer in the driveway next door.

She rises, goes mechanically to the sink, fills the teakettle. While the water is warming, she looks for Avis. The house is utterly quiet, with only the sound of her shoe heels tapping the hardwood floor. She finds the girl in the living room, on her knees, peering into the Victorian dollhouse. Her head is bent sideways, unaware of being watched. It is a perfect picture, a suspended, breathless moment of childhood. Helen stands quietly, guarding it.

There is a sharp knock at the door, a series of hammering raps. The girl looks up and finds Helen in the doorway.

"Hello, Mr. Tanner, Mrs. Tanner," a voice booms, "Old Cranbury Police."

The knocking ceases, giving way to an extended pause. Helen stands in place, holding the girl's gaze. The instinct to answer the door, that forceful inborn decorum, bubbles up in her. There is, however, something in the girl's eyes, some tunneling, bottomless need, that overwhelms it. Helen feels that she must not look away.

She is conscious of her figure being sheltered from view by the display cabinet. And as long as Avis remains crouched like that behind the dollhouse, she will not be visible from the living room windows. The sound of the doorbell peals through the house, and the hard knocking resumes. Avis begins to stand, but Helen gestures for her to stay down—and, miracle of miracles, she does. The police officer calls out again, less robustly this time, a note of futility in his voice. Then, there is quiet. Finally, the sound of a car ignition in the driveway.

Helen feels a fizz of relief. They will have one more night. It will be best to spend the evening upstairs, she thinks, behind the bedroom curtains.

She will talk to the police, of course, in her own time. When she does, she will simply tell the truth: that the girl was left alone, that she'd taken it upon herself, as a concerned neighbor, to look after her. It is the mother they should be questioning.

The mother. This is what she will tell them, what she will repeat and repeat, until they understand.

Gradually, a low whistle comes through the house. Helen startles, then remembers the teakettle. The whistle amplifies, gaining force like a strengthening wind. Avis is still crouched in place. The kettle's shriek rises, becomes penetrating. Helen takes a step toward the girl, extending a hand to help her.

Elevations

Mark is arranging terrier pillows in the back when the door chime jingles. A smartly dressed couple comes into the store, a parrot-faced blonde with a hard leather purse at her armpit and a neat man in clear Lucite eyeglasses—gay, or German. They exchange smiling nods with Harris, who is bent at the window over a vintage watering can display.

Abandoning the pillows, Mark retreats farther back to a box of new inventory. A cache of rubbery, handmade insects. Harris has made a case for their playfulness, their novelty, for the arthropod silhouette's outpacing the antler and the owl. Each piece is lovingly painted, some in iridescent shades of blue and green that to Harris are reminiscent of Fabergé. The insects were supposedly created as part of some larger installation that was gunned down by the town, and Harris is hopeful that their notoriety will appeal to customers. The people here love a conversation piece, a flash of rebellion on their own terms. Mark lifts a smooth-domed beetle from the box, Aegean blue, its underside so realistically ridged that he shudders.

After the statutory period of quiet browsing, Harris straightens himself in the window and addresses the customers in a creamy baritone.

"That's a nineteenth-century Russian sleigh bed," he says, stepping toward the couple with a shuffle in his gait that means his knees are hurting again.

The blonde exclaims in delight, and the dance begins: Harris's lavish descriptions and the customers' musical declarations, as if each object were hand-curated just for them.

"Oh, yes, I knew you'd find that. It's a Zapotec blackware olla pot. We were in Oaxaca last year, but didn't have enough room in our suitcases to bring back everything we wanted."

Here in the store, lined with wood wainscoting like an aged oak cask, objects from around the globe radiate casual exoticism. Harris's offhand way of cataloging them is designed to flatter, presuming the customers' shared worldliness. *Oaxaca*—naturally. He won't mention the security guards at the hotel. He won't mention the beggars on the street, the women with their snaking braids and smudged children. He won't mention the way he'd haggled with the vendor in his oversized sun hat, Mark cringing at his side; the way he'd gallantly conceded the last few pesos before tucking the rest back into the money belt under his shirt.

Oaxaca had been a turning point for Mark. Coming up the jet bridge at Newark behind Harris and his engorged suitcase, he'd felt that he was walking against a reverse magnetic current. The car service had picked them up and squired them back into this softest pocket of the continent, this deepest pouch of forgetfulness. They had closed the door of their house, unloaded their bags, and re-canopied themselves in the safe tarpaulin of their lives.

Since then, Mark has suffered from a dissonant feeling, something like the antipathy of adolescence. He remembers the first time he'd been nettled like this: during a childhood trip to Jamaica, when his family had driven through a shantytown, past cornrowed, bright-uniformed children walking barefoot on the side of the road—and his mother had locked the car doors.

"Oh yes, my partner and I discovered this beauty on our trip to Brittany in '95," Harris is saying, stroking the top of a cherry demilune table.

He pronounces "my partner" without any meaningful beat. Mark does not look up from the box of insects. Harris is in his tangerine polo shirt today, the one he thinks makes him look preppy and straight, but which has become conspicuously tight across his belly. It seems impossible that he hasn't noticed this, and yet there is no kind way to point it out.

While they are triangulating the demilune table, Mark slips out the back door for a cigarette. He feels an urge to call Camille, to hear her sardonic voice, something salted to neutralize the gush of self-congratulation in the showroom.

He calls, tells her about the box of bugs, plays up the bitchiness for her benefit.

"Oh, I *remember* those," Camille sings. "This old man glued them all over his neighbor's house. It was supposed to be an avant-garde installation but it turned into a big scandal. People said it was bringing down property values."

"Of course. Well, at least they're on consignment." Mark pulls on his American Spirit, the mellow varietal, a half-stride toward quitting.

"Are you smoking?"

Mark exhales. "God, you *people.* So what?"

"Just asking. Go ahead if you want."

Camille had been the first to leave the city. Mark and Harris followed later the same year—in the midst of the Wall Street encampments, the haphazard arrests—and joined her in the same cosmically quaint town an hour north on the train line. What incredible fortune, they agreed, that life should have washed them on this same high rock together. They would throw scandalous parties, now on ambrosial back patios rather than spongy rooftops, more *Gatsby* than *Bright Lights.* Then Camille gave birth, got divorced. Mark and Harris had never really liked her husband and toasted her freedom with a bottle of Cristal, but frolicsome times had not followed. Instead, over the course of the past year, Camille seems to have pulled away, succumbing to the plague of insecurity that besets all single women alike. Her foray into Internet dating has become something heavy, secretive. She no longer calls Mark with stories that make him laugh until he wheezes.

Harris appears in the doorway. Mark hangs up, stubs his cigarette.

"Come in," Harris stage-whispers, "I want to introduce you to these people."

"Why?"

"Oh, just come in."

Inside, the customers are smiling expectantly.

"Mark, this is Gretchen and Caspar Von Mauren."

Gretchen. Not what Mark would have guessed.

"They just bought one of those gorgeous old homes on Cannonfield and are looking for a designer."

"It's a bit of a mess right now," Gretchen says in a voice that is surprisingly deep. "But we have big renovation plans. Harris tells us this is something you do?"

Immediately, Mark feels exposed. Most likely he is the same age as these people, but inside he is still a boy, a student.

"Yes," he says as casually as he can, "and I especially enjoy working with historic homes."

"How serendipitous!" the woman pronounces, glancing at her gay German husband. "I'm so glad we came in today. You never know who you'll meet. Well, Mark, could we ask you to come by one day and have a look?"

Mark glances at Harris, who is smiling paternally at him.

"Of course. Which house is it?"

"Four-thirty Cannonfield."

Mark pretends to think, pulls out his phone, pretends to check his calendar.

"They're taking the olla pot *and* the demilune table. They put cash down on the spot."

"That's great."

"I had a feeling when they walked in. You know how sometimes you can just tell? I knew by the guy's shirt, the French cuffs, that he was all business. And the way the woman's eyes scanned around, quick like an eagle. She's had practice."

"Like an eagle sighting its prey."

"What? Why do you always have to mock everyone?"

"Who's mocking? I just didn't see anything so special about them. Also, I drove by the house. It's a disaster."

"So what? You don't have to deal with the outside."

Mark doesn't answer. It's true that he hasn't been hired for a big project in years. In a recession, even the eternal clamor for interior design is muted. Only high-end firms with physical showrooms can expect to thrive. So he's been spending more time at the store, helping with bookkeeping and inventory.

"It's perfect timing," Harris continues. "You'll probably finish up by next summer, just in time to go somewhere. We still need to do Africa. I was thinking Tanzania." Harris pauses. "While we're there, maybe we could go on a safari."

Mark's lips tighten. A safari will mean staying in a luxury lodge, surrounded by primitive villages with no access to clean water. It will mean dropping enough money to feed one of those villages for a year, in exchange for the indulgence of looking at wild animals that would prefer not to be looked at. He has no interest in feeling like a descended extraterrestrial again, touching ground just long enough to take something.

"I don't mind going to Tanzania," he pronounces carefully, "but only if we can stay in a village and do something useful."

"Oh, honey." Harris stares for a moment, smiling, as if at a child who has said something amusing. "You're not serious, are you?"

Mark is quiet. It is at times like these when he feels their age difference most sharply, feels a returning undertow of regret like a soft tug in his gut. It is at these moments, unbalanced and vulnerable, that Seth sweeps back to him in a flood, like a mythical ocean creature. No future there, no destination. It would have been like riding a sea horse, dipping and diving and drowning, over and over. He was in Nairobi, last Mark heard. He was in Cairo, Marrakesh, Damascus. It's been fifteen years. The choices that had seemed fungible, reversible, whimsical fifteen years ago have finally cemented. Time goes in only one direction; a hackneyed truth, but suddenly as dense as iron. Their bodies, young and beautiful as they were then, will never again be seen on this earth.

Mark looks at Harris, large and able. His autumn-brown eyes give the warmth of a thousand hearth fires.

"We used to talk about it, you know," Mark reminds him quietly. "We used to talk about how important it was to give back. You agreed that maybe we could join a volunteer service someday."

"Someday we could still do that."

"But why not now?" Mark bleats. "Why not rent out the house and go away for a while?"

"When you say volunteer service, do you mean like the Peace Corps?"

Mark lets a beat pass. "Yes, like that. Now that we're married, we can apply as a couple."

"Oh, sweetheart, you know we can't do that now. Not with the store."

Mark doesn't answer. He doesn't mention that he's begun filling out their applications for next year. He is hopeful that his architecture degree and sustainable design training might make him an attractive candidate. Perhaps there is a need in some far-flung outpost for environmentally responsible interiors. He imagines himself wearing a bandanna in an equatorial African village, reflooring huts with cork, lining walls with hemp board. As for Harris, his art history degree won't count for much, but with some volunteer experience at home and language training, he might make an adequate English teacher.

"I'm not saying we should *never* do it," Harris continues. "But there's plenty of time. We're still getting settled here, the store's just taking off." He pauses, then adds, "And your business is starting to blossom."

Mark nods his head, does not argue. On the Peace Corps website, there is a whole section detailing the strain on romantic relationships for volunteers who serve without their partners. Twenty-seven months is a long time. There are many scenarios to consider before one partner should embark without the other, many eventualities to discuss before sending in a solo application.

When he and Harris were first in love, they sometimes played a game called "Deal Breaker." What degree of sin or betrayal would make the other leave?

"What if I kissed your brother?" Mark would ask.

"What if I put up Laura Ashley drapes?" Harris would counter, laughing.

"What if I wanted a threesome with a woman?"

"What if I wore whale-print golf pants?"

It has been a long time since they've played "Deal Breaker." There is a comfortable formality to their evenings now, the two of them reading in bed, a stack of books and magazines upon each nightstand, a sense that every waking moment must be squeezed for gain of further information. Mark can't help but contrast this with their first helium weeks together, holed up in Harris's Bond Street apartment, lightened by the exertion of talk and sex, when he wondered if he would ever read a book again.

Harris accompanies Mark on his consultation visit with the Von Maurens. Together, they drive away from the dollhouse center of town, through softer acres with gated residences hidden in the trees. It's true that Mark loves the aesthetic refinement of this area. He loves the exquisitely restored farmhouses, the expensive masonry that makes new stone walls appear old, the blanketed show horses. He can't help but thrill to the effortless elegance of the weathered barns, the convertible sports cars—to his sheer proximity to this most rarefied class, peppered with private film stars, financiers, icons of fashion and design. There is an aphrodisiac in this aura of informal exclusivity that is absent from the city and its brassy rivalry.

They pull up to number 430, a flat-faced white saltbox with an ugly blue tarp on the roof. The Ezekiel Slater house, according to the plaque at the side of the door, built in 1740. The date alone, Mark admits, gives him a frisson. He has never worked on anything predating the Victorian era.

Gretchen opens the plank door before he and Harris can knock, her jeweled ears and neck discordant in the rustic doorframe.

She pulls them inside and begins talking. "The elderly woman who lived here didn't do *anything* to the house. I don't think anything's been changed for forty years." She clips over the wood floor in snakeskin pumps. "Anyway, we interviewed designers in the city, but none of them had a feeling for the history. They wanted to do everything new. Then we had a problem with the roof, as you can see, and the historical commission got involved. So now we're in the middle of a big exterior restoration in keeping with their guidelines. Of course that won't affect what we do to the interior."

Mark nods. "But you'll want to be sensitive, regardless."

"Of course," Gretchen chimes. "Anyway, let me show you what we're thinking, then you let us know if you can make it work."

She turns away, and Mark rolls his eyes at Harris, who smirks. They follow her up the narrow staircase, its steps groaning with age. Harris trails behind, his knee joints blasted by late-stage Lyme disease. Probably picked up in the garden during their first weeks in the house, before they'd learned to wear kneesocks.

Caspar Von Mauren appears silently at the top of the staircase, an apparition in white linen. The attic would become his home office. The walls separating the two smaller bedrooms would vanish to create a master suite, and the third bedroom would become a his-and-hers bath. The kitchen pantry would morph into a powder room, and the kitchen itself would grow a glassed-in sunroom.

"The front has to stay the same, I know that. We wouldn't want to change that." Gretchen looks at her husband, as if for confirmation. "And I'm already picturing some of the things from the store in here. The barn-door table right here in the dining room, with the Windsor chairs around it. Also, I'd love to enlarge some of the windows in the back, get some more light in here."

Mark makes notes on his little pad with a metal pen. He fills pages. If these people are serious about their plans, the job will take a good year.

At home, Harris opens a '93 Dom.

Mark shakes his head. "It's not official yet."

"Oh, you know it is. Cheers, and kudos to me for matchmaking."

"Thank you."

"Come on, let's take this to the patio."

They sit at the wrought-iron bistro table and drink. Here it is, their home. Their dream house, a restored Victorian in a neighborhood of restored Victorians, a perfect row of painted ladies. Theirs is yellow with sage trim, a pink-iced porch ceiling. They are bookended by other marzipan confections; their flowering backyard abuts other flowering yards. Their quarter acre is bordered by a lattice-top fence flush with hydrangea bushes and honeysuckle vines. Even the name of their road—Mercy—suits this particular kind of American paradise, this miniature encapsulation of English gardenhood. This is what had appealed to them, this manageable, modest utopia, this antithesis of trashy sprawl. It pains Mark to think that he has outgrown it so quickly.

It will take over a week to prepare an estimate for the Von Maurens. Mark sits in the garden each day with his laptop, staring at the bed of snapdragons Harris has planted. His head fills with fuzz, and his breath becomes shallow. Allergies, he wants to believe.

Three days later, he has not even finished an estimate for the kitchen. Harris returns from the store at six, like any commuting husband, portly and hungry, the king of his castle.

"The Von Maurens came in today. I told them how excited you are about the project." He grins. "They put a deposit on the Windsor chairs. When I mentioned that the woodworker lives in town, they flipped. They want him to carve their initials into the chair combs. These people love to support their local craftsmen, you know."

"And underpaid Mexicans, too."

"Mark, I looked them up today. Do you know who these people are?"

"Um, no?"

"*Gretchen* is a rubber heiress. Her father is a Texas tire baron. And *Caspar* is an actual baron. From Liechtenstein."

"Ha. I knew he was German."

"No, *Liechtensteinien*."

"Oh, please."

"I'm going to invite them for drinks."

"No, you're not."

"Yes, I am."

"Why, Harris? What do we want with these people?"

"Honey, you need to think like a businessman. These people are top rung. They're all over the gala pages. Your design could wind up in *Town & Country*."

"God forbid."

"Oh my God, when did you become such a snob?"

Mark opens his mouth but does not answer. It would be overly hostile to remind Harris that they'd come to this place with an understanding, a quiet contract, a shared touch of irony. They'd come as a pair of anthropologists to masquerade among the natives, or so Mark had thought, to mirror their culture and borrow from its abundance. They were not supposed to adopt it; they were not supposed to blend.

Harris opens a Bordeaux Blanc while the Von Maurens rave about the house and everything in it. Gretchen touches the objects on the tables, picks them up, turns them in her hands. She taps the Ghost chair with a fingernail and lowers herself finally into one of the antique fauteuils, letting her fingers splay upon the saffron Bergamo upholstery. She points to the flokati ottoman that rests like a sheepdog at her feet.

"Mark's design," Harris trumpets.

Through the avid eyes of visitors, Mark can't help but be pleased with their home. They have achieved an impeccable mix of new and old, sleek and textured, Mark's eye for classic symmetry counterbalancing Harris's more exuberant tastes. Mark has had to hold him back from too much Jonathan Adler, tempting as it is. Already, he regrets rubber-stamping the eight-by-ten Union Jack rug in the living room. It dominates, limits their options. Also, he would like to sell the third-rate Hirst spin painting that they'd bought at the height of the market, but which has lost its dimension over the years and become a flat thing.

As the swooning continues, Mark becomes resentful. Perhaps he should take their fixation on decor as a compliment to his designer's eye, but it is edging into a presumption that he and Harris have no other interests. He tries to change the topic of conversation to something political, global. It occurs to him that a Liechtenstein baron might have something to say about the EU crisis.

"The whole endeavor was misguided from the start," Caspar responds without expression or gesture.

"I just have to say I love your window seat there." Gretchen points. "Is that original to the house?"

Harris opens a second bottle of wine, a third. He is glowing. This is not what Mark had pictured when he'd pictured the parties they'd have. The baron seems to be relaxing a bit, leaning back in his fauteuil. Gretchen keeps touching Harris's arm as they talk, as if she is hungry for something.

Harris is now cherub pink. He leans in, and in a breathlessly intimate voice says, "So, tell me. Are you two youngsters thinking of having a family?"

Mark stares at him. During the bubble of silence that follows, he feels himself levitate slightly.

At last, Gretchen smiles serenely. "Not until the house is done."

Harris leans back, showcasing his jolly belly, and glances at Mark with a look that says, *How nice for them.*

A flame lashes Mark's insides. "We've talked about joining the Peace Corps," he pronounces.

The baron does not appear to have heard. Gretchen's eyes widen. "Oh," she intones in her deep-sea voice. "That's so admirable. I have so much respect for people who do that kind of thing. I can't even imagine."

They move on to Armagnac. The Von Maurens inhabit the pair of fauteuils like extensions of the damask itself. Mark rarely sits on these himself, for fear of flattening the cushions, taxing the bowed legs. His love for them is jealous. And yet he could sell them, he thinks. He *should* sell them, sell everything in the room, escort these guests away, divest himself.

The next morning, Mark confronts Harris. "I can't believe you asked if they want to have children."

"I don't think that's too intrusive, do you? People ask all the time. People ask *us.*" He looks meaningfully at Mark.

"What if they're infertile? What if they've tried and can't?"

"Like I said, people ask *us* all the time. And *we* obviously can't conceive children. There are other ways to have a family you know."

Mark is silent.

"I really think we should talk to Camille."

"I've already said I don't want to do that."

"Well, what *do* you want to do?"

Again, Mark is silent. Harris knows that Mark has never wanted children. Part of the relief of coming out at eighteen was knowing that he would never be expected to anchor himself that way. He'd be released from conventional latches;

free to travel, sleep with whomever he wanted, reinvent himself infinitely. That was the upside of losing popular approval. But then, like piercings and tattoos, gay culture had insinuated itself in the mainstream, and all at once, same-sex marriage had become legal. This, despite years of activism, had taken Mark by surprise—and had coincided with the deepening of his relationship with Harris.

"We have so much to offer. A stable home environment, a great town, financial security. It would be a shame to keep it all to ourselves."

He is trotting out the practical argument, but his eyes tell a different story. Mark has seen the way Harris melts over infants. It was amusing, at first, the way he behaved like a woman overtaken by maternal hormones. Now, it makes Mark's groin turn cold.

"What you want is a *baby*," Mark says. "But you're forgetting that they're only babies for five minutes, then they're snotty teenagers and have to go to college. Do you know how much college is going to cost in eighteen years?"

"What else would we do with that money?"

"Are you serious?" Mark goes quiet. He does not have the strength to continue this argument. If Harris can't think of a better way to spend—what? two hundred thousand dollars?—then they are truly ill matched.

The larger truth is that Mark is not interested in the kind of sentimental living, the relentless diminution, that parenting imposes. A child would drain all of their energy, all of their resources—both of which could be better spent on bigger issues. How could a man he loves bear witness to this ruptured, calamitous world without taking action? Their circumstances *are* perfect. They are two men in good health, somewhat young. The house can be rented, the store leased and reopened at a later date. There is no excuse not to go, not to make their best years count.

He thinks of Seth, sandaled and dusty in some medina. The thought makes him hate himself. To any observer, he has dwelled too long in pampered comfort to peel off the caul of materialism. He has terminally softened.

After a long moment, Harris says, "I know what you're thinking. That we should devote ourselves to saving the world." There is no sarcasm in his voice. "But the way I see it, having a child, or adopting one, would be a way to do that. It would be a meaningful contribution. It's no small effort, committing ourselves to a human being who needs us."

Mark is suddenly tired. It is too early in the morning to discuss this. He ends the conversation with a kiss to Harris's stubbled cheek, a stroke to the sleeve of his robe. Harris returns the kiss, his brown eyes softening, turning liquid with hope.

On Monday, Mark completes an estimate for the full scope of services. He will supervise the renovation and work with the clients to select furnishings, cabinetry, appliances, lighting. To justify postponing his own travels to the Third World, he is compelled to furtively raise his prices by 10 percent across the board. He pulls in his breath and types in the total—$342,000—plus contingency fees for special purchases.

The packet, printed on heavy stock, easily weighs two pounds. Rather than e-mailing it, he drives to Cannonfield Road and places the parcel into the mailbox. His logo, MARK TILLEY DESIGNS, in lowercase Courier, dwells in the bottom corner of the envelope like a centipede.

Gretchen Von Mauren calls the same afternoon. Only indignation could prompt such a call, Mark thinks. She is offended by his audacity.

"Hello, Mrs. Von Mauren," he says, his voice lowering involuntarily.

"Mark, I've looked over the estimate. I'd like you to throw it out."

He drops onto the Ghost chair. "My apologies, Mrs. Von Mauren. Perhaps I should have spoken with you in more depth about what you and your husband hope to achieve."

"No, no. That's not what I mean. What I want you to do is throw out the numbers, don't worry about the money, don't worry about completion dates. There is no budget, there is no timeline. We want this house to be a showstopper. Believe me, I wouldn't be talking to you if I didn't trust your instincts."

Mark's eyes rest on the Hirst over the mantel, a citrus vortex with an empty center.

"Well, I don't know what to say. Thank you, Gretchen, for the vote of confidence."

"So you'll draft a master plan for us?"

"Yes, yes." He has a nauseous feeling from looking at the painting. "I'll have to come over to take another look before I can start."

"Come tomorrow."

☆ ☆ ☆

He begins to hand-draft the interior elevations. It is already August. They'll have to skip Provincetown this year. Truth be told, they've both tired of the high-season flamboyance, the flapping colors, the vibrating sexual energy. They are no different from other middle-aged couples, perhaps, in obeying this instinct to slow down and turn inward.

Harris announces that he will need to hire someone at the store while Mark is working on the project. "I'll put an ad in the paper. Unless we know someone?"

Mark calls Camille.

"I don't think I'd be good at customer service," she says, "but I do know someone you might like."

The woman comes in for an interview. Madeleine, a transplant from Charles Street, near their old apartment. She doesn't have knowledge of vintage decor, but is attractive and poised.

"She might take away some of the gayness," Harris quips. "I didn't see a wedding ring, did you? She must be single, or maybe divorced?"

"Maybe she's a lesbian."

"Camille would have mentioned *that.*"

This is it, then. Mark smiles sadly. It's good that Harris will have the help he needs, he tells himself, a kind face in the morning, someone to admire his rubber insects, maybe keep one on her desk like a pet. It will make it easier to leave.

☆ ☆ ☆

Finally, in late September, Mark sits in the ancient kitchen of the Ezekiel Slater house and shows Gretchen Von Mauren the plan view, the walls of windows in the sunroom. She thumbs through them, nodding.

"And green design." She taps him lightly on the arm. "I'd like to hear your ideas for green design. Ways to incorporate environmentally sustainable materials, renewable wood and bamboo, et cetera. While retaining the colonial flavor of the house, of course."

"I'll put some examples into a portfolio. Then we can go through it together and start putting in orders."

"We really want a blend of the old and the new," Gretchen says, gesturing a circle, "and light. Lots of light."

"Do you want to enlarge the windows even further?"

"Mmm . . ." She trails off, as if staring through the kitchen wall. Her hair is glossy, cut in a carefully serrated fringe. When she looks back at Mark, there is a girlish snap in her eyes. "My cousin just married his boyfriend, you know. I think it's so wonderful that people are finally coming around. People should be free to love whoever they want."

Mark smiles uncertainly. "Absolutely." Gretchen holds his gaze for an uncomfortable moment. He shifts in his chair and pats the pages in front of him. "Okay, so larger windows? I'll revise the drawings and have them back to you by next week."

"Oh. Next week?"

"I can try for Friday, but I can't guarantee it."

Driving back into town, a shark-gray Lexus follows too close to his bumper, and Mark feels his neck muscles tense.

He sees the pouf-haired form of a woman driver and has an overwhelming urge to flip her the bird. Instead, he takes a long breath and pumps the brakes. The Lexus recedes behind him. It would be so easy to become a misanthrope, he thinks, to judge others by their Barbour jackets, their piano-key teeth. These are people with their own heartaches, he scolds himself, their own generosities.

Coming into the store, he finds Harris squatting on his haunches, singing with a little girl. The new shop assistant, Madeleine, stands beside them, beaming. Harris is going bananas, making hand gestures to accompany "Twinkle, Twinkle, Little Star." The child is giggling, twirling her skirt. When Harris glances at Mark, his eyes are ablaze.

Mark hesitates. "She's adorable," he offers.

"Harris asked me to bring her in," Madeleine apologizes.

This is the first time she has given them a glimpse of her personal life. Mark shoots a look at Harris, but he is blind to the message, distracted by his prolonged eye-lock with the child.

In their tradition of imagining the hidden lives of others, they have mused for weeks about their inscrutable shop assistant. She is always pleasant, but with the air of someone with a secret, they've concluded. According to Camille, her husband had been a coworker of Camille's own ex-husband in Manhattan, but underwent a radical change after moving to the suburbs. She delivered this information in a breathy voice, but when pressed for more, demurred. *Madeleine doesn't like to talk about it. It's been a challenge for her.*

* * *

Through the fall and winter, Mark draws and redraws the elevations for the Ezekiel Slater house. The Von Maurens have offered an hourly rate rather than a lump sum, which has been quickly compounding in his favor. He has been straining for ideas. Perhaps the clients will ultimately lose patience and fire him. Perhaps this is his private hope. If he were released from this job, there would be nothing holding him here. All winter, the desire to leave has been expanding in him, crowding everything else. It has begun to push against his diaphragm, constricting his lungs. The air of this beautiful place, now so cold, so oxygenated and clean—this brisk vapor of the country rich—has begun to sear his individual cilia.

He approaches Harris one last time. It is a wet night in March, in the dead space before spring. The air is so raw that it invades the living room. Mark finds Harris bending at the fireplace in his dragon robe and sheepskin moccasins, clumsily arranging kindling. From behind, he looks corpulent, effete. Mark sits quietly on the Ghost chair. When Harris turns and sees him there, he smiles broadly, but the smile dims as Mark begins to speak.

"Well, tell me then," Harris says gently, after a moment. He drags the shaggy ottoman closer to Mark and settles onto it. "Where would you like to go?"

"I don't know. It doesn't matter." Mark hears the petulance in his own voice.

"It sounds to me like you're down on yourself about the Von Maurens. You're afraid they won't like the work, and you're coming up with a contingency plan. Am I right?"

"You know that's not it. You know this is something I've been thinking about for a long time."

"Listen. How about we go volunteer somewhere for a couple of weeks so you can get it out of your system?"

Mark shakes his head. "That's not enough. That's not a life change."

"I understand," Harris says. "And it makes sense. It does. It makes sense for kids right out of college. It makes sense for retired people. But, honey, it doesn't make sense for us."

Mark stares at his fleshy cheeks, at the pink skin at his temple where the hair is thinning.

What if I became just like them?

What if I went away without you?

"But I've been thinking"—Harris touches Mark's knee—"and I do agree that we should find a way to help others. I was thinking we could donate a share of the store's proceeds to charity. Ten percent? You and I could pick a charity, or more than one."

Mark listens. There is a click of satisfaction on a buried level inside him—donating to charity is a fine idea—but the rest of his being is unmoved. He stares at the hairline of his partner, his *husband,* and feels possessed by a single imperative.

"I'm sorry," Mark mumbles. "It's not enough."

Harris takes his hands from Mark's knee and lays them in his lap. A long moment passes. When Harris speaks again, he looks tired.

"Listen," he says. "You can go if you want. If that's what you really want. I'll miss you, but I don't want to be the one holding you back."

Mark looks down at the Union Jack rug, that emblem of revolution and youth. A memory returns to him from their wedding night, lying naked on the sand of Race Point with a bottle of Tia Maria, beneath the stars at the tip of the land, suspended between sea and sky, spinning with the liquor and the hugeness of their future.

Harris pushes himself up slowly. There is an inward look on his face that means his knees are acting up. For an instant, Mark is ashamed. There is a soft concavity in the ottoman where Harris had been sitting. Mark listens to him go out of the room, hears the bathroom sink running.

Harris comes back into the living room, the sleeves of his dragon robe hanging limp, its silken sash taut around his middle.

"I meant to ask, have you seen the new shop where the chiropractor used to be?"

"No, what's there now?"

"It's a New Age thing. It's called New Altitudes."

"Well, that's brave," Mark says. They are speaking normally, as if the previous conversation hadn't happened. "Who would open a store like that in this economy?"

"There were people in there when I went. It's mainly books and CDs, but there are some interesting pieces, too. There's a charango from Peru. Gorgeous. I heard the guy saying he was down there with the tribe people. I was thinking, if you don't want Africa, maybe we can go to South America next year."

"Who is this guy?"

"Some strange bird, all dressed up like a guru. I've never seen him before. He's got plenty of charisma, though. He calls himself Apocatequil, after the Incan god of lightning."

"Really." Mark is surprised by a stab of jealousy.

"There were people there talking to him, a whole little cult. Apparently he's running drum circles and healing sessions."

"I shouldn't be surprised," Mark says. "The self-absorption of these people is truly limitless."

Harris pauses. "I'm thinking of signing up for a healing session."

"You are? For what?"

"For the Lyme. The antibiotics aren't working anymore, so what the hell?"

Mark is quiet. A picture comes to his mind of another man bent in front of Harris, massaging his knees. This is how it happens, he thinks. It would be foolish to imagine that Harris hasn't felt his distance, hasn't suffered over these cold months. This is how the script goes, the arc of every such story.

The spring issue of the local magazine runs a front-page profile on the shop, with a photograph of Harris and Mark flanking the big birdcage chandelier. Harris poses in a cream cashmere V-neck, arms over his chest. Mark is in plaid and jeans, leaning on a Chinese altar table. Both smiling, relaxed: men of style and success. The article is full of superlatives about Harris's eclectic taste and social conscience. There is a box insert about the store's contributions to global charities: International Rescue Committee, UNICEF, VillageReach.

In the weeks that follow, customer traffic surges. Harris nearly sells out of the painted insects, which he has tucked in surprising locations throughout the showroom. The birdcage chandelier also goes, and the twelve-piece Louis XVI dining set.

At home, they open the bottle of '95 Margaux, a wedding gift. They drink, go into the bedroom. For the moment, Mark allows himself to slide back into the old ways. It is a simple pleasure to feel Harris's hand on the small of his back, the familiar sensations returning to his body.

While Harris spends a preliminary moment in the bathroom, a feminine quirk of his, Mark undresses and waits. Perched on the bed, he opens the top drawer of Harris's night table and hunts through handkerchiefs for the bottle of sandalwood oil. Instead, he finds a glossy booklet entitled *Navigating Your Adoption Journey.* A folded piece of paper falls out, a "Pre-Orientation Information Form," with blanks filled out for each of them: their birth dates, heights, yearly incomes.

When Harris comes out of the bathroom, Mark is naked on the bed, holding the packet.

"Oh, honey, I was just curious," Harris says preemptively. "I was just doing some preliminary reading. I wouldn't send anything in without you."

Mark does not respond. After a moment, Harris gently takes the packet from his hands and slides it back into the drawer. Standing there in his robe, he glances at the bed and sighs. "Do you not want to do this now?"

Mark is trembling. He can still see the logo at the top of the form, two intertwined hearts with a third, smaller heart nestled between. He can see his own name inked in block print beside the heading "Parent #2." He cannot bring himself to look at Harris, whose dragon-print robe fills his field of vision.

Finally, the robe moves away. There is a whisper of silk upon silk as Harris lowers himself onto the trunk at the foot of the bed. After several blank moments, Mark turns his head to see Harris facing away, his back quaking.

Later, in bed, Mark lies awake. Harris's sibilant breathing deepens and turns to full-on snoring, as often happens when he drinks. Mark usually interrupts this with a shake of his shoulder, but tonight he lets it continue. How silent the room would be without its tumbling cadence. One day, he knows, that silence will come—they will no longer be together. Sooner or later, through his own doing or through the brute force of time, of death, it will come. There is no truth more absolute than this. Perhaps it is understandable that in days of serenity the heart seeks it own friction—whether in defense against, or in ignorance of, the ultimate blow that awaits it.

For now, they are here, defiantly close beneath the blankets. Suddenly, all else drops away—the dust and sweat of Africa, that hot squall of abstractions—and this is all that matters. This man who would have a child with him, grow old with him and say good-bye.

The next afternoon, just before closing time, the door of the shop opens and a man enters with an extravagant crown of feathers on his head. The red and green feathers appear to have been borrowed from a South American macaw. His chest is weighted with a collection of intricately beaded necklaces and a string of long pointed teeth, perhaps shark or wild boar. Beneath, he wears a plain black T-shirt and jeans. Mark glances at Harris, who mouths something to him and winks.

The man comes to a halt in front of the desk where Madeleine sits. It will be interesting to see how she handles this one, Mark thinks. He watches as she puts a piece of hair behind her ear, then stands and pats down her skirt. He watches as she smiles up at the man and collects her purse.

He glances at Harris, whose eyebrows arch. For a moment, the old energy returns between them, trembling like a guitar string.

Madeleine pushes her chair in beneath the desk, and the feathered man takes her hand. She steps toward him, tall and slender, classically pretty with the neck of a ballerina. There is something of a little girl about her, Mark thinks, being picked up by her father.

"Harris, Mark"—she gestures—"this is David."

The feathered man raises a hand to each of them in turn, as if in benediction. Then, without speaking, he touches Madeleine's shoulder. She allows him to pull her close, pressing her cheek against the ranks of beads. As they walk toward the door together, she turns to give Mark and Harris a little wave. A strange smile flickers at her lips. The bell tinkles as they exit onto the sidewalk, colors aflame in the early spring light.

Aether

When the car pulls into the parking lot, Bethany heaves her duffel bag onto one shoulder. "They're here!" she calls to her mother. The weight of the bag strains the straps although she has packed only the essentials listed on the festival website—sunblock, baby wipes, rain poncho—and there is nothing she can safely take out.

"Have a good time, honey," her mother says, catching her in a tight embrace. Her voice carries the same note of distraction that's been there for weeks. "I'll miss you."

"I'll miss you, too, Mom," Bethany says into her mother's hair, feeling a hard nut wobble in her stomach.

They come out of the condominium, and Rebekah and Amos step from the car to greet them. Rebekah grins and chats easily with Bethany's mother about her California college, the beauty of the campus, the diversity of the student body.

As Bethany squirms into the backseat, her mother gives her another dreamy kiss, lingering for a moment, then letting go. Bethany feels the nut topple and slide in her stomach as the car pulls away. Once they are on the road, Rebekah cranks the music and opens the window.

As far as her mother knows, Bethany will be accompanying Rebekah's family to a revolutionary reenactment this weekend.It is, ultimately, a harmless lie. There are, of course, many worse things she could be doing than going to a music festival. Later, when she is older and her maturity proven, she will confess the truth, and her mother will understand that there was nothing wrong in it, that she'd underestimated her daughter all along.

But now is not the time for rebellion. Since renting the condo, her mother has been making an effort: asking about her feelings, sitting with her before bed. Sometimes it seems that this outreach is more for her mother's benefit than her own—that she needs to prove to herself that she is a responsible, available parent. The first year had been bright and optimistic. It was as if, by taking a break from her father, Bethany's mother had shed a winter skin. That was what she'd called it: taking a break. But as the second year advanced, the sparkle was replaced by a kind of preoccupied quiet. Now, her mother has stopped going out. Her hands have been jittery, and she has been dropping things.

They drive north in the heat, leaving behind Old Cranbury's dense greenery. Within an hour they are in a different country. Wider spaces, smaller houses, indications of farming. A tractor supply store, an NRA bumper sticker. Between the howling open windows and the thumping stereo, the noise in the car is engulfing. The music goes around in a throbbing, screeching loop.

"I'm so excited that you're here," Rebekah shouts into the rearview mirror. "You just have to be at Aether to understand it. Then you'll never want to miss it again."

Amos pulls down the sun visor on his side. A little mirror reflects the top half of his face. Since Bethany last saw him, his hair has grown past his eyes in a flat black flap, and he keeps moving it to the side with his fingers. Bethany notices for the first time how thin and careful these fingers are. Most of his teenage acne is gone, and the forehead in the mirror is smooth and pale.

"I just hope it hasn't jumped the shark," Rebekah continues. "Last year there were a lot of posers, you know? Guys just looking to drink beer and hook up. But that's *so* not the scene, you know?"

Bethany does not know, but nods her head.

From the back, Rebekah's hair looks different, thicker and darker. "Did you do something to your hair?" Bethany asks.

"I haven't been washing it. Look," she says, and shows Bethany the matted beginnings of a dreadlock.

Rebekah has returned from her sophomore year with a wise, fugitive glint in her eye. As many questions as Bethany has asked and as factually as Rebekah has answered them, her friend's new universe remains shut to her. Bethany suspects that Rebekah is enjoying this bit of mystery, taking it as license to treat Bethany like a sweet, dim younger sister.

The community college was supposed to be a stopgap before Bethany's launch as an actress. It was her choice to forgo the prototypical American college experience—that halfway house to autonomy—in exchange for intensive auditions. But the auditions have been as fruitless as they are relentless. It has proven impossible to stand out among the pert, practiced girls who have done this since toddlerhood, and it has already begun to seem that her role as Holly Golightly in the high school play will be the pinnacle of her career. All the talk of her precocious talent—a junior snaring a leading role—now seems miserably unfounded. She was cast as Liesl Von Trapp in *The Sound of Music* her senior year, and nothing since. Fear of failure has begun to puddle cold in her chest. She is a community college student now, surrounded by hairsprayed girls and dull boys earning vocational degrees.

Rebekah had auditioned for Holly, too, but ended up in the chorus. While some of the seniors resented Bethany for stealing a part they considered theirs, Rebekah hadn't cared. Instead, she'd been impressed with Bethany's mettle. They went to the diner after rehearsals and Rebekah elaborated in hushed tones about her new, older boyfriend. She'd found him outside the Coffee Bean, on break in his apron. He'd been sitting cross-legged on the pavement smoking an Indian *beedi* cigarette and reading Ovid's *Metamorphoses*. Rebekah was breathless when she talked about him, about the high-minded discussions they had, about his global awareness, his zest for experience. He was, she whispered, twenty-five years old.

As it turned out, this zest for experience had included a complete survey of opioid and psychotropic drugs. Rebekah swore him off when she left for college, then took him back when he was hospitalized for an overdose. "He said he's a better person when he's with me, even if it's just summers and vacations," she said with a sigh on the phone, "which I think is true. And he's gotten more spiritual. He's been working with this guy in town. He's kind of his protégé."

As they approach the festival grounds, the traffic slows, and they find that they have joined a parade of allied vehicles with overlapping car stereos. Passengers smile and wave at one another. Rebekah thrusts her arm out the open window and gestures universally, triggering a series of whoops and hollers. She bounces in the driver's seat.

"I can already feel the vibe. Everyone's so happy to *be* here, that's the thing. A lot of these people have been waiting all year for this. It's like the highlight of their year."

They park in a vast field and emerge into battering heat. Serpentining on foot through the grid of cars, they are assaulted by the slap of sun on metal. It is predicted to be in the nineties all weekend. Bethany squirts sunblock onto her arms while walking. Her hair is already damp on her neck, but she doesn't want to tie it up without a mirror. This, she recognizes with a dip of embarrassment, is because of Amos. He walks in front of her, taller than she remembers, slimmer in his jeans. It's as if, while he was away, some inner crank has lengthened his body and rotated its cells so that the boy she looks at now has no relation to the boy she has known, indifferently, since kindergarten.

"Aren't you hot?" she calls. "I mean, in those jeans."

Amos looks back and smiles. "Nah, I'm okay. There's no other option for guys, anyway. What am I supposed to wear, shorts?"

"I love my pants," Rebekah comments. "They're so cool on hot days." The pants are vastly wide, composed of patchwork cotton squares. She lifts the fabric to her knees. "I made them myself, you know. There's a girl in my dorm who's teaching me to sew on her machine."

At the gate, they wait for their turn to give over their weekend passes, a sacrificial two hundred dollars each. The passes are emblazoned with the Aether logo—an alchemical symbol like a seated stick figure with bent knees—and its slogan, "We breathe immortal air." They have their bags searched. There are so many people here already, just waiting to get in, that Bethany feels woozy at the notion of what small nation must be waiting inside.

"I can't wait for you to meet Rufus," Rebekah says, jiggling Bethany's shoulder. "I can't *believe* you guys haven't met before."

This exuberance strikes Bethany as disingenuous, as if insurmountable logistics had constantly intervened in the past. In fact, it seems that Rebekah has been keeping Rufus squirreled away, considering Bethany unfit to meet him. She is gratified, if begrudgingly, that she seems to have passed some unspoken test now.

As they enter the festival grounds, Bethany surveys its citizens: colorful figures scattered to the horizon. They seem to have been here forever, moving to and fro on blissful errands. Rebekah lifts her yellow sunglasses to smile at Bethany and does a kind of skipping dance. Bethany returns the smile through a roll of panic. It is scandalous to think her mother had swallowed her weak fiction about the revolutionary reenactment. Had she really believed so blindly, or was she privately crestfallen by her daughter's daring deceit?

Bethany allows this tremor to rumble and fade, and returns her attention to the surrounding sensory blitz. There is a mechanical thrum that seems to come from the ground itself. She usually gravitates toward radio-friendly songs with beginnings, middles, and ends, sticky melodies and words she can belt out. She likes rising choruses and drums that palpitate before big anthemic melodies. She does not think these types of songs will be performed here. In fact, the lineup seems to include only a handful of bands playing actual instruments. The rest of the artists are electronic—DJs with names like Slap Elf, Mork, Yggdrasil.

Amos does not skip like his sister, but walks faster as they go over the trodden fields toward the campground. He is the musician in the family, with wide and discerning tastes that easily encompass this and every imaginable festival. In high school he'd played whatever necessary instrument—guitar, bass, keyboard—in at least three different bands.

They pause as they come into the campground, a hobo village of nylon tents. Rebekah stops and shields her eyes with a hand.

"Do you know where we're going?" Amos asks.

"Rufus said he's in the northeast quadrant. As if that's helpful at all. But maybe we'll be able to see his rage stick."

"What's a rage stick?" Bethany asks.

"You don't want to know," Amos says.

"It's like a totem thing, to help people find their friends at festivals," Rebekah explains. "There's never any cell service out in the boonies. But I think it's better that way. It's pretty rare that we get to unplug like this, just be with each other and the music, you know?"

Most campsites are just tents on the ground, but a few are more elaborate arrangements with tables, chairs, tapestries, Tibetan prayer flags, hammocks. One tent is painted with the word *PLUR*.

"What does that mean?" Bethany points.

"Peace, Love, Unity, Respect. Sometimes people add another 'R' for 'Responsibility.' As if." Rebekah holds a hand over her eyes. "There he is!"

As they come closer to their own campsite, Bethany sees that there are already three tents bunched together, along with a wide canopy on poles. Beneath the canopy a number of canvas chairs are arranged in a circle, with a number of unfamiliar men seated in them. One of the men stands up and smiles, stretching his arms out as if demonstrating ownership, or granting a blessing.

His nose ring is the first thing Bethany notices, the first thing, she presumes, that he wants anyone to notice. It pierces the cartilage beneath the septum, with two arms curving downward in a way that is both hypnotizing and deeply unsettling. He is shirtless, his body decorated with paint: green and gold stripes circling his biceps and crosshatching his pectorals. His hair is buzzed short. Bethany thought she remembered Rebekah describing him as having long hair. But perhaps after hearing about the *beedi* cigarettes and the *Metamorphoses,* she'd only pictured someone more romantic-looking.

Rebekah scurries into this man's outstretched arms and cuddles into his chest. Bethany thinks she sees her kiss a nipple and feels a revulsion, as if she'd watched her lick a reptile.

"Bethany, this is Rufus," she says breathlessly, pulling away.

Bethany begins to hold out a hand, but Rufus bounds in for a hug, pulling her against his painted chest. "So great to meet you. Agh, sorry about that!" he cries, swatting at the smudges on her shirt.

"Oh my God, is that your stick?" Rebekah squeals, pointing to a pole in the ground with something like a decapitated head on top.

"Yeah, do you like it?" Rufus pounces on the pole, hauls it up, and proffers the head. "I made it out of foam and painted the eyes on. It's Argus Panoptes, the hundred-eyed giant. Watching over our campsite."

"Argus," Bethany echoes. "That's the name of my dad's company. It's a home inspection business."

"That's right!" Rebekah cries, dazzled.

"Argus, watching over everything," Rufus muses, gazing at the severed head.

He helps them erect their tent and arrange their supplies. He talks fast, moves fast, and seems much younger than Bethany knows him to be. She feels a kind of disappointment at this, as if Rebekah had purposely deceived her, built him up as something greater.

Rebekah grabs her by the elbow. "Come on, I don't want to miss Barterhouse!"

"What about Rufus?" Bethany asks.

"He likes to stay at the campsite."

As Rebekah pulls her along, Bethany looks for Amos. "Where's your brother?"

"Probably already out in front of the stage."

They hurry out of the dusty campground and across the field of flattened grass leading to the main stage. Bethany is sweating, and the dirt has come through her sandals and made ankle socks. The festivalgoers throng around them. It is staggering to see so many young people in one place. There are girls in bikini tops, smiling at Bethany and Rebekah as if privy to a shared secret. One bikini-topped girl wears an enormous feathered Indian headdress. One walks by with no bikini at all, just yellow and black paint upon her breasts, two big black-eyed Susans. Bethany is demure in contrast, in the studded shorts and shirttail tee she'd agonized over.

"Look at that!" Rebekah points. Young men in Victorian clothing, women in leafy halter tops, all perched high on stilts. They strut in circles, gesticulating like circus performers. It is hard to tell the difference between regular people and entertainers here. It seems to Bethany that everyone is imbued with some stardust indigenous to this festival and inaccessible elsewhere. The beauty around her is not exclusionary but inclusive. Just by being there, she might absorb it through her skin and begin to glimmer.

They reach the main stage where Barterhouse, a bearded jam band, is riding an upward swell of guitar licks to heaven. Rebekah begins to sway. Everyone is dancing, the boys wiggling in place, the girls swinging their hair. And this, Bethany remembers with a thrill, is just the beginning of the festival.

Rebekah taps her on the shoulder and holds out a thin, warped cigarette that has materialized out of nowhere. Bethany shakes her head. "You know I don't smoke."

Rebekah rolls her eyes. "*Here*, just take it."

"Why?"

"It's all part of the experience."

Bethany puts the wet end into her mouth and pulls a few times, coughing, then hands it back to Rebekah, who shoos it away.

"Pass it on."

Bethany looks around, makes eye contact with a shirtless guy in a bandanna. He smiles and accepts the joint. "Peace, man," he actually says to her.

She is relieved, as if she's rid herself of a hot potato. There are no police in the crowd, she is sure, but glances around despite herself.

She lets herself sway now, feeling the splash of the cymbal. The weed has made her throat dry. She has tried it only once before, at a cast party. The colors around her are candy bright. A fuzzy rainbow totem joggles above the crowd like a neon caterpillar, along with an impaled beach ball and some crude puppets. People dance with foil pinwheels, dream catchers, bubble wands. It's as if they've all come together to achieve a giant resurrection of childhood. Bethany laughs. All at once she grasps something so basic: this is what people mean when they sing about *getting back to the garden*.

Bethany and Rebekah last for the rest of the set, until they are both parched. Back at the campground, they fill their Thermoses with water and drop into chairs under the canopy. Rufus is picking out a tune on a strange little guitar. The other men are still under the canopy, drinking out of Solo cups. Their sunglasses make it hard to tell if they are awake or sleeping. Bethany doesn't recognize any of them from town. There don't seem to be any girls besides Rebekah and herself.

Rebekah taps one of the guys on the knee and he turns toward her with a slow smile.

"Hey, Chris, this is my friend Bethany."

"Hey," he says.

"Chris is from Old Cranbury, too."

He shifts his sunglasses to nest in a sheaf of sandy hair. His heavy eyelids reveal half-pools of languid blue. The surrounding skin is pale where the sunglasses were; the rest of his face is the bronze of year-round exposure.

"Nah, my parents just moved there a couple years ago."

"But you're there now," Rebekah prompts.

"Just for the summer, then I'm going back to Vail." Chris looks at Bethany, openly sliding his gaze down her legs and up again.

"His parents are the ones who had that crazy art project, those insect sculptures all over their house, remember that?" Rebekah says.

"Seriously?" Bethany chirps, leaning forward. "I *loved* that. I'm so sad they took it down."

Chris chortles. "You're the only one."

"Naw, man, I liked it, too," the guy next to Chris interjects. "That shit was sick."

"How the hell do *you* know?"

"I saw the picture in the paper. Your parents rock." The guy drinks deeply from his cup and appears to go back to sleep.

Chris gestures to his friend. "He's from freakin' Dunfield. He's never even seen my parents' house."

"So, uh, how do you know Rufus—and these other guys?" Bethany ventures.

"They were all roommates at some point," Rebekah answers for him. "Right?"

"Yeah." He chuckles. "Crazy times."

Bethany is quiet. These crazy times, she surmises, must have included Rufus's overdose. These are very likely the people who were with him when it happened. Through the smoothing plane of her high, Bethany feels a millipede of agitation. She stays quiet with her Thermos while Rebekah tries to talk to Chris about his time in Colorado. He really mellowed out there, seems to be the gist of it. All that sun and snow.

He and the others seem to be well into their twenties—perhaps even thirty—resting like complacent tortoises. She allows herself to feel a sizzle of aversion, then willfully dampens it into something tolerable, something more like anthropological interest, like being embedded with another tribe. She studies the men. The one next to Chris wears mismatched tube socks, pink and orange. His dark hair is shaggy, too long to be fashionable, flattened at the top as by an invisible hat.

Rufus has now put the instrument down, and stands in the middle of the tent until he has the group's attention.

"You all know that I'm clean now," he begins. "But this is a special occasion, and so I brought something special, just for tonight. For everyone."

"Something *really* special," Rebekah adds.

Bethany looks sharply at her, and Rebekah grins.

"Yes, something really special. You can't even get it in this country. It's from the Amazon, a very ancient, medicinal brew. I made it at home from the caapi vine and some other imported ingredients. The tribespeople call it 'vine of the soul.'" He pauses. "It's not really a drug, more like a potion. It's supposed to be taken communally as part of a ceremony. My mentor went down there and drank it with a real *curandero*. He said it was like a soul purge, like ten years of therapy in one night. It cracks the whole world open."

"You done this before?" one of the Solo guys asks.

"No." Rufus smiles. "I've been waiting for the perfect time to try it, and I decided that instead of saving it for myself, I'd share it with you guys, do a real ceremony. There's no place I feel more comfortable and safe than this."

Rebekah looks admiringly at him. Bethany feels dread like a trapdoor opening beneath her.

"All right, bro, bring it on," says the guy in tube socks.

"Not yet, Stooge." Rufus holds up a hand. "Not till after the music's done tonight. Maybe midnight or so."

"Cool."

"Just to warn you, it's so powerful it can actually cure drug addiction."

The guy called Stooge laughs, exposing a set of stained teeth.

Rufus finishes his announcement and takes a seat. Bethany stares at the war paint on his chest while Rebekah reaches for his hand.

"Hey, babe," she says, as if they are alone. "Can I see that?" She points to the little guitar where it rests on a folding chair.

"Did I ever show this to you? Apocatequil brought it back for me."

"You told me about it, but I never saw it," Rebekah says, blinking her lashes. She turns the instrument over in her hands, then passes it to Bethany. It is made from some sort of animal shell.

"What—" Bethany begins.

"Armadillo," Rufus answers.

Bethany touches the scaly hull, the stiff hairs still attached, and feels a small shudder. The instrument is hollow, eerily light. She thinks of the armadillo that was sacrificed, its flesh scooped out.

"It's called a charango," Rufus says. "It's for courtship rituals." He points to a mermaid carved into the head of the instrument. "This is a totem to the sirens who can help the musician win love."

He takes it from Bethany and plucks a few wobbly notes. "Maybe we can use it in the ceremony tonight."

Bethany's pleasant haze has turned heavy. Her body sags in the camping chair and it seems possible that she won't get up again today. She hears her name being called and listens vaguely to this, thinks what a funny thing a name is.

"Bethany," she hears again, more distinctly. *"Bethany Duffy."* She looks up to find three boys standing beneath the canopy. She

knows that she knows them, but it takes a moment to fish their names out. Noah Warren, of course—what is he doing here? And the Hatfield brothers. Kurt. And the younger one—Jason? Martin? All three of them look too clean, too fresh for this place. She smiles.

"Hey, do your parents know you guys are here?"

Noah laughs, then Bethany. Noah's mother, too, would keel over dead if she knew. She is one of those exasperatingly buoyant women in town who volunteer for everything, cheer at every sports game, and behave as if no world exists outside Old Cranbury. The persistence of her budgetary dreams is one of the reasons Bethany's father finally quit the school board.

"I'm at *their* house," Noah says, nodding to the Hatfield brothers.

"We're at *his* house," adds the younger Hatfield. *Mason,* that's his name.

The older one, Kurt, is staring at Rebekah. "You're Rebekah Foster, right? You went to OCHS."

Rebekah gives him a queenly smile. "I graduated three years ago."

"I thought so. I remember you."

"Hey, fellows." Rufus comes over with a bunch of folding chairs and hands them out. "Have yourselves a seat. Chill with us for a while."

There is no space in the circle's perimeter for them, so they awkwardly open the chairs where they stand, in the middle of the tent.

"I thought I saw you from across the campground," Noah is saying, "but Kurt said I was imagining it."

Kurt is still looking intently at Rebekah, as if trying to decipher something. He is dressed for a sailboat, in khaki shorts and navy polo shirt.

"You're at college in California now, right?" he asks.

"Very good," Rebekah says.

"I'm going to Dickinson in a couple of weeks. In Pennsylvania."

"Well, that will be different."

Kurt smiles despite this teasing, which Bethany can tell has already bled into scorn.

"He's just here to pick up girls," his younger brother pipes in.

"And what's wrong with that?" Kurt smiles at Rebekah, then at Bethany.

"Plenty of those out there," Rebekah says, motioning beyond the tent.

Bethany feels the urge to kick her friend. She normally would have little use for these boys, but she likes having them here now.

"Are you guys thinking about college yet?" Bethany asks Noah and Mason in a kind, sisterly tone.

The boys look at each other.

"I don't know," Noah says. "I'll probably go to college eventually, but I want to travel first. For at least a year. Maybe go around the world, like, backpacking. It feels so claustrophobic in Old Cranbury, you know? I feel like I've been cooped up my whole life. Even this"—he sits forward and flaps his hands outward—"it's so homogenous. Have you noticed that it's all white kids?"

"No, it isn't," Rebekah snaps.

"Yes, it *is,*" Noah says. "Look around. People think this is such a wonderful melting pot or something, such a representation of our generation. That's why I wanted to come. I mean, it's fun and everything, but it's not, like, earth-shattering."

"Well, no one's gladder to be here than I am," Rebekah says, putting her hands to her heart.

Bethany meets her friend's eyes and smiles back. She knows that, at home with her fanatic parents, Rebekah would be churning butter or helping her mother weave yarn into the household loom.

"So, where do you want to travel?" Bethany presses on.

"India. Bangladesh. Then further east, I guess. Maybe China and Russia."

"I'm sure your mom loves *that* plan."

Noah rolls his eyes cheerfully. "I haven't exactly mentioned it. But soon it won't matter. I'll be eighteen and I'll just go." He pats his friend on the knee. "Mason here has ideas, too."

Mason is a good-looking boy, well built. He peers downward and shifts in his seat.

"Hey, do you guys have beer?" Kurt inquires, looking around.

Rebekah scowls. "You have to go to the beer tents and buy whatever cat piss they're selling."

Kurt shifts his gaze one last time between Rebekah and Bethany, then pushes himself up from the chair. "All right." The younger boys don't move for a moment, then reluctantly go after him.

Left behind on her drooping chair, Bethany feels a tug of disappointment. Rufus has disappeared into one of the tents to prepare his rain forest potion. Someone has rigged a phone to a boom box and watery music leaks out of it, a sad mimicry of the day's live performances. In a remote part of her brain, Bethany knows she should be out there by the stage, not wasting time here. Instead, she sinks into the chair and finds herself thinking of her father.

Bethany had known all along that there was trouble. For several months her mother had been saying foreboding things like, "I thought he was a different kind of man," as if talking to herself, trying out the words. "Or maybe I'm the one who changed. People change, you know." She would look sternly at Bethany. "How did I get to be almost fifty? I have to make things happen if I want them."

Her mother never explicitly said there was another man, someone who represented these unspecified "things," but Bethany couldn't guess what else she could be talking about. She wasn't making exotic travel arrangements or adopting a risky new career. She wasn't buying a sports car. Sometimes Bethany overheard her on the phone, using a murmuring, coquettish tone. She had never spoken to Bethany's father that way. When she went out at night in new clothing, sharply tugging off the price tag before picking up her purse, it was clear she was not going out alone. It had made Bethany feel grown-up to coharbor this unspoken understanding.

Her father was a difficult person, she knew that. He complained stormily and often, and was not otherwise expressive.

As far back as she could remember, whenever she was in any kind of pain it was her mother who rushed to her. Her father did not try to comfort, did not even ask what happened. In her memory, he stands blankly like an etherized animal. And yet, when she thinks of him alone in their house now—where? on the slip-covered couch beneath her framed baby photos?—she feels an intolerable scrabbling in her rib cage.

"Hey," Rebekah says to her. "Hungry?"

Bethany shakes off her fugue state to accept a salami sandwich. The sunlight is suddenly dim through the trees, giving the campsite an aquatic tint. She hears someone say the word *gloaming*. The word is unfamiliar—perhaps festival terminology, or something to do with drugs? There is a swirl of activity in the campground, people yelling and laughing. Bethany stands, reenergized by the sandwich. All at once, she is aware of the passing time. Soon it will be night, and she has seen only one band.

"Let's go back out," she says to Rebekah.

Rebekah looks crossly at her. She has been rambling to one of the men about the racial oppression of government surveillance, or something to that effect.

"You go," she says. "I want to stay in case Rufus needs help getting ready."

Bethany looks down at her friend, rooting for words. If all they were going to do was lounge at the campsite, she wouldn't have come to the festival. She wouldn't have lied to her mother. But she knows a confrontation will make matters worse.

"Okay, suit yourself," Bethany makes herself say, and leaves Rebekah and the comatose men in their chairs.

Alone, she winds through the city of tents, looking for the way out. It is like wading through a dream world, the darkening blue air emblazoned with colored points of light, tinseled with bright voices. At this brief moment before nightfall, she lets herself imagine that she has come upon a ghostly settlement of her own people. This is how it might be, she muses, in the future they've been warned about, following the degradation of society, after the plastic infrastructure of school and shopping has melted and marooned her generation back upon the earth. Perhaps this is how they will all live, in wide-open settlements, vast tribal blocs.

At last, Bethany exits the campground and approaches the crowd at the main stage. The music is of another species now, wheeling electronic parabolas. The people around her are not swaying and wiggling anymore, but dancing acrobatically, aerobically, pantomiming elaborate sign language patterns. It is impossible to emulate this cold, from a standstill. As much as Bethany loves music, despite her confidence as an actress and singer, she has never been much for dancing, can't help fixating on how moronic she must look moving in these artificial ways. Here, though, no one seems to be looking at each other; they all face the same direction, transfixed on a solo DJ: a boy in a hooded sweatshirt hunched over a machine. It seems to take all of his concentration to plug this puzzle of beats into his device, making them skip and twist and weave.

Laser lights from the stage periodically wash the audience in green, blue, red. The lights swing down onto their heads, then lift to the sky to communicate with extraterrestrial entities. Glowing things are everywhere—necklaces, batons, body paint—as if the greatest fear of all, the surest route to death, is to not be seen.

The beat picks up and achieves a manic pace. The swinging lights quicken and the hive-mind dancing accelerates. Just standing in place, Bethany feels her heart jig in a way that is almost frightening. Then the hooded boy hunches lower over his box and the rhythm begins to slow, finally coming to a dead stop. The boy slumps, wound down. There is a breath of anticipation in the crowd, a moment of collective suspension. Then, like a thundercrack, the beat comes roaring back and the full spectrum of laser lights flares out. As if a string has been cut, the people fall back to dancing, possessed.

This time, Bethany cannot resist the current. Her body abandons her and goes into the music, finding caverns and waves and silver needles within. She is distantly aware of not making physical decisions, but following the motions of her limbs at a curious remove. When, at last, the DJ turns a knob that causes the crabby loops to join together in a final, booming tsunami, she feels as if she could lift off the ground. This, she understands, is the reason people flock here like pilgrims.

She thinks dimly of her father at home, her mother in the furnished condominium—all those cushioning, stifling trees around them, separating them from each other and from this. A stream of pity seeps through her euphoria like ink, shading it, giving it depth. Her parents are ruined children, stiffened in their bodies, ossified in their rituals. They are impossibly far from the sparkling truth that she is holding right now.

At this moment, she sees Amos. She thrusts herself through the crowd to where he is dancing, throwing his arms down as if ridding them of fire ants. She catches his eye and smiles, seizing his hand. He smiles back, bewildered. There is nothing specific she wants to say to him, really. It is enough just to be with him now, in the middle of this. She begins dancing again, a little less freely, waiting for him to join her. When he doesn't, she yells, "What's wrong?"

He shrugs and shouts, "The set's almost over."

He puts a hand in his pocket, and, suddenly, a look of terror darkens his face. He digs into the other pocket, then the pockets in the back. He looks at the ground, turns a circle in place. His eyes, when they meet Bethany's again, are panicked.

"What happened?" she yells.

He shakes his head, slaps his hands against the sides of his jeans. He turns a fast circle again, like a dog, scanning the ground. He pushes the person beside him away and examines the ground there.

"Did you lose something?"

He doesn't answer, but she sees him mouth the word *fuck*. He puts his head in his hands for a long moment, then looks at her again, glazed.

"Come on." She pulls him through the crowd toward the back. "There's got to be a lost and found somewhere."

He allows himself to be pulled. Once they are away from the crowd, he says, "It's my pocket watch."

"You have a pocket watch?"

"It was from my mom."

The simple way he says this makes it sound like his mother is dead, that no further explanation is needed.

"It's gone now," he says bluntly. He flicks his hair to the side, dismissing it.

"Well, let's at least check the lost and found."

"Forget it. It probably fell out in the crowd and it's trampled now. No one's going to see it in there."

The music has stopped—Amos was right that the set was ending, the seemingly infinite galaxy of it—and the stage behind them has gone dark for the intermission.

"We should go back and look for it," Bethany presses.

"Just never mind," he says.

They wander away from the stage into a stand of trees, an area that has been sectioned off as a chill-out space. Here, there are things hanging from branches, beaded strings and helixes. Floodlights have been strategically placed to shine upon rubbery objects of art, sea creatures and amoeba-like globs that suction the tree trunks. In a clearing, they come upon an enormous, translucent brain lumped upon the ground, made of clear resin. There is a crevice in the frontal cortex wide enough for people to slide through, and silhouettes are visible inside. The surface of the brain is hard and smooth when Bethany puts her hand to it.

"Let's go in," Amos says.

Bethany feels a clamp in her chest. There might not be complete privacy here, but it is comparatively isolated. He wouldn't suggest going in unless he wanted, at the very least, to talk closely with her. He stands back and lets her duck through first. She is aware of her backside directly in his line of vision and is glad she chose the long T-shirt. Inside, people are sitting on the ground. Amos has to stoop down low to get through the entrance and cannot stand fully straight once inside.

"Hey, Amos," someone calls to him.

"What the hell? I've been looking all over for you guys," he cries. He turns to Bethany. "These are my bandmates. We were supposed to meet up, but apparently they've been hiding in a brain."

This will just be a quick hello, she hopes. They will find another, more secluded place to go. She waits patiently, smiling at the bandmates, some of whom apparently have traveled from other states. To her dismay, Amos settles down upon the ground with them. They talk about music, using cryptic language. After fifteen minutes or an hour of this, Amos has made no sign of decamping, and Bethany stretches her arms meaningfully.

"Time to go back to the campsite, I think," she says.

He looks carefully at her. "Yeah, you look tired. Rest up for tomorrow, it's a great lineup. I'm gonna hang with these guys awhile, maybe crash at their site tonight."

She sits for a moment as the boys continue their prattle. Then she rises and exits the brain. She stands outside, dazed. After counting slowly to ten, she makes herself walk away.

Tramping through the woods, she feels newly irritated with the people gallivanting through the trees like elves. Off to one side a great number of neon hammocks dangle like cocoons. Here, she comes across the boys from Old Cranbury, each seated awkwardly in a hammock with an unfamiliar girl. These are girls of the skimpy clothing set, each thoroughly groomed and less-than-beautiful in her own way. They peer suspiciously at her. Kurt already has an arm around the hip of the girl beside him, the hammock swaying. Noah looks as guilty as a puppy caught digging in the yard. He inches away from his companion, but she quickly scoots back against him. Bethany, feeling an odd spike of betrayal, turns away.

When she arrives back at the campsite, she finds Rufus leading the others in a drumming session. Rebekah slinks over and whispers, "We're about to start."

"Are you going to do it, too?"

"No, I'm going to stay with Rufus while he does it. I'll be his sitter, kind of. Well, kind of the sitter for the whole group. Somebody has to stay sober, to keep people calm and make sure they have what they need."

"Do you think people will throw up? I mean, aren't the neighbors kind of close?"

"Believe me, we won't be the only ones vomiting tonight."

The drumming ceases and the drummers enter one of the tents—a yellow one—in single file. Rufus comes back out with a big insulated jug. He pours the contents into a stock pot and lights the propane stove.

"He's edgy," Rebekah confides in Bethany's ear. "He's been fasting for a couple days, including sex."

"Aha."

"Anyway, you can stay if you want. You can try it yourself, or you can help me sit. We have blankets ready in case people get chills, and a bunch of pails. We're going to put on a recording of the kind of stuff a *curandero* would play during the ceremony. There's an instrument he shakes, like a bunch of dry twigs."

"A *chakapa*," Rufus calls out.

"Right. We're going to play a recording of a *chakapa*."

"Okay. Well, good luck." Bethany backs away. "I'll see you when it's done, I guess."

The ecstasy of the dance music has completely receded from her veins now. The rejection from Amos has fuzzied her brain, and the bizarre, umbrous doings at the campsite exhaust her. She retreats aimlessly from the yellow tent as Rebekah and Rufus disappear inside.

"Hey," someone calls, and she turns to see Chris sitting on a log with a beer and a cigarette, the sunglasses still in his hair. She is unaccountably happy to see him.

"Aren't you going to do it, too?" she asks.

"No fuckin' way. I'm not going near any of that jungle shit." He smiles at her and shifts over on the log, patting the place next to him. He reaches into his pocket and offers her a flask of bourbon.

"I thought we weren't allowed to bring our own liquor in?"

"Shh." He holds a finger to his lips.

She takes the flask. The first sip burns. It ignites a new indignation at Amos's behavior, the giant brain and the juvenile hammocks, all the silly toys provided for them as if they were infants. A reckless flame travels through her. She tilts the flask and drinks in quick little gulps. Chris, pleased by this, moves closer and puts a hand on her back.

She finishes the bourbon. "Sorry," she murmurs, turning to him. His face looms very near. The first kiss is surprisingly gentle, then more insistent but still soft, causing a confused flutter inside her. "C'mon," he says, lifting her from the log. She steps behind him on rubberized legs toward a dirty white tent.

He has a slow-motion way about him, moving with his eyes closed like someone sleepwalking, acting out a dream. She finds herself lulled into unthinking response, mirroring his movements. Maybe because his eyes are closed, she has the sense that she could be anyone—that she is a temporary body in his arms. She is not even sure that he remembers her name. There could be something liberating about this, but the bourbon flame has died down and been replaced by her usual, maddening caution. She watches Chris's face as he moves his hands over her body like a blind person.

She thinks of Amos, wills back to mind the sharp immediacy of the look on his face when he noticed his pocket watch was missing. She feels an ache, a pining for the bright and precise black-and-white lines of this face. She understands exactly, painfully, who he is.

A rhythmic rattle comes through the walls of the tent from outside. An instrument being shaken in another continent. A rising moan.

Chris is at the zipper of her shorts now. It is a ridiculous zipper, no more than an inch long, but he fumbles at it regardless. Instinctively, she stops him, puts a hand over his hand, and he withdraws it obediently like a redirected animal. Now he is at his own zipper. It is suffocatingly hot, and the ground has begun to rock. More mysterious sounds drift over from the yellow tent—lower moans and strange barking noises. More than anything, Bethany does not want to go outside. She would rather be done with this and go to sleep right here. Whatever caused her to follow this man into this tent she doesn't remember, but now it is a job she has gotten herself into. It seems absurd, even funny, that she should put her face near this stranger's open zipper, a ridiculous posture for any person. But once she has consented, once she has begun, she realizes that she can't exactly, politely, just stop. Slowly, a tickle develops in her throat. It creeps down through her esophagus and grows, until she comes up for air, gasping. Chris puts a hand to the back of her head, pressing gently. She braces her hands on either side of his hips and takes shallow breaths. A drop of sweat falls from the tip of her nose. Unmistakable sounds of violent heaving are now entering the tent from outside. All at once a dirty wave swoons up in her and she retches and vomits in place.

The next few moments are a confusion of mopping and swearing. The tent is tropical, noxious with stink. Chris bundles his soiled camping pad and sleeping bag together with his shorts and underwear. Bethany watches, prone on the damp nylon floor, as he crouches around, naked from the waist down. Finally, he pulls on a pair of cotton pajama pants and looks at her with a kind of flustered reverence. "Are you all right?"

She nods, her head rubbing the ground, the nylon making static in her hair. He nods back and ducks silently out of the tent with his bundle. Relieved depletion overtakes her. She falls asleep to the lullaby of the susurrating *chakapa*.

* * *

In the morning—much too early, only a hint of daylight through the moldy tent walls—there is a stir at the campsite. Bethany lies, stiff and cotton-mouthed, upon a circuitry of roots and stones. Through the hammering of blood in her brain she hears agitated voices. *"I don't know, I don't know,"* someone is saying over and over.

She crawls to the tent door and peers out. There is a bleak indigo cast over everything, and it seems that objects have been rearranged in the night: the propane stove and log and plastic cups on the ground. Rebekah is standing outside the yellow tent, arms hanging at her sides. When she notices Bethany, she stares at her for a long black moment. Even at this distance, Bethany recoils from what she sees in the gaze.

"Only three people ended up drinking the brew," Rebekah tells her when she comes into the white tent. If she notices the rancid smell, she does not mention it. Her fingers knit and unknit themselves as she speaks, as if deciding whether to pray.

"Rufus was hysterical the whole time, rocking back and forth and trying to run away. That took up most of my energy, just trying to keep him calm. Then Holmes kept puking, like three or four times, and I had to deal with that, too. Stooge just kind of fell asleep, so I thought, *Good, I don't have to worry about him.*"

"Rebekah, what happened?"

Rebekah looks at Bethany. "He never woke up. He hasn't woken up."

"But you tried . . . ?"

Rebekah's mouth pulls downward. "I knew the tent was too hot," she cries, and bangs a fist on the ground. "I fucking knew something was going to happen."

When they emerge from the tent together, Chris is outside with Rufus and the other one, Holmes.

"He was probably on something else, man. We should've asked," Holmes is saying.

Rufus does not respond. He turns to look at the girls.

"What are we going to do?" Rebekah says calmly.

Rufus stares at her. His face is pale, and he is wearing a shirt now. The shirt is white with a big blue eyeball in the middle of it.

"I think we should go to the medical tent," Rebekah answers herself.

Rufus stares another moment, then says, "No, they'll send the cops."

"What else are we supposed to do, Rufe?"

"All right, I'll go to the medical tent," Rufus says quietly. "Let the cops come."

The ambulance arrives, barreling through the campground. Curious people gather nearby and murmur as the EMTs hunch into the yellow tent and, after a few minutes, slide out a stretcher with a sheet strapped over a body. That's what it is, Bethany realizes. A body.

"This happens every year," Bethany hears someone say in a hushed, authoritative tone. "There's always at least one person . . ."

The police come. When it's her turn to talk, Bethany feels like she is reading lines in an audition. She listens to herself telling the story of her evening, pointing to the white tent, pointing to Chris. The officers seem serious but unsurprised. Their tone wavers between sympathy and contempt. They unceremoniously take down her name and address in case they have further questions. She gives her home address—her father's address—without thinking, then feels a blade of fear that her parents might find out about this.

The police move on to Rufus. They speak to him for a long time. After they finish, one officer remains with him as the others poke around the tents. Bethany wonders what has happened to the magic brew, whether they'd drunk all of it last night, or if Rufus—or, more likely, Rebekah—had poured the remainder somewhere. Maybe a dog would sniff it out, attuned to whatever telltale chemicals, but the officers have not brought dogs.

After the police lead Rufus away, people from other campsites begin to infiltrate, rooting for information. Rebekah will not talk to them, but walks around in circles shaking her head. She is still in her patchwork pants and tank top. Her hair is snarled down to the tips.

"Well, it's bound to happen, with people mixing drugs," one girl is rattling on in a regular voice. "Not everyone knows what they're doing. People make dumb mistakes all the time. It happens every year."

"He was probably one of the Yggdrasil crew. I heard they had some bad Molly."

"Did you know him?" someone asks Bethany. She shakes her head mutely.

"We need to find Amos," Rebekah says, suddenly insistent. Her voice is high and strained. "You know, not having phone service fucking sucks. What the fuck are you supposed to do in an emergency? Walk around with a freakin' totem until someone sees you?"

"I think he's with his bandmates," Bethany offers. "He said he was going to stay at their campsite."

With a growl, Rebekah grabs the Argus totem. She holds it aloft as they wander the campground, until at last they find Amos and his friends playing guitars around a little table of bagels. Amos looks clean and rested. The breakfast setup strikes Bethany as neat and civilized; the mugs appear to be filled with real coffee. Bethany wishes intensely that she could sit down with them and pretend nothing has happened.

Amos looks up with innocent surprise.

"Let's go," Rebekah says to her brother. "We're leaving."

"What? Why?" His brow knits, and he keeps strumming the guitar.

Rebekah yanks him up by the arm. She takes him aside and talks quietly. Bethany can see her back quaver as she starts to cry, and she sees Amos put an arm around her.

They collect everything they can from the campsite and lug it out with them. Rebekah carries the Argus totem, now an unwelcome beacon. As they walk, it seems that some people are whispering, watching them with a curiosity bordering on envy. Others look on ignorantly, blinking like dumb cows, wondering why they are leaving the festival early. The story will spread through the campground, through the festival, eventually reach the ears of the performers themselves. It will dampen the mood for a while, or—possibly—enliven it, add new fuel to the manic dancers. Perhaps this direct news of death will underscore the present moment for them. They won't be surprised, that much is certain. This happens, apparently, every year. If that is true, Bethany thinks, then the festival itself is nothing but an enormous glittering gambling table where life is traded roughly in order to inflate its value, remove its guarantee.

Rebekah walks with a look of grim focus. Amos, too, is quiet. Bethany feels no sharp emotion, just a general numbness. Only in an abstract way does she understand that a man is abruptly dead—a man who was alive in front of her just hours ago, only a few years older than herself. The idea beads on the surface of her consciousness like oil on water.

A girl in braids approaches them. "Hey, are you leaving already? Here, take this." She holds out a fan of glossy postcards. *Did you become someone else at Aether?* the postcards inquire, showing a picture of a purple-wigged woman with butterfly wings. *Send us your photos!*

With every step toward the exit, Bethany thinks, she is fashioning a permanent memory that will remain with her. She *is*, in fact, a different person coming out of the festival. Now, walking beside Amos, she catches herself considering the unexpected advantage of having witnessed something he has not. This is such an unscripted moment that anything could be excused. She could grasp his hand right now, and he would have to hold it.

She does not grasp his hand. They continue walking, apart from each other, toward the parking lot. The sneaking light of dawn is gone, replaced by the white slab of morning. There is no special color in the sky. There are no cloud formations or intimations of a higher firmament. It occurs to Bethany that this story will make the news. There will be something about it on television. There will be a spin about the danger of music festivals, and she will have to sit silently while her mother obliviously warns her about it.

Eventually, she will distance herself from the incident, tamp it into a story she tells at parties. She will put herself apart from the man who died. He was fundamentally different, she will rationalize, not from Old Cranbury, unanchored by good parents and constructive surroundings. As they approach the gate Bethany thinks of the town, small and safe, awaiting their return. It is cloistered, oppressively familiar, but maybe—and her mother's trembling hands return to her—mired with its own dark disturbances. It is its own kind of restive campground, in a way, its properties penciled upon common land, impinging on one another despite the fences meant to hold them apart. Huddled in that encampment are their families, steely cohorts within the greater clan. Even Rufus must have parents of his own, although this seems improbable. He seems parentless, born from nothing, sprung from the thigh of some god.

Far off to the side, before the parking lot, Bethany notices a gathering of people on an open field. This would be the morning yoga session, offered to those able to rise early enough, still interested in breathing. The rows of people move in sync, adopting the same poses, configuring and reconfiguring their limbs like children experimenting with their bodies. Bethany watches as they all bend at once to plant their hands upon the battered field, then arch up in unison, a hundred arms saluting the sun.

Moon Roof

Lori Hatfield takes a different route home. She isn't sure what inspires her, after pulling out of the bakery parking lot, to turn onto a quiet side street connecting Edgeware Drive to Cannonfield Road. Part of it, no doubt, is impatience. It's rush hour, for what that's worth in this town, and the red light at Mercy Avenue is notoriously long; she once timed it at two full minutes. Or perhaps, after a long week of car errands, she just wants to pry open a tiny new vein of experience.

The road is called Iron Horse, a name that to Lori evokes the image of a horse cast in a high-kneed pose, mane sculpted in waves. In eleven years as an agent, she's never driven it. Somehow she hasn't had the occasion to bring buyers to a listing on this particular road. When returning from town, she always takes Mercy home. This is a more scenic route to be sure, she now sees, as her Lexus climbs a hill lined with loose stone walls. The trees are mature and generously leafed. She feels a lightness of heart as she drives and commends herself for doing something as delightfully simple as taking a new road home.

Too quickly, she reaches the end of Iron Horse. The hill has attained its crest and now slopes to a stop sign. She brakes and comes to a gentle halt at the intersection where, with a faint sense of resignation, she waits to turn left onto Cannonfield. A steady stream of cars approaches from each direction. These are people returning from work, coming home from the small city to the east and the larger town to the west. Lori keeps her foot on the brake and waits for a lull in traffic.

The car smells good. On the dog-haired passenger seat is a box of fresh cookies from Amici Bakery, the most expensive bakery in the area, where she went as much for the embossed sticker as for the quality of the cookies. She'd intended to bake something from scratch for the Christensens' party tonight, but ultimately aborted the plan, certain that no lemon meringue she achieved would equal the sunburst in August's *Bon Appétit*. It's probably gauche, anyway, to bring food to an event like this. Still, she fears arriving anywhere empty-handed.

Harold Christensen is the head of her husband's company, a private equity firm. Lori has heard many anecdotes about Harold but has never met or seen him, though he and his wife presumably live in the same town as Lori and Mitch. It occurs to her that she may have encountered Mrs. Christensen—Carol—without knowing who she was. Lori pictures her as one of the ageless capri-panted blondes who populate the town and who seem to have dwelled here, with their headbands and quilted bags, since its founding by the Pilgrims.

This is the first year Mitch has made the guest list for the party, an annual affair that the Christensens stubbornly bill as a backyard barbecue, an informal gathering to acknowledge Labor Day, the unofficial end of summer. Lori considers this a terrible purpose for a party. What is there to celebrate about the slow drying of greenery, the sneaky flash of autumn, the onslaught of another New England winter? *Bring your bathing suits!* the invitation commands in breezy cursive. Lori knows that the Christensens live on Pelican Point, on the waterfront, and this will not be a casual cookout. There will be passed hors d'oeuvres and a tuxedoed bartender. Whatever in-ground pool is offered for the guests' enjoyment will be rimmed with bluestone and rock outcroppings through which will flow a simulated waterfall. No one will bring a bathing suit.

The traffic continues to hurtle along Cannonfield. Lori holds the steering wheel, waiting to make her turn, but the cars are traveling too closely together for her to safely enter. The nature of the left turn, too, requires her to wait for simultaneous gaps in both eastbound and westbound traffic. Adding to the difficulty is the presence of a blind curve to her left, obscuring the eastbound cars until they are almost upon her. For this reason, she focuses on the westbound traffic—watching the distant cars as they approach and noting any promising spaces as they draw closer. Almost without fail, by the time the promising gap has reached Lori, it will have been narrowed to nothing by the accelerating car in the rear. And in the instances when the space remains, a quick check to the left reveals a new cavalcade swinging out from the curve.

The turn signal blinks on her dashboard with a lazy, plinking sound. Lori watches as vehicle after vehicle appears over the eastern horizon with twin headlamps like unfriendly eyes. A red sedan, followed by a silver SUV, pursued by a white pickup truck. She becomes aware of the pressure of her foot upon the brake pedal. It hits her that only by continuing this pressure is she preventing her car from gliding into traffic, becoming a jumble of steel. Perhaps this is what distracts her from acting when a suitable opening arrives in the wake of a Mercedes convertible. The opportunity registers in her brain, and yet the appropriate neurons do not fire, and her foot does not rise from the pedal. Instead, she stares at the empty road in front of her until a moss-green Subaru approaches and closes the gap irretrievably. Behind the Subaru comes a van, and behind that another Subaru. Lori reprimands herself. She could have made her turn twice in the amount of time she had. Now, who knows when the next opportunity will come. She breathes out and pumps her foot impotently on the brake.

Just one more minute and another chance will come. She will have to be patient. Well, she is good at that. She is patient, in little ways, every day. And she has been patient in a large way for years, waiting for her children to become independent. She has waited through midnight crying spells, failed toilet-training programs, food-flinging phases. She has waited through driver's ed. That is what motherhood is about, she reflects: patience. If she is not patient, no one is.

Now, suddenly, her boys are on the brink of manhood, and time will be hers again. Soon, she can do what she wants. She can give more attention to clients, really make a name for herself. She earned her real estate license after the kids started school, but has worked only as a buyer's agent, never taking listings of her own. Mitch was doing so well at his job—the firm was so crazy about him, giving him generous raises each year, plus bonuses—that it seemed unnecessary. She knows that some women find self-worth through work, pegging their identities to their careers, but she has never needed that crutch. And, in all honesty, she's become accustomed to her time at home. There is plenty to do with even just one teenage son in the house. Mason has his driver's license now and doesn't need rides anymore, but still needs his dinners cooked and clothes washed. In her free time, Lori enjoys doodling around the house, choosing new paint for an accent wall, finding new ways to organize the linen closet. The more open houses she attends, the more ideas she gets. No home is ever truly finished, as so many women her age are fond of saying. And she alone is the steward of their home, tirelessly pushing it to its potential, singlehandedly keeping it from regressing into chaos.

She has also begun the job of badgering her younger son about college. As expected, he is more interested in playing football than filling out applications, and she fears that any lapse of persistence on her part will lead to the casual trashing of his future and—more profoundly—to the reversal of her bloodline's ascent. Lori was the first to attend state college; it rests with her children to pierce the private sphere.

She is gratified to have succeeded with her older son, whom they dropped off at a well-regarded, very expensive university just two weeks earlier. Perversely, her reward for this success has been Kurt's empty bedroom, finally tidy, but so vacant that she cannot look in. For the past two weeks, she's struggled against telephoning him. She knows it's better to stay cool, to wait for him to make contact. Again, patience! And her waiting has paid off: he'd finally called the day before, although she has to admit that the conversation had been short and unsatisfying. He is planning to take a class in a subject Lori didn't quite catch—social biology? bio-anthropology?—and she hung up the phone with a strained good-bye and the feeling of a gauzy cluster in her throat.

The cars keep coming. Lori sits erect in the driver's seat, calm, like a good student, still silently berating herself for the missed opportunity to make her turn. Now she is going to be behind schedule; she is going to have to rush when she gets home. She has already chosen a dress for the party, but she hasn't actually worn it in centuries and is concerned that it might need ironing, or might not fit the way it used to. She should have tried it on earlier in the week. But, really, how was she to have guessed that she'd be held up tonight, and for such a silly reason? When she'd rushed out of the house that afternoon, she hadn't intended to be gone for more than twenty minutes. She hadn't even brought her cell phone.

And, really, this is getting ridiculous. People *live* on this road. How do they contend with this intersection day after day? She looks for evidence of previous trouble—skid marks on the road, bark shaved from trees—but finds none. Her current difficulty must be a fluke. She considers turning around, going back down Iron Horse, back to Edgeware, back home via dependable Mercy and its protracted but functional stoplight. If she had only taken the usual route in the first place, she would be home by now; she would already have tried on the dress and begun fixing her hair. A broken-down Volvo comes past with a patchwork of bumper stickers on its rear. No. If she goes back now, the traffic will relent the instant she is out of sight. She's lived long enough to know that's how the world works. And she's committed too much time to waiting already. How much time *has* it been? It feels like ten minutes, maybe more. It's better, she thinks, not to look at the clock.

Again, a space approaches, but this one she judges to be too tight. The decision is made: she will not accelerate; it's not worth the risk. Instead, she sits and waits as the Toyota speeds past, followed by a long brown Cadillac. She sits and waits as the Cadillac approaches, and realizes too late that it is traveling at an exaggeratedly slow speed, that she could have gone in front of it politely at least three times. As it passes, she sees the driver's head in profile, straining forward in the way of the elderly. Somewhere, she imagines, are the man's worried adult children, exasperated by their father's refusal to give up his license, by his insistence that his reflexes are still sharp as knives.

Lori takes a deep breath and holds it, calling up reserves of patience. It is not so easy to control the proud and aging. Her own parents are still stubbornly upstate, holding on to the decaying home of her childhood, despite its staircases and sunken living room, despite the Hasidic families swarming the neighborhood like black ants. Her mother has fallen twice already, bruising each hip. And yet they refuse to visit the assisted-living facility Lori has found for them here in town, where they could have an apartment with its own kitchenette. They don't want a kitchenette, her mother says. They want to stay where they are comfortable, and stay there until they die.

The traffic on Cannonfield is still dense, but there seem to be slightly longer intervals between cars now. With new hope, Lori waits. She notices that the sunlight is changing, taking on a warmer, angular quality. Across Cannonfield is a wall of trees. This is still considered the country, more or less, and it comforts her somehow to know that there are birds in these trees, and any number of undiseased rodents. Lori lets her eyes blur out of focus as she stares at the deep green foliage, discerning patches of shade and light. She sits like this for a long moment, until a movement in her frame of vision catches her attention, and she is startled to notice a vehicle in her rearview mirror. It is surprising, really, that no unlucky driver has yet gotten stuck behind her. Now she feels the renewed anxiety of her situation, compounded by the presence of a waiting stranger in a black BMW. She sits up straight and returns her attention to the physics of approaching traffic. How frustrating that the driver behind her has no way of knowing how long she's been sitting here, how laughably impossible this left turn has been, how stupendously patient she is.

The cars continue to flow steadily in both directions. Finally, a space approaches—it is tight, yes, but it's now or never—and Lori's foot again does not respond to the command to accelerate. There must be some contradictory command interfering with it, beyond her conscious control. For an instant, Lori understands herself as a split being, with a gulf between her voluntary and involuntary selves, between that which can be helped and that which cannot.

She glances at the mirror, sending an invisible apology to the driver behind her. And yet when another eligible space approaches, she again lets it pass, dumbfounded. The BMW honks and, at last, pulls alongside her, idles for a moment, and moves ahead onto Cannonfield, making a smooth left turn and disappearing around the bend. Lori feels her face flush in humiliation. Really, it couldn't have hurt the BMW to wait more patiently. Sometimes other drivers are terrible, forgetful of their shared humanity, their common fallibility. Too many people honk the instant a light turns green, make responsible people feel incompetent.

And yet, what is wrong with her today? She has never been so timid behind the wheel. It's as if she's entered a variation of that common nightmare: anchored feet, the sucking of quicksand. The stop sign looms, its message like an existential injunction for her alone. She takes a deep breath and closes her eyes. The thing to do is relax. It will do no good to think of the passing time, of the fact that the day is now visibly darkening, the patterns of sunlight disappearing from the road and trees.

Now, another car comes up behind her. It lurks in her rearview mirror, its black grille scowling at the back of her head. A moment later, another appears behind that, and then another. Two, three—maybe more—drivers are now depending on Lori's judgment, Lori's decisiveness, Lori's lifetime of experience on the road. They have places to be, perhaps urgently. Lori struggles to keep her focus on the streaming traffic, but her heart is pounding too heavily now, the blood surging in her skull, and her vision seems strangely blurred, her depth perception skewed. With a trembling hand, she presses the hazard button on the dashboard. A moment later, the first car noses tentatively alongside her and passes, followed by the others.

The clack of the hazards is stereophonic and insistent, over-ruling the turn signal's tinny tick. Lori holds her foot firmly on the brake and draws a long breath, relieved to be alone again with her stop sign. She finally allows herself to glance at the dashboard clock: 6:50. A shot of terror goes through her body. The party begins in ten minutes. Mitch will already be dressed, even as Mason continues to goof in his room. Without Lori there to nag, Mitch will have to be the one to remind him to change out of his sweat-stained T-shirt, to put on something befitting the son of a managing director. Lori pictures her husband in a clean shirt and chinos, face re-shaven, checking the Rolex she bought him as a birthday gift that summer with the excess of money he'd earned. The watch is still bright gold on his wrist, its bezel notched and fluted, almost feminine. She thinks of it now with a kind of nostalgic longing as she pictures her husband pacing the floor of their kitchen, just a few miles away but bizarrely out of reach. How long will he wait, she wonders, before going to the party without her? He will, after all, have to go to the party. He will leave a note, Lori thinks, in his boyish scrawl, telling her to call the minute she gets home. Or perhaps he will wait until nightfall before phoning the Christensens, keeping the fear out of his voice as he explains the situation. Whichever Christensen answers will express concern, as party sounds jangle in the background, then offer assurance that Mitch's wife will be home soon, that she probably just ran into a friend and lost track of time, and that they should come anytime before ten, really.

Lori opens the compartment in the center console and takes out a stack of CDs. She chooses the most relaxing music she can find: a New Age orchestral album with a snowy horse on the cover. As the synthesizer arrangement drifts through the car, Lori tries to relax her eyes. The vehicles on Cannonfield are passing less frequently now. With a moment's preparation, it will be easy to join them. The music is beautiful, transcendent. As she stares at the trees ahead of her, they impress her as meaningfully sublime. These are the kinds of trees the old artists painted, worshipfully, in a time when America promised different kinds of riches. One tree is at a slant, its trunk bowing to a neighbor. Another is tall against the sky: a horse's head. These trees have stood, frozen in their God-given poses, for years, decades, centuries, overlooking this same thoroughfare. Lori considers this. These same trees have watched horses pass over dirt, then cars over asphalt. And, today, they watch what must be a curious sight—a woman alone in a silver-gray Lexus, paralyzed.

It is now well past seven. Maybe they're at the party now. They'd be there with kebabs, Mitch standing firm beside Mason, being strong for his sake, holding the same warming beer bottle. If he could just stand like this long enough, he would have done what he needed to do; he would have gone to the party. Then he and Mason could go home, and they would find Lori waiting for them, apologetic, embarrassed, with a story to tell. Then they would get into bed, he and Lori, and pull the blanket up around them and go on together to the next day. Saturday. September.

It feels good to sit like this. One more moment won't make much difference now, and it's such a rare pleasure to simply enjoy music, to be still. What, after all, is the rush? There's the party, yes, but otherwise, what? The next chapter of her life hardly beckons seductively. Lori imagines the likely content of the years to come, the long hours at her parents' bedsides, the beginning of physical ailments of her own. There will be sporadic, rushed visits from her children as they enter their futures like swimmers shoving off a pool wall. Is this all that life promises at its far end? She blinks her eyes at the thought of such imminent, unpopulated years. She will, she supposes, have to do what every underutilized, terrified woman has done throughout history: find volunteer opportunities, become an involved elder citizen, vigorously resist the twilight slide to oblivion.

For the moment, however, she is still relevant. After some span of time, Mitch and Mason will set out to look for her. They will, eventually, call the police. The certainty of this gladdens her. She allows herself, from the safety of her unmoving car, to imagine their fear of her death. They would not mention it aloud, of course, but it would be in the kitchen with them as they sit at the table, unspeaking. Wrenching scenarios would play out in their minds, each ending with her permanent absence from their lives. Perhaps it's wrong to derive a flowering kind of warmth from this idea. All Lori knows is that, for the span of her unexpected absence tonight, she will be prominent in the minds of her husband and son, and perhaps that is all right. Let them wait. Let them think deliberately of her for this one extended moment before time begins again and she is thrust into the dark.

The trees have gone black. The CD ends, and the car fills with the crude ticking of the hazard signal. Lori touches a button and begins the music again. From time to time, a car rolls up behind her and passes incuriously. There is little traffic on Cannonfield now, but she thinks only abstractly of making her turn. She just wants to stay for another moment. Every so often, she tells herself, we need to stop and sit. There should be pauses between chapters, white space on the printed page. Even a wave of water needs an instant of suspension before crashing down.

Lori's right foot aches. It's like a brick on the brake, unattached to her body. She closes her eyes for a moment, looks at the faint, conjured faces of her husband and sons, then opens her eyes again to the wall of darkened trees. The stop sign, too, has gone dim, its authority muted. Lori gazes at its letters, aglow in the dusk, until they become strange and lose meaning. She puts the car in park and, just like that, removes her foot from the brake. It feels light, grateful, hers again. She just wants to be quiet for another moment. If she could just be quiet for a moment, she would see a space between cars and slide into it. She would go home.

But for now, she turns off the ignition. Her stomach rumbles audibly. It's been hours, she realizes, since she last ate. Ah, but here are the cookies. No one will notice if the box is one or two short of a dozen. Lori loosens the red string and withdraws a jelly cookie, its red blotch like a stoplight. She eats three of these, then reclines her seat. From here, she stares up through the car's moon roof. *Moon roof,* she whispers to herself. *Moon roof.* Mitch had paid extra for this feature at the dealership, though Lori was never sure of its benefit. Now, its value is clear. Through the rectangle of engineered glass she sees a neatly framed portion of sky, a handful of static stars.

Kurt is in Pennsylvania, two hundred miles away. Lori is proud to have dropped him off without crying. Now, she finds herself replaying the day in her memory: the fast westward drive over polished black highway, the abrupt stop at the campus whose gate rose into view like a halting hand. Lori hadn't cried when they located Kurt's concrete dormitory, breathtaking in its ugliness. She hadn't cried when they laid eyes on the cinder block cubicle where he'd sleep for the next ten months, out of her sight and protection, at the mercy of Quaker gods. She had adamantly not cried. This moment of separation, she told herself, had been scripted from the beginning, contained in the very moment of his birth. It was the destination, the destruction, of parenthood.

But now, Lori cries. Sobbing, she allows herself the dangerous luxury of remembering the first months of Kurt's life, when she—her looming smile, the warmth of her body—was all he knew. She would watch his little face, its twitches and flashes of dawning comprehension, and wonder at the shadowed, textured mysteries that were evolving there. His little mind would be labeling everything it encountered, eliminating possibilities, whittling the world into its proper shape, its ultimate, disappointing narrowness. She would stare, as if she might witness the transformation as it occurred. But it was too fast, it was too slow. And one day he became a boy, kicking a bicycle to the ground. From an infant at effortless swim in the world, he'd become a stout little person with a name, a wish, at odds with everything.

It is the story of every mother. Lori leans against the headrest and puts a hand over her eyes. It seems, at times, that everything ends the minute she thinks of it. The minute she considers a thing's eventual end—no matter how far in the future—it ends. She takes her hand away from her eyes and looks through the moon roof at the stars. Those stars may as well be dead the minute she considers their death. The remaining thousands of years are only a technical distraction.

Lori lets her body sink farther into the driver's seat. It is a surprisingly comfortable seat, the headrest expertly contoured to the shape of a woman's skull. She allows herself to be cradled by the upholstered foam and focuses on relaxing each muscle of her body, beginning at her toes, the way she learned to do as an insomniac girl. Like this, she could become a floating being, weightless and free.

As Lori shifts her focus to her abdominal muscles, she feels suddenly and irreversibly tired. It's as if all the years have piled upon her at once, the accumulated hours of lost sleep. She lies with her eyes closed, her brain requesting the release of the cinches that hold her abdomen together. As she does this, a maw of exhaustion opens in her core. It would be so easy to just go to sleep. In the corner of her consciousness, she is aware of being a woman alone in a car at night. She thinks of locking the doors, but her hand disobeys the order to move.

Distantly, she wonders what time it is. Perhaps her husband and son are already home from the party or, more likely, out looking for her. The childish pleasure of this thought is undercut by a feeling of trepidation. Her family will be distraught by now, convinced of the worst. What, exactly, is she doing? An animal whimper comes out of her as she strains helplessly against sleep, its steady velvet tug.

Hours pass. Lori sleeps shallowly. Half dreaming, she drives out onto Cannonfield, then snaps back into place at the stop sign, over and over. When she partially surfaces from sleep, she senses that the black screens of her eyelids are changing, becoming reddish. Possibly, the morning sun is approaching, lighting her blood vessels. She allows her lids to remain closed. Groggily, she understands that the residents of this town, invisibly sleeping in the houses surrounding her, will be rising soon. The Christensens will be waking to hangovers, to a fresh-faced cleaning crew ringing their doorbell. Two hundred miles away, Kurt will be starfished upon his narrow dorm bed, possibly working toward a hangover himself, but for the moment still lost in dreams, his mind enviably clear.

The sound of a car engine registers in Lori's awareness. Someone going to work on a Saturday morning, or to an early breakfast at the pancake house. The engine idles behind her for several moments, the sound of anticipation itself. If she had the ability to sit up, she would lower the window, wave the car past. Perhaps it isn't a car, but the hum of her own dreaming. But then, unmistakably, the sound of a door closing. Someone is finally coming to check on her. A concerned neighbor, or perhaps the police. It's a wonder that it's taken this long, a wonder that so many others have driven past indifferently. From behind this thought stalks another, darker possibility. This is no concerned neighbor, but a stranger with malign intentions. She lies helpless in her seat, conscious of the distance between the door's locking mechanism and her own immobilized fingers. She is the perfect victim, supine and defenseless.

The inside of the car is silent as she waits, adrift in space. The passage of time has become strangely palpable, each moment billowing around her. In these suspended instants before a tap on her window, any outcome remains possible. And yet she is certain it's Mitch who has come. She knows, in her blood, that it is her husband behind her, emerging from their old Acura, the one Mason drives to school with the mysterious gash on the passenger door. That's the car he would have chosen for the hunt, for trolling through town for hours. Now that he's found the Lexus here on Iron Horse Road, he will be walking toward it, his chest thundering with gratitude and fear. This can't be good, he will be warning himself. If she'd simply broken down, why hadn't she found a way to call, or walk home?

Lori is awake now, more awake with each second. At last, she opens her eyes to the moon roof and sees the gentle blue sky. It's a sweet morning, she can see, very sweet. He will have almost reached the driver's side window by now, preparing himself to look in. She'll be seeing his face any minute, unslept and creased with worry, brown eyes as soft as the day she met him. He will peer in at her with an expression of relief and concern, of decades of life already lived and decades remaining, and then he'll open the unlocked door and lift her out of the car. Just like that, he'll lift her and take her home. She turns toward the window and waits. His face will appear any minute now.

Wampum

Michael has already unlocked the pistol case. He keeps his eyes pinned to the road, to the vague weavings of the car in front of them, as they cross through town to the address on the invitation. The gate is open, winged by stone pillars and carriage lanterns. As Michael navigates the driveway, Rosalie surveys the grounds through the passenger window. Michael knows that she has seen other fine properties of course, but this is of another tier. He is aware of the weeks she's spent preparing for this evening, having found the invitation where he'd buried it deep in the recycling basket. *This is not something you ignore,* she chastised, holding the card aloft.

The tennis court comes as no surprise. The green clay blends into the surrounding emerald acreage, the pleasant dips and hills, a miniature Ireland here on Pelican Point. The Christensens are the type of people who would build a court whether they play tennis or not, he thinks, the type who trust they will learn the game eventually, hire a private instructor, spend weekend afternoons rallying together. They are determined to reap their rewards, seize each moment as their due. They are, in this way, so much like children, Michael thinks. When the final collapse comes, they will simply and effortlessly crumble. It would be a kind of liberation to live like this, free from the burden of constant vigilance. He exhales audibly and Rosalie flashes him an admonishing glance.

They are met at the end of the driveway by a dark-skinned man in a bomber jacket. Michael's grip on the steering wheel tightens. The man signals to them, gesturing alongside his body.

"Ah, a valet," Rosalie says, keeping the dazzlement out of her voice.

Michael knows he will have to be fast. The valet opens the passenger door for Rosalie. The moment the door closes behind her, Michael reaches under the seat and slips the subcompact into the outer pocket of his sports jacket. He is out of the car before the bomber jacket has reached the driver's side. He feels a rush of relief. Let the guy adjust the seat and change the radio station all he wants.

As the BMW slides away, he takes off his glasses, which are strictly reserved for driving and theater performances. He and Rosalie circle the house on foot, following the valet's direction. It's a sprawling Tudor with severe, half-timbered gables over a hulking stone base. The effect is heavy, almost medieval, out of sync with the waterfront setting.

Sunlight is fading already. The operatic end of summer, the perennial pinnacle of romance and youth. They circle the house and stand at the top of a granite staircase. Lights are strung in the trees. Jewels glitter on the women. Michael idly contemplates the total dollar value upon the bodies of these collected guests. A group of armed interlopers—perhaps even one bold villain—could hold up the lot of them and divest them of millions. Before he steps down into the mix, he calls the scene to mind. His raiders are equipped with ski masks and black rifles. The women slip necklaces over their heads and drop them to the flagstone. The men unclasp wristwatches with as much slow dignity as possible. Michael knows that, if it weren't for the Ruger, he would have to do the same. Letting Rosalie step briefly ahead of him, he deftly transfers the gun from outer pocket to inner. It is so slim that it barely makes a bulge.

Carol Christensen appears at the bottom of the steps, beaming up at them, illuminated by a footlight. She looks good, hair all grown back, dressed in a snug flower-print number, still shapely for a woman her age. If she has had work done on her face, it is of the highest quality.

"Dr. Warren, we're so glad you could make it," she says, brushing her cheek against his. He keeps his torso pivoted away. "Your husband is a miracle worker," she informs Rosalie. "We're honored to have you both here." She gestures and leads them into the crowd. Michael glimpses the place near the ear where the incision had been, where he'd peered through a window of bone.

They pass batches of faces. Most are attractive, none beautiful. From behind, the women could be young. Their hair is dyed in lustrous blacks, golds, and auburns. Michael's eye is hooked by a woman in red, and he balks. From behind, the shape of the shoulders, the russet hair like a tapered flame, suggests Diana.

This is what he was afraid might happen. He's been reckless, playing too close to home.

He sidesteps, causing Rosalie to look. There is no way Diana could be here, he tells himself. There is no feasible link she could have to these people. And even she would not drop so far as to track him down this way. The shape in red rotates a few degrees, exhibiting a horse-nosed profile, and Michael snickers aloud.

But isn't it possible that she would do it? Diana's campaign has stretched out for months. Her phone calls and texts have been unpredictable. Rosalie has been reporting hang-ups at home. He's put a new cell number into service, but kept the old one to throw her off the scent. As far as he knows, she is still in the rented apartment with her daughter, hostage to her own amateur error.

Off to the side, a swimming pool glows. A stone cabana the size of a town house has its double doors open. The main residence is apparently closed. Smart people.

Rosalie troops quietly at his side in a matte silver dress that reminds him of a fish. The dress is out of character for her, but she'd come home one day elated to have stumbled upon it in a consignment shop in town—perfect for this party. A long silver chain with a squiggly pendant rests upon the unified mogul of her breasts. Matching squiggles hang from her earlobes. She has applied some kind of metallic makeup that adds to the marine effect.

"I wonder if we know anyone," she mutters.

"I'm sure you'll find someone you know," Michael answers, putting a hand to her elbow. He has, after all, never accompanied her to an event where this has not been the case.

They have already lost Carol. A waiter zeroes in on them like a drone with a filigreed platter of bruschetta. The women are all beginning to look familiar to Michael now. There is a wavy-haired blonde like Camille—but he dismisses this possibility, too.

Rosalie is spirited away by a sparkle-toothed specimen rhapsodizing about the school board. Then Harold Christensen appears. He envelops Michael with a hearty, patriarchal greeting—a hand to the shoulder, a booming hello meant to be heard by all those around them. Michael has the unmistakable sense that their power dynamic has shifted. He is on Harold's turf now, among Harold's people, where Harold reigns. It occurs to him that Harold views his single, privileged visit to Michael's operating room as something inevitable from the start, to which he was always entitled. He had paid good money for it. Very good. And there is no residue between them. A quick wink is the only evidence of their secret compact. Carol is fine, yes, he says. The seizures have not returned. Michael is the best of the best.

"The best of the best," he repeats, drawing another man into the conversation. "Bill Gregory, I want you to meet Michael Warren. He's the one who fixed Carol." Harold hits the man on the upper arm and says to Michael, "I'm so glad I lured this one to town. Already he's making waves. The town council nearly sued him for some sort of art"—Harold gestures, looking for the word—"exhibit on his property."

"Installation," Bill corrects, smiling.

"He's a firebrand." Harold grins. "One of the finest businessmen I know. He finally gave in and joined my board."

They all know each other, of course. This is the nature of *society* as Michael is given to understand it. A nebulous flow of acquaintance and event. A rigorously upheld air of casualness, coincidence, serendipity—of gleefully "running into" one another. To circulate among them is to witness finely wrought identities held aloft by mutual scrutiny. In every exchanged glance is a judgment of financial prowess, social capability, personal fulfillment. Michael is both repulsed and fascinated by it all. Mostly, he is grateful to be spared, ensconced in a comfortable, unassuming home kept presentable by his wife. He has never gone in for the usual pretentions. It would feel like a lie, trying too hard to please. He is not from this world and would not pretend otherwise.

And being in the presence of these men, complacent upon their moneyed peaks, makes him uneasy. Indeed, he is most admired by his colleagues for the phenomenon of his success out of dingy beginnings. His life story, having leaked somehow to the hospital staff, has become legend: his father's sudden brain hemorrhage when Michael was twelve; his widowed mother cleaning houses, going on food stamps. The consensus is that Michael was activated by poverty's humiliation to rise above his station. Given the nature of his father's death, it seemed logical—and admirable—that he would pursue medicine, and neurosurgery in particular.

Now, he stands upon a square of flagstone on Pelican Point and watches in horror as his host retreats into the mass of guests, leaving him alone with the art insurgent. There is a long, vacant moment during which it occurs to Michael that it must be his duty as the lower-ranked male to carry the conversational burden.

"What's your line of work?" he finally ventures.

"Banking," Bill Gregory says, his focus snapping back. Despite the relaxed stance and soft-jowled face, despite the pink shirt and navy blazer—that uniform of the ages—there is something hawklike about him.

Michael mirrors his stance, one hand in a pocket, the other holding a tumbler of Scotch. "Rough time lately?"

"It's a memorable moment, that's for sure." Twinkling smile. Of course no one of Gregory's rank would feel a pinch of any kind. They are the ones delivering pinches.

Michael considers, for a brief moment, whether to ask this man's advice about gold bars. Most likely he has his own cache. Anyone with insight into the current financial debacle would know how to hedge—and gold, after all, is the hedge of all hedges, the only sure thing. When the crunch comes, no one will want to see a dollar bill. Anyone with a stock certificate or government bond will get a laugh in the face. If anyone would know this, it's Bill Gregory.

"Hell, I hate talking shop," Gregory says. "But now Harold tells me you're quite a prodigy with the scalpel. I heard you saved a girl's life? Some new type of surgery?"

"A hemispherectomy. Not new, but unusual. The disconnection of an entire hemisphere of the brain."

Bill Gregory nods. "Yes, that's right. That's what I heard. She was almost gone, she was seeing angels, and you brought her back."

This is what everyone has heard. It has become less about the procedure, less about Michael's life-saving work, than about his patient's glimpse of the afterlife on his operating table. There was a national magazine feature about it, which mentioned Michael's name only in passing. There was no praise for the heroism of modern medicine, or of the surgeon who yanked the little girl back from the brink and secured a semi-normal life for her. Rather, the article went into raptures about the existence of God, as proven definitively by the words of a child.

The girl gave everyone what they wanted. She hovered near the OR ceiling, traveled to the waiting room and observed her anxious parents. She floated to a night sky and passed the planets of the solar system—Saturn was a floating ball of milk ringed with ribbons, she said—and beyond. Then the light and tunnel. She entered this light, of course, and felt the usual sense of warmth, perfect peace. She met the relatives she'd never known in life, all of whom fluttered with wings. The long-dead grandmother turned her around and sent her back to her body.

It would have seemed petty to contradict all this, to offer the probable scientific explanations: The malfunctioning of the girl's remaining parietal cortex would have created a feeling of union with the universe and the sensation of flying. Adrenaline from a distressed brain would have dilated the pupils, causing the appearance of bright light. The diminishing supply of oxygen would have been to blame for the closing of the girl's peripheral vision field and her trip down the quintessential tunnel.

"The surgery was a success, yes," Michael tells Bill Gregory. "She'll need plenty of therapy to regain the use of the left side of her body, but will otherwise be like any other child."

Gregory puts a hand out, pumps Michael's. "Well. It's an honor." He smiles. A trim blonde appears at his side. "Excuse me, my wife." Gregory winks, claiming her. As they retreat, Michael allows his imagination to swoop into their bedroom, then back out, to what he presumes are Gregory's extracurricular pursuits.

Michael stands in place, training his gaze over the heads of party guests. Between the pool house and Tudor mansion a swatch of the Long Island Sound is visible. From here, it is a fragment, an ornamental splash of color. Still, its presence agitates him in some primal way. Just the suggestion of sea, the undertone of its faraway thunder.

There is one woman who keeps looking over. Bottle blond, in a dress with a complicated green-and-navy print. Despite the wrap design that creates a deep plunge at the chest, Michael distinctly dislikes the dress. Its pattern, he realizes, is like a crude illustration of the sea. The woman's chest is so smoothly rounded beneath the fabric that there must be some sort of padding in her bra, or beneath the skin. The over-bleached hair lies flat against the sides of her head like paper. Still, he returns her glances. The woman disengages herself from her conversation and approaches.

"You're the brain surgeon, am I right?"

"I'm Michael Warren, yes."

She touches his arm. "The Christensens have told me about you. And I read the story of the little girl you saved."

Her hand remains on his arm, the fingers impressing themselves through his shirtsleeve. She holds his gaze, and he feels the usual stirrings. Despite the unappealing sleekness of hair, the toned upper arms, the terrible dress; despite the lurking presence of the husband in blocky eyeglasses—or maybe because of it—he does not look away. He feels the woman's fingers against the flesh of his arm like a reassurance: the old passages will always remain open to him.

She talks in an undulating voice about the little girl and her audience with angels. "So amazing, don't you think?"

Michael finds himself pulling his arm away in punishment, bringing the Scotch glass to his lips. He has nothing to say about the attractions of heaven.

He had pushed for the surgery. It was a long-thwarted ambition of his to perform a hemispherectomy. Most patients opted to travel to Johns Hopkins, but he was determined to persuade someone to stay at St. Joseph's. At age eight, the girl was somewhat old for a surgery best suited for infants whose brains have not yet calcified into task centers. But Rasmussen's encephalitis was causing debilitating seizures, and the parents did not want to travel. The girl resembled his youngest daughter, with the same shade of maple wood hair. During the surgery, with the patient's head concealed by blue sterile drape, he kept lapsing into the thought that it was Hannah's cerebrum beneath his knife.

It was after the frontal and parietal lobes had been disconnected and he was cutting the corpus callosum that intraventricular hemorrhaging began. The team's first attempts to cauterize were insufficient. They went into silent focus. For just a fleeting moment, Michael slipped. He allowed himself to think of the child, of the little memories tucked into the folds of her brain tissue, and his fingers went stiff. Standing over the open skull, he imagined having to tell the family. If he lost her, he would have to be the one to tell them. He had lost only one patient before, but there had been no relatives to inform. Meeting the grave eyes of the attending surgeon at his side, he felt a crater open inside him.

The hemorrhaging finally, magically, ceased, and the girl's heartbeat returned to normal. After they fastidiously replaced the section of bone and sutured the skin of the scalp, Michael left the OR without a word. The attending surgeon called after him, but he kept walking, exiting through the radiology wing to avoid the family in the waiting room.

It was after eight in the evening. He raced his BMW over the roads that led to his own family. He felt a vertiginous impatience to see them, to wrap them in an iron embrace that would never weaken. When he got home, he would pull them close and talk to them. He would say and do what a husband, a father, might say and do. Coming through the door and standing in the entryway, he could hear the voices of his wife and children, the younger ones getting ready for bed. He stood for a long time in the foyer, listening. At last, Rosalie came down the stairs and glanced at him. He stood, mesmerized. Her gaze lingered for a moment, as if reading something, then slid away.

Now, standing with the blond woman, the same unmoored sensation returns. The name she gave him has faded out.

Something unbeautiful. *Gertrude,* or *Greta.* For the past few minutes she has been relating the story of a dream she had as a young girl.

"They were angels, I'm sure of it. They came to my bed and talked to me. They explained the difference between right and wrong." She cocks her head to the side. "I really believe they gave me my first lesson in morality." She has the faraway look of a woman traveling on three margaritas.

"What did you say your name was again?"

Her gaze spirals back. She moves a piece of hair behind her ear, exposing a cluster of icy gems. "Gretchen Von Mauren."

"It's been nice talking with you, Gretchen. Will you excuse me?"

Despite the gravitational pull to remain in any woman's orbit, Michael steps away. He is careful not to make eye contact with anyone as he drifts to the periphery of the crowd. But, as if supernaturally attuned to the defection of any of her guests, Carol Christensen appears at his side.

"Lovely party, Carol," Michael offers, producing a smile. "And you look wonderful."

She grins like a teenager. "I'm *feeling* wonderful." Stepping closer, she lowers her tone. "You know, I never mentioned it to you, but I did have some bad headaches right after the surgery. And some very dark moods."

"No, you didn't mention that."

"I'm afraid I might even have been clinically depressed for a while." Carol blinks. "But thankfully that's all gone now. I'm better than ever."

"Well, I'm glad to hear it."

Carol pauses, gives Michael a long look. "I feel a little bashful telling you this, but I ended up finding a holistic healer. Well, I guess he'd call himself an *indigenous* healer." She quickly puts a hand to Michael's sleeve. "Honestly, I never thought I'd go in for the New Age stuff. That's not the kind of person I am. But I have to say, I'm so glad I kept an open mind."

Michael feels he has no choice but to prod further. "So, what kind of healing was this exactly?"

She smiles and draws closer. "He did something called a soul retrieval, which sounds very spacey, I know, but afterward I felt like a completely new person. It seemed like everything was brighter around me. Even my complexion has improved. People have noticed!"

Michael looks sternly at her. "You should have called me about the headaches."

"That's what Harold said." Carol tilts her head. "But, anyway, they're gone now. The healer said that sometimes, with some conditions, there's a point where Western medicine can't really help anymore, and you have to address the root cause of the problem. He said that the surgery may have been an effective solution for the epilepsy on a superficial level. But he perceived some deep-seated spiritual issues, too. I'm sure that must sound implausible to you, but whatever he did, it worked for me." Carol touches Michael's sleeve again, as if in apology, then scans the crowd. "I invited him tonight, actually. I'd love to introduce you, but it seems he's not here yet."

"That's all right," Michael says, raising his Scotch glass and disengaging Carol's touch. He has cut open more than one shamanic skull in his career, short-circuited more than one carnival in the temporal lobe. He can predict just the kinds of interictal spikes that would appear on an EEG if Carol's healer were monitored during one of his so-called retrievals. Michael considers the irony here, of one epileptic healing another.

"His name is Apocatequil, in case you meet him. Hard to forget that! It means 'god of lightning' in the Incan language. He's really a very interesting person."

At this, Carol summons a nearby crescent of guests to her, and, as they begin to congeal into a ring, Michael lifts his chin as if suddenly remembering something. With a quick backward step, he melts out of the circle toward the edge of the pool. He stands, feeling the cut of Carol's insult. There is an acidic taste in his mouth as he watches the flux of revelers.

He spots Rosalie, mingling happily. She always looks good in her diligent way, but in a social setting like this a kind of nimbus surrounds her. He watches her for a few moments in wonderment. He is aware of her quiet power, the daily feat she performs of parenting his children, of navigating the politics of schools and township, what she refers to as *the community*. He becomes aware of her partnership as a boom to which he clings. She alone has made it possible for him to join gatherings like this, gatherings that to him court all manner of attack—crazed gunmen, terrorist sieges, biological pandemics—and send his imagination reeling.

He knows that this feedback loop is its own biological pandemic, likely caused by deficient serotonin in his amygdala. He has learned not to fight the fear, but to welcome it as an inborn advantage, compelling him to prepare where others might procrastinate. Still, once the panic begins, it takes all his will to push it away. He is seized by the myriad ways he could be killed at any moment. Car accident—blunt trauma to the brain, impalement by the steering wheel column, snapped rib through the heart. Electrical fire—third-degree burns, asphyxiation from smoke inhalation. Brain aneurysm—subarachnoid hemorrhage, intense headache, collapse. Nuclear blast—immediate dismemberment or slow, painful death from radiation poisoning. Just the sound of fireworks out of season makes him jump. The apocalyptic moment is skulking closer all the time. There is a script of actions that he is prepared to take when it finally appears like an ornate rising dragon, breathtakingly hideous. It is almost a feeling of welcome, of feverish anticipation for the beginning of something. He has charted the variables so studiously that there would be a certain disappointment if they did not occur.

Standing beside the pool, he pictures the sky lit up, bleached like a photo negative. The atmosphere would flare white-hot, sending radioactive particles raining down within seconds. Standing there, he does the calculations. It would take several minutes to locate their car in the assemblage on the front lawn. He and Rosalie would have to split up to find it. Being the first into their vehicle would be crucial if they were to avoid the inevitable jam of guests bottling the Christensens' elegant driveway. If they succeeded, they could be back on Whistle Hill Road in twenty minutes, more or less, allowing for detours onto back roads. If those roads were also clogged, they would proceed on foot via wooded shortcuts. Once home, it would take another five minutes or so to get the kids into the dugout under the tool shed. Not fast enough, but better than it could be. And although the underground bunker itself is not yet finished, it would be serviceable—large enough for sardine-tight sleeping pads—and more than what most others would have. When Rosalie sees what he has done for them, how thoroughly he has seen to their safety, she will be dumbstruck.

He has, over the course of a year, reinforced the tool shed walls with concrete blocks. The supplies are hidden behind a false wall: a waste bucket, bins of clothing, a pyramid of water jugs, three months' worth of shelf-stable food, and first aid kits with iodine tablets. He is always adding, little by little, to the survival kit: an assortment of pocket knives, fire starters, flares. The gold—about fifty Good Delivery bars with serial numbers, twenty-seven pounds each—is buried a hundred feet away in a spot marked by a loose triangle of rocks.

And he has done even more with the money from Harold Christensen, who had wanted to attend his own wife's surgery. After months of persuasion, Michael had finally accepted his donation, then put it toward an arsenal to keep roving mobs at bay: a .38 pistol for each of his boys, plus his own Ruger; a .22 rifle, a Remington 700 with Leupold scope; and his newest acquisition, a set of four AR15s, one for each male in the family. He has rubbed the weapons with rust-preventing grease and secreted them in a cache tube made of industrial piping, itself buried in a cavity adjacent to the dugout. With the rest of the cash, he has bulked up his ammunition supply. There is no such thing as too much personal ammo, or too much wampum for barter.

It might take another year of digging, removing buckets of dirt after dark, before the bunker is up to standard. He will need to go down far enough for earth arching to protect against radiation. He will need to install some sort of ventilation and, crucially, create a second exit. Even with two exits, however, there is always the possibility of the shelter collapsing, of being buried alive—a scenario that has already bored its way into his imaginative repertoire.

He breathes deeply. The rise and fall of conversation and laughter, like ocean waves, insist on normalcy, the stubborn continuation of the world as it is.

With an effort, Michael steps back toward the party. As he joins the swarm, a woman brushes past him, a new brunette like a draft of cool air—loose hair, scant makeup—a natural beauty. Tight at her side is a ponytailed freak in some kind of pajama set. This man gives Michael a direct, penetrating look. The jealousy is unsurprising, given the disparity of the pair: the man has a narrow, miserly face, his hair pulled too tight in its choke hold. A cracked leather cord girdles his neck and disappears down the front of his tunic. This can only be Carol's medicine man.

He tracks the strange couple as they navigate through the crowd until, at last, Carol Christensen falls upon them. After her effusions, she pulls away, keeping a hand upon the man's narrow shoulder as if to hold him in place. Michael watches her survey the surrounding guests, alight with her new self-image, burning to display her guru to some benighted soul. Her eyes spark upon Michael, and as she raises a hand to wave him over, he swivels away.

He will be sorry not to meet the brunette, but has no need to engage with Carol's god of lightning. He knows the type. Like all fanatics, they want only to sermonize. Trying to pin them down is like playing racquetball on a buttered court. There is no way to win, no arguing for the validity of medicine or the supremacy of biological systems. There is, for these people, no such thing as brain disease—least of all in themselves. The spirit world is something external, untouchable, a higher order of reality beyond the mundane perception of science. When their own brain scans show unusual electrical patterns, they consider their point proven: their spiritual experience made manifest. It's not a biological flaw; it's a gift.

Before Carol can seize him, Michael circles around to the far side of the pool. From there, he ambles over the grass, away from the party, willing invisibility upon himself. Finally, he takes refuge in a shadowy place near the privet hedges and stands alone with his Scotch glass. Too late, he notices the glass is empty. Still, he feels an intoxicating breeze here, away from the crowd. He breathes deeply of the rich, darkened air and instinctually scans his surroundings. As if in a dream, his eyes catch on a shadowy figure near a hedge several yards away. A dart of adrenaline pierces him, and hot blood slams out to his extremities. Just like that, he is fully, poundingly alive. His right hand goes across his chest, feeling for the pistol at his heart.

The figure turns slightly, and the pool glow illuminates the profile of a teenage boy. Stepping closer, Michael sees a polo shirt and khakis. Their eyes meet, and the boy glances away. Michael lets his right arm drop to his side, but the adrenaline is still circulating and needs a place to go. Without thinking, he walks toward the boy with a little jig in his step. He smiles sociably and nods. The boy hesitantly returns the nod. Michael can see the Adam's apple burrowing in his throat. The boy has obviously come to this spot to be alone, and Michael feels suddenly sorry for having approached. Standing there, he rubs his hands together as if to warm them. He is bristling with the urge to run, to do a lap around the pool, to sprint all the way to the end of this feeble spit of land, to swan dive into the sound. Instead, he turns and adopts a relaxed pose alongside the boy.

"Which ones are yours?" he asks, nodding toward the crowd.

"Sorry?"

"Your parents."

"Oh." The boy points toward the pool house, where there is a unit of men. "That's my dad, in the blue shirt."

Michael points to Rosalie, who is laughing with Bill Gregory's wife. "That one's mine."

"Your—?"

Michael laughs. "My wife."

The boy has an easy, symmetrical face, eyes that are brown and lamblike.

"Are you at the high school?"

"Yeah. I'm a junior."

"Ah, good year," Michael says ludicrously. "What are your plans after school?"

The boy gives him an incisive look. The Adam's apple goes up and down. "I don't know." There is a pause. "Maybe the army," he mumbles.

"Did I hear you say *army*?"

The boy folds his arms over his chest and stares into the pool water.

"You know there's a war, right?"

"Well, yeah," the boy says without looking at Michael. "That's what armies do." His voice strums a low register of notes, like a saw blade going through wood.

"How about college?" Michael hears himself ask. "Have you thought about college?" It is insane, he knows, to be grilling the boy this way. It seems to arise from an instinct he cannot readily identify. Not fatherly, exactly, but something approximate.

"I'm afraid college isn't right for me," the boy answers. He looks at Michael with a shimmer in his eye. After a moment, he breaks his gaze. "You don't know my father, do you?"

"I don't recognize him, no."

The boy nods. "Well, if you do meet him, please don't say anything. I haven't told him about it yet."

Michael's mouth crimps into a smile. He is mystified by these young men who volunteer themselves for the armed forces, who willingly put themselves in harm's way—not necessarily through love of country or desire to serve, but in some kneejerk rebellion or plain lack of direction. He supposes that legions of youth have lazily ricocheted into service to their country this way; there is a reason the armed forces target the young, after all.

Michael looks back to the party, singles out the boy's father. What has that man done, he wonders, to drive his son to war? Rather than thinking of his own sons—immersed in battles on athletic fields to the exclusion of all else—he reflects on his own teenage years. Whereas this boy seems driven by muscle and instinct, Michael's body had adopted the features of manhood while slouched indoors on a stained basement couch, day after sunlit day, playing Atari. He would choose a single game and flog it single-mindedly until he had conquered every level. More than shooting aliens out of the sky, he'd gleaned the greatest satisfaction from climbing the cubes of a pyramid and strategically making them change color. He believes that the addictive pleasure of repainting those squares and standing at the summit each time—a squat little creature with a tubular nose, invincible—may have tinted his worldview in some permanent way.

He and the boy loiter in silence. Michael scrapes his mind for another question, something to keep the kid standing here. He is not sure why, but he does not want the boy to move away. Perhaps there is something Michael could teach him, if they hit on the right vein.

As they stand together watching the mingling herd on the far side of the pool, Michael spies a woman in white—tall, long-haired—he hadn't noticed before. He feels a tingling begin at the tips of his ears, hears a ringing. He takes out his glasses and finds the woman through their lenses. At once, he identifies the coppery hair in its licentious cascade. The dress is too long for a cocktail party, too much like a bridal gown, or the robe of a ghost. Only Diana would make this mistake. He sees the resolute smile on her face as she makes her way along the edge of the crowd, near the lip of the pool. The reflection of her dress accompanies her, an ice floe on the water. At the other end of the pool stands Rosalie, in animated chatter. Michael feels a gelid lump in his chest, which drops swiftly into his groin. The ice radiates, freezing him in place. He watches the space between the white figure and his wife shrinking. It is a disaster beyond any he might have concocted. About to happen.

There is no drill for this. He runs through the obvious actions first—interception by foot or by water—but sees that he cannot run around or swim across the pool in time. Shouting would do nothing. He stands in place, feeling the chill ascend to his head. The tinkle and chatter of the party is amplified as if it were taking place inside his skull. A switch flips. His hand goes to the inner jacket pocket and finds the pistol grip. There is a dreamlike feeling as he slides the weapon out and exposes it to the air, as if revealing his genitalia. His thumb releases the safety, his arm lifts, and the barrel points to the sky.

The shot is followed by a pixel of silence. The faces turn toward him. Diana stops. Then the screams of women. The next moment, he is on the ground, gasping dirt, a weight like an anvil rammed into his spine. Through the thrum of blood in his ears comes an underwater confusion of faraway shouts and near, beastlike panting. His vision is blackened, reduced to the tight study of grass roots. The smell of the soil through his crushed nostrils holds the deepest and darkest of messages, the raw beginning of things.

He feels the gun being taken from his hand. His white shirt, he thinks dimly, will be streaked beyond rescue. The anvil leaves his back, but a stabbing pain remains. Perhaps a broken rib, or worse. He lies still for a moment, a rare thing. For a moment, he postpones whatever will come next, clutching a peculiar bead of gratitude for this small respite, this fleeting breath of defenselessness. Finally, he is being helped up. Two men, one on either side of him, grip his arms and pull him to his feet.

"What the hell was that about?" one barks.

It hurts Michael to straighten his back, but he does it. "Nothing, nothing," he murmurs. "Just having a little fun. Just making fireworks, you know?"

He does not recognize the men from the party. Security, maybe. Christensen is wiser than he thought.

There is another figure, a polo shirt. Michael meets the teenage boy's eyes, bright with fear or exhilaration. "I-I'm sorry," the boy stammers. "I mean, I'm sorry if I hurt you."

Michael stares. Beneath the polo shirt, the boy's chest is broad, the torso tapering to a muscular abdomen. His arms are athletic without being sinewy. His face is radiant from exertion. The stabbing pain returns to Michael's ribs.

"What's your name?" he gasps.

The boy swallows. "Mason Hatfield, sir."

Michael nods, keeps nodding.

"We'll take you to your car," says a man at his arm.

The women are still on the far side of the pool, a wall of gaping faces. He does not see Diana among them. There is no one in a white dress, short or long. She must have run, he thinks. In the roil of his brain, beyond the distant congratulation, is another, more distant thought. Perhaps she hadn't been there at all.

The men shepherd him over the lawn toward the front of the house. Rosalie comes running in her wobbly heels, her face ashen. Her mouth opens, but nothing comes out. She takes a few backward steps, then pivots and marches out ahead of them. As they walk in this awkward phalanx, Michael thinks briefly, bizarrely, of Carol's healer. He hates, for some reason, the idea of that man witnessing this.

Suddenly, as if remembering something, Rosalie halts and spins around.

"He has a stalker," she announces with sudden force, standing in front of them like a barricade. "That's why he did it. There's someone who's been stalking him, I don't know who. Ever since the magazine article."

Michael's escorts do not respond, and after a moment his wife turns away and continues walking. He is ushered forward again, albeit more slowly, the torque on his arms slightly reduced. He stares at Rosalie as she walks with aristocratic carriage, the back of her dress like a dull mirror. For the first time in their married life, she is entirely opaque to him.

He thinks about the bullet. Where would it have finally landed? He hadn't absorbed enough of advanced physics class to hazard any estimate of a .40-caliber shot's degree of curvature, or to reckon the height of its apex. Perhaps just a slight tilt seaward would have placed it on the sliver of beach beyond the house, where it would rest for the duration, commingled with the clutter of gray stones. Or a small cant north might have landed it on the tennis court. Michael pictures the bullet striking the pristine green clay and creating a divot. He sees it bouncing over the painted white lines, coming to rest at the base of the chain-link fence, harmless as a thimble. It may not be discovered for days or weeks or months, or whenever one of the Christensens or their offspring happens to jog to the spot and bend to retrieve a ball.

Or maybe—is it possible?—the bullet hasn't yet landed. Maybe it is still streaming upward, freewheeling, unchallenged by any impediment in the clear night. He thinks of this last possibility with a kind of wonderment, like a boy releasing a bottle to the waves. He tilts his face briefly to the sky as the men press him on toward the blue-shadowed lawn where the car is.

Acknowledgments

Enormous thanks to all at Grove Atlantic who helped bring this book into the world, especially Virginia Barber, Elisabeth Schmitz, Morgan Entrekin, Katie Raissian, Deb Seager, Judy Hottensen, Charles Rue Woods, Gretchen Mergenthaler, Amy Vreeland, Patsy Wagner, and Justina Batchelor.

I'm deeply grateful to Bill Clegg for his abiding faith, wisdom, and guidance, and to Chris Clemans for his always invaluable assistance.

I'm fortunate to have the support of many brilliant friends, and would like to thank Melissa Hile, Anne Fentress Nichols, and Deborah Shapiro in particular for their responses to these stories. For invaluable writing time during playdates, thanks to Karen Ruscica Haitoff, Sara Carbone, and Andrea Jaffee.

Thanks to Irini Spanidou for her inspiration and enduring belief. For solid advice and encouragement, thanks to Susan Choi, Michael Cunningham, Jenny Offill, Jonathan Baumbach, Emily Mitchell, Sara Shepard, Cari Luna, and Bryan Charles.

I am indebted to the MacDowell Colony for the calm before the storm of parenthood and for providing the time and space for my characters to gestate. Thanks to Evelyn Somers Rogers at the *Missouri Review* for her editorial help. I'm grateful to Dr. Daniel Spitzer and Mike Cho for their help with neurology and neurosurgery details; any inaccuracies in this arena are my own. Thanks also to the Wilton Historical Society for insight into colonial New England and historic home renovations, and to the staff of 02 Living, who allowed me to turn their café into my office.

Loving thanks to my mother, Mary Ann Acampora, for all that she's given me over the years and for her careful reading of these stories. This book is dedicated to the memory of my father, Raymond Acampora, without whose unconditional love and faith I would never find myself writing these words.

To Amity, for brightening my days.

And to Thomas, who is at the heart of everything.